THE
LAST
SWORD
MAKER

ALSO BY BRIAN NELSON

The Silence and the Scorpion:
The Coup against Chávez and the Making of Modern Venezuela

THE
LAST
SWORD
MAKER

...

BRIAN
NELSON

BLACK STONE PUBLISHING

Printed in the United States of America

First edition: 2018
ISBN 978-1-5385-0766-7
Fiction / Thrillers / Technological

1 3 5 7 9 10 8 6 4 2

CIP data for this book is available
from the Library of Congress

Blackstone Publishing
31 Mistletoe Rd.
Ashland, OR 97520

www.BlackstonePublishing.com

For Ben
and Lucas

What need is there for responsibility? I believe that the horrifying deterioration in the ethical conduct of people today stems from the mechanization and dehumanization of our lives, a disastrous by-product of the development of the scientific and technical mentality. We are guilty. Man grows cold faster than the planet he inhabits.

—Albert Einstein

AUTHOR'S NOTE

The innovations in genetic engineering, artificial intelligence, and nanotechnology described in this book are consistent with forecasts made by leading scientists.

In 2003, the Naval Research Laboratory (NRL) in Washington, DC, opened its Institute for Nanoscience. The laboratory is at the forefront of a global effort by governments and private companies to develop advanced weapon systems using nanotechnology and other "cross-disciplinary opportunities."

Finally, all historical information about the People's Republic of China and Tibet is accurate.

PROLOGUE

THE LETTER

In August 2018, Nobel laureate and biochemist Bill Eastman hosted a conference for some of the greatest minds in science at the Millennium Institute in San Francisco. The theme of the conference was the anticipated growth in technology over the next half century. The predictions of the attending scientists—who ranged from physicists to geneticists to computer scientists—prompted Eastman to draft a letter to the president, warning him of the possible dangers from emerging technologies. "We are in the early stages of a technological transformation that will dwarf the Industrial Revolution," he wrote. "A revolution that will change economies and societies in ways that are difficult to imagine today." The letter, modeled after Albert Einstein's 1939 letter warning President Roosevelt about the possibility of an atomic bomb, was signed by Eastman and twenty-seven other leading scientists. It described how the combination of genetics, artificial intelligence, and nanotechnology (manufacturing on an atom-by-atom basis) would enable the creation of microscopic machines, smaller than a single cell.

As soon as 2030, these three sciences will merge. Advances in nanotechnology will make the construction of these microscopic devices possible while innovations in genetic engineering will enable them to make copies of themselves. Finally, developments in artificial intelligence will guide them with computers that exceed human intelligence. While these tiny devices will have tremendous benefits—including the ability to greatly prolong life by entering the bloodstream to fight disease—they will just as easily be designed as a new breed of biological weapon.

Eastman predicted a new arms race between the major powers as each strove to tap into the military applications of the new science. But his most sobering predictions addressed what would occur *after* the arms race was over.

Unlike other weapons of mass destruction, which are extremely difficult to make, these devices will be cheap and simple to acquire … Instead of rogue states and terrorist groups developing nuclear or biological weapons, we will have small groups or even individuals (such as those who create computer viruses today) capable of engineering viruses that can target people with a specific genetic trait.

The letter stressed that, while the invention of new biological weapons was a foreseeable possibility, these microscopic devices would be so versatile, and evolve so rapidly, that thousands of other hazardous scenarios would arise that we cannot even fathom today. To prepare for these contingencies, Eastman called for the creation of a new government agency to regulate their development. He concluded, "We must accept the likelihood that the future will be a place where a few clever individuals will gain access to astonishing power."

While the letter caused a stir within the scientific community, media attention was sparse. Only a few major papers bothered to cover the story, and many prominent scientists—including some who had attended the Millennium Conference—denounced Eastman and scoffed at his predictions, calling him paranoid.

It was 2018, after all, and with so many doomsday predictions come and gone, the world had grown skeptical. Still bruised by the global recession and under the constant bombardment of news about terrorism, climate change, and rogue nuclear powers, people were too exhausted for yet another pending catastrophe. Besides, most people believed that the answers to the world's problems would come by turning *toward* science, not away from it. Humankind had learned, and had the lesson reinforced many times, that the more its progress was intertwined with its dominion over nature—the atom, the cell, the genome—the brighter its future would be.

But in a college dorm room overlooking the Charles River, a twenty-year-old college sophomore named Eric Hill happened upon a summary of the letter in the *Boston Globe.* For reasons he could not quite explain, it enthralled him. Over the next few weeks, he scoured the internet, reading everything he could about Eastman and his predictions. He quickly noticed that while Eastman's detractors dismissed his dystopian vision, none of them questioned his predictions for technological change. No one disputed that artificial intelligence would eventually exceed human intelligence, or that the human body would soon be integrated with intravascular microscopic devices. Eric knew there was something important here. Bill Eastman, the man who had accurately predicted the rise of biotechnology a generation ago, had a new vision of the future. And while the inventions he foresaw might not be realized for decades, their antecedents were already being designed in universities and laboratories across the globe.

A month after the letter's publication, Eric made the change. He switched his major to chemistry with a concentration in systems analysis. At that moment, he could not have imagined just how far he would rise, or how his life and Eastman's would come together. How, despite their best efforts, Eric's work would help bring Eastman's worst nightmares to fruition.

PART ONE
THE ENDS
OF PEACE

SEVEN YEARS LATER ...

The principles of physics, as far as I can see, do not speak against the possibility of maneuvering things atom by atom. It is not an attempt to violate any laws; it is something, in principle, that can be done; but in practice, it has not been done because we are too big.

—Richard P. Feynman, 1959

JANUARY 13, 2025

Dear George:

I know you've been getting the updates on Tangshan. I wish I could dismiss their progress as exaggeration, but ▮▮▮▮ is our best, and his reports are confirmed. I'm still trying to swallow it: a programmable virus within the next seven months and full replication within eighteen. I have to admit, I'm worried about this one. The more I learn about this stuff, the more it scares me. Worse, the boys at NRL say that second place isn't good enough. Whoever replicates first will likely stay ahead, as these things learn and grow by themselves. It's sobering to think that military supremacy could pass entirely to the Chinese.

What's the word on funding? I'm hoping you can do your magic between NSA, Homeland, and DOD.

Working to get Eastman on board as soon as possible. Considering Curtiss as Project Lead. Thoughts?

My regards to Katherine and the girls.
Michael T. Garrett
CNO—UNITED STATES NAVY

JANUARY 14, 2025

Dear Mitch:

I share your pessimism on Tangshan. We've been screaming about this for years, and it's only now getting the attention it deserves. The good news is, we finally got the right people scared and the funding is secure for at least three years, so go get the best you can.

While you get things up and running, I'll investigate ways to slow down our friends in Tangshan. We may have to sacrifice ███ and the other operatives, but those losses will be acceptable if it gives us the time we need—perhaps six months to a year.

While I agree things look bleak, the good news is that ███, ████, and ████ are feeding us excellent intel on almost everything they're doing, which means we should be able to catch up quickly.

Was surprised to hear you are considering Curtiss. I have to strongly recommend against it. That son of a bitch should never have kept his stars after what happened in Syria. I know he's done some impressive things, but you'll never be able to control him, which frightens me, considering all the money and power that is coming your way. Pick somebody else.

Warm regards,
George

CHAPTER ONE

January 27, 2025
US Naval Academy, Annapolis, MD

Rear Admiral (upper half) James Curtiss awoke with a gasp, instinctively reaching for the FN Five-seveN pistol on the nightstand, pulling the slide with a metallic clank, and sweeping the room. His heart pounded against his ribs as the tactical light of the pistol illuminated ghostly circles in the dark room: the dresser, his uniform hanging on the closet door, the TV. Then he saw a flicker of movement. Someone was here, in the room. He acquired the target, center mass, and began to squeeze the trigger … Then he saw his own face, painted with fear, reflected in the mirror. He lowered the pistol and let out a long exhalation.

It had taken him a bare second to go from deep sleep to "the hardness"—to the soldier with his weapon cocked, teeth clenched, ready to kill. But just as quickly as he had filled with violence, he deflated. Reality flooded in. *It's just a dream,* he reminded himself. *Just a fucking dream.* But not just any dream. It was the dream he couldn't shake. Ever since Syria.

He was standing in a huge tunnel: the enormous gray fuselage of the C-17 Globemaster. He was dressed in his ceremonial whites, a wide rectangle of colored ribbons on his left breast. In the dream, there was no sound. Someone had muted everything but the staccato click of his heels on the corrugated metal deck. Click, click, click ... *Attached to the fuselage, surrounding him like giant bullets in the cylinder of a revolver, were six coffins draped with American flags. Ramírez, Chen, Thompson, Anderson, Day, Edwards. As he moved forward into the belly of the plane, another six coffins appeared, draped in flags just like the first six. Moses, Brewer, Hoffman, Vargas, Lightfoot, Jackson.* Click, click, click ... *On it went. Every few steps, another six coffins would appear out of the gloom, each name conjuring a hard drive of images: a smiling young face, a joke told at a picnic, a man pushing a child in a swing.*

The cargo door opened, and he raised his hand to shade his eyes from the light. He couldn't see, but he knew what was out there: fathers, mothers, wives, husbands, and children. They were waiting for what was left of their boys and girls—their husbands, wives, fathers, mothers. He didn't want to go out there, but he made himself. There were hundreds of them, and they were, like his soldiers, all races and creeds—white, black, Hispanic, Asian, and, like him, Native American. They stared at him, their faces blank, expressionless. No one spoke, no bugle played "Taps." But now, in addition to the clap of his heels, he heard the wind blowing—a lonely, solitary sound that whistled and echoed inside his head.

As an honor guard carried the coffins from the plane, a little girl in a white dress emerged from the crowd. She came to him and took his hand. It felt like forgiveness, her small hand in his, and he followed her willingly. She led him to a small lectern. But he had no speech prepared because there were no words that could soften this. He fumbled. He saw an interminable line of hearses moving like an assembly line toward the open aircraft. The girl was holding a present: a red box with a white bow. He took the box and untied the ribbon. Inside was a revolver. He took it, cocked it, and put the barrel in his mouth. It seemed the right thing to do; a fair trade for what he had taken from them. He glanced down at her then sideways at the families. Then he pulled the trigger.

He sat on the edge of the bed, the sudden sweat on the inside of his T-shirt cooling, making him shiver. Nothing in the room looked familiar.

Where the fuck am I?

You're back in Annapolis, you stupid Indian. He ran his left hand through his hair, then looked down at the pistol in his other hand. It had been eight years since he had last led his soldiers into combat—eight years since he was promoted to a maker of PowerPoint presentations, since he became a senior officer who conducted warfare from a command center in Florida, watching live satellite and webcam feeds as his soldiers risked their lives in dusty streets nine time zones away. Eight years, but the training was still there—the reflexes, the familiarity. The gun felt so comfortable in his hand … and the dream. He put the barrel into his mouth, just as he had done moments ago in the dream. He tasted the cold polymer and Gunslick. Just for a second, he considered pulling the trigger, but he stopped himself and put the gun down gently on the nightstand.

One thing was for sure: he needed to get that little bitch out of his head. If she hung around in there much longer, he was going to take her up on her offer.

"Jim, as your commanding officer, I think you should consider seeing a psychiatrist."

"Shrinks are for pussies, sir."

"That's what I thought you'd say."

"Then why'd you open your goddamn mouth?"

A shrug. "All right. I won't force you, but if Evelyn takes the boys and leaves you, don't come bitching to me."

He looked at his watch—4:15 a.m. *You've slept enough, old man.* The chopper would be here in an hour anyway.

He got dressed, and twenty minutes later he was standing on the seawall on the east side of the Yard, looking out at the Severn River and the Chesapeake Bay beyond. It was bitter cold, the temperature just south of zero. He shivered and his teeth chattered, but he didn't care. He welcomed the discomfort; he felt he deserved it. Beyond the snow-covered stones, the bay was undulating in gray scale, rolling high and beautiful and forbidding, as only the deep water could.

He had been summoned. Ordered to report, but without details or explanation. At his rank, that was unusual. It annoyed him, but it also piqued his curiosity. Something was up. But what, he wasn't sure.

The world was more or less at peace. The eighteen-month civil war in Saudi Arabia had turned into a stalemate, and—much to the relief of global markets—both sides were now exporting oil as fast as they could pump it. The rest of the Middle East was as stable as it ever was. There were monsoon floods in Bangladesh, and China was rattling its saber over PACFLT operations in the South China Sea, but that had become routine. Whatever they wanted him for, it was something else. Mitch's call had come late, and while the CNO's voice had been cool, Curtiss had still detected an urgency there.

Behind him, snaking across Dewey Field, were the footprints he had left in the snow. They led back across Holloway Road to Bancroft Hall—to Mother B, the biggest dormitory in the world. She was mostly dark and still at this hour, with only a few windows lit. He imagined the cadets inside clutching desperately to their last moments of peace before reveille, just as he had done when he called the place home thirty-seven years ago.

It had changed little since then. It still sat huge and daunting, at rest but never sleeping. It struck him now as it had when he first saw it. The building was a living thing—a massive respiring organism. It held not only the entire brigade of over four thousand midshipmen, but also the residue—the pain, humiliation, tenacity, and tears of every cadet who had ever come through its doors. A huge aggregated mass of emotion that encompassed everything those boys and girls had been when they arrived—brave, frightened, optimistic youth—and everything they became: hardened, beaten, and burned into officers of the United States Navy. Inside those walls, you felt their essence like a layer of greasy paint: their victories and their tragedies, wherever they had gone, even if they had gone nowhere.

All cadets hated Annapolis, but he had hated it more than most.

And year after year, he had avoided coming back here. But this year, when they asked him to give a guest lecture, he had agreed. Now he knew it had been a mistake. Whatever he was looking for, whatever he needed, it wasn't here. *Jesus, you do need a shrink.*

He supposed he had come looking for himself, for the man who had arrived here in 1988. The young man who had believed the recruitment posters. *Join the navy. See the world. Adventure.* As well as the thing the posters didn't say: that along with that life of adventure, someday, in some distant port, far from the shitty Oklahoma reservation he had escaped, he would meet a beautiful girl and live happily ever after.

That was the boy he wanted to meet now. The boy who had looked on the veterans with envy and saw ribbons and medals as things to strive for, not as reminders of pain and suffering and destroyed families. He saw traces of himself in the cadets, but the way they looked at him made him uneasy, because it was just the way he had looked at the decorated Vietnam vets in 1988: as heroes, as someone to emulate. They could read the ribbons and medals on his uniform like a résumé, and to them, he knew, he seemed the epitome of a badass: Bronze Star with "V." Combat Action. Sharpshooter Award. Navy Cross. "The Budweiser." Bosnia, Afghanistan, Operation Enduring Freedom, Syrian Liberation. As the cadets had huddled around him after his lecture, pestering him with questions, he suddenly felt that he was on the other side of a great and terrible lie.

That was when the CNO had called. He had excused himself and gone into the wings. "Jim, I'm gonna send a chopper up for you in the morning. Something's come up, and we need to talk."

Now, standing in the bitter cold, he turned his attention away from Bancroft Hall and back to the Chesapeake. It was rolling rough and surly, with long, deep swells, as if huge humpbacked monsters were roving just beneath the surface, stretching, trying to break free. A bit of orange sunlight reached his face, and he felt the slightest change in temperature on his lips. At that moment, he heard the approaching thump of rotors, steady and smooth. A minute later, the Sikorsky SH-3 Sea King appeared just over the treetops and banked majestically over the roof of the Nimitz Library.

It was a beautiful sight, and he was touched by a sudden sentimentality. Taken all together—his sleepless night, the history of this place, the brooding Chesapeake, the white Sea King in flight, and the way the sun flash refracted through its dragonfly rotors—it stirred something in his chest. Beautiful. But he dispelled the romantic feeling almost immediately and strode across the snow to meet the chopper. It flared up a moment, then settled onto the snowy field. The door opened immediately, a gangway was lowered, and a marine sergeant stepped out and saluted him. He returned the salute and climbed aboard. Then they were off, rising quickly.

As they banked to the west, he looked down over the Yard. He still hated the place, yet he had to admit, grudgingly, that Annapolis had also given him a great deal. He drew on this place—particularly the fact that he had survived it—over and over again. It came down to something very basic. *It had trained him to do things he didn't want to do.* It sounded simplistic, but it was the truth. There was a wide gap between a man who could force himself to do difficult things, and other men who could not. And not just the horrible things he had done: killing a young man with a knife, extracting a bullet from a friend's guts with rusty pliers, sending men off to die. No, it was the day-to-day things that made the difference: getting up at four thirty every morning, voluntarily going five days without sleep, swimming six miles. Over a lifetime, that discipline added up.

But now, as the school and his past shrank behind him, he feared the meeting with Admiral Garrett because he feared that they were once again going to ask him to do things he didn't want to do. Terrible, terrible things.

"These are images from a village called Dagzê, in the Nyingchi Prefecture in the Tibetan Autonomous Region," Commander Holder said, stepping toward the huge iSheet mounted on the wall. Curtiss was in the Pentagon, at a huge conference table with CNO Garrett and a group of high-level officers and spooks. "The official Chinese media says that these are victims of a new disease, which they are calling *Tibetan fever*. They claim it only attacks Tibetans and that everyone else is immune, including the ethnic Han Chinese."

The images were haunting: hospital wards full of sick Tibetans—men, women, and children. Then a scene from a filthy morgue: bodies stiff and stacked like lumber, not even covered with sheets. The camera had caught a weary hospital worker, a young man who looked sick himself, with his eyes open wide, horror legible on his face. Next, an image of a schoolyard with a playground made from wood and plumbing pipes. Four girls in colorful Tibetan clothes: white blouses, sky-blue silk skirts, elaborate beads in braided hair. They lay unmoving on the ground, apparently struck down while at play.

Curtiss found himself pushing his coffee away. As much death as he had seen, he should have gotten used to it. But he never did. In fact, the older he got, the more it seemed to bother him. And those Tibetan girls' clothes—they were so familiar to him, almost identical to Choctaw dress.

He had seen a briefing on the outbreak yesterday, but he had considered it minor. Wrong assumption. But how could it kill so quickly? It didn't make sense. Unless …

"This is satellite footage from near the Ganden Monastery, close to Dagzê."

Now Curtiss had to lean forward to sort out what he was seeing. A green, windswept hillside dropped away to a huge valley with sharp white mountains in the distance. It would have been strikingly beautiful if not for what he also saw there: five huge funnels of black smoke, rising off five distinct hillsides, each ascending like a black tornado into the stratosphere. Massive towers of smoke. And there was something else in the air, also swirling and rotating—a huge column of them. The commander gave an audible, and the image began to zoom down toward the earth. The things in the air were birds, he realized—thousands of them. No, tens of thousands. Tan and brown, resembling eagles with enormous wingspans. The camera seemed to pass very close to them as it fell through their mile-high vortex.

Tibetan vultures.

On the hillsides there were thousands more, in a seething, squabbling mass. Shoulder to shoulder, they pecked and clawed and fought among themselves. Only here and there did he see what was underneath: the red and pink and white of human corpses. Rib cages and spinal columns.

He had to rack his brain to remember his East Asian history. Sky burials. Most Tibetans didn't bury their dead; it was not the Buddhist way. They laid them out on hillsides, prayed, and sang mantras while the vultures came and devoured the remains. He remembered that nothing was left behind; that would be bad karma. Even the bones were ground up, mixed with meal, and fed to the birds. It had struck him as a ghastly custom, but then again, he supposed being stuck in the ground and fed to worms wasn't all that pleasant, either. Supposedly, it was soothing to the Tibetans to know that the remains of their loved ones were flying over the earth, quickly recycled into the living.

"When was this footage taken?" asked Brigadier General Corey Wilson.

"This is live," the commander said, "and it has been going on for three days. The funeral pyres you see are for people of high status, since wood is scarce in this part of Tibet."

The commander's words sent a chill through the room. There was something about watching things live that hit you harder.

"Officially, the Chinese say that seven hundred people have been infected and a hundred have died; however, these images show that's impossible. Our estimates show at least four thousand infected, with almost one hundred percent mortality—sometimes happening very fast, as you can see.

The screen went blank for a moment, as if to emphasize the sensitive nature of what the commander was about to say. "We have a man—I'll call him *the Fly*—inside the Tangshan project, who has been updating us on the Chinese program.

"His report of yesterday gave us a shock. The Fly stated that the outbreak is not a real disease at all, but a new weapon system—a nanovirus, designed in the Tangshan lab, that can selectively kill based on a victim's genetic code. This synthetic virus was intentionally released in four villages in the Nyingchi Prefecture as a weapons trial."

This caused a stir, and the officers began to whisper and mumble among themselves. Curtiss kept his mouth shut.

"We believe his report is accurate for many reasons. We already knew that the Chinese were working on a weapon system like this, but we thought they were at least seven months from completing it. Also, the choice of villages is significant—this was the epicenter of the 2021 uprising and the headquarters of the Gedhum Freedom Movement (GFM), which has been sabotaging Chinese infrastructure projects for years.

"Indeed, our reports say that while the four villages have been decimated in the literal sense—with one in ten citizens dying—the GFM has been completely wiped out. All the members that we track, which is close to three hundred people, are believed dead, along with most of their families. The Fly says that the nanovirus was able to seek them out specifically from blood samples taken when many of them were arrested after the uprising.

"As you know, there is a complete media blackout in Tibet, and the only news that reaches the outside world is what the Chinese government decides should be released. However, an attaché from State obtained this video, taken yesterday in the house of Kwetsang Rinpoche, the leader of the GFM."

A shaky image appeared on the iSheet. Admiral Curtiss saw a modest kitchen, a card table with mismatched wooden chairs, and peacock feathers decorating the walls.

And bodies.

A woman lay on the floor near the sink, and a girl was sprawled out at the table with her hands over her head. The cameraman was speaking in Tibetan, his words indiscernible but feverish with emotion. He seemed to be saying the names of the dead, his voice cracking, holding back tears. The camera spun into another room. At a desk, head down, face tilted toward the camera, was a wide-eyed man of no more than forty. This, the admiral somehow knew, was Kwetsang Rinpoche. Although he wore no robes, his head was shaved like a monk's. He had a gentle face that struck Curtiss as too kind for a guerrilla leader. The camera panned. A crude bassinet stood in one corner of the room. Mercifully, the camera did not approach it.

The camera moved down a dark hallway and turned into a bedroom. On the floor lay a teenage girl. Her posture, now frozen, spoke of incredible pain—her back was arched too far, like an overextended gymnast's. On the bed was the body of a teenage boy, facedown, naked from the waist up. Curtiss involuntarily leaned forward in his chair. Of all the images he had seen today, from the morgue until now, this one affected him the most. That young man … There was something about him. It was in the shape of his back. He must have been sixteen or seventeen, with the look that boys have at that age: lean, sinewy, and strong, but not yet as bulky as a man. Logan, Curtiss's oldest son, was sixteen, and he had a physique that was almost identical. He knew that back. He saw it when Logan leaned into the refrigerator after soccer practice, his sweat-soaked shirt over his shoulder, he saw it when the boy walked down the hall after a shower with a towel around his waist, and he saw it when he woke the boy in the mornings.

"Jesus," he muttered under his breath.

"As you can see," the commander continued, "the nanovirus must have killed Kwetsang and his family almost instantly. The Fly's report indicated that this was unexpected. The Chinese were surprised that it killed so quickly, and they actually hope to slow it down for future, um, *applications*. They also hope to design different viruses that will mirror the symptoms of other diseases, so that the deaths do not raise suspicions and are essentially undetectable.

"Of course, the impact of all this is enormous. With just one sample of a person's DNA, the Chinese can assassinate anyone they wish, and only the most detailed autopsy would be able to prove foul play."

Everyone started talking at once, but the commander raised his hand for quiet.

"While it does look bleak, it's important to remember that this virus is crude compared to what will be possible after replication. Yes, it can identify DNA strands and decide whether to switch on or off, but it is not truly programmable, and the Chinese are still a long way from replication. Which, of course, is the real prize." There seemed to be a hopeful gleam in Holder's eye when he said, "*the real prize*," which Curtiss didn't like. *Be careful what you wish for.*

Curtiss looked around the room. There were eight officers and two suits—Edmund Peters from Langley, and Bill Dawson from NSA. He knew them all, had worked with them (and occasionally against them) for decades, across wars and conflicts covering much of the globe. He checked off his assessment of each of them as he glanced at their faces: prick, asshole, prick *and* asshole, insufferable sycophant, pussy.

There were only three he admired: CNO Garrett, his boss; Edmund Peters (CIA), the most competent spook they had; and Lieutenant General (marines) Ellis Carlson, admittedly a bastard, but a straight shooter and one of his only true friends from Annapolis. All the officers outranked him (O-9s or higher), and all but those three hated his guts. That made him a little uneasy. He still didn't know why he was here, but he suspected he wouldn't be leaving this room without a size-seven asshole.

"Which is why we have to move fast," the commander continued, breaking Curtiss from his thoughts. "With the right team and the right leadership, we can still beat the Chinese."

Admiral Garrett crossed his huge meaty forearms and leaned back in his chair. He was looking straight at Curtiss now, and Curtiss didn't like it. Garrett was the head of the whole damn navy, and he was made for the part: a huge, fat Texan with a bald head and dazzling blue eyes that should have belonged to a movie star. He was known as the Preacher because, most of the time, he was gregarious and affable and could make you feel all warm and fuzzy. Duty, honor, country, and all that shit. Enormously likable—people wanted to please him. Which was perfect for him. In fact, most of the time, you didn't even feel as though you were receiving orders; he'd make it seem as if you had thought it up yourself. "What we maybe oughta do is …" or, "You might want to consider …" And the next thing you knew, you were busting your hump for him, but you didn't care, because it just seemed like the right thing to do, and besides, you certainly didn't want to disappoint the Preacher, because you knew he had another side to him, a side you didn't want to see.

Garrett's stare, combined with Holder's last words—*with the right team and the right leadership*—was enough to make it click.

They had chosen him. They wanted Curtiss to lead the project. They knew everything he'd done in his thirty-seven-year career: Annapolis, Dive School, BUD/S, SEAL Team 4, Bosnia, Afghanistan, Iraq, his Purple Heart, the Navy Cross, and, of course, Syria. They knew what kind of sailor he was. The navy was split into thirds: engineers, bureaucrats, and soldiers. He wasn't an engineer, and he wasn't a bureaucrat. That alone told him what they thought about this little project. This was war.

But Syria. He had been sure they would never give him another command after Syria. Now he realized they wanted him not in spite of Syria, but *because* of it. Even for those in the room who hated him, Syria had solidified his reputation as a man who was ruthless, calculating, and, when necessary, very, very cruel. To them, he was not the man who had returned with so many body bags, but the man who had ended the war so succinctly, annihilating the enemy.

Looking at their faces, he knew they had fought over the decision. They had fought, and Garrett had eventually gotten his way. Because it was Garrett who knew him best. Garrett knew what he had become—the change that had started in Annapolis and ended in Syria. And Garrett alone knew the whole truth.

Curtiss stared into Garrett's eyes, and in that moment, he hated him. He hated him for insisting that he come back, that he reach into himself one more time for the *hardness*, for making him once again become the man they wanted, the man who would sacrifice other men and women for a greater good.

It was Garrett who spoke, realizing that Curtiss understood full well why he was here. "Jim, this is now the nation's top security priority.

The job is straightforward: make sure our team wins this race. No matter the cost, no matter the consequences. To do that, the first thing you have to do is get one man: Bill Eastman. He's got more smarts than a rattlesnake whip, and that's more than most of those Chinamen put together." Garrett leaned forward for effect, his meaty forearms heavy on the table. "Get me Eastman and you're halfway there.

"Now, I realize all this nano-crap might be throwing you for a loop, so Ed is going to fill you in on what it's all about. If you thought this little trick in Tibet was impressive, you'd better pucker up your o-ring, because what Ed's about to tell you is gonna knock you on your Indian ass."

Ed Peters got up, cleared his throat, and began to speak.

Seven hours later, Curtiss left the Pentagon. Shaken. Foggy. Overwhelmed. And a little angry. *Why didn't you put all the pieces together yourself?* A part of him kept rejecting what they had told him. That was his gut reaction: to deny that it was true. It would be much easier to return to his old understanding of the world. To go back to the world of this morning, to that sunrise in Annapolis … But that was what other men would do. And wasn't that the sort of denial that had gotten them here in the first place? That was why they were so far behind the Chinese: because people refused to see what was happening.

His assistant opened the car door for him. Vacantly, he got into the black Lincoln. Safe behind tinted glass, unseen by any subordinate, he pulled his hand down his face.

Again, he lectured himself. *Why didn't you see it coming?*

He had always prided himself on being keenly aware of the evolution of warfare. He had studied it with a professor's discipline ever since Annapolis. He had measured it in the changes from one war to the next—the fits and starts and sometimes startling leaps in technology, and their gruesome effects. It was plain to see in specific battles, usually in the first encounter between sides: the musket wars of New Zealand, the German invasion of Poland in 1939—the Polish cavalry against the machine guns of the Wehrmacht. The rate of technological change since that day, September 1, 1939, was equally startling. War had been the great catalyst. World War II had begun on horseback and ended with a B-29 Superfortress dropping an atomic bomb on Hiroshima six years later. Only fifteen years after that, the world was locked in mutually assured destruction, with ICBMs poised to make their insane volleys over the North Pole.

But then it seemed that technological change had slowed. The same B-52s that had bombed Vietnam in the 1960s also bombed Afghanistan and Syria. Yes, there were drones and webcams and real-time satellite footage, but the rate of change did not feel quite so awesome as before.

Now he realized that this perceived deceleration had been an illusion. The changes had been happening all along. He just hadn't seen them, because the changes were, quite literally, not visible. They were *in*visible, microscopic. Since World War II, technology had moved away from things that people could see and appreciate (aircraft carriers, submarines, thermonuclear explosions) toward the invisible— the molecular, atomic, subatomic, quantum.

But were they really on the cusp of doing what they hoped to do? Were the Chinese really almost there? It was so big—not just one or two additions to the arsenal. No, the whole arsenal would change, and most existing weapons would be useless against those who wielded the new science.

And it would come from a single major breakthrough—what they were calling "replication"—when they figured out how to bring these things to life.

He reminded himself that he didn't have to take the job. He could tell Garrett to go to hell. The Preacher would sigh and shake his head and say he was disappointed, but he would let Curtiss out because he wouldn't want a man who wasn't fully committed to the project. Then Curtiss would be free to retire in peace. Yet, it was clear there would be no peace. The peace was ending. That much was evident in the image of the dead Tibetan boy on the cot, in his shape, his strong back.

★ ★ ★

That night, Curtiss lay in bed beside his sleeping wife, running over everything he had learned. The spiraling vultures, the rib cages and spinal columns, the bassinet in the corner.

At 4:30 a.m., Curtiss found himself in Logan's doorway, looking at his son as he slept. It was a ritual he had performed religiously when the boy was younger—the evening check that he was safe, a ritual that began when he was a newborn, fresh out of the hospital. Back then Curtiss would check three or four times a night just to make sure the boy was still breathing, often stepping into the room and placing a hand on his back. And that simple act, that simple piece of evidence—the rise and fall of his son's chest—was still the most soothing thing in the world to him.

Logan was snoring loudly. Curtiss looked around the dim room, saw the silhouettes of the boy's soccer trophies amid all the things that he knew were there, yet were concealed in the darkness: the prize he won for a state writing competition, a picture of the boy and their dog, the Pink Floyd prism poster, the life-size cutout of Lionel Messi.

He gave a heavy sigh as he remembered the Tibetan boy. He didn't want the job, but he was going to take it. It came back to Annapolis and Bancroft Hall. It was the way he had been trained: to do the things that he didn't want to do.

CHAPTER TWO

February 28, 2025
Advanced Micro Laboratories, Sunnyvale, CA

Two men sat on a rooftop overlooking Silicon Valley.

From here, they could see the top floors of the other tech giants—silver-and-glass towers jutting above the trees like Mayan temples above the rain forest. On the streets below, workers were pulling out of parking lots and heading home for the day—a long stream of red brake lights making their way to the foothills. To the east lay the San Francisco Bay and the vibrant green wetlands that made up its southern tip.

But the two men weren't looking at the buildings or the traffic or the bay. They were gazing out at the fiery sunset that filled the western sky. A warm high-pressure system had moved up from Baja in the afternoon, colliding with cooler air from the north. The effect was astonishing. The clouds were stacked up like shelves, each tier refracting a different hue of red or purple or orange, reaching high into the troposphere. Between the layers, shafts of light broke through, spotlighting distant patches of earth and water.

The two men sat in rapt silence. They had come here as part of a ritual, to mark the end of an era. Thirty-two years ago, they had been on this very rooftop together, confident young men celebrating the launch of their first company. It had been a big party: two thousand invitees, thirty tables of food, a swing band, and 120 gallons of ice cream. Reporters from all the major magazines and newspapers in the country had been there for "the startup of the decade," and the party had run late into the night.

Now, the scene was very different. The building was abandoned—the electricity, water, and gas turned off. There were no witnesses, no reporters. The only light was a single candle on the plastic table between them. And while the company would live on under new leadership and in a new facility, for these two men it was over.

Finally, when all the light had drained from the sky and the first stars began to shine, Jack Behrmann stirred. He was a massive man, over seven feet tall and built like Paul Bunyan. He had a thick beard and spoke with a deep, gravelly voice.

"Can we trust him?"

"Curtiss?" Bill Eastman asked.

Jack nodded.

"It's still bothering you, isn't it?"

Another nod. "I suppose it's not really him, exactly. It's the whole idea. Weapon systems? I just never imagined …"

It was the big question, the one that had been plaguing both of them. It had been a frenetic six weeks since Admiral Curtiss had started calling—a disconcerting and emotionally draining process of staunch refusal, reconsideration, and, ultimately, acceptance. In the end, it was the images from Tibet that had persuaded them.

"You're right to be worried," Bill said. "Believe me, so am I. But it's really the only option we have. The venture capital for this is all over the place: we have Procter and Gamble trying to use nanosites to make better toothpaste, and Merck trying to use them for erectile dysfunction. The only players with a real shot at replication are the national governments. That means China and the United States. And if our goal is to create a safe and sustainable postreplication world—which, of course, it is—then we can't let China win. That leaves us with the US government."

Jack grunted unenthusiastically. He knew all this, yet he kept trying to shuffle and reshuffle the possibilities until he got a different result. "It still doesn't feel right."

Bill gave him a reassuring smile. "You asked me if we can trust Curtiss. We can trust him for one thing: to do his job, which is to get us to replication. I think he'll do everything in his power to help us, and that could be a tremendous asset. But after replication …"

Jack watched him closely. Bill had a habit of rocking back and forth in his chair as he spoke. He would lean forward to make a point, and his face would come into the candlelight; then he would lean back, and his face would be consumed in darkness again.

"It's after replication that we have to be very careful with Curtiss. That's when our goals will diverge. That's when Curtiss and the people who control him will have their new big stick, when they'll have the power to make weapons the likes of which this world has never seen. My fear is that they might be tempted to use those new weapons." He leaned into the light. "First it was Gatling, then Nobel, and finally Oppenheimer. They each believed that their inventions would make combat much too destructive for the likes of 'civilized' humans." Bill leaned back, and the hollows of his face filled with shadow. "I hope we're not remembered for making the same mistake."

CHAPTER THREE

March 14, 2025
Tangshan Military Laboratory, Hebei Province, China

General Meng Longwei strode back and forth across his office, examining a single piece of paper. It was only a short paragraph, a snippet of data, yet he had been fixated on it all day. *It has finally happened,* he thought. He had known that it would. It had to, sooner or later, but that didn't make it any easier to accept.

He turned to the far wall and looked at the faces there: dozens of eight-by-ten-inch color photos. They were arranged in a pyramid, a bureaucratic hierarchy. The kind of thing one might expect to see in a detective's office, displaying the faces of an infamous crime ring such as la Cosa Nostra. It *was* like that, but different.

Jessica M. Berg—Head of Artificial Intelligence
Formerly full professor of integrated systems, Duke University,
Durham, NC
PhD Yale University, 1991
National Medal of Science, 1997

Olexander Velichko—Head of Genetic Engineering
PhD National Technical University of Ukraine, Kyiv (Kiev)
Polytechnic Institute, 2010
MD Johns Hopkins University, Baltimore, MD, 2013
Wolf Award in Medicine, 2016
William Allan Award (ASHG), 2020

And so on. Next was Jack Behrmann, the head of Nanotechnology. Meng found this man's face particularly disturbing. There was something about the huge head and bushy beard that he found grotesque. He was smiling too broadly, and with those big, puffy cheeks, he was like a caricature of Santa Claus.

But the face that Meng was drawn to, the picture that pulled his eyes to it over and over again as he tried to work at his desk, was tiers above that. No, not Eastman, who looked serene and self-assured. No, the face above that. Meng had memorized its shape, its lines—the small mouth with thin lips, the nose that looked as though it had been broken at least once, the brown skin, the deep-set dark eyes.

Rear Admiral James Curtiss.

"How much do you know?" he said aloud, his own voice surprising him in the quiet office. In light of the piece of paper in his hand, it was the most important question in the world.

It was true that he felt a deep contempt for most Americans. Theirs was a nation of capricious children, obese, arrogant, and spoiled, who could be distracted by the simplest of things: fast food, Hollywood movies, video games, and sparkly gadgetry. Pampered, undisciplined, and stupid. *Yu chun.* It was Americans like these who had been his adversaries until now, moving forward with their own replication project in pitiful fits and starts. And so, he had, he now realized, grown complacent. He had had nothing to worry about.

But their choice of Curtiss worried him because it demonstrated a perspicacity that he had not thought his enemy possessed. Curtiss was a cruel, cruel man—a man who, like Meng himself, had been tempered by a huge military institution. A man who knew war, had survived it, and had gone far. They were very similar, really. And while they would likely never meet, they were now viciously committed to defeating each other.

He looked down at the paper in his hand. It was mostly gibberish, random characters. Only here and there a word that even meant anything:

（こやま　けいいちろうてごし　ゆうΣΓ　や、11月11日 - ）形象顔藍TARGETTING　　KFMLEADERS委批作賤自己色為為粉紅色。[同時屬於∝♥♡ョム子團體手越增田]　餘波TEST SITE ABLE:DAGZE　重ббFILL辦38TESTSITE98艦08形象BAKER 顔色為長:BEILA 冷血役男 隔天ÆΩΣΓ續尋歡TESTSITE890CHARLIE:鄰娃墜樓　　BAINA.伊朗國家電視ㄥㆆㄅ臺當天援引伊朗石化行MORTALITY業官員納西100PERCENT裏的話報道說RECOGNITION TUNNELING事故係天ACCU然氣泄97　　PERCENT漏起火導致ÆΩΣΓфюЩ^{ㄨㄨ} ㄥㄅREPEAT ㄬㄥㆆㄅ∝♥心ョムマケ。納西裏說, 火勢目前已得到控制, 事故未對該石化廠處理設施造成損壞。他表示, 事故原因

This small packet of data, a droplet in the torrent, had been snatched out of the ether by a government satellite because it had no clear recipient or sender. Suspicious, General Meng had ordered it decoded, and after a month this was all that had been, or could ever be, recovered.

But it had been enough.

Since his first day as project leader, he had assumed that there were spies among them. He suspected everyone and kept them under the tightest surveillance. Yet to know without a doubt that he had a traitor was still disconcerting. Like a man who discovers his wife has been unfaithful, he felt a complicated mix of distrust, betrayal, and, most of all, anger.

Two words particularly disturbed him: "RECOGNITION TUNNELING." Those words jumped off the page at him. It was the technique that the new virus used to spin rapidly through the genome and read the entire double helix in a fraction of a second, thereby identifying the victims. It was a revolutionary step—something that took a large computer in a laboratory eight hours to do.

Mention of it suggested that the spy was high in his ranks and was likely passing on some of their most important design secrets. Of Meng's more than twenty-four thousand employees, only two hundred knew about it.

But who? He looked at Admiral Curtiss again. "Who is it? I know he's one of yours." Then his voice changed. He coaxed sweetly, as if talking to a lover, "Why don't you tell me who it is?"

Admiral Curtiss did not reply.

"It doesn't matter," Meng said abruptly, "because I will find him. Yes, I will find him, and then …"

The poor man—or woman. It was the most inexcusable of treasons in Meng's eyes, given the history of his country. China had been the greatest nation in the world, its oldest civilization, its most advanced culture—at least until the Western powers had forced their way in, dividing them, pitting them against each other, destroying their culture in the name of their markets. It was what they all had been taught in grade school as "the Great National Crisis." Beginning with the Opium Wars and culminating in the devastation and humiliation of the Second World War. Everyone knew it. China's fall was the fault of the colonial powers.

And now, three quarters of a century after that great humiliation, after more than seventy-five years of the People's Revolution, China was once again back in its rightful place—on the cusp of surpassing all other nations. So, to find a Han Chinese willing to trade their greatest technological advances—indeed, their nation's very future—to the Americans … The thought brought up a fierce contempt in him, and the urge to do violence. When he found the spy, there would be torture and execution, then prison for his family. And the spy would be caught. Meng was supremely confident of this, just as he was confident that China would reach replication first.

Regardless of the Americans' sudden awakening, regardless of their recruitment of Curtiss and Eastman, and regardless of the presence of the spy, Meng still remained largely unfazed. And why shouldn't he be? For the past five years, *he* had guided the Tangshan program with tact and precision. *He* had pushed and cajoled and manipulated his scientists, who were some of the best in the world, to overcome obstacle after obstacle. *He himself* had conceived the synthetic virus as a weapon system that could be used either as an instrument of assassination or to subdue large populations. *He* had convinced the politburo to make it a research priority. And *he* had pushed to test the prototype on the Tibetan separatists, skillfully killing two birds with one stone.

And his success had not gone unnoticed.

No less than the president's personal secretary, Tan Wei, had called to congratulate him. "The president sends his personal congratulations to you. He wants you to know that the people's government treasures men like you—men who inspire us all with your service and dedication. Your work in Tangshan, as well as in the Tibetan Autonomous Region, ridding the country of the terrorist threat, will not be forgotten." Tan Wei went on to insinuate that Meng would soon be promoted from brigadier to major general.

Meng had thanked the secretary profusely, reiterating that he was always ready to fight terrorists—although the truth was, he had an ulterior motive in targeting the GFM separatists. For it had been the peace-loving Tibetans, a people who supposedly dedicated themselves to compassion for all life, who had killed his wife and daughter twelve years ago.

It was the night his life changed forever, during the May 2009 uprising, when Meng was just a captain stationed in Lhasa, in charge of the Najin barracks. He and his men had been outside the Tsuglagkhang (central cathedral), trying to quell the anarchists, when, unbeknownst to him, a band of them had stormed the barracks, overwhelming the few remaining soldiers and setting the place on fire.

That night, he had returned home to look for Li Xia and Lien. At first, he was sure they had fled like most of the other families. It was only late in the night, when he returned to his fire-gutted house, that he found them dead in the bedroom closet. They must have gone there to hide. The image of their faces as his flashlight crossed over them was forever cauterized in his mind. For the next five years it had persistently reappeared at least every hour, until he was quite sure it would drive him mad.

I'm sorry.

He could only guess what had happened. They had gone to the closet to hide, that much was certain. But once the fire started, Li Xia must have been too frightened to come out, despite the smoke, likely hearing the whooping and shouting of the Tibetan *Mantze* outside.

I'm sorry.

Lien, his daughter, had just turned two and, that morning, had learned the expression *duì bu qǐ* (I'm sorry). But she didn't understand what it meant or in what context to say it, so she had gone around repeating it for everything. When her favorite cartoon ended: *I'm sorry.* Talking to her stuffed bunny: *Wǒ ài nǐ. Duì bu qǐ* (I love you, I'm sorry). When Meng had left the house in his uniform: *Bye, Daddy, I'm sorry.*

He had chuckled at that. *I'm sorry, too, Lien.*

And so, he was forever haunted by scenarios of their last moments. He imagined them in the closet. The sounds of the fire: the wind roar and the occasional startling pop. The shouts of revelry outside. And the smoke as it began to make its hypnotic curlicues under the closet door.

I'm sorry.

The bodies had not been burned—the fire had been put out before that. But they had been asphyxiated, their skin turned a milky purple. That was how they were when he found them, when he had opened the door—just checking, not really believing—and shined the flashlight inside. He knew immediately that they were gone. He did not call for help, didn't even look away. He simply got down on his hands and knees and crawled into the closet behind his wife, pulled them both close, and turned off the flashlight. He had to use every ounce of his willpower to ignore the coldness of their skin.

After the weapons trials, Meng had gone to Dagzê personally to witness the effects of the new virus. He had gone into the morgues, seen the sky burials, seen the trucks full of dead, and watched his doctors perform autopsies to confirm the efficacy of the virus. None of it aroused any empathy in him, only satisfaction. He was doing what a good soldier did: killing the enemy.

In his conversation with the personal secretary, the man had given him something else that he wanted, something that reminded him of how well they knew him. It was a gift he wanted even more than the promotion.

"The president would also like you to know that if you should choose to have another child, that child would receive all the benefits and privileges of a first child."

Again, he had thanked the personal secretary profusely for the president's great generosity.

Meng had married again, wed to a beautiful woman whom he loved half as much as his first wife. And she had given him a son, which had made all the grandparents happy. Yet, despite the blessing of a boy, he still wanted a girl. It was a dangerous desire, he knew, because the child would not be Lien, yet he wanted a girl all the same, so that he might love her as he had loved Lien.

He shook the memories from his head and turned again to the wall, to his new enemy: Admiral James Curtiss.

"How much do you know?" he repeated. "You know that we have the nanovirus. You know how we plan to use it. Okay, now I know that one of your spies is here. But tell me, Admiral, do you know how many spies I have with you?"

CHAPTER FOUR

January 27, 2025—Six weeks earlier
Nyingchi Prefecture, Tibetan Autonomous Region

The seventeen-year-old Tibetan boy awoke facedown in a ditch. Sand and dirt clung to the cuts and scrapes on his face. He started to get up, then thought better of it.

Everything hurt. He took a deep breath. That hurt, too. One of his ribs wasn't right. No, definitely not. Each time he breathed, he felt as if he were being stabbed. He turned his head. More pain, but at least his neck wasn't broken. Fingers, wrists, toes, ankles, knees—he tested them one at a time. As for his face, he didn't have the courage to touch it. He knew that the news from his fingertips would not be good.

It took him several minutes to get up on his hands and knees and then to struggle to his feet.

He could see out of only one eye, and that eye told him it would be dark soon. That was one bit of bad news; the other was that they had taken his prison uniform, leaving him naked except for his underwear. Tibet in January. He needed to get moving, find shelter, or he would die. He could already feel a stiffness in the skin, a coming frostbite.

"Congratulations, Sonam, your reeducation is complete. We are going to release you."

Released, and already facing death. Wouldn't that be something! Surviving six months in Drapchi prison only to freeze to death. He imagined how it might play out. When the sun went down, it would soon drop below freezing. If he froze quickly enough, maybe someone would find his body come spring. Blue and stiff, yet perfectly preserved. He had heard of that happening to lost herders. But then he rejected the thought. The birds and mice would take care of him long before spring. *You must have been a real son of a bitch in your last life, Sonam.* But at least he was out. He would take death here in the cold over death in prison. Six months of forced labor, beatings, humiliations, endless study sessions of Communist verse, Mao's "Little Red Book," and the *Tibet Daily.* Forced to sing party anthems every dawn and before every meal. *"Socialism is great; socialism is good."* Interrogated over and over as they tried to coerce him to turn in friends and relatives. "Atone for crimes with worthy deeds," was the party slogan. "Inform on others, and you will be repaid with leniency." He had not, although many had. Some even confessed to things they had not done, in the hope that it would reduce their sentence. That had been a grave mistake, because they then suddenly discovered that their sentences had been lengthened or that they faced execution.

He looked around. He was on an abandoned mining road in a valley with steep hillsides all around, dried-out grass, windswept junipers, and wilting buddleia. Nothing looked familiar. He could be anywhere.

Climb, he told himself. *You have to figure out where you are.* He moved uphill, but darkness was coming on quickly. The jagged summits to the east still caught the alpenglow, but where he stood was already deep in shadow. Every few minutes, he would look up to see the sunlight receding up the sides of the peaks—a solar hourglass—while the temperature steadily dropped. He crossed his arms over his chest. Another ten minutes' walking confirmed his fears that the road was long abandoned—he came across a thirty-meter section that had been washed away by the rains. By the time he had negotiated the wash, the sun was almost gone from the eastern hilltops. He had covered pathetically little ground. He felt so small in this place where the mountains ran in indistinguishable rows across the top of the world. He could wander around for weeks and not see another soul. But he didn't have weeks. He had perhaps a few hours. He kept looking up and up, watching the slopes of the nearby hills, searching their silhouettes for some peak or landmark that would tell him where he was.

Finally, the road rounded to the north, opening up his view to the west. Now he could see that the hill he was on was really quite small. Higher hills loomed in front of him, black and impenetrable, pushing his gaze up to the purple night sky beyond. Then he saw them: thousands of swirling shapes in that blue-black sky. Falling, spinning. A huge cylinder of dark angels, reaching ever up and up. There seemed to be no end to them. Only when his eyesight failed did it seem to stop. As he watched, he realized they all were slowly gliding downward as the coming night stole away the thermals that kept them aloft.

Simultaneously, he realized where he was; the dark angels were descending on his village.

"There's a little surprise waiting for you at home. I hope your immunizations are up-to-date." Laughing and snickering.

He was seized by a sudden panic, and what little store of adrenaline he had surged through him. He wanted to run, but he didn't have the strength. He had to know what the Chinese had done. He had to know whether his father and little sister were safe. He had to know whether *she* was alive.

But walking was the best he could do, and even that was a struggle. Going downhill was fine, but uphill was torture. Every time he lifted his right leg a little too high, he felt the rib stabbing in his side. He was weary and hungry, and the strain from the exercise brought every bruise and cut to life, particularly on his face, which throbbed like a huge heart. And his brain was not working right, either, his lucidity coming and going like a camera that wouldn't stay in focus.

"Your study group leader says you are completely rehabilitated. You are free to return to your family—if there is anything left of it."

What had they done? He had prayed every day to be released, to return home to the small sheep farm, to help his father and sister, to return to her. Many times, he had simply given up hope, resigned himself to dying there in Drapchi prison like so many others. And now to be out, to be so close, yet … His heart ached at the thought that it was still not over. That he would arrive home to find that they had robbed him of much more than they had already taken.

"Congratulations, you are free to go—after one last thamzing, *one last struggle session."*

Yéshé heard someone fumbling at his door, the sound of a key. How? Had some burglar found the spare key he kept hidden in the barn? And the dogs—why hadn't they barked? He heard the door open slowly, tentatively. He sat up with a start. His heart, brought too quickly out of sleep and into fear, thumped like a drum. He grabbed the plastic flashlight and looked at it for a moment. He supposed he could use it as a club.

"Pa pha … pa pha."

Now his heart really did skip a beat. The voice was weak but unmistakable. "Sonam!" he called. He had almost given up hope.

He scrambled from the bedroom. There in the kitchen was a figure, shivering and much too small to be his son. The light of the flashlight danced over him, then held steady. Yéshé struggled to focus on what he was seeing; then his knees became like water.

He quickly grabbed the blanket from the bed and threw it over both of them and took his son in, held him close. The boy was so cold. Yéshé tried to send the heat of his body into him. Yéshé's body knew how his son should fit against him. His skin had memory, of course, a memory laid down from every embrace since boyhood. But now his skin was telling him this was not his son—the body was too light, the face too swollen—and he had to fight an impulse to push this sick animal away.

"My Sonam, my Sonam," he repeated, half to reassure the boy, half to reassure himself.

Be thankful. Just be thankful that he is alive, that he is finally home. But what have they done? He had to resist the urge to weep. *Save that for later. Now is not the time.*

He tried to see his son's face, but the boy pulled away. "It's okay," he said. "Let me see. It's going to be all right now."

Slowly, the boy turned. He was barely recognizable. One side of his face, where it had been burned, had shrunk like an old apple, while the other side was cut and bruised and swollen—mangled as if by machinery—with splotches of purple and yellow, and a deep gash from jaw to temple. One eye was swollen shut, while the other was flooded red with blood. *My boy, my beautiful boy.*

It had been six months since they came for him. Three hours before dawn, as was their way, loading him into an army truck. Six long months, and Yéshé had feared that his son had been "disappeared" like so many others, like the Dhamdul boys, the town constable, and the Lhasa nuns. Now he was simultaneously elated and brokenhearted. But why had they beaten him so badly? Yéshé knew their ways, knew how some of the other prisoners had returned. And he had tried to prepare himself. But this was much worse than any beating he had ever heard of. It was another humiliation in a lifelong string of humiliations: that they should treat the thing he loved most in this life, one of his children, like a mongrel dog. They had even taken his hair. Tibetan men never cut their hair—only the monks when they took monastic vows. Long hair was a source of pride. The Chinese knew this, and it was one of their favorite ways to demean young Tibetan men.

He brought Sonam butter tea and some *thenthuk* soup. At first, the boy was too weak to hold the cup to his mouth, but then the yak butter started to do its work, and the boy was soon sipping it by himself. He sat by the hearth, wrapped in the blanket, the gold light from the fire softening the bloated profile of his face.

The old man went to his bedroom cabinet and got out the medical kit. From the kitchen, he took a stool, a cloth, and a bowl of soapy water.

Sitting beside the boy, he began to clean the wounds. Sonam didn't resist or even seem to notice—soap and water, soap and water again, the cloth turning reddish black from blood and dirt. Then alcohol, then honey on his burns. They had placed an iron on his face. He could see the telltale triangular shape and circles from the little holes that vented steam. He could tell that they had done it repeatedly, letting the wound heal a bit, then doing it again, coming very close to the eye. Yéshé worked for almost an hour. Sonam's one seeing eye remained fixed on the fire, never moving, not even when his father pushed the fishhook into his cheek and began to stitch up the gash.

Finally, when he had finished, the boy spoke. His voice was pained and dry.

"Bhasundara?" he said, asking for his eleven-year-old sister.

"She is at your grandmother's in Lhasa," he replied. "She is safe."

The boy asked about the vultures.

"Tomorrow," he said. "Just rest now."

"I need to know, *pa pha.*"

"Tomorrow."

There was a long beat of silence.

"Chodren?" he asked, looking straight into the fire.

The old man cringed, suddenly drained of energy. It was as he feared: the boy had been in love with the Khédrup girl. He had suspected it but had said nothing, knowing that if it was true, they would have to keep it secret. In Tibet, secrets could be deadly, and even the most trusted person could break under torture, condemning dozens of others, even family members, to terrible fates. Information was also currency. The Chinese paid handsomely for it, and many Tibetans were willing to sell it for profit, for favors, or to save their own skins. So the two had kept their relationship secret, rarely going out in public together and never engaging in the same protests. She had joined the Lhasa protests in 2021, gotten arrested, and had her blood taken. Sonam had stayed home. And although Yéshé and Sonam didn't know it, that was the reason she was dead and Sonam was alive.

"She's gone," Yéshé said. "The fever took her ... quickly."

Sonam nodded and looked into the fire. Even now he would not let on that he had loved her.

Just be thankful, Yéshé reminded himself. *Just thankful that he is alive.*

Sonam saw his father bow and clasp his hands. The boy stiffened. He had so longed to be home, to be with his father and sister again. But the old man's genuflecting changed that. It meant that he would do nothing. He would not get a lawyer to contest his son's illegal detainment and torture; he would not go down to city hall and complain to the Chinese-appointed mayor. He would not go to Lhasa on the anniversary of the uprising. Instead, he would accept it as karma, part of his fate, something that had been decided since birth. Something he could do nothing about.

Sonam was sick of it, sick of his father and sick of his people for rolling over and letting themselves be subjugated by the Chinese. Hadn't the Dalai Lama himself admitted that the nonviolent path was a failure, that he had accomplished nothing in his life to relieve the suffering of his people? Sonam felt the same way about his father: that he had wasted his life. In fact, three generations of Tibetans had wasted their lives. Seventy-five years of lying on their backs while the Chinese kicked them, a repression interrupted only by the occasional feeble protest or by a monk setting himself on fire. The whole time waiting—waiting for what? For the Chinese to suddenly realize their error? *So sorry, you can have your country back again.* For international sanctions against the Chinese? Another joke. No one was going to help them. They all were too afraid of upsetting the great economic behemoth. So what were they waiting for? To Sonam, it was just cowardice, because whatever they were waiting for, they were hoping it would come from the outside. Which was delusional. The change had to come from within.

"I don't believe it," he said. "Even now you won't stand up to them?" He had meant to sound hard and defiant, but his voice cracked and the words came out as a supplication—the pleading of a boy much younger than he was.

The old man knew his son's disappointment. It had been a growing wedge between them. "No," he said. "I will not stand up to them—at least, not the way you want me to."

The boy shook his head in disbelief, but Yéshé would not let this old argument separate them now. He embraced the boy again and he wept, letting some of his sorrow out. For several minutes, Sonam remained stiff, but his resolve was weak. He also felt ashamed. He knew it was a bad time to pick a fight. Yes, he hated that his father would not take a stand, but he also knew that he and his sister were the reasons why. The old man would do anything to keep them safe, and turning up his belly to the Chinese had seemed the easiest way to keep them from hurting his children.

Sonam gently patted the old man's back, letting himself inhale the familiar smell of him, a smell of dry earth and smoke. "It's just so hard," Sonam said, his voice cracking again. "So hard." Before he knew it, he was crying, too. Softly at first, but soon he was crying uncontrollably, the way a little boy cries. It did not last long. He simply did not have the energy for it.

Within minutes, he was asleep, snoring over his father's shoulder. The old man picked him up—much too easily—and carried him to his bed, tucked him in as he had when he was just a boy, and went to work. For now there was much to do.

His son had returned to him. It was a moment he had dreamed about every day for the past six months: the fantasy of seeing him in the doorway or coming up the road. Home. Where he belonged. But it was a bittersweet homecoming, because he knew that the boy couldn't stay.

He could see the boy's path clearly: he would continue to fight, and sooner or later they would kill him. He had seen it dozens of times with the boys and girls of other Dagzê families. But he could not let that happen to his son. That was what the Chinese wanted: to get rid of all the true Tibetans, all those who held on to their culture and would not be turned. That was why they had arrested Sonam in the first place: because they knew they hadn't assimilated him. And that was why they had beaten him so savagely: because even in jail he had resisted them.

But there was something else he now realized—something

important: an opportunity. The boy was literally unrecognizable. What was more, he would never look the way he had before. It was a wild idea, and it had struck him as he stitched the wounds and applied the honey. His son need no longer be Sonam. In fact, he need no longer be Tibetan. Perhaps, unwittingly, the People's Liberation Army had given him a path to a new life.

He would have to leave as soon as he was strong enough—in a week, two weeks at the most. Yéshé could hide him for a time, claiming that he had not returned from prison, but the Chinese liked to keep tabs on former prisoners. And even though the guards had meant for him to die, they still had to report his release, which meant that a political officer would start coming around, looking for him.

The dark days have returned, Yéshé thought. He had feared that it would happen, when the Chinese began to slaughter them openly once again. It had happened before, in '57, after the Khampa uprising, when the Chinese had committed the most terrible atrocities against the Tibetans—crucifixions, live burials, vivisection, pushing them from airplanes. Those terrible days when Tibetan children were forced to shoot their parents, when monks and nuns were forced to shoot their lamas and *rinpoches.* Now the dark days had returned.

"Tibetan fever."

He did not know how, but he knew the Chinese were to blame. And because he had always known that the dark days could return, he had taken steps to protect his children. They were all he had, his fortune and wealth, and he loved them above all things—partly because they were the future of Tibet, but mostly because they were half of their mother. She had been taken from him too soon, killed by the Chinese doctors who had botched her sterilization after she "illegally" bore a second child. In his children, he still had a little bit of her, in their eyes and their smiles and their mischief. If they died, then Tibet would die, and so would the last remnants of his wife.

But to get off the Tibetan Plateau was a nearly impossible task. There were more than a dozen security checks, and anywhere the army wasn't watching, its informants were. So in the faint glow of dawn, he drafted two letters: one to a fellow Tibetan who worked for the Chinese lumber conglomerate, and the other to a Han Chinese man. If the letters were opened by the Public Safety Bureau, they would appear to discuss simple things—the winter's light snows, the accomplishments of the children in their fine Chinese schools—but there was a second message within these innocuous words that would cause things to move.

The boy would not want to leave. He would resist. But for the old man, it was decided. As soon as Sonam was strong enough, Yéshé would send him on a journey that would take him far from Tibet. And there his life would ultimately intersect with scientists who practiced a magic that, at that moment, neither he nor his son could comprehend.

CHAPTER FIVE

April 15, 2025
Naval Research Laboratory, Washington, DC

> We knew from the outset that we were out to make history. We
> knew how important it was to the nation and to the world, and
> that made it a little frightening. But we also knew that this was a
> once-in-a-lifetime opportunity to push science to a new frontier,
> and if we could win this race, we would likely determine the
> direction of the world for decades to come.
>
> —Bill Eastman, January 30, 2025

An orange dusk was fading to darkness as three men walked across the
tarmac toward the Moffett hangar. Even though he was now one of the
leaders of what would soon become the most expensive military project
in history, Jack Behrmann felt small and insignificant next to the huge
hangar they were approaching. Seeing it up close for the first time, he
had to admit he was impressed. In the growing darkness, the colossal
structure reminded him of something out of a science fiction movie,
a monochromatic plated beast, one of the great sandworms of Dune.
It was nothing like a normal aircraft hangar, not the ground-hugging

half cylinder of a Quonset hut. This was a massive thing, over 150 feet high, 80 feet wide, and 1,200 feet long. From the front, it looked like a huge omega sign—Ω—with the front and back ends rounded like the head of a torpedo. It had been built in California in the 1930s to house one of the huge zeppelins that the navy was experimenting with at the time—enormous airships that could launch and recover five or six fighter planes from their platforms. Jack had been told the hangar was so big that clouds formed inside it, and now, as he craned his neck upward, he believed it.

When they were still some twenty paces from the massive front doors, a warning siren sounded. This was not the small, annoying beep of a backing truck. It was like the siren of a warship, a sound pushed by a great bellows and meant to be heard for miles, like the deep wail of a prehistoric beast.

Jack cringed.

Then a series of warning lights, each encased in a metal birdcage, began spinning, throwing a yellow strobe along the seams of the huge doors.

As the warning siren began to fade, they heard the revving of great turbines, followed by a deep *thump-thump* as thick metal cables suddenly exhausted their slack and began to pull the hangar doors apart. It was such a huge structure and they were so close, Jack had to resist a sudden urge to turn and run. It was like standing next to a speeding train.

He leaned down to Eastman's ear. "Couldn't we have just come in through the service entrance?"

"Now, Jack," Bill said, smiling, "what fun would that be?"

Light poured out from the growing fissure, dazzling the three men and bleaching them in whiteness. Jack raised his hand to shield his eyes. It took a few moments for his vision to adjust, and when it did, the scene took his breath away. They stood on the threshold of a great cathedral of light. At first, it seemed as though the huge arched walls were actually *made* of light. Then he saw that they were not really walls at all, but an intricate webwork of triangular supports and trusses that crisscrossed again and again, at least nine feet deep. It reminded him of the cross-linking lacework of the Eiffel Tower. But where the Eiffel Tower was a drab iron gray, here every beam, rod, and bolt had been polished to a chrome-like brilliance. It was as if he were looking into a huge domed spiderweb, its gossamer strands wet with dew and refracting light in preternatural ways.

In the foreground, two thousand brand-new employees, *their* employees, were waiting for them, standing in front of their chairs. Beyond them was an elevated stage, and hanging from the ceiling above it were three enormous banners, each one some 50 feet wide and 130 feet tall, colored navy blue and adorned with lighter, Egyptian-blue designs—each one dedicated to one of the project's three core sciences.

Genetics: a double helix.

Artificial Intelligence: the left hemisphere of a brain.

Nanotechnology: a geometric carbon nanotube.

Behind these, at the back of the hangar, were several historic fighter planes in storage, blue and silver with the US insignia on their wings and fuselages: a circle and star over a red and white ribbon. Three F-4 Phantoms, an A-4 Skyhawk, and three F6F Hellcats.

Jack felt instantly uneasy.

Taken all together, the symbolism of the place couldn't have been clearer: the three pillars of science inside a military womb. He looked apprehensively at Bill Eastman, who was looking straight ahead and grinning. *You should never have agreed to this,* said the voice in his head. *This is not what science is for.*

Bill and Admiral Curtiss stepped forward over the threshold and into the hangar, but Jack couldn't. There was something about taking that next step. He looked down at his feet. Somehow, this was more significant than leaving California, or selecting his new team, or moving into his quarters on base. Doing those things had not really meant that he was fully on board. But taking the next step meant that he was really going to do it. He was really going to make weapons for the military.

With another frightening *thump-thump,* the doors stopped moving. The mouth of the hangar was now wide open. On cue, a snare drum began a military march. *Tap-tap rat-ta-tat tat.* It was a hypnotic rhythm, urgent and patriotic, and it was soon accompanied by trumpets, flutes, and French horns, all full of stars and stripes and amber waves of grain. Jack didn't know his military marches, only that they were written to inspire soldiers into battle. Designed to pull at their heartstrings while bypassing their minds. He knew this, yet he also felt—very much against his will—a patriotic stirring in his breast. As Bill and the admiral made their way to the stage, the crowd began to clap. The applause quickly fed on itself, rising and rising, accentuated by whoops and cheers and whistles. Joy. Exultation. It was for Bill, of course. He was their icon, their leader, their guru. He had gathered all these great minds to this place. They could see, just as well as Jack could, the possibilities that such a group might accomplish, the high plateau that they might attain.

The energy of the crowd, the rousing music, the dazzling cathedral of light, finally pulled Jack in. It was like standing knee-deep in a river and feeling the persistent pull of the current. He took a step forward, then another. As he crossed the threshold, there came a new surge of applause. They had seen him. The Big Man. There was no mistaking it. This was not *all* for Bill. He quick-stepped and fell in beside his friend, his apprehension dissipating. How could all this energy, this beauty, and this combined intellect be wrong?

Some people stepped into the aisle to greet them, to shake Bill's hand, to touch him. Bill greeted them warmly, taking his time with each one. He waved, pointed, and winked. Soon, Jack was doing the same. They had done this many times before, of course, working the crowd, but never a crowd with so many great minds.

How had they gotten them all? There was Jessica Berg from Finland, perhaps the top computer scientist in the world. He saw Rebecca Zhu from U. Penn, a leader in cognitive intelligence systems. And there, sitting quietly in front, was Olex Velichko, an insufferable prima donna but without doubt the world's greatest mind in genetics.

Perhaps more important than the famous ones were the not-yet-famous ones. God, they looked young. In many ways, the postdocs and grad students would determine the fate of this project, because the cutting edge of science was in many ways like the world of professional athletes and musicians. The greats tended to peak young. Jack had never quite figured out why this was. Perhaps it was chemistry, a hormonal imbalance, or perhaps they just wanted it more. Maybe they were still too ignorant of all the distractions and pleasures of the world. Whatever it was, the young had it: ambition that took them to the outer wall of science, where they pushed and prodded and hammered until they found a way through. Over and over again he had seen it: young scientists doing groundbreaking work in their twenties and early thirties, then fizzling out. *Einstein's disease,* some people called it. For Einstein was the most famous example of the phenomenon. In a single year, at the age of twenty-six, he published major papers on light quanta, Brownian motion, mass and energy equivalence, and the special theory of relativity. Annus mirabilis. His miracle year. He never reached such brilliance again. At thirty-seven, he shone briefly when he published the general theory of relativity, but after he turned forty, it was generally agreed that he wasted the rest of his life.

So, this project was about recruiting the greatest known minds, but also about finding those who were on the cusp of greatness. It would likely come down to the young, and Jack knew that his role would be to inspire, cajole, and squeeze every drop of brilliance out of these young minds. At times, it would get ugly. They were going to churn and burn them. He didn't like that, but it was the nature of the job. There was just too much at stake.

As Jack clasped hands and waved, he knew that these people, whom he scarcely knew, were relying on him. But he was relying on them, too.

The three men climbed the steps to the stage, where they turned and waved to the crowd. The cheering swelled to a roar, like the sound in a ballpark when someone hits a home run. Jack couldn't help but grin. It was the hope of beginnings, the start of a great journey. The joy of setting out for the unknown with a group of fellow travelers who were capable and strong, deft and daring.

Admiral Curtiss stepped up to the podium and spoke briefly,

knowing full well that this crowd looked to Eastman for leadership and were not predisposed to trust a military man. He reassured them that he was here to help and that if they needed anything at all, he would get it for them. His tact impressed Jack. Maybe the guy wasn't so bad after all.

Then Bill Eastman stepped up. He had them enthralled at the first word. A gifted orator, he spoke with great insight and clarity, yet he was also funny and self-deprecating, sharing silly mistakes he had made and times when he had made a fool of himself.

Now, he told them they had to work fast. He had faith that they could win, but there was no time to waste. The crowd was spellbound. Just as they had roared at his humor, now they were solemn at his seriousness.

"Eight months," he said.

The crowd stirred at that, and even up on the stage Jack could hear the whispers and murmurs: "*It's too soon.*" "*That's not enough time.*"

"Eight months to replication," Bill repeated. "Between now and then, I will ask you to work harder, longer, and smarter than you have ever worked before. You will struggle through many nights and days. At times, you will feel exhausted and overwhelmed. Your resolve will weaken and grow brittle, and you will be tempted to quit. Yet you must press on! The importance of the deadline cannot be stressed enough. The owner of the first functional device will have an influence unsurpassed in history. With it, they will immediately jump ahead of all the others."

Now Bill's eyes had an icy intensity. "We all know how coveted the prize has become, and that one nation—you all know which one I mean—is already ahead of us. If they win, what will keep them from selling their technology to hostile nations, as they have done in the past? What will keep them from exercising their newfound might against their weaker neighbors, or even against us? After all, they will have nothing to fear from anyone." He let that sink in. Jack saw heads nodding. "Eight months to secure the balance of power in the world. Eight months to give us time to protect ourselves and create countermeasures." Bill stopped and gave them a hard look. "Can you do it?"

The response was instantaneous. The crowd thundered. "*Will* you do this?" he shouted over the din. They roared louder. Resting his elbow on the lectern, he turned to Jack. "Well, do you think they're ready?"

It was one of their old tricks. A showman's stunt to fire up the crowd. Jack rubbed his big beard in a show of skepticism, then shook his head. *Nah.*

Bill turned back to the crowd and shrugged his shoulders. They roared louder than ever.

Jack cupped his hand to his ear. Two thousand voices cheering as loud as they could. Then Jack smiled and nodded his head as if impressed, which, in fact, he was. The crowd laughed and cheered.

Four hours later, the crowd was gone and Bill and Jack were alone in the immense hangar, except for a few maintenance people stacking chairs and sweeping the floor. There had been a huge meal, and afterward the band had played Glenn Miller, Benny Goodman, and the best of the Casa Loma Orchestra. The men had loosened their ties, and the women had danced with their heel straps laced between their fingers.

But now it was quiet, and Jack Behrmann felt his euphoria beginning to ebb. His mind was coming back to the monumental task ahead, of keeping his team focused, motivated, and as happy as possible. And the biggest problem, the perennial problem: finding more talent. He felt as if he were casting a great motion picture, in which each of his six hundred actors had a unique role to play. Each one had a specialty that they would need in building the nanosite. It was not unlike specialization in medicine, really, except that instead of taking care of a patient, they were *building* one. He had specialists for data processing (the "central nervous system"), for power distribution (the "circulatory system"), for system regulation (the "endocrine system"), for energy conversion (the "digestive system"), and for replication (the "reproductive system").

And Jack was still missing his most important cast member. An architect. He needed someone who could envision the whole organism, who would direct and guide the other groups and integrate all their ideas into one superefficient organism. The architect was a critical piece, and Jack had been trying to fill the slot from day one. But he had not found anyone who truly impressed him, so he had been reduced to hiring several people, hoping he could train them up so their combined talents might equal the one person he really needed.

As the group of workmen began disassembling the stage, Bill and Jack began the walk back toward the residences.

"Oh, I almost forgot," Bill said, producing some folded papers from inside his suit. He had a sudden glint in his eye. "I have something for you."

It was the draft of a journal article. Jack stopped to look at the title, which was simply "What Will It Look Like?" Then he read the abstract.

"This looks perfect!" he said, his cheeks rising with color. "Where'd you get it?"

"A few months ago, I told Pierce Craig at *Nature* to let me know if he had any submissions that might be security sensitive. You know, stuff that could be useful to us but that we didn't want made public. He sent it to me yesterday—said he'd love to publish it."

"I bet he would," Jack said, looking at the byline. "Eric Hill? Who is he?"

"He's under Kathy Masson at Stanford. Set to graduate next month. I think we can get him."

"This was written by a grad student?"

Bill gave a slow nod and smiled.

There it was again, Jack thought as they left the light of the hangar. For a graduate student to do work worthy of publication in *Nature* was extraordinary. It was the type of publication that would get the author an immediate tenure-track position at a top university.

"Should I get Curtiss's boys to start the background check?" Jack asked.

Bill gave him a sheepish look. "I hope you don't mind, but I told him to get started this morning. He says it'll take at least a week."

"You seem pretty sure about this one."

"Eric? Well, I've been keeping my eye on him for a while now. I heard him give a paper a few years ago. He struck me as a good egg."

"Well, let's hope he's our boy."

"Yes, let's hope."

Jack looked at his friend for a moment. He knew there was something Bill wasn't telling him. He had known him long enough to recognize the signs. Something about this Eric Hill. But Jack decided not to push it. It had been a long evening, and tomorrow they would begin the hardest project of their lives.

CHAPTER SIX

April 19, 2025
Palo Alto, CA

Eucalyptus trees crowded the low-rise apartment blocks in Escondido Village, the principal housing area for graduate students at Stanford University. In a tiny apartment, a young man lay asleep on a mattress on the floor. He was tall and lean with thick black hair and a handsome, but boyish, face. He was naked except for a black polyurethane brace on one knee.

The only light in the blacked-out room came from an oversize computer monitor that was quietly flipping through a series of images. Eric at age six with his father, dressed up for church in a blue suit and squinting in the sun; Eric with another young man and two pretty girls—tuxedos and prom dresses, all of them laughing at some forgotten play on words; Eric holding up a trophy at the State Wrestling Championship; Eric receiving his degree from MIT; and finally, an image of Bill Eastman with a superimposed caption: "When I grow up, I wanna be just like Eric Hill."

Under the faux wood desk that held the monitor was the cpu—a plywood box with a single red switch, above which was scrawled THE WHOPPER, in permanent marker.

A phone rang. From under the covers, Eric Hill gave an involuntary kick. He moaned in protest and tried to ignore the sound, but the phone kept ringing. On the fifth ring, he opened one eye and looked at the clock on the floor: 6:17 a.m., and on a Saturday! *Son of a bitch.* He burrowed his head under the pillow. It didn't help. Finally, the ringing stopped. *Sleep. More sleep.* But a minute later, the phone rang again. He sat up in bed, wanting to throw something.

The floor was littered with clothing, books, and trash … There, in the corner—his gray sweatpants were glowing. He snatched up the phone. *Caller: Chris Hatter.* He knew it! Once again, the Merck recruiter had forgotten that New York and California were not in the same time zone. He silenced the phone and climbed back into bed. *Sorry, Chris, like I told you, not interested.* He punched the pillow a few times and tried to get cozy, but it was no good. He was up now. Thinking. He knew his own brain. Once it kicked in, it wouldn't stop anytime soon, not with all that was going on in his life. *Not interested.* God, was he a fool? He was two weeks away from getting a PhD in chemical engineering from Stanford fucking University, and he wasn't interested in the twenty-one job offers he had. Twenty-one. They had started coming during his very first semester of grad school. Six figures, corporate car, eight weeks' vacation, profit sharing, *write your own ticket.* How many times had he heard that? They all must have said it. Most of his friends were gone now. Few had bothered to graduate. Nanotech was just too hot. They'd gone pro, hit the majors. They called to say how great it was, that he was an idiot for staying. *Who cares if the suffix after your name is only MS?* The offer from Merck—that was the sweetest. He could pay off his student loans in six months.

Not interested. But he *was* interested. He was obsessed—by one job, which may or may not even exist. He was obsessed with finding Bill Eastman.

For the past six weeks, many of the greatest minds in nanotech, artificial intelligence, and genetics had been disappearing. Two of his Stanford professors and one from MIT had suddenly taken extended sabbaticals and moved away. He didn't know precisely where they had gone or what they were doing—only that the disappearances had come shortly after a rumor began that Eastman was going to lead a big project for the government. Then he too, had suddenly dropped out of sight.

It had to be self-replication, he thought. The government had finally realized what was at stake. And the man they had chosen was Eastman.

He lay on his side, his mind turning over the problem. How to find Bill Eastman?

His phone rang again. This time, he sat up with a start. He could have sworn he'd silenced it. He decided to ignore it, but then he noticed that the call had a different ring, the way it sometimes did when he got a call from overseas. His curiosity was piqued. "Listen in," he said, and the phone chirped its compliance. Now he could hear the message as the person was leaving it, and if he wished, he could still answer it.

"Hi, you have reached Eric Hill, I can't—" his greeting began.

Then he heard a man's voice: "Hello, my name is Jack Behrmann—"

Eric scrambled to his feet, stumbled, fell over, recovered, and grabbed for the phone. "Dr. Behrmann?"

Jack Behrmann. A quarter of Eric's bookshelf held volumes either by or about this man. The first scientist to manipulate a catenane through chemical self-assembly. MacArthur Foundation. National Medal of Science. Possibly the most brilliant nanotechnologist in the world. But more than brilliant—he was Bill Eastman's best friend. Wherever Behrmann was, Eastman had to be close by. "Hello, Eric, I hope I'm not calling too early."

"No, sir. I've been up for a while now. Getting some work done."

"Very good. I'm calling to talk to you about something rather important. Do you have a secure video line?"

"Yes, just a minute." He was trying to stay cool, but his heart was racing. *How many times had he dreamed of this?* It almost didn't seem real, and he feared that at any moment one of his friends' voices would break into the line and reveal that it was all a prank. He fumbled about, scavenging for a presentable shirt, then whacked his shin on the desk so hard it sounded like a base hit. Grimacing and fighting back a string of expletives, he managed to pull a *Star Wars* T-shirt over his head and sit down at his desk, the better to conceal the fact that he hadn't put on his underwear. "Connecting now," he said. He set the phone by his desk. It immediately interfaced with the computer.

A moment later, the image of a man appeared on the monitor. It was Behrmann, all right. There was the thick beard, the soft eyes, the bald head. Although he could only see Behrmann's head and shoulders, he was reminded that this was a very big man. You could hear it in his voice—a deep, comforting sound.

Behrmann was sitting in front of a green screen. The newer video-conferencing software had selectable backgrounds, in case you didn't want the other person to see your real background. Instead, you could pick the location you wanted to "call" from: your office, your house, Cancún.

Behrmann was studying something on his desk, and Eric realized that it was his own picture. Behrmann was confirming his identity. Finally, he looked up. "Let's get down to business, shall we? I saw the paper you submitted to *Nature*. I liked it, and I may have an opportunity for you."

Eric tried to hide his shock. He had submitted the paper hoping that its publication would get Eastman's attention. He never imagined that could happen before it was even published.

"However," Behrmann continued, "I need to ask you a few questions. I've had a chance to talk to Otto, Kathy, and other people who know your work. They have nothing but good things to say, but I … well, I need to be absolutely sure."

Eric nodded ever so slightly, and his eyes narrowed in concentration. Behrmann was about to put him through his paces. But he was ready for it. He had expected this—dreamed of it, in fact. He was going to rock Behrmann's world. "Shoot," he said.

Behrmann picked up an iSheet and set his glasses on the end of his nose. "First question …"

Eric breezed through the first set of questions. Phase equilibria, Brownian motion, sliding friction—things any decent grad student in chemical engineering would know. With each right answer, his confidence grew. After Behrmann had quizzed him for almost an hour, he paused, and Eric figured it was in the bag.

But Behrmann was just warming up. It was going to be a game to see if the great Jack Behrmann could stump him.

They moved into mathematics and physics—the real core of advanced nanotechnology. He asked about quantum entanglement and Bohr orbits, then about Maxwell's equations and the Klein-Gordon equation. Eric's answers started coming slower, and he started to worry. Any minute, Behrmann was sure to nail him. Eric had been lucky on the last two questions. He had seen Maxwell's equations by chance just a few weeks ago, and the Klein-Gordon equation was something his father had taught him in high school.

Then came the moment that made Eric's heart skip.

"Why don't you write out a set of six possible paths for a particle using Feynman-Dirac propagators."

Eric felt suddenly queasy. The Feynman-Dirac propagators were some of the toughest equations in quantum mechanics. They were path-integral formulas that charted possible trajectories to compute quantum amplitude—complicated extensions of the famous Schrödinger equation. And Behrmann wanted not one, but six of them. It was a task that could easily fill a chalkboard and, these days, was always executed by a computer. Eric hadn't written out an equation of that size in years.

"I'll give you twenty minutes," Behrmann said, looking down at his watch.

Eric felt the inside of his skull heat up. It was a sickening feeling that threatened his concentration. *Twenty minutes!* He dashed for his backpack, not caring whether Behrmann saw his bare ass, retrieved an iSheet, and began writing furiously, his fingers suddenly sweaty, slipping on the stylus.

As he filled each page, he sent it to Behrmann with a swipe of his hand. Behrmann studied the printouts meticulously, scribbling on them and occasionally asking questions to prove to himself that Eric really understood the equations and had not simply memorized them. "Why did you compensate for the relativistic arc length?"

"Because you are dealing with imaginary time—that's why you need the heuristic."

A nod.

By the time he reached the eighteen-minute mark, his fingers were so cramped he was shaking. He had one more full equation to go. He began writing faster than ever, his mind a focused tunnel of effort. When he next glanced at his watch, he had forty-five seconds to go. He might just make it. With a flurry of effort, he finished the last equation and swiped it over to Behrmann.

Now he waited, watching as Behrmann reviewed the equations, scrutinizing, jotting notes on each page, like a professor grading exams, occasionally grunting or nodding or squinting at his handwriting.

Eric waited, flushed with nervousness, and felt tempted to make excuses for what he was sure was a poor performance. He glanced at the clock. He couldn't believe it. They had been talking for more than three hours.

At last, Behrmann pulled off his glasses and looked up, but Eric could not read his expression. "Believe it or not, you are the first person to actually finish the technical part of the interview. In fact, the last person started crying when I got to Klein-Gordon." A warm smile grew across Behrmann's bearded face. "You missed a few, but they were understandable mistakes. So, to put it bluntly, I'd like you to join my team. Interested?"

Eric let out a long exhalation, a roguish grin broadening across his face. "Yes, sir, I am." He couldn't believe it. He'd done it!

"There is one more thing," Behrmann said, "and I want you to think very carefully about what I'm going to say. If you do this, if you agree to come work with us, then you have to give me everything you have. We are taking only those who are willing to give every ounce of themselves to this project. You will live on-site, and you will be expected to work harder and smarter than you have ever worked before. Six- and seven-day weeks, up to sixteen hours a day. In short, only if you can make this your life's work do we want you here. Are you willing to do that?"

Eric didn't honestly know whether he could, but this was what he had wanted ever since his sophomore year at MIT. He looked around the cluttered apartment and thought of the solitary life he had led to get him to this place.

He said what he had to say, the only thing there was to say.

CHAPTER SEVEN

February 2, 2025
Nyingchi Prefecture, Tibetan Autonomous Region

Sonam shifted anxiously beside the old truck driver.

"Hurry up," the man said, looking around nervously. They were standing on the back of a logging truck, bracing against the cold, their breath pouring out of their mouths like smoke. Under their feet were snow-covered tree trunks—massive pines and hemlocks, six feet thick at the base—so long they jutted out from the end of the flatbed.

"Go on, get in!" the man said.

Sonam hesitated. At his feet was a hole in one of the pine trees, the opening scarcely bigger than a dinner plate. Just looking at it made him claustrophobic.

"I won't fit," he said.

"Yes, you will," the driver said, placing a hand on his shoulder and urging him down. "Now, please hurry. If this truck isn't back in the convoy in five minutes, the political officer is going to suspect something, and then we'll both rot in Drapchi prison."

Sonam looked at the man's weathered face, the skin almost black from a life under the high mountain sun—leathery, worn, and cracked.

Sonam didn't like the man's touch, but he said nothing. He knew that the man was taking an incredible risk helping him. Whatever debt he owed Sonam's father, it must be very great. Sonam mumbled a prayer then wriggled his way in, feetfirst. As emaciated as he was from prison, he still had to squeeze his elbows together to get his shoulders through. He fit, but just barely. There was no way to extend his legs, and it was a struggle to move his arms at all. It was also cold and damp inside. The only thing that didn't completely repulse him was the soothing smell of pine.

The driver handed him a thermos, a small bag of food, a fur blanket, and a funny-looking medical bag. "My wife stole this from the hospital for you." Sonam eyed the bag and its little hose curiously.

Reading his expression, the driver said, "Put the end of the tube over your dick and piss in the bag." Sonam flushed with embarrassment.

"Now, remember, you *must* stay inside the whole time. The convoy will stay close together, and if your head pops up out of this hole, the driver behind me will see you."

Sonam nodded. He lay back, pulled his hands to his chest, and watched as the lid descended toward his face. He took a big gulp of air, like a man about to be submerged in water, and the man fitted the lid into place, a mere inch from his nose. Darkness. He thought he could do this, but something inside him rebelled. *No!* It was too much like death, like *bardo*. He shoved the lid open, gasping, and started crawling out.

In a second, the driver was beside him, but now his tone was not so harsh. "Breathe, Sonam. That's it. No, don't get out. Wait a minute … just wait. You can do this."

"No, I can't!" He sat on the lip of the opening, legs still inside.

"I know you can. Breathe. I know it seems bad, but I've taken many people off the plateau this way. If they can do it, so can you."

Sonam shook his head. *No.* He looked at the man's face. It had struck him as an ugly face at first. But now he saw tranquility in the eyes, and he suddenly realized that this haggard old man was a strong Buddhist. He would have to be to risk his life over and over again for others. Sonam breathed. Waited a moment. Breathed again. His heart began to slow. He exhaled, looked at the man, and nodded. "Okay, let's try again."

"That's it," he said. "Use your training."

Again the lid was lowered. Darkness. He concentrated on his breathing and began to recite his mantras. *Oṃ maṇi padme hūṃ* ... He thought of bardo, of death, the forty-nine days between one life and the next. If a mind was untrained and unprepared for bardo, then it became hell—forty-nine days of nightmarish torment that culminated in a bad rebirth. But if one could find serenity and control one's fears, then a teacher would appear—a lama who could guide the soul. Then bardo became a sublime space of transcendence, leading to a good rebirth.

Sonam tried to remember the meditation techniques his father and the tutors had taught him. He reminded himself that this was not as bad as death, not even as bad as prison.

Outside, he heard the driver shoveling snow on top of the log, followed by the rustling sound of a hemlock bough being brushed over the snow to conceal their footprints. A few minutes later, the diesel engine clattered to life and the truck began to move. That was good. It meant that every minute he endured brought him that much closer to getting out. Between his breathing, the meditation, and the movement of the truck, he remained calm. As his eyes adjusted, he realized it was not completely dark. There was a circle of pink around the rim of the lid. It had been made to allow a little air in so that he did not suffocate. He thought of the others who had made this journey before him, and he began to believe he could do it after all.

He thought back to last night, parting with his father. For days, they had been fighting bitterly over his leaving. Last night had been no different.

"I don't want to argue anymore," his father had said. "You must go. Can't you see what will happen? You are stubborn and proud, and a subjugated people cannot be stubborn and proud. You will continue to fight, and soon enough they will kill you."

"I'm at peace with that path," Sonam said. "In the next life, I will be stronger and I will fight them again. I will never stop. I will return again and again."

"Fighting the Chinese is not the way to nirvana."

"And rotting here while they systematically destroy us—that is? While they humiliate us and brainwash us and steal everything we have created—*that's* the way to nirvana?"

But the old man was unmoved. "You are my son, and I forbid you to forfeit your life."

Sonam turned his head in disgust. He was arguing merely to argue. He knew that. He would not disobey his father. Yet arguing was his way of telling him he didn't want to go, that he was scared. Couldn't his father see that?

Yéshé went to his son and stood very close to him. "Stand up," the old man said.

Sonam stood. A long moment passed, and he shifted uncomfortably, half expecting his father to strike him.

His father cupped his hand behind Sonam's neck and pulled him closer until their foreheads touched.

"I don't want to let go of you. Know that. If I could have my way, I would keep you here with me forever. My little boy, the one who learned to walk in this very kitchen, holding on to your mother's hem and gripping the floor with your strong little toes. But it is more important that you live. You have a chance now, a chance to make much more of your life than so many other Tibetans. I want you to live—for me, for your mother. So let's not argue anymore. Just be my son for the few hours we have left."

Yéshé opened his arms, and the boy embraced him.

Three hours later, in the dead of night, they said goodbye. They stood out in the courtyard in the cold, the Milky Way hanging above them like a crystal river.

"You may return when the Dalai Lama returns," his father said. Sonam knew that this meant never. He would never see their little farm again. Never again see the sloping hillsides, the painfully beautiful mountains beyond. He would never experience another day here, the feeling he had when he returned each afternoon with the sheep, hungry and tired, but content with the simplicity of life. He would never see his sister again, never again tease her and play pranks on her.

"*Na kirinla gaguidou*," the boy said.

"I love you, too." The old man clasped his hands and inclined his head in the Tibetan way, blessing him and his journey.

The truck rumbled over a series of potholes, and Sonam was shoved violently in one direction, then another.

How long had they been moving? He had lost all track of time. It was still daytime, which seemed impossible. Yet the pink circle of light around the lid told him so. The truck had stopped four times so far. Once for petrol, he was sure, because he had smelled the fumes and heard men talking and laughing. The other stops had been government checkpoints, each one more terrifying than the last. With no way to see what was going on, his imagination had run wild. It was maddening to think that someone might be inspecting the truck, looking for him; that some soldier might have moved onto the log without his hearing, and that at any moment he might hear the *eureka* shouts of soldiers and see the lid suddenly open.

Then came the fifth stop. It was after dark. The pink circle of light was gone, and the temperature was dropping fast. He heard the driver talking to someone, joking and laughing, but whoever he was talking to did not laugh in response. He heard talking in Chinese. Another checkpoint. Then he heard the whimper of a dog and three short barks.

Sonam felt a chill run through him. More barking, then a man shouting orders in Chinese. "Yú, check this one here." He heard the scuff of boots on the logs coming closer. He stared into the darkness, listening with all his might. Waiting. Suddenly, the pink circle of light around the opening throbbed for a moment then faded. Throbbed and faded again. A flashlight was being swept over the lid. More footsteps.

Coming closer. The wood gave a long creak, and the pink circle of light returned. The man was right on top of him. Suddenly, a new fear gripped Sonam. Perhaps the warmth of his breath had melted a circle in the snow. The searcher would surely see it. He would open the lid at any moment. Of course he would. And then Sonam would go back. Back to prison. *Please, no,* he thought.

He couldn't go back. Six months in Drapchi had almost killed him. If they caught him again, the sentence would be much longer, and anything more than six months was a death sentence. That was because the Chinese prisons were not designed to reform or reeducate. No. The motto written in iron above the prison gate—REFORM THROUGH LABOR—was a lie. The prison was designed to kill, and they kept you until you died—usually not from the work or the beatings or even the torture, but from starvation. It was all about math. Caloric math. There was simply no way to survive on the amount of food they rationed. All the prisoners were slowly starving to death, from the moment they arrived.

It had been clear the very first day, when they had opened his cell and looked at the twenty prisoners inside. Those who had been there only a few weeks looked healthy and strong, but those who had been there longer—two months, then four months, then six—were wasting away in steady increments. Anyone jailed longer than six months was just a bag of bones. Many of them couldn't even walk because their legs would no longer support their bodies. They crawled.

Yet, he had soon learned that some *did* live longer. They survived nine, ten months, some a year, and a few even longer. But that was only because they were getting extra calories from somewhere. Some made deals with the guards, others managed to smuggle food in, and some pilfered from the meager stashes of other prisoners. But you could be sure that anyone who looked too healthy for the time he had served was eating more than their ration.

He would never forget that first night, when the inevitability of his own starvation was driven home. It was around ten thirty, almost lights out, when the rumor ran from cell to cell that there was going to be an inspection. Any prisoner who had stashed extra food under his floor mat rushed to eat it lest it be confiscated. An older man from Kham had just received two balls of butter bread from his family—a prize that could be stretched for a week. He quickly shoved them in his mouth. He was fine throughout the inspection, but he was unaccustomed to so much rich food, and after the guards left he became sick and threw up on the floor. Sonam watched in horror as the other prisoners scrambled and fought over the vomit, pushing and scooping it into their mouths. But the greatest horror for Sonam was not what he was watching, but rather the certainty that within a few weeks he, too, would be hungry enough to fight over another man's vomit. And with that realization came another. Now he understood the prison's second leading cause of death: suicide.

No, he could not go back there. He looked up, transfixed by the ring of pink light, scarcely daring to breathe. Only an inch of cold pine separated him and prison. And in that moment he knew, with a profound sadness, that he could not let them take him. If the lid should open now, he would fight them. He would fight, run—whatever it took to provoke them into shooting him. He would not go back. He would do the thing he had wanted to do in prison: take his own life. He had stayed alive for Chodren, but now that she was gone ...

The sudden bark of the dog made Sonam flinch. Then he heard a string of Chinese curses. "Get back here!" Then he heard the driver laughing. "It was a hare," he cried. "There he goes! Go get him, boy!" More laughter. "You aren't feeding him enough." Sonam heard the dog growl, followed by the scrape of its claws on the pavement, and the receding sound of its barking.

Sonam felt the soldier's boot grind on the wood as he turned; then the circle of pink was gone. Only after he heard the soldier swing down to the roadway did he finally breathe normally. He sighed with relief and thanked the hare that had saved his life, and he thanked the three jewels for the little bit of good karma he still had.

On and on the truck rolled through the night. And all night long Sonam shivered and squirmed inside his cocoon. His body ached from the constant jostling of the truck, and the cold seeped into his bones until he could not stay focused on the mantras. He would begin a recitation, but then his mind would spin away wildly, pursuing its own whims. He faded between consciousness and dream. And in the cold and the shuddering of a strong wind that shook truck and log and man, his weak mind returned to the dark places, to the things he tried to keep locked away—to the windowless room in Drapchi prison. To Lieutenant Bai. He had felt so small then, at his first torture session, naked except for his underwear, the men standing over him, armored in their uniforms. He remembered how Bai had waved his hand absently and the four soldiers descended on him, picking him up under the armpits and taking him back toward a stainless steel table. How cold the table was. Bai had selected a straight razor—to start with.

"But I told them everything. I swear."

"Oh, I understand, but you see, it's my job to be absolutely certain."

As the night reached its darkest and coldest, so his mind delved into its darkest nightmares of Drapchi prison—which were not the things that were done to him, but the things he himself had done.

He would never forget the woman … her face. She had been a schoolteacher, and they had brought her in for *thamzing,* a "struggle session," in the prison courtyard. They had tied her neck to her ankles so that she was bent at a right angle. Then they had strapped a full-size chalkboard to her back and listed on it her supposed crimes. "Poisoner of children," it read. "Instrument of the imperialists." "Refuses to give up *the four olds*: old customs, old culture, old habits, old ideas."

Other prisoners and officials surrounded her, taunting her and humiliating her, trying to get her to confess to her crimes. A party official guided Sonam through the crowd toward her. When they reached the bound woman, the crowd grew quiet. The official leaned forward and grabbed the woman's hair, trying to pull her up. The ropes creaked and she moaned in pain. It was then that Sonam's heart jumped in his chest. He knew this woman. She was a nun from the Ganden Monastery, and she had tutored him when he was eight years old. His father had insisted that of all the nuns, he learn from this woman. For a moment, their eyes met. *Please don't recognize me,* he thought. *Please.*

"Sonam," she said, "help me."

An anger had welled up in him then. A brutal sense of betrayal. She was not allowed to do that. In this perverted play, she was not allowed to name him, to return him to his old life. He kicked her hard in the face. To shut her up, to teach her not to violate that one vital truth: that here, we are no longer the human beings we once were. The crowd had cheered; the political officer smiled. And that had been just the beginning.

The logging truck ran ever eastward, toward the edge of the Tibetan Plateau. Assailed by the nightmare visions, Sonam pushed and heaved against the unyielding wood. The dreams were so clear, so vivid. It was exhausting to live it all again: the school teacher, the torture sessions, the hot iron, the knives, the electricity.

He began to weep, and once he started he couldn't stop. He wept and wept until it became his normal state, the way he was—until there seemed to be no reason in the world *not* to cry. He gasped for air and his whole body shuddered, but it kept going, an outpouring that he could not control or understand. He could only let it take its course. There seemed to be a reason for it—a reason that his body needed to do this here, now.

Finally, something in him snapped—a cathartic breaking—and a door in his mind opened. And there she was, standing in front of him. It was her, Chodren, and she was alive again. His beautiful girl with black eyes, his spirited fighter, his *khandroma,* warrior, goddess, lover. Her beautiful skin seemed to radiate light. She was sky walking, alive in bardo. She touched his cheek. "Sleep now," she said. "You have done so much. You don't need to carry the weight anymore. Let it go. Sleep and know that I love you and I am proud of you."

He tried to keep the image of her in his mind: her dark eyes, her hair with the single knot in it. He had protected her those long months. He had never given her name to Lieutenant Bai, never. And Bai had known it. He had sensed that Sonam had something more to give, and that was why he had never stopped.

"You saved me," he said. "You saved me, but I couldn't save you. Oh, Chodren, how can I move on from this? How does one move on?"

Inside the truck cab, the music had stopped, and the driver thought he heard the boy weeping. Or was it just the wind? He listened hard and even dared to slow down a little. Then he thought he heard it again. He felt sorry for the boy, because he knew firsthand what the boy had been through. He himself had served two long sentences in the labor camps. But the boy's story was so common that it did not shock him in the least. Former prisoners were everywhere. If you sat twelve Tibetan men down, all but two or three would have served some time in the Chinese jails. He would have liked to stop. To check on the boy and comfort him. But there was no way to do that without causing suspicion. The boy would just have to hold on.

He put a fresh CD in the stereo and turned up the volume.

★ ★ ★

When Sonam awoke, he felt cleaner somehow. His mind was not so cloudy. The dreams had been so real and her face so clear, he knew that he had come through the sacred sleep. That Chodren had come to him as a *khandroma,* a Bon Mother.

It was daylight again, warmer, and the air had a weight to it that he had never felt before. Just then the truck took a long turn back on itself, and he realized that it was a familiar feeling. While he dreamed, the truck had been making many such turns. He could also hear the deep, flatulent sound of the truck's air brake, working to slow the heavy load. They were coming down off the plateau.

Suddenly, he couldn't take this confinement any longer. He had to see out, to breathe fresh air. He began to push on the lid, but then he remembered the driver's warning. *If your head pops up out of this hole, the driver behind me will see you.* Reason checked impulse, and he took a deep breath. He waited for the next switchback, for the exact moment the truck behind them could not see them; then he popped the top off the hole.

The sun was up, filling the world with yellow dawn. It was a wonderful sight, and he dared to put a finger on the lip of the hole, to feel the sun's warmth on his skin. He breathed the air hungrily. The beauty of the world. It was still here. He did not know his place in it, but it was still here.

Then he looked up the long hillside, and his heart sank. He saw the switchbacks rising as far as he could see, a great twisting snake of a road, going up and up and up the side of the plateau. And every hundred yards he could see a logging truck. He could see no less than seventy of them, and he knew there were many more below him. He was filled with a sudden sadness, which turned quickly to anger. Forests in transport. Tibet's huge forests, clear-cut, strapped to trucks, and bound for China's factories, to be turned into everything from their daily newspapers to furniture; from cosmetics to turpentine; from toilet seats to chopsticks, then packaged and shipped to the far corners of the earth with the stamp, "Made in China." The sight made his heart ache, for it made plain that even if China quit Tibet at this very moment, it would take a lifetime, if not a century, for the country to recover.

The more he thought about it, the more enraged he became. He had felt a serenity from the night before, from his visit from Chodren, but now that serenity was gone, replaced by hate. It was a shameful emotion for a Tibetan, but he could not shake it, and he knew that it would never leave him. Like the scars on his face, it was permanent. He was too young and too unwise to be forgiving. He hated the Chinese government, the PLA, and every damned Han who benefited from the Chinese occupation.

He was a Buddhist, dedicated to peace, sworn to revere all life, and all he could think of was revenge.

PART TWO
THE RACE

The power of nanotechnology has always been with us. We knew it was there. For thousands of years we saw it in ourselves, saw our wounds heal, our food become energy, watched our bodies age. We saw it in the gait of the lion and the growing of the trees. As with coal and steam before the industrial age, we hadn't made the leap. We didn't know how to harness it—until now.

—Bill Eastman, 2023

CHAPTER EIGHT

INITIATION

May 9, 2025
Naval Research Laboratory, Washington, DC
Phase 1 Deadline: T-minus six months and fifteen days

"This is the most difficult job on my team," Jack Behrmann said. "So if you get the feeling that I'm asking more from you than I'm asking from anyone else, you're right."

Eric sat up straight in his chair, scarcely believing what Jack was telling him. *The architect.*

"You must have an intimate knowledge of all the other specialties," Jack continued. "That means propulsion, data processing, system regulation, energy conversion, and replication. You have to be good at all of it. That's what impressed me about your paper: your understanding of how the systems work together.

"Here, you can start with this." He handed Eric an iSheet. "Keep it. It has all the design plans from each of the teams. As you'll see, replication is our biggest headache."

Eric scanned through the links. It was hundreds of pages. He felt a sudden queasiness.

"Bill has us on strict deadlines," Jack added. "Every month. Sometimes every two weeks. We've met them all so far, but if we don't figure out these replication errors, we are going to miss. And that looks *very* bad for me."

The big man sat behind his desk. Behind him, Eric could see the Potomac River and Reagan National Airport beyond.

"What's the problem?" Eric asked.

"Error rates. They're much too high for efficient replication—too many mutations from parent to offspring. I need you to help me figure out what's going on, and how to fix it."

"I'll get on it now," Eric said.

He went to work. At first, he felt a rush of amazement. Architect— it was his dream job. But soon, the full gravity of it sank in. The complexity was overwhelming. The replication equations alone totaled 320 pages. He barely knew where to start. He tried hitting the books, but that got him only so far. Why? Because there was no textbook for what they were doing. No one had ever done this before. So he began interviewing every team member he could. He took copious notes, organized them, and reviewed them every night. He was learning, but his weakness was replication. He just couldn't get his head around the equations.

He spent five long nights in the library with those equations, but it was like trying to learn Japanese without a dictionary. With each day he failed to make progress, the voice in his head grew louder and louder. *Well, well, well. Having trouble already, are we? You thought you were such a hotshot, what with the full ride at Stanford. Now look at you.*

At his weekly meeting with Jack, he had to admit that he was lost.

"Yes, I've noticed," Jack said.

Great, he's noticed.

"In the other areas, though, you're doing quite well. In fact, I'm impressed by how much you've assimilated in just a few weeks. The propulsion and data-processing groups both say you've been a great help. But the replication group tells me that all you've done is ask questions."

Eric felt the silence grow too long. He wanted to tell Jack that the equations were just too complex, that he lacked the basic genetics background, and that he just didn't have time to learn it and keep up with all the other groups. But he didn't say those things, because it was clear that Jack wasn't interested in excuses. Indeed, it was clear that Jack was testing him. He would have to learn to swim on his own. If not, Jack would let him sink.

"I'll work harder on it," he said.

Jack gave him a reassuring smile. "Keep pushing and I think you'll start to figure it out."

Over the next week, he redoubled his efforts. But it got him nowhere. He just grew more and more distraught. He lost his appetite and started popping antacids to settle his stomach. And all the while, the inner voice grew more insistent. *Just accept it, Jack made a mistake hiring you. Just tell him you aren't cut out for it. Go work in the industry, like all the other mediocre PhDs.*

He tried to tell the voice to shut up, but as each day passed without progress, it was harder to keep quiet. The voice seemed to know the truth: that he was not really a scientist. He was merely a faker, an impostor.

It was late Friday afternoon when she appeared. He was at his desk, and she ducked into his cube. "Hey, I know you don't know me," she said, "but I need a big favor." She was hunched over so no one could see her head above the maze of cubicles. She popped her head up like a gopher, scanned the floor, then hunched down again.

Her badge read, HUNTER, JANE, PHD GENETICS.

There must be over six feet of her. Tall and fit, with tanned skin stretched over muscle. She was dressed in a hodgepodge of influences: expensive running shoes and army fatigue pants that clashed horribly with a purple Fisher Scientific T-shirt, the kind they gave away free at conferences. And he thought he heard a hint of a Southern accent that she was trying to cover up. No makeup or jewelry. Her ears weren't even pierced. And she had beautiful, thick blond hair, the kind that most women would kill for, but it was disheveled and messy, as if she couldn't care less.

"That depends on what the favor is," Eric said, although he was intrigued.

"Here, this is Olex's cell number. I'm leaving town for the weekend; I've got a triathlon and I need to escape without him seeing me. Call him and find out where he is. Please. Make up a story. Anything. Tell him you need supplies or something. If he sees me leaving, I'm dead."

"Who's Olex?"

"*Who's Olex?*" she said with disbelief. "Wow, you must be new. Olexander Velichko? The devil of the Ukraine?"

Eric gave her a vacant stare.

"Evil incarnate?" she offered. "The unhappy blending of Joseph Stalin, Adolf Hitler, and Lord Voldemort?"

Eric shook his head faintly. She kept going.

"The man who steals other people's work and publishes it as his own, then uses his station and fame to get away with it? The man that no one has ever seen laugh, and who relishes any opportunity to ridicule and torture his underlings?" She pointed at herself. "I give you exhibit A."

"Sounds like someone to avoid."

"Precisely. If he sees me, he'll keep me here all weekend. Then no triathlon, which I have been training for … for three months."

"Well, you're in luck," Eric said, pulling out his phone. "I have a trick for you." He entered Olex's phone number and typed a few commands. "Olex is up on Connecticut Avenue, north of Woodley Park."

"Wait—how'd you do that? Olex's phone is encrypted. You're GPS-ing people without their permission?"

Eric gave her a knowing smile.

"That's illegal," she said, shocked, "and super illegal on base. And your name is …?" She squinted at his badge. "Eric Hill."

Eric's smile vanished. If she told the marines, he'd be in big trouble. They all were under the navy's jurisdiction here, which meant military law.

"Very cool," she said with a big grin.

Eric exhaled so hard it pushed up his hair. "Technically, I'm GPS-ing his phone's IP address, not the phone itself."

She gave him a *yeah, right, buddy* kind of look. "Call it what you want, it's totally illegal." She smiled again, and now, since she didn't have to worry about Olex, she hopped up to sit on his desk, cupping her hands over the edge and leaning forward, arms locked at her sides. Her triceps emerging like thick cursive *T*'s.

"So you're Jack's newest NUB?"

"NUB?"

"Yeah. You. Me. All the postdocs and lab techs. We're called NUBs. Olex heard it from one of the marines: 'new useless body.' It's an insult, of course, but one that we've proudly embraced—at least for the short time we're here."

He gave her a quizzical look.

"Until we're fired. You know your life expectancy is about the same as a fruit fly's, right? We're cheap labor. They churn us and they burn us. I've been here two months and I feel like a war veteran."

"That bad?"

She nodded emphatically. "That bad. Just wait till the last day of the month. That's when they do the *re-opt*—reorganization and optimization." She enunciated it dramatically. "It's a purge—a few people get promoted, a few more get demoted, and a whole bunch get a cardboard box and their final paycheck. Looking out over the parking lot, you can watch them go by. It ain't a pretty sight."

Eric looked down at his notebook and thought of the four hours he'd just spent trying to understand a single equation—unsuccessfully.

Reading his expression, she said, "But I'm sure you'll do fine. After all, that trick with the phone was pretty good. You saved me!"

At just that moment, a short, plump Asian man popped his head into Eric's cube. He wore thick glasses and a Spider Man tie. "There you are," he said to Jane. "Nobody's seen Olex."

"Oh, I know," she said, hopping off the desk. "Eric cleared that up for me." Then she said, "Eric, this is Ryan Lee. He's an idiot." She said it so casually that Eric thought he misheard. "Ironic, actually," she continued, "since he works in Artificial Intelligence. So I guess that means you create Artificial Idiocy, isn't that right, Ryan?"

"And this is Jane," Ryan said, not missing a beat. "The only daughter of a Marine Corps colonel who desperately wanted a boy. As you can see, he didn't change his child-rearing strategies when he didn't get what he wanted. The result: it looks like a woman but acts like a man."

She punched him on the arm.

"I rest my case."

The banter continued, with Jane teasing him about his devout belief in the universe according to the prophet Stan Lee. He reminded her that arctic camo could not be used like blue jeans for mixing and matching.

When their available stock of insults had been exhausted, Ryan said, "So, Eric, what do you do?"

"Apparently, nothing well," he replied. "I just joined Nanotech."

"Oh, you're Jack's new architect? I don't envy you, brother. That job sounds like a headache."

It struck Eric how much both his visitors knew about the politics and the personalities of the lab—things he was thoroughly ignorant of.

"I was just telling him about the re-opts."

"Oh," Ryan said, shaking his head. "You'll find this place is crazy. We're all under the great eye." He made a circle with his thumb and forefinger. Eastman and Behrmann know all. If you go even three days around here without making a contribution, they notice. And then there is the great maelstrom of evil: Olex."

"I warned him already," Jane said.

"Whatever she said is a gross understatement. Olex gave me hell for two months. Tried to get me fired. Luckily, Eastman found out the truth about me—right, Jane?"

"About being an idiot?"

"Au contraire—that I'm a genius."

Jane rolled her eyes.

"Now Olex can't touch me."

"Unfortunately, he's right about that," Jane said. "Ryan has something going on—super top secret—that has Eastman excited."

Ryan crossed his arms and gave a smug grin. His bravado was so incongruent with his short, pudgy stature that Eric couldn't help but smile. He decided right then that he liked him; in fact, he liked both of them very much.

Jane looked at her watch. "Shit! The race!" She threw her weekend bag over her shoulder and was out the door. Ryan raised his eyebrows twice and said, "See ya around," and he, too, was gone.

When Eric arrived at the next Nanotech team meeting, the room was too quiet. There was none of the normal premeeting chatter—no talk of sports, politics, or science news.

That was when Eric saw him, sitting at the head of the table.

He had the look of a man who is chronically underfed, with frail, papery skin that pulled at his skull and created a hollowness around his eyes. But his most distinctive feature was a thin black goatee that gave him the look of a Spanish conquistador. But he wasn't Spanish. He was Ukrainian. This was Olexander Velichko.

Sitting beside him was Jane, scribbling notes on an iSheet. The seats closest to Olex and Jane were conspicuously empty.

Eric took the seat next to Jane.

"Ah, someone with guts," she whispered, then added, "Jack asked him to help with your replication problems."

At that moment, Olex looked up, straight into Eric's eyes. Eric felt an intense uneasiness. He had dismissed much of Ryan and Jane's grievances about Olex as hyperbole. Could anyone really be *that* bad? But now it was occurring to him that yes, perhaps someone could.

Olex leaned over to Jane. She whispered something in his ear. Olex stroked his goatee, and Eric saw his lips silently form the name *Hill.* He nodded slowly, examining Eric.

Eric shifted a little in his seat and looked down, suddenly very interested in his pen. At that moment, to his relief, Jack arrived, and the meeting began.

Isaac Zyrckowski started by reviewing the mutation problem and some recent experiments he had done. Isaac was an older postdoc who had gone back to graduate school in his midthirties. Ryan called him "the professor" because he favored a tweed jacket complete with suede elbow pads. Isaac was smart but permanently disheveled: untucked shirt, frayed pant cuffs, and hair that rose up from his scalp as if by some static charge.

Just as he was presenting his first slide, the door opened, and Bill Eastman himself stepped in. Isaac stopped midsentence, but Bill waved him on. "Continue, please. I'm just auditing the class." He said it in a lighthearted tone, but no one laughed. Eastman's appearance was painfully obvious: he was worried that the Nanotech team was going to miss its deadline. The fact that they had wasted almost a month on the replication problem had gotten his attention.

Isaac cleared his throat and continued. People were excited about his work because he might have solved at least some of their problems.

But he spoke only a few minutes before Olex waved his hand dismissively. "Please, please, just shut up. It's all wrong. All of it." He had a thick Slavic accent, and for a second Eric assumed that the blatant disrespect was a product of his poor English.

Olex put his fingertips to his forehead and closed his eyes as if he were suffering from great pain. "You strike me as a very 'highly functioning' ignoramus," Olex began and on it went. He gave a vicious dissection of Isaac's work, explaining with amazing clarity why it would never work, how his experiments were flawed, and how the team was right back where it had started. All the while, Isaac stood facing the audience—all forty-five members—his look of defiance slowly withering. Soon, he looked like a little boy who has lost his parents. His jaw quivered for a moment when Olex forced him to acknowledge that he had been wasting their time "with your mental masturbations." He nodded and apologized, looking as if he had somehow shrunk in size.

Olex seemed ready to go on, but Jack cut in. "I think you've made your point, Dr. Velichko. Let's refocus our attention on the problem, shall we?" Olex made the slightest bow with his head.

Olex's attack had been cruel, yet the scientist in Eric had to acknowledge his awesome perspicuity. Bill and Jack must have known Olex's reputation—that he was impossible to work with, condescending, and utterly egomaniacal—before they hired him. But they had hired him anyway. In fact, Bill had made him chief of the Genetics Team. Which meant they felt he was worth it. And that was what Eric had just witnessed. Olex, a geneticist, had just walked into a Nanotech meeting and, within minutes, had identified a major flaw in their work.

Jack continued: "Arundhati and Jian-min did some experiments last week. What did you find?" Jian-min Xu stood up confidently, apparently undaunted by the thought that he might well be Olex's next victim. He was a handsome young man, well put together, in a suit with matching tie and pocket square—overdressed for the crowd, yet he seemed to radiate poise. Eric noticed Jane rolling her eyes as he prepared his presentation. With a lift of her nose, she whispered a quick impersonation. "Did I mention I went to Yale?"

Jian-min began, his voice confident and cool.

Eric had been briefed on Jian-min and Arundhati's experiments but was struggling to understand them. Still, he didn't want to appear clueless in front of Bill Eastman, so he racked his brain for something to say, some insightful question to ask. But since he barely understood the material, he could think of nothing. Olex seemed to perceive his mounting anxiety and eyed him suspiciously. At that moment, Jian-min posed a good idea. Well, Eric didn't really *know* whether it was a good idea or not, but people were smiling and nodding, so he nodded, too.

"Hill," Olex said, "tell us why you like that idea."

The room grew very quiet.

Eric felt a heat on his cheeks, as if he were sitting too close to hot coals. He was screwed and he knew it. He wanted to say that it wasn't fair, that they were asking too much of him.

"I guess I don't know," he admitted.

"Well, what is it about the relationship between the higher magnetic field and the graphene ribbon that makes you think the idea has merit?"

Eric shook his head. He had no answer. He couldn't even bullshit his way out. Anything he said would just expose him further. Now Olex had a self-satisfied smirk on his face. "Hill, do you know the replication impediments of Grätzel cells versus Bregnin photovoltaic cells? Do you know why zigzag graphene nanoribbons should replicate more easily than diamondoid? Do you even know how magnetism will affect the replication cycle?"

Eric looked around for a moment, but no one would make eye contact with him. Jane kept her eyes down at her iSheet. Jack Behrmann's expression was unreadable. But Bill Eastman had a disappointed frown on his face. Now they all knew what the whispering voice had been telling him all along. *Faker. Impostor.*

"It appears that good trees do not always produce good fruit," Olex said.

For the rest of the afternoon, Jack thought about the confrontation between Eric and Olex. Several things about it had upset him, though his anger and frustration were focused not on Eric Hill or Olex Velichko but on Bill Eastman. Around midnight, he went to meet Eastman in "the brig," the NRL's biocontainment chamber. He boarded an elevator on J level and, inserting a special key, hit the button for Q level. The elevator car chimed rapidly as it descended into the earth: N, *ping* ... O, *ping* ... P, *ping* ... Then there was a long pause. Jack waited. He was still descending, and he felt his ears pop as the elevator plunged deeper and deeper underground. Over half a minute passed before it chimed again. By then he almost felt the weight of all that earth and rock above him. Jack found it soothing—a caveman's sense of protection.

The elevator opened. Outside was a small antechamber, with high concrete walls and a massive stainless steel door. The door read, in huge stencil font,

DECK V

BIOCONTAINMENT LABORATORY (BSL-4)

Etched into the door was a large yellow biohazard triskelion. A notice on the wall read:

AUTHORIZED ACCESS ONLY.
VIOLATORS WILL BE SUBJECT TO DISCIPLINARY ACTION
UNDER THE UNIFORM CODE OF MILITARY JUSTICE (UCMJ).

Jack swiped his pass card. He felt the deep thud as the door unlocked. Then came the hiss of rushing air. Stepping inside, he felt his clothes being tugged forward by the negative air pressure inside—one of the deck's many safeguards to keep nasty things from escaping. He walked down a narrow hallway that reminded him of a giant Habitrail. It had glass walls and a glass ceiling. As he walked, inverted U-shaped brackets slid back and forth around him, dousing him in ultraviolet light to break down any stray viruses that might have hitchhiked in on his skin or clothes. Then he was sprayed with a thin mist of chemicals.

From this prep corridor, Jack could see the main lab with its forty-foot ceilings, long rows of "benches"—biochemical workstations—and, every twenty feet or so, an emergency shower and "dunk tank." Across the lab, he could see the test-animal vault, now just empty cages waiting to receive mice, rabbits, cats, dogs, chimps, bonobos, and gibbons. The lab was not yet complete—that would take at least another month. But Jack could already imagine how it would look: scores of technicians in yellow and red pressurized suits, playing with some truly scary stuff. As he walked past the cages, he realized that the animals would have front-row seats to the action. He imagined the larger primates behind soundproof glass, watching their distant cousins—likely uneasy, but not quite grasping their inevitable fate.

Jack stepped through another air lock. Along both walls, rows of pressure suits, about a hundred on each side, sagged on their hangers, looking like condemned prisoners. This was the part he hated most. To get to the end of the corridor, you had to walk through them, and as big as he was, they always brushed against him. Jack tried to get it over with as quickly as he could. He had heard stories about people who had exposed themselves working with viruses like Marburg and Ebola. He shuddered at the thought. They put you into quarantine if that happened, sometimes for weeks. He considered it torture. Confined away from the world while doctors in suits like these came to examine you. And with nothing to do but think about how the virus you exposed yourself to was replicating inside you.

Finally, he reached a spacious changing room and the final air lock. Another biohazard triskelion and a warning: *do not enter without wearing ventilated suit.*

He swiped his pass card one last time and stepped into the main lab.

And there, sitting calmly at a huge table with three iSheets open in front of him, was Bill Eastman. "Ah, Jack, there you are."

"I can't believe you like it here," he said, shaking his head.

"Love it! It's the first place I've found in ten years where I can get some peace and quiet."

"Yes, because the place scares the bejesus out of everyone else."

"Precisely."

Jack tossed his own iSheet on the table to show his annoyance and sat down heavily. "Did you notice I'm irritated?"

"Immediately," Bill said.

"And do you know why?"

"I've got a pretty good idea."

"You should have told me Eric was Monty Hill's son." Jack said, giving Bill a hard stare. He remembered the night in the hangar, when he sensed that Bill was holding something back. This was a side of his friend that often grated on him: when he played puppet master, using that formidable brain of his to manipulate people.

Bill shook his head. "No. If you didn't already know, then it wasn't for me to tell you. Don't you see? I didn't want it to influence your decision to hire him. What's more, there was Eric to consider. Not only does he not want to be in Monty's shadow, but a suicide like that, when the person is so well known, becomes a very public event. He's never brought it up, has he?"

"No, never."

"Of course not," Bill said, putting his elbows on the table and leaning close. "And please do me a favor and don't go pressing him about it, either. The family really disintegrated after Monty died. A lot of pointing fingers about what pushed him over the edge. In many ways, Eric lost a lot more than his father. He lost his whole family."

"All right," Jack said, his anger dissipating. He remembered when it happened. The headlines. "It's a shame. I heard Monty was brilliant."

"Oh, he was one of the smartest men I've ever met. An incredible mind, until …" Bill trailed off. "Did you notice Eric's age?"

Jack shrugged. "I assumed he was twenty-eight or twenty-nine like most of the postdocs."

Bill shook his head. "He's only twenty-six. He graduated a semester early from MIT with a double major, then shaved a year and a half off his PhD."

Jack's eyebrows went up. "He's driven. That's good."

"Or he's afraid he's going to run out of time."

"Out of time?"

"No one knows exactly what Monty had, but the cycles were getting worse every year. I saw it myself. Eric must have seen it, too. Monty was losing his mind. That would explain why Eric's in a hurry. He thinks he's inherited it." Bill took a long drink from his coffee. "But this is all beside the point. It's almost time for the re-opt. Are you going to keep him, or let him go? I had very high hopes for him, but after today …" He trailed off, thinking about the meeting. "Olex certainly doesn't like him."

Jack gave a snort. "If we kept people on the basis of what Olex thought, we'd have only one employee: Olex. Besides, the architect job is a tough one."

Bill smiled. "Yet I noticed you didn't come to his rescue today like you did with Isaac. You let Olex humiliate him."

Jack gave a slow nod. "Yes, I did. Because on this occasion, I think Olex might have done us a favor. I've seen this type of thing before. Either Eric's going to channel all that emotion into something positive, or he'll give up."

"So you want to keep him?"

Jack waited a moment before he answered. "I haven't decided."

CHAPTER NINE

THE SPY

June 19, 2025
Tangshan, China

The Fly looked again in the rearview mirror. They were still there, four cars back: two stone-faced men in a black BYD sedan. At first, he had laughed at himself. It was so cliché. *I mean, come on: two secret policemen in a black BYD?* Everyone knew it was their vehicle of choice—the way all the stories began when people talked about the disappeared. But now, as they matched his third turn since leaving the base, he felt his fear escalating.

Just a coincidence, he told himself. Besides, would they be so obvious? You're just being paranoid. Meng doesn't suspect a thing.

Then why are they following you?

Asking the question made his gut as heavy as lead. *But what about the drop?* He had made two dozen identical drops over the past two years, all brilliant in their simplicity. But now? *Don't do it. It's too dangerous.*

But, you have to warn them.

Just yesterday, he had gotten a lucky peek at General Meng's own files. Project Crimson. *You have to warn them.*

But how?

He turned right onto Xinhua Road. The black sedan made the turn leisurely, then closed the gap. He could see them in the rearview mirror. At the wheel was an older man with a fat, round face and invisible eyes. In the passenger seat was a younger man, with short hair that bristled up like a brush. He wanted to look closer for some clue that would either confirm or dismiss his rising fear, but he dare not let his eyes linger in the mirror. One thing he knew was that he could not let his disguise break. He had to keep up the illusion that all was normal. Of course, he hadn't noticed the sedan. Why should he? He had nothing to hide.

But they were definitely following him. He could deny it no longer. He decided against making the drop. He would just keep driving, go to a different restaurant. But then they would notice the change in the routine. After all, he went to the same restaurant every Thursday afternoon. The simple act of varying his schedule would heighten their suspicion. *Shit. Shit. Shit.* In the movies, being a spy was always glamorous and thrilling. And truth be told, it *had* been thrilling. He got a high off the danger. Sure, there were those first few months, when he had made himself sick with worry, but with each success he began to enjoy it more and more. He loved outsmarting General Meng and all his cronies, stealing right from under their stupid noses. He had grown confident, even smug, so certain they would never catch him. But, suddenly, within the span of three or four minutes, all that had changed. Now his insides twisted like wet clothes wrung by strong hands. *Fool, you should never have gotten into this. The risk was too great. Your wife, your son ...*

Then the adult, the rational side of him, regained control. *Don't be stupid,* he told himself. *They know nothing. That's exactly why they're being so obvious: to spook you. If they knew that it was you, you'd be strapped to a chair on level forty-nine with Meng himself holding the alligator clips from the car battery. Just keep up the mask. It's normal to be frightened; just don't show it. Remember, you're good. You can handle this. Just don't give them any reason to suspect. Once they suspect you, really suspect you, it will bring a cascade of scrutiny until ...*

He exhaled and drew in a long, slow breath.

He really was good. It was no exaggeration. In many ways, he was the perfect spy. An affable, likable man, charming enough that women liked him, but not so charming that other men hated him for it. He made people laugh, put them at ease. And then, of course, there was who he was. Who he knew. He was the most powerful man in the Tangshan lab—if political connections were the measure of one's power. For he knew half the members of the Central Committee and had known them since he was a child. They called him *Xiaolong,* the little dragon, and treated him like a nephew. His father had been the governor of Tianjin, and his grandfather had served Mao loyally for twenty-five years *and* been one of the few to survive the purges. It was unthinkable that he would betray his country. And that kept them all blind to the truth.

And there was one last thing that made him the perfect spy: his job. The irony of it. He was a spy hunter: a party official assigned to the Tangshan lab to ferret out informants.

Despite these advantages, outwitting General Meng and his cronies was no small feat. Information in the lab was strictly compartmentalized so that few scientists could grasp the big picture and thus aid the enemy. The computers themselves could not talk to one another. Important files were stored in a virtual library, and authorized users could only check out the files pertinent to their specialty. It was also impossible to make copies of any file. Memory sticks, phones, iSheets, and visual enhancements were strictly controlled. Employees could us phones and iSheets, of course, but these were issued to them by PLA Security, and all the information they contained—call history, texts, and photos— was accessible to Meng at any time.

Finally and most crucially, there were the hundreds of cameras, all equipped with facial recognition, that constantly tracked the physical location of each employee. If anyone entered an area where they were not permitted, it triggered an immediate alarm.

And yet, the spy could still move about the lab undetected. "Xiaolong, why can't I find him?" Meng had asked one day.

Because you are looking in the wrong place, Bo Li thought to himself. Meng still suspected one of the scientists—he had even jailed two of them. It had not occurred to him to watch the watcher, the man who checked the scientists' files for evidence of sabotage or copying. And this was perhaps the sweetest part: Bo Li was capturing terabytes of data without ever copying a file, without ever plugging his phone or iSheet into a computer. It was brilliant. It was genius. It was perfect. And they had no idea how he did it.

"I don't know, General," Bo Li had said, "but we'll have to keep looking. I'm beginning to suspect a network of spies, all scientists, who are working together, sharing information, and meeting on the outside." Meng had nodded in agreement; it made sense. Bo Li had suppressed a smile.

But now he was suppressing his fear instead as he parked in the trendy shopping district known as Phoenix Heights, north of downtown. It was the wealthiest area of the city, filled with sports cars, chrome-covered motorcycles, and American Jeeps and Buicks. He got out of the car and put on his sunglasses, resisting the urge to look at the black sedan just a few cars back. Instead, he turned around slowly, taking in all the glitter and commerce, as if he were thoroughly enjoying his afternoon off. On the sidewalk, he saw the usual: rich, skinny women with oversize sunglasses, and businessmen full of swagger. He fell into the stream of pedestrians with his typical lazy confidence, feeling more and more certain that he was safe.

It was logical, after all, that Meng should begin expanding his surveillance beyond the core scientists. Bo Li would be just one of a dozen people now being tailed by the Secret Police. When he saw Meng tomorrow, he would compliment him on the idea, make a joke about it. He knew they would follow him around for a month or so, and when they found nothing, they would leave him alone.

Halfway down the block was the restaurant—red and white, decorated with the image of an old man with a white chin beard. Fetching dark-eyed girls in tight pants stood outside with coupons, welcoming a steady stream of customers. The wonderful smells pulled Bo Li toward the door. *KFC.* He loved their Peking duck and the "Taste of Ireland," a whole chicken bathed in Irish cream.

This was where the drop would be. Do it in a conspicuous place, doing a mundane thing. Stay in plain sight. Meet no one. Touch no one. Leave no evidence of your transaction. He was going to do it, he reminded himself—and right under their stupid noses.

He ordered the Taste of Ireland and took it on its red plastic tray to a table right in front of the window. He looked out at the busy street and the bustling traffic. A minute later the two secret policemen settled into a corner booth. They hadn't bothered to order anything. They were just sitting there, the fat one with the round face talking on his cell phone. The younger one, Bo Li now saw, was outrageously fit, the veins on his forearms visible from here. Bo Li gave an inner sigh. *Amateurs.*

His chicken was wrapped in wax paper. He picked it up with both hands and bit into the breast. Though his stomach was still feeling queasy, he made a point of eating every bite, even sucking the meat off each individual rib bone. When he was done, he cleaned his fingers one by one with a napkin.

It was time.

Bo Li rubbed one eye and then the other, just as he had practiced, then wiped his fingers one last time on his napkin. He leaned back in his chair. A pretty girl wearing the Colonel Sanders logo over her ample breasts came and asked if he was finished. He nodded dismissively, and his tray disappeared.

He stood and dusted some crumbs from his lap, then walked out the door into the street. There. It was done. He began to relax a little, his calm expression no longer a false front. In just a few hours, the Americans would be warned. They would know about Project Crimson. Bo Li checked his watch: 2:15 p.m. The two idiots in the corner had seen everything. And nothing.

Bo Li gave thanks to the man who made it possible: David Evanston, a man he had never met.

Five years earlier, Evanston had been working for Hydro Polymer Designs as a biochemist when he made an amazing discovery: a morphing synthetic plasma (a liquid plastic) that could copy the characteristics of half the periodic table. It was a revolutionary discovery: a plastic that could behave like silicon, copper, antimony, platinum, mercury, or strontium, among others. Not only that, it could switch forms in the blink of an eye. The young scientist had quickly realized the potential of such a plastic. Within a year, the first prototype was unveiled at the 2021 World Tech Forum.

It was an ordinary-looking piece of transparent lamination, the size of an 8½" × 11" sheet of paper and only slightly more rigid. Touch a button or give an audible command, and the page filled with text. It was a fully functional computer. Unfold the edge, and it became twice its original size. Unfold it again, and it was the size of an opened newspaper. Very thin. Very slick.

But that wasn't even the half of it. You could fold it down, too. And you could keep folding and folding. Each time, the plasma would reorganize inside and create a new device. Fold it eight times, and it was the size of billfold and functioned as a phone or camera. Unfold it a few times, and it was a screen and keyboard for a laptop. Fold up the keyboard and it was a tablet. At any stage, at any size, it was a computer, a camera, a phone, a music player. Light and super thin, you could even wad it up into a ball and throw it across the room. Just unwrap it, flatten it with your palm, and it was ready to go.

Twenty-seven hours after the prototype was showcased, Hydro Polymer Designs was purchased in a hostile takeover by Apple Inc. The rest was history. When the iSheet hit the market nine months later, it was an overnight success. People did away with their laptops, tablets, phones, and cameras for one simple featherweight device that did it all.

It was currently believed that the smallest functional iSheet was two inches square. Everyone said it was impossible to make them any smaller. But Bo Li knew that this was not exactly true. At the behest of the US Navy, Apple had created a functional iSheet that was a tiny disk twelve millimeters in diameter—the size of a contact lens. Bo Li knew this because just a few minutes ago, he had had an iSheet over each eye.

CHAPTER TEN

THE HORSESHOE CRAB

May 27, 2025
Naval Research Laboratory, Washington, DC
Phase 1 Deadline: T-minus six months and ten days

Eric left the staff meeting with his eyes down, avoiding everyone's gaze. He headed for the apartment block, struggling to act normal, to keep his appearance neutral, so that the anger and frustration didn't show. *It was no big deal. Stay cool.*

As he tried to put his key into the lock, it fell from his trembling hand. He let out a seething breath and tried again. Once inside his apartment, he threw his back to the door, trying to control his breathing, trying to control his temper.

It didn't work. He exploded in a wild fury.

First, he yanked up the mattress and flung it aside. Then he plunged his fingers through the thin fabric of the box spring, heaved it up, and hurled it against the wall. But just as he was releasing it, a spring cut into his palm, making a nasty gash. Howling, he stomped on the box spring until he heard the wood crack. Next, he gave the closet door a hard kick, then beat it with his fists. He felt the skin split and saw blood. He didn't care. The pain felt good. It was release. His eyes fell on the desk chair, then the closet door, and he decided impulsively that he would split the door apart with it. His bloody hands made it difficult to grip the leather-backed chair, but soon he held it over one shoulder and swung it like a bat against the door. He heard the satisfying pop and crunch of splitting wood. *Good ... good.* Then he heard a loud knock on his door.

"Hey, you all right in there?"

He ignored his neighbor but dropped the chair. He stood there for a moment, chest heaving, and looked around at the wreckage. He felt the blood dripping from his battered hand. *Breathe, breathe. Control it.* He sucked in air loudly through his nose. *That's it, deep and slow.* But then the rage surged again. With a savage kick, he sent the battered chair cartwheeling across the floor. It hit the radiator with a resonating crash. Again the knock on the door. *Okay, enough.* He wanted to go on, but that would just bring more trouble.

He headed for the shower, smearing his bloody palm across the wall as he went, and turned on the cold water. He wanted the numbing, the constriction of his lungs. Gasping in the icy water, he felt his body wanting to get out of the freezing jet. But he fought it. *Don't you dare move.*

He wanted to be tough and angry, primal and savage, but under the cold water those feelings began to erode ... until something inside him—a dam he hadn't known was there—gave way. The next thing he knew, he was standing there shivering and weeping.

He was filled with an overwhelming frustration. He was furious at Olex for what he had done. But he was also disappointed in himself—for letting Olex play him, for being powerless to find a single word to defend himself. He had known the answers to some of Olex's questions, but he'd been too petrified, in a state of intimidated shock, to speak. Perhaps worst of all, he hated that he hadn't seen the position that Jack and Bill had put him in. He was another piece in their intricate machine—a piece they would replace if it didn't function right. It was all an elaborate game to them. But it was his fucking *life*.

★ ★ ★

For the next three days, Eric remained a little unhinged. He avoided everyone, including Jane and Ryan. He was sure that they, like everyone else, were whispering about him. *There he is. Did you hear what happened?*

He came and went quietly, worked in a carrel in the library, even ate there. With nothing to counter it, the dark voice in his head had free rein. *Nice going, Hill. Way to show 'em just how brilliant you are. That dazzling Hill brain is really something. Face it, pal. You are way out of your league.*

It was the first time in his life that he couldn't tame the voice. And that frightened him, because he had inherited the voice from his father. It was what drove him, pushed him, made him reach higher than others. Yet it was also a curse, because it was rarely satisfied, always telling him he wasn't good enough.

He would never know why his father had killed himself, but he was quite sure it was that inner voice that had told him to pull the trigger.

It was around ten thirty in the evening on the third day after the incident when he heard a knock on his door. He asked who it was, but got no reply. He cracked the door open. It was Ryan and Jane. "Guys, it's really not a good time …"

Jane pushed her way in as if she owned the place.

"Where have you been?" she said. "We've been looking all over for you. We need to talk strategy. Ryan and I have been thinking. What you need most is tutoring on the replication. I can help with that."

"And I think I can help you with some of the equations," said Ryan.

"Right," Jane continued, "but we decided the equations are frustrating you because you don't understand the genetics behind them. So we'll do genetics first—a couple of weeks at least—then come back to the equations."

Eric smiled. He had completely misjudged them. Yes, others may have written him off, but not them. "Thanks," he said. "But I can't ask you guys to do that. I have to accept the fact that I might not be the best architect."

"Oh, no, you don't," Jane said. "You're not rolling over yet. Don't you see? Today was the re-opt, and you didn't get cut. That means Bill and Jack have given you another month. You have to use it. And as for Olex, you can't let him get under your skin. That's what he wants. He tried to do the same with both of us."

Eric nodded slowly. It was true. They both had suffered under Olex and survived. "Okay," he said. But he was looking at the floor. Jane reached out and lifted his chin.

"You sure?"

He looked at her and smiled. "Yeah, let's do it."

"That's better," she said.

"You'd better get crankin'," Ryan said. Then he seemed to suddenly notice just how trashed the apartment was. "I must say, I like what you've done with the place." He tented his fingers like a self-absorbed art aficionado and began speaking with a French accent. "The bloody palm print evokes, for me, Warhol with a touch of Dachau." He put his fingertips to his lips and blew out a kiss. "Überchic!"

Eric had a month. For the first ten days, he worked with Jane, who pushed him harder than any prof he'd ever had. Chromosome cleaving, mapping, Punnett squares. Night after night of advanced genetics. When she felt he was ready, they started back on the first sixteen-page equation. They got through the first four pages well enough, but then Eric got bogged down. Jane could read his mounting frustration and told him to be patient. They pressed on. But by one in the morning, Eric realized that all the genetics in the world wouldn't help him crack these equations. He tossed down his stylus. "It's no use. I appreciate all that you've done for me, but this isn't working. I just need to face it: I'm not cut out for this." He knew it was the other voice talking, and he felt ashamed for quitting, but there it was. He'd said it.

"Why are you so convinced you can't do this?" she said.

"It's just too much to get my mind around."

Jane pushed back from the table and examined him. "You wanna know what I think?"

He didn't really. He just wanted sympathy.

"The problem isn't these equations or the genetics or even Olex. The problem is your attitude."

Eric exhaled. He didn't like where this was heading. "Maybe you should go," he said.

"I'm not going anywhere," she said. "You wanna know something? I saw the paper you submitted to *Nature*—the one that got you this job. I found it on one of Olex's iSheets. I read it and I thought it was incredible. Incredible and beautiful, and not just the way you imagined it, but the science behind it. It was one of the best papers I've ever read. I knew instantly why Jack wanted you to be the architect. But whatever attitude, whatever confidence, you tapped into to write that paper—it's gone." She paused, letting her words sink in. "Now, are you going to get in touch with that again or not?"

Eric felt embarrassed and angry at the same time. But he said nothing. There was a long silence.

"You know what?" she finally said. "You asked me to leave, and on second thought, I will. Because the guy I came to help was the guy who wrote that paper, the guy who tracked Olex's encrypted phone—not the guy who's sitting next to me now."

She calmly gathered up her things and put them into her backpack. A minute later, she was gone. She didn't slam the door, but the sound of it closing seemed to hang in the air.

Eric sat there for a long time in silence, the conical reading lamp spotlighting the equations. He saw them but didn't. After a long while, he nodded slowly to himself, turned out the light, and went to bed. On the iSheet, he had written a line: *Strength is the outcome of need.*

★ ★ ★

The next morning, he got up at five forty-five and went for a four-mile run. After breakfast, he went back to the library with a copy of the equations. He stayed there for the next twenty-two hours. He slept for six hours, then did it all again: workout, eat, work. Checking and recalculating. He started at the beginning, teaching himself everything he needed to know, downloading several books on advanced algorithms, energy coupling, and cloning. By the third day he understood every term, every assumption, and, finally, every equation. In fact, he rewrote each equation out by hand on a long ream of dot-matrix paper he found. And in doing so, he made them *his* equations. They were no longer Arundhati's. They were his. He checked the time. It was three forty-five in the morning. He could have sworn that the last time he lifted his head it was still light out. He was exhausted and had to pee. But he had done it. They were the toughest he had ever seen, but he'd done it. And that was the key: *he* had worked them out himself. No shortcuts, no calculators, no computers. He realized that the very complexity of the thing had been what frightened him. But it also reminded him that one of the reasons he had succeeded so well at Stanford was because he never assumed anything. He questioned all existing methods and often tweaked them or designed his own.

And that was where he found the answer (at least part of it): in their assumptions. At first, he thought he had missed something, but after double-checking it, he realized that Jack had made a very controversial assumption. It was right there on the second page: that the leptons (electrons, muons, and neutrinos) would have a spin quantum number of one-half. But it was known that some leptons could have different spins. When he gave the muons and neutrinos a spin of 3/2 and 5/2 respectively, he found he had only a .004 percent rate of error as opposed to Arundhati's 16 percent. It was that simple. The team had been working on the problem for so long, no one had bothered to review the assumptions.

But Eric waited. He still had to figure out the remaining .004 percent error. He wasn't going to settle for half the answer. He was going to do it all.

And he was sure he would. Something in him had changed, and the dark voice, for now, was quiet.

He picked up his phone and dialed.

He heard a long string of expletives, followed by, "It's the middle of the night. Whatever you have to say, say it quickly."

"You were right," he said.

"Of course I was right." And she hung up.

The next morning, he got to work on the other half of the problem. He tried to step back, to go to the place where he got so many of his ideas for Nanotech: from his horseshoe crab. That is, he tried to look at how nature did nanotech, because the truth was all organisms were made by nanotechnology. A bluebird, a blue whale, a man. They all were machines. But not the antiquated notion of a machine with gears and clockwork. They were molecular machines with billions of synchronized parts—machines made from protein, using the DNA/RNA/ribosome system. DNA was the master program, and RNA transmitted the instructions to the ribosomes, which, in turn, built all the protein molecules that made up our bodies.

The work at the lab was all about making tiny machines—assemblers—that could grab and rearrange atoms in any way that man wished. Certainly complex, but something that our proteins and enzymes did within our bodies already: taking nutrients out of our food, moving iron across a cell wall, and breaking down ATP to ADP to fire our muscles. Nature had been doing nanotech for billions of years. And once the team figured out how to program assemblers using the model that nature had given them, they could do *anything*. After all, the difference between hazardous waste and seawater, the difference between cancerous cells and healthy cells, was merely the arrangement of atoms. The awesome power of nanotech would come from this versatility. As Otto Mayer often said, "Anything that can be imagined can be made."

And made better.

While nature was good, it could certainly be improved on. This was because evolution was locked into using protein as its building material, and once it started, there was no turning back. No creature could exchange its calcium bones for steel or its dendrites for copper, not once the program had been hardwired for protein. But Eric and the other scientists at NRL had no such limitations. They intended to build their nanosites faster and stronger than anything nature had produced.

The horseshoe crab was Eric's reminder of the roots of his science.

He had been nine years old when he got it—on the Hill family's summer vacation to Cape May, New Jersey. His sister, Ellen, who had just turned six, was wading in the shallow water with Dad when she stepped on the poor creature. She screeched in horror and tried to bolt for shore, but Dad held her by the wrist, likely knowing exactly what had frightened her. Intrepid in the name of science, he had fished through the ankle-deep water with his free hand until, a moment later, he pulled up a handsome specimen of the Precambrian arthropod. He held it up proudly by its hard tail, its spindly legs moving in the air like typing fingers while its armor plates clanked and flapped about. Ellen shrieked with renewed vigor at this monster that was now joined to her father—who was still joined to her.

"Settle down," Dad said, or some such thing, but Ellen was having none of it. She squirmed until she broke free and raced up the beach crying, straight to their mother. Dad had shrugged and lumbered up the beach after her, still holding his struggling prize. "Eric, I want to show you something."

Eric was instantly intrigued. *Cool, it grosses girls out!*

The horseshoe crab had been marvelous to him even then. Dad had explained everything. Its beauty was in its simplicity: an armored exoskeleton with toothed ridges that protected its sensitive belly, primitive gills that had evolved only in horseshoe crabs—book gills, each with one hundred leaves. Water was circulated over them by the movement of the legs. The long tail, the telson, was used to right itself during mating—not for defense, as many thought. Simple. Perfect.

Eric listened, storing every word so that later he might impress his father with his memory—so that his father might suddenly hug him as he sometimes did, and say, "*Yes! That's it. That's my boy!*"

He had kept the crab with him ever since. Junior high, high school, MIT, Stanford, and now the Naval Research Laboratory. It was still amazing to him: a living fossil that had survived all five of Earth's mass extinctions. It was the quintessence of masterful engineering, because it had been made right the first time. Most protein machines, whether human, virus, fish, or insect, had to be continually redesigned, upgraded, and tweaked to ensure their survival. By comparison, the horseshoe crab was a beta version, release 1.0—a molecular machine so perfectly constructed that it didn't need to adapt to environmental pressures. And so, over time, it had outdistanced—lapped and then relapped—all the other creatures that we consider primitive. The horseshoe crabs had seen the dinosaurs come and go. They were older than sharks, older than the crocodiles, older than the cockroach and the dragonfly, and older than the splitting of Pangaea.

He suddenly caught a whiff of it, the smell salt and sea life.

He made himself focus on the problem.

An error rate of even .004 meant that replication could never take place. The key to making assemblers was volume. Just as the human body needed trillions of proteins to function, building with assemblers required trillions of flawlessly identical copies—which meant that a .004 percent error rate would not do. It had to be *much* lower. But how did nature manage it? How did the horseshoe crab handle errors in its cell replication? What was the difference?

Then he knew, and he was mad that he hadn't thought of it before: an error-checking program. In horseshoe crab cell replication (in all DNA replication, really), the DNA copied itself and then the cell pinched itself in two. Yet the copied DNA in most of these cells made less than one error in one hundred billion, or .000000001 percent. The key to that accuracy was that certain enzymes, such as DNA polymerase I, proofread the new DNA and corrected it for errors.

That was the answer: a subgroup of assemblers would have to be designed that mirrored the error-checking enzymes in the natural world. Then Arundhati's error rate would be within tolerable limits.

It was now June 23, a week before the next re-opt. For the next two days, he worked almost around the clock on a general design for an error-checking nanosite, getting help from Jane on the biology of existing proofreading enzymes. He had no doubt that it would work; he had covered every base. But he had to be tactful, especially with Olex. He had gone so long without making a contribution, he feared it might look suspicious. Solving one part of the problem was impressive, but two?

With four days to go before the deadline, he went to Jack's office.

"Eric!" he cried. "Come in. Have a seat." Jack seemed genuinely happy to see him.

Eric began telling him about the energy-coupling problem, explaining how he had been reviewing the equations. Then he asked if, just perhaps, Arundhati might have made a mistake in her assumption about the lepton spin.

"Hmmm." Jack leaned back and folded his arms across his chest, his poor chair yawning under his weight. His eyes narrowed for a moment—thinking it through. Then he broke into a grin that pushed his cheeks up into his eyes. "Oh, yes!" he said. "Yes, that would bring down the error to less than five in ten thousand." Eric nodded. "Excellent." Jack laughed, and his beard seemed to grow whiter as his face went pink with embarrassment. "I certainly should have seen that … But what about the rest of the errors?"

"I've got some ideas," Eric said, knowing he needed a gap between the two parts of the answer for it to seem plausible. "But let me do some more testing."

"Very well," Jack said, still smiling. "Keep me posted."

★ ★ ★

At the next Tuesday talk, when the discussion was heating up about the remaining .004 percent error, he spoke up at last. He immediately felt the heat of Olex's eyes on him. But he proposed slowly and deliberately—a speech he had rehearsed five times with Jane the night before—explaining how the proofreading nanosites were the only way to get the margin of error within acceptable parameters.

Olex scoffed. Preposterous. But Eric could tell by the nods, by Jane's reserved smile, by the way that Jack slowly nodded his head with an expression that might have been pride, that he had won them over.

A ritual had been played out. An initiation. He was now one of them. After a few questions went around that reinforced the merits of his idea, Olex gave a grunt. A conditional acknowledgment. *Even a blind squirrel finds a nut.*

CHAPTER ELEVEN
THE FOURTH OF JULY

July 3, 2025
Naval Research Laboratory, Washington, DC
Phase 1 Deadline: T-minus five months and seven days

Nanocomputers will be smaller than synapses, and assembler-built wires will be thinner than the brain's axons and dendrites…It seems that a structure similar to the brain will fit in less than a cubic centimeter…[and will be] over ten million times faster…Every ten seconds, [this] system completes as much design work as a human engineer working eight hours a day for a year…In an hour, it completes the work of centuries.

—K. Eric Drexler, 1986

Rear Admiral Curtiss slammed his fist on his desk. "God-fucking-damn it!"

Admiral Garrett raised an eyebrow but didn't say anything. He knew Curtiss had every right to be angry.

"You told me when this all started that I could run it my way, that you'd let me call the shots. But now you're telling me I have to let this ride. *This?*"

"I'm sorry, Jim, but you know as well as I do that there's too much at stake."

Curtiss picked up the Fly's intelligence brief one more time, then crumpled it in his fist. Project Crimson. God, a part of him wished it weren't true. But he knew it was, every word of it. It was good intel. Fucking perfect. And that was the whole problem: it was *too* good.

At eleven forty-five tomorrow night, on the Fourth of July, a genetics postdoc named Xu Jian-min would enter the Anderson Hall Library with a janitor's pass card. He would take a bag to the third aisle of the engineering section, between call numbers TP 248.25 .S47 and TP 248.25 .Z25. The bag would contain a clever bomb that would explode downward through the deck, spewing, and then igniting, a mixture of gelling compound and jet fuel—a little like napalm but nastier—into the cool room below, where the NRL kept its biggest supercomputer. The ensuing fire would be unstoppable, consuming the whole building and—the enemy hoped— destroying all evidence of the bomb, leading the Americans to assume that it was an accidental fire that started in the library.

Curtiss shook his head. The enemy knew precisely where to hit them. There were four Cray supercomputers on base, but the one under the library was special. The 75,000-cpu system was hands down the fastest computer in the world, the SR-71 of computers, far surpassing the Crays at both Oak Ridge and Sandia. But more than its speed, the Cray housed the lab's prototype artificial-intelligence system. While not nearly as fast or as compact as the AI systems would become after replication, it was getting faster and smarter every day. It was an ingenious piece of work, coded largely by a single NUB named Ryan Lee. In the past month, it had helped solve some of their toughest design problems. It was the main reason they were catching up to the Chinese.

But the hardest thing to stomach about this whole shit sandwich was that he could do nothing about it.

"I'm sorry, Jim, but our hands are tied," Garrett said. "The situation in Tangshan is too delicate. If we thwart the plan, Meng will know too much."

"But he already suspects Bo Li. It was in the report."

"The secret police are *watching* him, that's all, just as they're likely watching forty others. If he plays it cool, he'll come away from this clean. But if we prevent the bombing, that puts them too close to putting their finger on him. We can't risk it, and you know it. We'll win a battle but lose—"

Curtiss slammed his fist down again. He was tired of platitudes. He suddenly wanted to lift up the huge conference table and heave it on top of Garrett, crushing the CNO and his goddamn baby-blue eyes.

"You're just going to let him *do* it?" Curtiss said. "Let Jian-min plant his bomb … let the Cray burn … and let people die."

Garrett nodded. "That's exactly what I'm going to do. And so will you. That's an order."

There it was. If there had been any chance of saving innocent lives, along with their single biggest asset, it was gone. He'd been given a direct order to stand down. *Obey.* It was a word conditioned into him since his first days at Annapolis. The word that everything in the navy depended on.

"Fuck you, Mitch," he said, and stormed out.

"Let's go to the fireworks," Ryan said.

This brought sardonic laughter and shouts of "Forget it" and "Wouldn't *that* be nice."

Eric, Jane, Ryan, and Isaac were holed up in a conference room, busting ass to finish a prototype for Olex and Jack that was due by noon tomorrow. No more excuses, or heads would roll. They had been working on it all week, sleeping only an occasional hour or two. They were exhausted and frazzled. Worse, with less than sixteen hours left, they were completely stuck.

They kept looking at the clock: 8:27 p.m. … 8:29 … 8:32. It had become a nervous tic.

"No, listen," Ryan said. "It's only a twenty-minute walk from here.

We go, watch the fireworks, and run back. By ten fifteen, we're back, refreshed and ready to go. Have you ever seen the fireworks on the mall? They're the best in the country."

"Can't do it, guys," Isaac said, "I have a wife and four-year-old at home. Can't afford to get purged."

For a moment, Ryan looked deflated—but only for a moment. "Fourth of July," he coaxed. "A national holiday. Look around. The whole base is deserted. Everyone in the country's out having a good time."

That struck a chord with Eric. Ryan was right. It wasn't fair how much they had to work. "Let's do it! I can't think anymore, anyway."

"It's settled," Ryan said. "Come on, they're gonna start in half an hour."

"Forget it, you two," Jane said, "It's no joke that we could lose our jobs."

Five minutes later, Jane and Eric were outside on the lawn, waiting for Ryan and Isaac. "We shouldn't be doing this," she said again.

The sun was setting over the Potomac—orange and red and beautiful. It was stiflingly hot, the air heavy with moisture, but Eric was just grateful to be outside, breathing real air. He looked at his watch. "How long does it take that little Korean to pee?"

But Jane's attention had turned to the other side of the quad, where four workmen were coming out of Anderson Hall. "I wonder what they're doing," she said.

"Uh, maybe whatever it is that electricians do," Eric said. "You know, like fix the lights."

Jane rolled her eyes. "At nine o'clock on the Fourth of July? No, they aren't electricians."

"What?"

"They're some kind of military team."

Eric took a closer look. The men were dressed in white coveralls with "Dynamo Electric" printed on the back. "What makes you think that?"

"When you spend eighteen years of your life on military bases, you learn to spot them. See the long hair and beards? That's called *minimal adult supervision.* Plus, there's something about them, the way they move. They're very relaxed in their skins."

But Eric wasn't buying it. "We're in a high-security military facility. Why would they be in disguise?"

"I don't know," she conceded. "But apparently, they don't want anyone to know what they're doing."

Isaac and Ryan came bounding out the door and down the steps, moving past them at a run. "Come on," Ryan said, tracking Jane's eyes. "You can check out the beefcake later."

"Damn NUB," Jane muttered.

That began a mad dash to reach the Lincoln Memorial before dark. The humidity was so thick that within moments they were drenched in sweat, hair slick and faces glistening as if they had been running for miles. As they hurried through East Potomac Park, they each gave their responses to a question that Ryan had posed. He loved to challenge them with the most random questions. Tonight's question: *If you could design anything you wanted after replication, what would it be?*

"That's easy: synthetic meat," Isaac said.

"What?"

"That's right, meat. Then my damn vegan wife (whom I love with all my heart) might get off my back. God help me, every time I eat anything with meat—and I mean *anything* with even a molecule of animal tissue—she's all over me. She loves to sing that Smiths song, 'Meat Is Murder.' Even when I'm at work, she'll text me right before lunch with a link to the song."

They all laughed.

"What about you, Hill?" Ryan said.

"Ah, it's kinda silly—an idea I had when I was an undergrad."

"Well, let's hear it," Ryan said.

He hesitated. "You're gonna laugh, but I'd make minifabricators, shoebox size, that only made Twinkies, and I'd have them airdropped over Ethiopia, Sudan, wherever, on little parachutes. And in one fell swoop, Twinkie the Kid and I would end world hunger. I always imagined the cover of *Time* magazine. Men of the Year: me and the Kid."

"Thank you, Miss America," Ryan said, "That's the worst answer I've ever heard."

"My turn," Jane said. "I'd develop a cure for Alzheimer's."

"You, too?" said Ryan. "Isn't the world overpopulated enough?"

As was always the case whenever Ryan said something Jane didn't like, she tried to hurt him. She grabbed his shirt with one hand and made a fist with the other, but he squirmed free and went tearing off into the baseball field they were passing. "No, I didn't mean it!" he cried. "It's a great idea, really." He ran around the backstop and headed for first, but Jane caught him in right field. "Please don't beat me!" he yelped. "I take it back. No, not the face. *Ow-ow-ow-ow!*"

Ryan lay there in the grass, trying to catch his breath. Jane standing over him. "My grandmother had Alzheimer's," she said. "It ain't pretty."

Ryan got up cautiously and dusted himself off. "While all of your ideas have merit—well, except Hill's—they nevertheless lack the entrepreneurial spirit that has made this country great. In dramatic contrast, *my* idea"—and here he pointed his thumb at his chest like a proud little kid—"will fill an important niche in the global marketplace."

"Here it comes," Isaac said.

"Ladies and gentlemen, I am going make the world's greatest virtual sex machine and become filthy rich. I'll have nanosites take up residence in your nerve cells—"

"But in some nerve cells more than others," Eric offered.

"Absolutely, and I'll project different images on the eye and directly stimulate the brain. People will forget about food and sleep and other people. It'll be great."

"A sex machine—how original," Jane said. "You've already chosen your theme song, haven't you?"

"*Yeeeeooooow!* That's right! James Brown's my man!"

They couldn't help but laugh, even Jane.

They crossed Independence Avenue, and the crowd grew thick around them, slowing them down. By the time they reached the Lincoln Memorial, they had to push and shove to get through, but they soon found that every inch of available space was taken. By the time the fireworks started, they found themselves on the lip of the reflecting pool, teetering between the water and the wall of people. But the overhanging trees blocked the view, so they couldn't see a thing.

"Glad we skipped work for this," Isaac said.

Eric sighed. It had been a dumb idea after all. Then he felt a shove from behind, and in he went, thigh-deep in unpleasantly warm water, his sneakers sinking into mud before hitting the concrete bottom. "What the fu—"

He turned and saw Jane with her hands on her hips, laughing— obviously very pleased with herself. Then she jumped in after him. "The view is much better," she cried back to the shore. And it was. Isaac and Ryan shrugged at each other and hopped in.

A group of teenagers pointed and laughed, then jumped in, too, and that was all it took. Soon, there were scores of people standing in the water. The ducks gave them a wide berth, their quacking inaudible over the boom of fireworks and the music.

They were the best fireworks Eric had ever seen. He felt a wave of bliss roll over him, here with his friends, feeding off the euphoria of the crowd ... the Washington Monument celebrated in kaleidoscope color ... Copland's "Fanfare for the Common Man" so loud it fibrillated his heart ... and all God's colors reflected in the water around them. Near the end, he caught a glimpse of his friends: the perspiration on their faces, the way their wet shirts sucked to their skin, and the proud way they all looked to the sky. He felt blessed to have them.

His eyes lingered on Jane, and he was reminded of something he had felt when they first met: that she was beautiful but didn't know it.

She turned and smiled. "Okay," she admitted, "it was a good idea."

After the fireworks, Ryan suggested they go for a beer.

"You guys, we really can't afford to waste any more time," Jane said. But even as she said this, she was leading the way to her favorite bar in Foggy Bottom.

Inside the Parish, surrounded by dark wood and stained glass, Isaac went for a pitcher of beer and a basket of wings. When he got back, Ryan held up his iSheet. It was playing the Smiths.

"It's death for no reason and death for no reason is MURDER ..."

Isaac gave him the finger, and everyone laughed.

For a good hour, they joked and laughed and drank. Now that Isaac had a few beers under his belt, he began talking about his favorite subject: his four-year-old daughter, Amanda.

"I met her," Jane said. "She's adorable."

Isaac beamed. "She's still wetting the bed, so I told her, 'You need to listen to your body. When it tells you you need to go, you know, do what it says.' To that, she said, 'Daddy, it's not my fault. My body needs to talk louder.'"

On and on he went. Eric and Ryan and Jane would alternately laugh and congratulate him at each story. "That's hilarious."

Isaac finally gave a sideways smirk and said, "Thanks for humoring me. I know I'm boring you, but when you have kids you'll be doing the same thing."

It was past midnight by the time they made it to the wooded grove on the north end of the base.

Just as they were emerging from the woods, they saw him.

"Is that Jian-min?" Jane said.

They watched as he shuffled to a stop under one of the walkway lights. He was looking every which way, clearly nervous and unsure of himself. Not the confident Yale grad Eric remembered. He had on a blue backpack, and whatever was inside, while not large, was so heavy it pulled the bag into the small of his back. After a moment, he swung it off, unzipped it, and looked inside. A long moment later, he nodded his head as if steeling himself for a difficult task, rezipped the pack, and slung it back over his shoulder.

At that moment, he lifted his eyes toward them. They drew back with a collective suck of air—but then relaxed. It was obvious he couldn't see them. They were in the shadows of the trees, while he was bathed in the walkway light.

"Now, what in the world is Mr. Ivy League doing at the Science Library at midnight on a holiday?" Jane said.

"He's probably trying to keep his job, like the rest of us," Isaac said. "People pull all-nighters in there all the time."

"With Sputnik in his backpack?" Jane said. "Look, if it were anyone else, I'd give them the benefit of the doubt, but not Jian-min. He's always asking me bizarre questions about my work and what the other teams are doing. He's up to something."

"It's probably nothing," Eric said. "Come on, we can't afford to waste any more time."

"No, I want a closer look." And without another word, she moved out of the shadows, slipping from tree to tree, then she made a quick dash for the left side of the building. With her back to the red brick wall, she inched up to the corner. Jian-min was in the entryway, and Jane was just around the corner. It was an odd image, like something out of a cartoon: the two of them only three feet apart but unable to see each other.

Jian-min swiped his badge, and the electric lock clicked open. He gave a last furtive glance around, then slipped inside.

Jane peeked around the corner, then quickly caught the door before it closed.

She motioned them over.

Ryan whined, "But I don't wanna stalk people." But Eric and Isaac were already moving toward the door. Ryan gave a groan and followed.

"Hurry up," Jane hissed as they drew close. "He's heading toward the library."

"Wait a minute," Ryan protested. "There must be a hundred Chinese Americans working at the lab. You can't go stalking everyone who decides to pull an all-nighter."

Jane shook her head. "No, this can't be a coincidence."

Eric remembered the "electricians" they had seen earlier, and realized she might have a point. "Let's just call Marine One," Eric said. He thought of the security posters plastered all over campus. *Security is common sense. Don't take chances.*

"Stop being such a bunch of pussies," Jane hissed. "Jesus! I've got more balls than the three of you put together."

That shut them up, and they moved down the hallway together. Eric was struck by how eerily quiet Anderson Library was. Usually, regardless of the hour, there were people working here, talking in the halls, caffeinating themselves, or rummaging around the vending machines.

At the first bend in the corridor, they peeped around the corner. Seeing the coast was clear, they filed into the hallway.

They had gone only a few steps when Jian-min emerged from a doorway. He must have heard their footsteps.

Eric would never forget the way he looked at them over his glasses. Exhausted and conflicted, his hand inside the backpack.

"What are you doing here, Jian-min?" Jane asked.

No answer.

"Jian-min, we're talking to you," Isaac said.

Still no answer.

"The Cray," Ryan muttered as he suddenly put the pieces together. "Oh, no! You can't."

"My parents," Jian-min said. "They have my parents."

"Please, you can't do this," Ryan said. "It'll ruin everything."

"You'd better leave," he said. "It's not safe."

"We're not going anywhere," Jane said. "And neither are you."

Eric found that he literally could not move. It wasn't fear, exactly, but something very close: a numbing confusion, a sense of not knowing what to do and of having no memory or experience to guide him. He knew that death was very close, yet he didn't know how to save himself or his friends. He was merely a spectator, watching as if it were a movie. And just as if watching a movie, he was waiting like an idiot for the next thing to happen, hoping someone else would do something so he wouldn't have to act. So he wouldn't have to be brave.

Then Ryan lunged forward, and fire and death followed.

CHAPTER TWELVE
PROJECT CRIMSON

July 4, 2025
Naval Research Laboratory, Washington, DC
Phase 1 Deadline: T-minus five months and six days

> No bastard ever won a war by dying for his country. He won it
> by making the other poor dumb bastard die for his country.
>
> —George S. Patton

For some reason, the drinking fountain was important. It was an old one, tall, with gray sides, a stainless steel basin, and a white toggle on the spout that said PUSH.

Ryan rushed toward Jian-min.

"Wait!" Isaac cried, going after Ryan—not to help him stop Jian-min, but to pull him away, to get him to safety. But Ryan swung and clawed at Jian-min before Isaac could pull him back.

Jian-min emerged with blood oozing from his eyebrow. Blocked from getting into the library by Ryan and Isaac, he began to retreat down the other hallway.

That was when the drinking fountain became important.

As Jian-min moved past it, Eric saw a subtle movement against the cuff of his pants. Jian-min must have felt it, too. "No," he whispered.

Eric would never know how he had sensed what was about to happen, but it was he and Isaac who acted quickest. Eric grabbed Jane, and Isaac grabbed Ryan. On Eric's side of the hall, there was an entryway to an office, but on Isaac's side there was nothing. That made all the difference. Eric spun Jane into the recessed entryway. As he fell on top of her, he caught one last glimpse of Jian-min before he disappeared at the center of the light.

There were at least two explosions; he was pretty certain of that. But they were right on top of each other. The first was a deep thump in his chest, like being hit by a big fist. The second was a hot iron locomotive, unfairly, brutally matched against his soft flesh—an unstoppable wall of force. His brain sloshed to one side of his skull, and all the air was sucked out of his lungs. Something sharp smacked into his shoulder. Sudden pain. Then all went quiet and he was in a silent movie ... a silent horror movie. The lights had gone out, but the walls had been splashed by an orange liquid fire.

Can't track ... Can't focus ... Can't see. Breathe! Breathe!

Reflexively, he made short, desperate sucks, but he couldn't get enough air. *Breathe!* The smell of melting plastic, and paint and burning clothes, and hair and skin underneath. Light coming from strange places, light coming from his leg. *Get out!* his inner voice said. More desperate sucking. The sprinklers came on. Rain. A red light: EXIT THIS WAY. He wanted to move, but his body wouldn't respond. His mind not firing on all cylinders, thinking stupid things. *Wow, cool colors.*

His shoulder. There was something very wrong with his shoulder. He didn't want to move it. That would be bad. So he kept it pinned to his side.

Then someone was pulling him. Under his arm, *not that shoulder.* He tried to cry out, but there was too little air in his lungs. Things began to blur. Black smoke billowed.

★ ★ ★

One hundred eight miles above Washington, DC, a Chinese SAR reconnaissance satellite slid silently through space, its synthetic aperture lens sending crystal clear images of the Anderson Library to General Meng's command center in Tangshan, China.

Meng sat on the edge of his seat, waiting.

There!

The explosion. Debris and dust erupted around the target building as if it were a dirty rug being whacked on a clothesline. The general nodded, deep satisfaction and relief washing over him. Several of his staff raised their fists and cheered. It was shaping up to be a good night. Now they just had to hope she burned. They waited a minute, then two. "Burn, damn it, burn." Slowly, the building began to blur as the rising heat signature distorted the satellite's infrared imaging. Yes, it was burning. Getting hotter. That was when he noticed a door swing open and two people stumble out. The figures were white in the infrared, white against a dark gray earth, moving like ghostly apparitions. Their heads seemed oddly distorted. Why? Ah, he realized, their hair was on fire.

"Zoom in," he ordered.

The image sharpened. Now he saw that it was not two people, but three. One of them, a woman, was carrying a full-grown man. Meng marveled at her strength. He could see her long hair burning, yet she did not drop the man she carried. *What self-control!* Meng wondered whether his best soldiers would do the same.

The woman set the man down gently, then pulled her shirt up over her head to smother the flames. He had never seen such composure in his life.

Soon, several MPs arrived and began giving them first aid. Then came the firefighters and their big rectangular trucks. Then came Curtiss.

Meng recognized him immediately. His gait. His presence. How the heads turned to him. He recognized him the way one soldier recognizes another. "There you are! Well, Admiral, I hope you are ready. The show is just starting."

The next thing Eric knew, he was on his back in the grass. He was soaking wet. Jane was kneeling beside him, and so was a man he didn't know. Jane's hair was half gone, her scalp black and red. It disturbed him to look at her. The lights from the emergency trucks were dancing on the side of the building. *God damn,* his shoulder hurt. The other man, a paramedic, was snapping his fingers in Eric's face, trying to get his attention. His mouth was moving, but no sound came out. The pain in his shoulder was too much for him to focus through. He tried to turn his head to look at the pain. He didn't like what he saw. There was a thin trail of black smoke coming out of his shoulder. He wasn't on fire, but something inside him was smoldering. *What the—!* Then it went dark again.

The fire sent pounding waves of heat against Admiral Curtiss's face. It was so hot that, at sixty yards, he felt sure his hair would burst into flame. He watched as the iron light posts closest to the building began to bend on their stalks like wilting flowers. Despite the heat, he found his eyes seduced by the inferno, drawn to the raging towers of orange and yellow and blue. And the sound. It had an unearthly roar that made him feel small and insignificant.

Focus, damn it. He tried to appraise the situation. Jian-min was dead, and the entire library had been destroyed. The enemy had succeeded, which meant their precious spy was safe. Lee and Hunter were burned but on their feet. Hill was seriously, perhaps critically, injured. And Isaac Zyrckowski was still inside, certainly dead, consumed by the fire. Curtiss spat bitterly. Was it worth it all to save one spy? Yet he knew what Admiral Garrett and the rest of the Pentagon brass would say: that these were perfectly acceptable losses.

Just then the lights all over campus went off. *Clap, clap, clap, clap, clap.* The glowing fire and the twirling lights of the fire trucks were now the only lights he could see. People stopped and looked at each other, unsure what it meant.

It was at that moment that Curtiss understood. With vivid clarity, he knew the mind of his enemy. At that moment, he *was* General Meng.

Cutting the power would provide no tactical advantage in any of the research facilities on base, because they all ran on auxiliary power. Even as he thought this, the lights were coming back on as the emergency generators kicked in. The only place—the *only* place—affected by a power outage was the row of bungalows that ran along River Drive, where the senior officers and head scientists lived. The only reason the enemy would cut the power was if they meant to assault the bungalows. *Son of a bitch!*

Meng was going to assassinate Bill Eastman.

Curtiss had been fully aware that the bombing of the Cray might be part of a one-two punch—a diversion—and that Project Crimson was even more than the Fly had discovered. That was why Curtiss had increased security around the base, including assigning a personal bodyguard to the lead scientists. Johnny Cloud, his very best SEAL, was guarding Eastman. His number two SEAL, Tommy Evans, was guarding Behrmann. But now he feared it would not be enough. He had spread his resources too thin because he didn't know the real target. He had underestimated the Chinese general. Why? Perhaps it was the rather amateurish use of Jian-min as the bomber. It had blinded him to the second blow that Meng had planned. Something smarter, more professional.

Curtiss touched his earpiece. "Alpha Dog to Buster, come in."

There was no answer.

"Alpha Dog to Buster. Code black. I say again, code black."

The seconds ticked by. Were Cloud and Evans already dead? The tactical and personal implications of the thought made his mouth go dry. If they got to Eastman, it would all be over. Without him, the project could only limp, lame and pathetic, toward a distant finish line.

And then there were Evans and Cloud, especially Cloud. The intimate wound that his death would cause … He was almost a son to Curtiss. The admiral had been guiding him through the navy for more than a decade, ever since Curtiss rescued the recon marine from a heroin addiction, a court martial, and a dishonorable discharge. One dysfunctional Indian looking after another.

Curtiss looked around. He could call the special-reaction team—that was SOP—but they were much too far away. He imagined them getting the call, way down by the main gate, scrambling for their body armor and M4s, hopping in their jeeps, and driving down to Eastman's bungalow. No, it would take way too long.

He looked to the river. Eastman's bungalow was only five hundred yards from where he now stood, on the far side of the woods. He began barking orders. "Adams, Patel, Sawyer, Loc! With me. The target is Eastman. Walters, give me your goggles." Curtiss snatched the heavy night-vision goggles out of the air. "Walters, you're in charge here. Let's go."

The five men set off at a sprint toward the woods.

Meng watched as the men set off, disappearing under a canopy of trees.

"I'm afraid you're too late, my friend," he said. "It will take you at least three minutes to get there. But in sixty seconds, it will all be over. I've already got Behrmann. In another minute, Eastman will be dead, too."

In Bill Eastman's bungalow the lights went out and the steady blowing of the air conditioner stopped, creating a sudden silence. Johnny Cloud reacted. Coolly, calmly, but quickly. Out came the night-vision goggles, which he strapped to his forehead, ready. Then out came a small penlight, and then the Heckler and Koch P2000 .40-caliber pistol. "Gentlemen, follow me."

Eastman and Behrmann were sitting in the study, passing an iSheet back and forth. Now the glow from its screen was the only light in the room. Both men stood with no hesitation. The soldier's tone was enough to make them move.

Cloud had to get them to the basement quickly, to Eastman's small private laboratory. That was the safest place and the easiest to defend.

"Tommy, I need a sitrep here. We are on the move."

Tommy "Gun" Evans, the other SEAL in the house, was Behrmann's bodyguard. He had been on the front porch when the lights went out. A wiry little Texas boy, Evans was the best shot of any SEAL Cloud had ever seen. The man never missed.

"Tommy, come in," he repeated. For reply, he heard the sharp crack of Tommy's Mk 11 rifle. One. Two. Three shots.

Three shots for Tommy meant he had three targets. Cloud's adrenaline surged. This was real.

Two more shots.

They were being overrun.

He turned off the penlight, lest it give away their position. He slipped it into Eastman's back pocket and eased his night-vision goggles over his eyes. "Gentlemen, we are running." Cloud let them go first, placing his hand on Behrmann's shoulder and guiding him down the first flight of stairs toward the basement. Halfway down the stairs was the landing to the back door. Cloud didn't like that. What if another squad was heading for the back door right now?

Just as Eastman and Behrmann made the turn toward the cellar, the door exploded inward from a small explosive charge.

For Cloud, time slowed. "Combat time." He was entering a different consciousness—a consciousness heightened by adrenaline, yet calmed by countless hours of repetition and training. He knew instantly what he was up against: a fire team of at least four men. He himself had practiced entering and clearing houses with the same type of team at least two thousand times. Now he was on the other side: one man trying to protect two civilians. The enemy would try to get through the door frame—the breach. His goal was to keep them there, in the kill funnel.

They would be good. He would have to be better.

Cloud pushed Behrmann down the steps, then threw his back to the wall just inside the door frame.

The number one man came in, green and ghostly in the night vision, rifle stock at his shoulder, panning left, textbook perfect. Cloud came off the door frame, stood the man up—*crowd the doorway*—pushed the man's rifle barrel up with one hand, and placed the snout of his HK under the man's chin and fired. Blood sprayed white in the night-vision goggles.

The second man would be just behind the first man, coming from the right. Cloud fired at him through the first man's neck, holding up the body, hoping that the second man would hesitate to shoot his buddy in the back. He fired as fast as he could. *Bang-bang-bang-bang.* The second man went down.

Cloud pivoted the body to shoot at the third man, knowing he would come off the opposite shoulder. He kept firing through the first man's neck—no time for anything else. *Bang-bang-bang.* He wasn't really thinking now; it was all instinct and training. He felt the first man's body jiggle in his grip. The third man was firing into it, but the man's body armor was protecting him. Cloud kept firing; then he heard the third man cry out. That was good, because the third man was usually the team leader. The fourth man (and the watchover team, if there was one) might pause at the loss of the leader.

The fourth man typically hung back and would be armed with a bigger, automatic weapon. There he was, coming up the steps—a big fucker, a jade menace in the night vision, lugging a Soviet-era RPD with a round ammo drum.

Cloud gave the corpse in his arms a hard shove with all his strength, and the body went backward while the head, held on only by thin bands of flesh, flopped sickly forward. The fourth man vacillated just long enough for Cloud to put the man's nose in his tritium sights and pull the trigger. He heard a clang like a cowbell as the bullet slapped the back of the man's helmet. The man fell backward, his legs still trying to run.

Cloud retreated. He had to get out of the exposed door frame. He backpedaled, firing into the yard, giving himself covering fire. *Bang-bang-bang-bang-click-click.* He was empty.

Then came the deafening burr of automatic fire from the back of the lawn, so fast it melded into one long *BRRRRRRRRRRRRRRR*. Cloud saw tracer rounds tear past him—over his shoulder, under his arm. He dived for the stairs, sliding and bumping his way down, but then slammed into a body. Jack Behrmann was slumped facedown, holding his belly and moaning deeply.

Holstering his pistol, Cloud grabbed Behrmann under the arms and heaved with all his might. The giant hardly budged. Around them, the walls were disintegrating under the ravaging fire from the machine gun. Wood splinters and chunks of plaster and insulation rained down on them.

"Help me, damn it!" he yelled in Behrmann's ear.

He heaved again, and with a sharp cry of pain, Behrmann kicked with his feet, and both men went bouncing down the rest of the stairs, Behrmann issuing sharp cries of pain all the way down.

Cloud had to think. What was going on? He had killed four men—a typical fire team. But the machine gun meant there was probably an overwatch team as well. He likely had five to ten seconds before this second team tried to breach the doorway. He pulled the Glock 30 SF from his rear holster and lay on his back at the bottom of the stairs, Behrmann moaning beside him. There was no time to help him now. He waited, looking up through the night-vision goggles at the emerald frame of the back door, the pasty-green sky beyond, and the stars of the summer night, burning extra bright in the goggles. Waiting. He considered trying to find a better position but discarded the idea. He dare not move. The seconds ticked by. Where was the other fire team? Mind racing, he began to doubt. Maybe there wasn't another team. Maybe he'd gotten them all except for the machine gunner. And Tommy—had he bagged *all* the bad guys at the front of the house? No. If that were the case, why hadn't Tommy come to help him? No, there were more. This thing was far from over.

He refocused on the door. It was then that he felt a sudden fatigue—a great weariness that he should not feel at a moment like this. And he knew what it meant. He tried to bring his consciousness back from the doorway, back from the outside, to look inward with his mind. And in the process, he felt it: pain, a wetness. The tracer round he had seen, the one that appeared to go under his armpit, had not missed him. He'd been hit, and he was losing blood fast.

He shook his head. *More time. I need more time.* He returned his focus to the outside, peering through his tritium sights at the door frame.

The first man came in. They locked eyes. They both fired, but Cloud's aim was better. The man's head sprouted white liquid like a fountain. Cloud waited for the second man, but he didn't come. The Glock began to tremble in his hand. *Hold on. Hold on.*

Another long beat of silence. He heard Behrmann moan. The image in his goggles began to fade. They were losing power. But no, that wasn't it. It was him. He was dying. A narrowing tunnel of awareness. He was losing too much blood. He squinted and tried to shake it off. Tried to will more blood to his eyes. He thought of his wife, Steph, and their son, Josh. He thought of the new bicycle that remained unridden, in a box in the basement for the past month because he hadn't taken the half hour he needed to put the thing together. *Damn it, damn it, damn it.*

The second and third men came in almost simultaneously. Green ghosts without eyes. He fired, but too late.

He felt their bullets this time. Three-round bursts. He felt them pass through, scrape off the concrete underneath him. He felt their heat, then cool air where you should never feel air. The muzzle flashes temporarily overloading his goggles. He fired up where he thought the doorway was. Only a few seconds left now. He fired until his clip was empty. Then the darkness consumed him.

Bill Eastman turned around in the dark basement, frantically trying to orient himself. *Get a hold of yourself,* he thought, but then another deafening gunshot made him jump and he was disoriented all over again. *Don't let it consume you. Don't let it ...* He tried to think. He was out of his element, certainly. What did he know of guns and soldiers? Yet he had to do something. Jack was hurt, and Cloud couldn't hold them much longer. It was him they were after. He had to stall them, slow them down. Help would surely come if he could just delay them long enough.

But what could he do?

He had converted the basement into a small laboratory. Perhaps there was something in the lab. But without a light ... He dug into his pockets and found Cloud's penlight. He remembered the night-vision goggles on Cloud's head. The enemy would have them, too. Yes, of course. That was why the power had gone out. It was their advantage. Or so they thought. What if he could change that? What if he could ...

He went to his bench and began pulling at chemicals, the penlight in his mouth, its pitiful circle of light dancing over the labels. He needed a metal oxidant—something that burned bright. There. Top shelf. Magnesium powder. Now for an oxidizer. He scanned the glass vials, then grabbed the ammonium perchlorate.

Mind racing, hands trembling, penlight shaking, he poured the ammonium perchlorate powder into a glass vial. Then he grabbed a rag, got it damp in the sink, and spread it out on the counter. He poured the magnesium powder on it and folded it tightly—the wet cloth would slow the reaction just enough to keep it from detonating too soon—then he shoved the rag into the vial and pressed the stopper in as hard as he could.

He heard more shots, then Cloud's return fire. Then it grew quiet. The next sound he heard was footsteps slowly descending the stairs. He scrambled to the far end of the bench and ducked down. He held the vial in one hand and shook it. It grew warm in his hand almost immediately.

He listened in the darkness. One, two, three sets of boots. He heard a cool voice speaking Chinese, and the boots moving in different directions, spreading out across the room. He had only a few seconds. He had to throw it, but he couldn't. He was too afraid.

Come on! He tried to will his body to act, but he couldn't. His instincts—his stupid instincts—told him that if he remained perfectly still, like a child playing hide-and-seek, they might not see him. *Do it! Do it now! Do it or they will kill you!* At last, the spell broke. It was the vial that did it. It had become so hot, it was starting to burn his hand. He turned and threw it toward the doorway. He ducked down quickly, closed his eyes tight, clapped his fingers to his ears, and dropped his jaw open.

In the confined space, the explosion was staggeringly loud. It knocked over chairs and filing cabinets, and the flash was so bright that even through his closed eyelids, Eastman could see the room in photonegative.

The soldiers cried out and tore at their goggles. Even to the unaided eye, such a flash would cause blindness, but the night-vision goggles amplified the effect tenfold, ensuring that every photoreceptor in the eye was overloaded. Two of the three men stumbled around, the explosion having also ruptured their eardrums and destroyed their equilibrium.

In his command center, General Meng saw the flash of light through the soldiers' head cams and heard them cursing.

"What's happening?" he ordered. "Report!"

"Blinded," the commander gasped.

"Stay calm," he said. "It will wear off. Just wait."

And then Meng saw the most incredible thing. There. Right there. Walking slowly in front of his video screen was Bill Eastman. Meng could see him clear as day, but his commander, who was right next to him, could not. How infuriating! To be so close, yet incapable of finishing the task.

"He's there!" the general hissed. "He's right there!"

"Where?" The man spun, and Eastman disappeared from Meng's view.

"No, you fool, behind you."

But when the man turned again, Eastman was gone.

Meng wanted to scream with rage, but he had to keep calm. Eastman was still close. There was still a chance.

"As soon as you can see again, I want you to finish off Behrmann."

"Yes sir."

It took only another few seconds before the commander began to make out the room around him. He went over to Behrmann. Meng watched as the big man looked into the darkness, searching but unable to see the rifle muzzle pointed at his nose.

Admiral Curtiss and his men rushed into the woods toward Eastman's bungalow. All around him, guns were coming out. He heard the sharp metal clank of rounds being chambered, the click of safeties thumbed off. And one by one, the men donned their goggles and entered the watery green world of night vision, where the trees where white with heat and the night sky was filled with suns.

They moved through the trees like a hunting pride. Shifting, surging, covering; each man aware of the rest of his team, doing his part so that no one was too exposed, no one caught off guard. Curtiss ran at the center of their diamond formation, his Five-seveN up and ready. After only two hundred yards, his lungs began to burn and his heart began slapping against his ribs. God, he felt like an old man, but he wouldn't show it, not for a second. *You are in command here.* Reminding himself of that simple fact gave him strength. He felt it coming on, like a Jekyll-and-Hyde transformation: the hardness. They were soldiers going to protect … to protect and to kill …

Curtiss began to spot things in the grass: a mouthpiece from a respirator, a pile of gray parachute silk, a pressure suit. And he began to piece together how Meng had done it: a HALO drop—high altitude, low opening—likely from a stealth aircraft. Teams could be dropped from as high as twenty miles above the earth and would be undetectable to radar.

It was then that he heard a deep boom, like a car bomb going off, from the direction of Eastman's house. He had to resist the urge to rush in. *Hold on, Johnny.*

General Meng looked at Behrmann's face on the monitor: the big ugly beard and the glassy eyes. The image reminded him of a big dog that is about to be put out of its misery. *Time to end this and find Eastman. He must be hiding somewhere in the house.* But finding him with only one fully functioning soldier—that could take an hour, which he didn't have.

"Wait!" he shouted, and the gun muzzle lifted from in front of Behrmann's nose. "I have a better idea."

Forty yards from the fence line Curtiss spotted the sniper perched in an oak tree just outside the back fence. He gave a hand signal, and Patel knelt on one knee and fired two silenced rounds. The body pitched forward and fell to the ground. The sniper was dressed completely in black. Even his face was covered with a black mesh, his eyes covered by goggles.

A moment later, Curtiss and the SEALs were over the white picket fence, their infrared sights bobbing toward the back entrance of the house. There in the doorway were the bodies of four enemy soldiers that Cloud had killed, still warm in the infrared.

Cautiously, Curtiss and his men entered and descended the steps.

He found Cloud's body, riddled with bullets, the eyes open and vacant. Curtiss's mind raced ahead to the repercussions of this. Steph would never forgive him. He had brought this man through three tours in the bloodiest wars of the past decade, and now he had died on US soil. *There's another one you let get killed.*

But he forced the thoughts aside and channeled the emotion, as he had been trained to do, into more hardness. *Keep leading your men. Your job is to save Eastman and Behrmann.*

They entered the basement lab. A soldier in black was there, trying to stand up. He fell, tried to pick himself up, and fell again. He still clutched his rifle and seemed to see them, but only vacantly. Patel shot him in the head with another silenced round, then approached the body and put two more rounds into the chest. Curtiss motioned for the men to search the basement. It was empty except for a strange splash of light on the floor. Eastman or Behrmann must have concocted some sort of bomb.

Then they heard a voice from upstairs. "Bill, it's me, Jack. You can come out now."

Curtiss listened. It was Behrmann's voice, all right, but it sounded fatigued and somehow hollow.

"Bill, come on out. It's safe. I need your help."

Curtiss thought he knew what was going on. Up until now they had been totally silent. The remaining attackers had no idea his team was in the house.

Quiet as cats, he guided his men up to the first floor. First, they entered the kitchen, Patel on point, then Loc, then Curtiss, then Adams and Sawyer. At home in the darkness, checking corners, covering. Curtiss now hungry for revenge.

They moved into the dining room.

There was another Chinese soldier. This one, too, was disoriented. They came up behind him silently; only when they were about five feet away did he turn. Patel shot him in the head, and the body landed with a hard thump.

They heard a voice call out in Chinese, then Behrmann's voice again. "Bill, is that you?"

Curtiss gave a signal, and Adams and Sawyer separated from the group and eased up the staircase while he and Patel and Loc moved toward the voice.

There in the study, standing in front of the fireplace, was the last assassin, the surviving commander. He stood behind the kneeling Jack Behrmann, the long thin barrel of his Steyr AUG A3 assault rifle pointing at the scientist's neck. Behrmann's eyes were glassy and his eyelids flickered spasmodically, from either pain or loss of blood. He held both hands over his gut and seemed to be making a great effort not to double over.

Through his goggles, Curtiss studied the commander's rifle. The barrel still glowed with heat, and its translucent magazine showed that more than half the forty-two rounds had been fired. Curtiss wondered how many of those rounds had gone into Johnny Cloud. He had to check an impulse to take the shot then and there.

The soldier was hiding behind Behrmann, using him as a shield, fully aware that one of them might try to snipe him. He had reason to be afraid. A few minutes ago, he had been one of many. Now he was the sole survivor. He was so nervous that he had begun shifting back and forth behind Behrmann, one of his goggled eyes appearing to the right of the big man's head, then a moment later, to the left. Curtiss noticed that he had fallen into a steady rhythm. *One ... and two ... and right side. One ... and two ... and left side.*

"Eastman!" the soldier said. "Bring me Eastman."

Curtiss lowered his pistol and put it in its holster. He raised both hands to show he meant no harm.

"Take it easy, son. We don't want any more violence." He had to play this just right. "You want to talk to Dr. Eastman? We'll bring him to you just as soon as we find him. I've got two men upstairs looking right now."

At that, the commander seemed to relax a bit. He was getting his way. But then he suddenly stiffened and slid further behind Behrmann's massive frame. Curtiss realized that someone was talking to him. He saw the thin camera on the soldier's helmet. *Meng.*

Curtiss looked into the soldier's eyes, into Meng's eyes. Their plan had been to kill Eastman, but maybe Meng was tempted to take him instead. Meng might order the soldier to take the shot—bag the admiral. It would never work, of course; with Patel's rifle trained on him, he'd never have time to shift the barrel off Behrmann's neck. So perhaps Meng would just settle for Behrmann. Neither scenario would do. Curtiss had to keep both the soldier and Meng believing he would deliver Eastman.

"I'll get Eastman for you. I swear."

Just then Curtiss's radio came back to life. It was Sawyer. "Alpha Dog, we have Prophet. I say again, Prophet is secure." Curtiss touched his finger to his ear theatrically. "Okay, son, we found him," he smiled at the soldier. Then into his mike, "Bring him down."

The soldier continued to shift. *One ... and two ... and right side. One ... and two ... and left side.* Curtiss took a step back and raised his left hand in a soothing gesture. "Just relax, son. He'll be right down." But even as the left side of Curtiss's body was capitulating—*One ...*— even as his mouth was uttering words to sooth and reassure—*and two ...*—his right hand moved in a blur of motion, and the Five-seveN came up and out of the holster—*and left side.*

Jack Behrmann felt the hot ball of compressed air blow past his cheek as the bullet whizzed by him and into the lens of the soldier's night-vision goggles. Then he heard the crack of the gunshot. The soldier gave only the slightest jerk, teetered for a moment, then pitched backward, knocking over the fireplace tool set before settling on the floor.

Behrmann collapsed forward in pain.

Curtiss was there in an instant, shoving the Steyr aside with his foot, easing Behrmann into a comfortable position.

"Loc here is a first-rate medic," he said. "He'll look after you until the ambulance gets here."

Loc went to work quickly, pulling away the saturated shirt to inspect the wound. "I think you're gonna be just fine, sir," he said. "Can you do me a favor and try to roll on your side?" With a grunt, Behrmann complied. "Take a look at this, Admiral." Loc pointed to the small exit wound on Behrmann's back.

"Armor piercing," Curtiss said. "Went right in and right out. You're a lucky man, Dr. Behrmann. One of the drawbacks of armor-piercing rounds is that if you don't have armor on, they can pass right through you without tumbling around inside."

Behrmann gave a pained nod and exhaled with relief.

Curtiss stood and looked around at the wreckage. He thought of Johnny Cloud, as well as the wounded—Behrmann, Hill, Lee, Hunter—and, of course, the body he knew he would find on the front porch: Tommy Evans, another exceptional man. He wanted to scream. But more than that, he wanted revenge. He wanted Meng.

He went over to the assassin's body and stared down at the camera.

"General," he said, "Eastman is safe." He paused for a moment, choosing his words. "I'll be coming for you, General—you and everyone who works for you. I'm going to kill all of you. No one will be spared. Not one soul." Then he ground the heel of his boot into the camera.

Curtiss was out on the front porch, sitting on the floor with his back to the wall. Tommy Evans's body was beside him, and Curtiss was holding his hand. His skin was still warm—not as warm as it should be, but warm.

"I'm sorry you had to die alone," he said aloud. "I'm sorry we weren't here." They placed such an emphasis on teamwork in all their training—you never left a man behind—that it felt wrong, almost criminal, that one of them should die alone. Yet both Evans and Cloud had done exactly that.

Evans had been a great kid, the youngest of Curtiss's SEALs, enlisting at seventeen and finishing basic underwater demolition training at eighteen. Patriotic to the point of naïveté, he drove a red, white, and blue Ford F-250 with two bald eagles custom painted on the hood. He was the type of guy who would tear up every time he heard the national anthem. He was in the navy to fight for liberty, justice, and the American way. The other men teased him incessantly, but to him it wasn't corny—he believed it. It gave him purpose, and it made him a great SEAL.

Curtiss dropped his head, a great sadness coming over him. He didn't want to let go of Tommy's hand, and he decided he wouldn't until the hand was truly cold.

The aluminum screen door creaked open, and Curtiss heard Bill Eastman walk out on the wooden porch. Curtiss couldn't look at him. He wasn't angry at him; he just didn't want to deal with him. Eastman waited there for a long time. *Jesus,* Curtiss thought, *what did he want, a fucking debriefing?* Curtiss felt like reminding Eastman that the dead man on the ground had just given his life for him. The words were on his lips, ready to hurl at Eastman, but when Curtiss raised his head, he saw the white tears streaming down Eastman's face. Curtiss said nothing.

CHAPTER THIRTEEN

THE SOUVENIR

July 6, 2025
Bethesda Naval Hospital, MD

"It's about time you woke up," Ryan said.

"Eric!" That was Jane's voice. Such a sound—the emotion in it, the relief. It brought up Eric's emotions, too. Before he could even open his eyes, tears started to well up.

They were huddled around his hospital bed. He had an IV in his arm. A heart monitor beeped.

Jane spoke again, but she was already back to her normal self, a note of irritation in her voice. "Finally! We've been waiting forever. Can you hear us? The doctor said your hearing might still be gone."

He could hear, but everything was muffled, like being underwater.

He tried to move his head, but pain shot through his whole body. It was as if his brain was surrounded by shards of glass. Any movement caused stabbing pain.

"Take it easy, now. You've had a tough couple of days," said another voice. A nurse came into view. She was older, with sandy-blond hair and a kind, weathered face. As she checked his IV drip, she gave him a smile that, by itself, made him relax. He was going to be okay. "You've been out for about thirty hours. It's July sixth."

He looked himself over. His right arm and shoulder were thick with bandages. There were more bandages on his left leg, and the skin around his kneecap felt tight. He knew he had been burned there. Ryan and Jane both had baseball caps on, and he realized why.

"Do I still have hair?" he asked.

"A lot more than me," Jane said. She pulled off her cap and proudly displayed the damage. Her beautiful blond hair was mostly gone, except for a fat clump on the left side. Her scalp glistened with ointment. "I know I look ridiculous, but I just can't bring myself to cut the rest off."

"I just lost a little bit," Ryan volunteered.

"How's Isaac?" Eric asked.

The color drained from Ryan's face. Jane dropped her head. That was all Eric needed to know.

"He saved me," Ryan said. "He grabbed me just as ..." He wanted to say more, but his eyes flashed to the nurse. Eric understood. *Security is common sense.*

"You know," Eric said to her, "I'm starving. Could I get something to eat?"

"Of course," the nurse said.

As soon as the door was shut, they began to tell him what happened. "You *carried* me?" he asked Jane. "How?"

"Fireman's carry," she replied matter-of-factly. Eric was impressed. He outweighed her by at least forty pounds. "I'm sure the adrenaline helped," she added.

"Well, however you did it, thanks."

"Well, you saved my life, too," she said. "If you hadn't thrown me into that doorway ..." She trailed off, not wanting to say it. Then she smiled. "So we're even."

Eric grinned. "Sure," he said.

They explained that Isaac had shielded Ryan, but that meant he'd taken the full force of the blast. Both he and Ryan had been blown through the glass doors of the library. Ryan wouldn't say any more, but Eric got the feeling that the shock wave had blown Isaac apart.

"And then there's Curtiss," Jane said. "He's been acting really weird. He's been coming to check on you, *acting* really concerned. But the night of the fire, he was furious. He wanted to know what the hell we were doing in the library. He said we could have ruined everything.

"And that's not all. Something else happened that night. Behrmann's in the hospital, too. They say he had appendicitis, but I don't buy it. Something happened at Eastman's house. They've had work crews over there fixing it up."

A nurse came in with a sandwich and some juice, and they couldn't talk about the fire anymore.

Eric nodded at the bandaged shoulder. "What's the story here?"

"Oh, you're gonna love this!" Jane said, suddenly excited. Ryan rolled his eyes as she dug into her pocket and pulled out a plastic bag with what looked like a black tortilla chip in it.

"That was inside me?"

Jane nodded dramatically. "Yep!"

"What is it?"

"They think it's part of the drinking fountain. That's what was smoking when the paramedic was working on you. Isn't it cool?"

The pain woke Eric sometime in the night. He fingered the switch on the bed's safety rail that sent more painkiller into his IV. *Thank God for Big Pharma,* he thought. He stared at the ceiling, waiting for the pain to ease. He was alone. Both Jane and Ryan had wanted to stay, but he had insisted they go home.

Lying there alone, he tried to make sense of it all. Jian-min had carried a bomb into the library to destroy the Cray supercomputer. That much was clear. But Eric couldn't shake the feeling that there had been *two* explosions. And the electricians that Jane had seen—who were they working for? Jane had said that Curtiss was furious. "You could have ruined everything," he'd said. But ruin what?

Eric suddenly felt a presence. He turned to the door, which was open, and saw a man standing there. Perhaps it should have frightened him, but it didn't.

"I didn't mean to wake you," Admiral Curtiss said.

"No, I was up." He motioned to his shoulder.

Curtiss nodded. "I went for a drive to clear my head and …" He paused. "Well, I suddenly found myself driving here. How are you feeling?"

"Like I tried to wrestle a freight train."

Curtiss gave a short laugh. "A fitting description." He paused. "I'm very sorry this happened to you and—"

Eric cut him off. "You knew, didn't you?"

Admiral Curtiss sucked up a breath. He didn't feel particularly inclined to explain himself to someone like Hill. In fact, security dictated that he shouldn't. But he had come here to make sure that Hill—essentially one of his men—was okay, and … well, he realized that Hill deserved some kind of explanation. He had almost died and that alone can make a man unstable, especially if he doesn't understand why.

He stepped closer to the bed, took off his cap, and tucked it under his arm. "Yes, I knew. I locked out all the pass cards except the one Jian-min stole. I thought that would be enough to keep everyone out of the library, but I didn't plan on the four of you tailgating him and getting in before the door closed."

Eric shook his head in confusion. "You knew he was going to plant a bomb, and you didn't stop him? Not only that, but you planted your own bomb?"

"This might be a little hard for you to understand, but what happened the other night was only a minor battle in a much larger war." Curtiss paused, as if deciding how much he should say.

When he spoke next, his voice had taken on an edge that gave Eric a chill. It was creepy, the sound of the man's voice. But at the same time, he suddenly realized why this man was an admiral and why men did as he commanded.

"What I am about to tell you, you will never repeat to anyone." It wasn't a question. "If you do—and I mean to *anyone*—then I will make sure you spend the rest of your life in a military prison. Let me be clear: You will never become a prestigious scientist. No one will remember you. You will die in prison, alone. Do you understand?"

Eric nodded.

"I need to hear you say it."

Suddenly, Eric was not so sure he wanted to know. Yet, he wanted answers. The scientist in him needed to understand. "I will never repeat it to anyone."

The admiral's cold eyes lingered on him a moment, searching his face, trying to validate his trustworthiness. "Very well," he said, and he put his coat and hat down, pulled up a chair, and sat down.

After a few moments, he began to speak. "If I had stopped Jian-min, the enemy would have become suspicious. They would have asked how we knew ahead of time. They know we have a spy among them, and they may have been able to track him through this very specific piece of intelligence. We couldn't take that risk. If I had acted, we would have won a battle, but just a battle, and it could likely have cost us the war."

"But the Cray," Eric protested. "Ryan says without it, we don't have a chance. We *will* lose the war!"

Curtiss shook his head with disbelief. God, he hated dealing with civilians. "First of all, you shouldn't even know we have that Cray, so you tell Ryan Lee to keep his damn mouth shut." Curtiss's tone softened a little. "However, I agree, which is why I moved the Cray on July third. It's safe and running smoothly in a location not to be named. I was ordered not to interfere in Jian-min's attack. Ironically, I've never been very good at following orders. And I decided that as long as it *appeared* to the Chinese that their plan succeeded, we wouldn't risk our spy. What's more, the situation allowed me to eliminate Jian-min. If I had done nothing, if I had not booby-trapped the building, he would still be running around spying and planning more sabotage in order to save his parents. I didn't want to have to do this all over again, so I made sure he didn't come out of the library alive."

Eric shook his head with a reaction halfway between amazement and disgust. It was true that Curtiss's efforts had minimized the damage to both the project and potential victims. Yet he couldn't shake the feeling that his life and the lives of his friends had been toyed with.

A tingle ran up Eric's spine and made his scalp bristle as he realized just how cold the man sitting next to him was. "You saw us," he said. "You knew we had entered the building. You watched us yourself." As thorough as Curtiss was, he surely had the building under surveillance. Yet he hadn't intervened. "Was that an easy choice for you? Sacrificing the lives of four NUBs?"

Curtiss's face turned hard, and he had to remind himself that Hill was oblivious to what else had happened that night. He didn't know about Johnny Cloud or Tommy Evans or Jack Behrmann. He didn't know how it had felt to go to Stephanie Cloud's house in the middle of the night and tell her that her husband was dead. Or to call Tommy Evans's parents and tell them their only son was gone.

And he reminded himself that what had happened to Hill—the blast and the fire and the loss of his friend—was probably the most frightening and traumatic thing that had happened to him in his twenty-six years of existence.

So for a brief moment, he was tempted to explain it all: how it really felt to lose a man, to have a pain that never went away. How the pain of each death lived under your rib cage, where it throbbed for months before leaving a hollow place. He thought of telling Hill how that felt. About the nightmares, the flag-draped coffins, the times he had put his pistol in his mouth. How it haunted you and found you in your happiest moments: with a child in your arms, in the middle of a slow dance, watching a sunset over the water. The awareness that another man has been robbed of this because of the orders you gave. That he will never see, touch, smell, or feel what you are feeling now, because of you. The shame of still drawing breath. He would add Isaac Zyrckowski, Johnny Cloud, and Tommy Evans to the list that now stood at 241, and he would think of two more orphans—Cloud's and Zyrckowski's—a boy and a girl who would gradually forget how their fathers' voices sounded.

But he said nothing about that to Hill. He had said too much already, and besides, it was none of his fucking business.

"No, it was not an easy choice, Dr. Hill," Curtiss said finally in a voice devoid of warmth. "It was a terrible moment, watching the four of you enter that building, knowing that I had made a mistake. But to send in more men to save you would have risked their lives as well. Instead of risking four, I would have risked six or eight. And yes, if you must know, I would trade the lives of four NUBs for the project. Just as I would trade the lives of four Jack Behrmanns or four Bill Eastmans or my own life. That is what I do, Dr. Hill. I make decisions that have terrible consequences. But I do it in the hope that it protects and serves more than it hurts. Listen, nothing would make me happier than if the United States had no enemies, and the US and China were good buddies. But that's not the world we have. The world we have is a place where dozens of groups would love to get their hands on what we are doing here, and where one country has no problem killing as many as it takes to get there first. So I'm going to tell it to you straight: there are going be a lot more bodies before this is over. I guarantee it. It's my job to make sure that most of those bodies are Chinese."

That night, Admiral Curtiss began to lay his plans. His threat to Meng had not been just an eruption of anger. No. He would do exactly what he said. It had taken the deaths of three men—Johnny Cloud, Tommy Evans, and Isaac Zyrckowski—but now the transformation was complete. The hardness had filled him once more.

He worked through the night at his desk, encased in darkness except for the cone of light from his reading lamp on the pages of his journal. He had discovered, through his long career, that the dead of night was the best time for this type of work. The still hours gave precious space for his thoughts to entertain the darkest, bloodiest fantasies and nurture them into reality.

CHAPTER FOURTEEN

THE PROFESSOR

May 5, 2025
Xinjiang, China

It had been three months since he came down from the plateau. Three months since his long night as a chrysalis in a tree trunk, hurtling through wind and snow. Three months since he arrived in Chengdu, a megalopolis that took four hours to traverse.

He should have made it to India by now, connected with the other exiles in Dharamshala, but he hadn't. He was still in China.

It will be best if you stay with me for a while. The documents will look much better if you are fully healed.

He had been suspicious of the professor from the moment he laid eyes on him.

When he had entered the man's living room that first time, Sonam had sat close to the door, a tiger halfway inside a cage, ready for the door to slam, his knife ready in his sleeve, watching the man's every move. How could this man be the one his father trusted so much? He was Han Chinese. Just the sound of the words coming out of his mouth had repulsed Sonam.

The professor, warm and friendly and effusive, had seemed to sense this and had giving him plenty of space. He kept his hands in the open, very much aware that a wild animal had arrived in his parlor.

"I know you don't trust me, Sonam. But please give me a chance."

Sonam had said nothing—only stared at him, at the room, around the house. The place was seductively comforting. Dark rosewood panels under subdued light. High cabinets of old books. Leather chairs. Artifacts and statuettes from remote aboriginal cultures. And at the back of the house, a sunroom with huge sheets of glass, looking out on a quiet stream. The sun was setting there, and the effect of it all was so inviting, so soothing, that he was sure it couldn't be true. He had expected to travel in the underbelly of the Dragon, hidden in poor settlements, fighting for food and survival, connecting with others who had been pushed down by the government, yet he had arrived in a rich man's house. It made no sense. This was a man who had much to lose. Why would he risk his life to shelter a fugitive?

"I can't stay," Sonam said forcefully in Chinese. He was in charge here, he told himself. "I'm going to India."

But the professor had shaken his head. "That would be most unwise. Just imagine for a moment that you are a border guard. You see a young man trying to leave the country. He catches your eye because it is clear he has recently been beaten. You look at his papers, which are all new. That, too, is suspicious. Even his passport photo shows him with the same beaten face. Yes, the papers are technically correct, but the guard decides to hold you nonetheless. They do some checking and find out that before a few weeks ago, you didn't exist. Eventually, they figure out who you are and they send you back to prison, where this time you will surely die."

Sonam couldn't accept that. How could freedom still be so far away?

"No, I have to go," he said, but now his voice was not so forceful; it was supplicating. "I have to get out of here."

"I'm sorry, but I can't let you go. You are my responsibility and your father would never forgive me if I let you get captured again. I can get you the papers you need, and they will get you across the border, but we have to do it my way. If you try it now, it will all be a waste. All your suffering will have been for naught. You will lose, and the *party* will win."

Sonam put a hand over his eyes and pulled it down over his cheeks, feeling the hard clumps of scars under his fingertips. He was intensely weary and now he felt trapped, hijacked by the fact that the professor held the keys—the documents and passport—that he needed in order to make his escape. He entertained an impulse to flee on his own, to set off on a two-thousand-kilometer journey alone, but without the right papers, it was hopeless. He knew no one in this strange land. Not a single person.

"You will be safe here," the professor assured him. "You don't have to worry about that. Give yourself a few days to rest from your journey; then we can talk some more."

That night he lay awake. His eyes alert in the dark, the back porch light painting the shadows of the trees on the ceiling. The knife under his pillow, a dresser slid in front of the door, he listened to the house sounds and the professor's snoring, ready to slip out the window at any moment. He had intended to stay awake all night, but shortly after he heard the 3:00 a.m. train, he drifted off to sleep.

He awoke with a ravenous hunger that was immediately intensified by the delicious smells coming from the kitchen downstairs. He looked out the window. The sun was coming up. No, that wasn't right. The sun was *going down.* He had slept through the whole day. Fifteen hours. Oh, that heavenly smell of food!

He shuffled groggily into the kitchen, hair plastered to the side of his head, his face sticky from sleep.

"He lives!" cried the professor. Sonam grunted in reply.

The professor wore an apron—SICHUAN HIGHER INSTITUTE OF CUISINE—and from the copper pots and pans stacked in the sink, it looked as though he had been cooking all day.

"Let's see if this will breathe new life into the zombie lord!"

He placed a small plate in front of Sonam with three tiny pieces of bread topped with something green and yellow. Sonam shoved one into his mouth. It caused a thirty-second chain reaction of pleasure as hints of butter, cinnamon, raw brown sugar, and mushroom rotated around on his palate. It was delicious beyond words. He quickly inhaled the other two pieces and mumbled through stuffed cheeks, "More, please."

The professor smiled. "It speaks!" He next presented Sonam with a bowl of dumplings. Sonam took a bite, and again his eyes rolled with pleasure. It was not simply that he was ravenous; they were the best dumplings he had ever tasted. He finished the bowl within a minute. "More … please."

The professor brought more and more, and Sonam ate for the next two hours: noodles; a stir fry with asparagus, carrots, ginger, and soy sauce; rice pudding; and a single unassuming egg that made him moan. Finally, as a special treat, the professor made tsamba, the Tibetan staple of barley flour mixed with butter tea.

At the end of it, Sonam sat in a stupor. His cheeks hurt, but it wasn't from all that chewing; it was from the grin that wouldn't leave his face.

"I take it you liked the food?" the professor asked.

Sonam's grin only widened.

After that, he never missed a meal.

Subsequent dinings were punctuated by exclamations of amazement—not from Sonam, but from the professor.

The next night: "You ate almost twice as much as yesterday!" The professor cried. He came around the table and rapped on Sonam's leg. "I knew it! It's hollow!"

The next night: "You just ate two whole ducks"—he glanced at his watch—"in ten minutes!" The professor scratched his head in sincere astonishment.

Sonam found the professor's theatrics very funny. "That was duck?" he said, laughing. "I barely had time to notice. Delicious!"

The professor gave him a warm smile. "It's good to hear you laugh," he said holding his gaze. "It looks like I'm going back to the store—again. Aren't you Tibetans supposed to be vegetarians?"

"Some in the cities are," Sonam said. "But in the country, we eat what we can. My father butchers a sheep every couple of months."

Over the coming weeks, eating became Sonam's job. He would spend all day in the professor's library or the sunroom, listening to the clang of pans, the hiss of steam, and the quick *thumpthumpthump* of an adroit hand cutting vegetables, while the smells of garlic, ginger, cinnamon, and cloves whirled around the house. The professor's specialty was sauces—hoisin sauce, XO sauce, and plum sauce. Over the years, the aromas from his sauces had infused everything in the house: the wood paneling, the books, even his clothes.

Two weeks after Sonam's arrival, over breakfast, the professor said to him, "I want you to come to campus with me today and attend my class. Our cover story is that you are a visiting student from Yanchang, so you might as well start playing the part."

"I don't know," Sonam said. A part of him was dying to get out of the house, but he was still afraid of being in public, surrounded by Chinese. *You are behind enemy lines,* he reminded himself.

"Before you decide, I have something for you." The professor left the table and soon came back with some new clothes: brown winter slacks, a white collared shirt, and a gray sweater, set off with a knit cap and Ray-Ban sunglasses. "This is what all the rich kids your age are wearing," he said.

A few minutes later, Sonam was transformed. The professor squared the sweater on his shoulders and took a look at him. "Now, walk around for me."

Sonam took a few steps around the parlor. "Not bad," the professor said with a smile. "Despite everything, you're still a confident young man. My advice to you is, always act as if you belong here. In fact, almost swagger—it will go a long way in keeping people's attention off …"

The professor needn't finish the thought. Sonam knew what he meant.

Sonam had never worn clothes like this before, and he felt like an inexperienced actor pushed out onto the stage. Surely, everyone would see right through him. But when he looked in the mirror, it was like seeing a new person. That was good and, in a way, empowering. He felt the thrill that a child has donning a mask for the first time: the power of anonymity and a certain mischievousness—the feeling that he could get away with just about anything.

"Everyone, this is Sòng Píng," the professor said. "He's staying with me this semester and wanted to sit in with us today."

There was a chorus of "hellos" and even some smiles. The classroom was simple: bench desks with two chairs apiece, a whiteboard, a computer, and an overhead projector. Sonam sat in the back near the door, ready to make a quick escape. He half expected some student to point at him suddenly and shout, *Separatist!* But no one did. In fact, they soon seemed to forget about him. He watched them closely. The blue jeans, the overstuffed backpacks, the sweaters, and the sweatshirts advertising famous brands, sports teams, and bands. There were a few more boys than girls, and a few of the girls were so beautiful that Sonam could barely look at them. He felt conflicted. These students were *gyaro,* he reminded himself—Chinese corpses. Yet, at the same time, he felt a strange pull to win their acceptance. He tried to push that desire aside. *You don't want anything from them.*

Near the end of the class, the professor stumped them with a question. "Who was responsible for bringing Vladimir Lenin to power in Russia?"

There was a long pause.

The professor tried to coax the answer, mentioning that it was in the midst of the First World War and that Lenin was given ten million dollars by a foreign power.

When it was clear that none of them knew it, Sonam spoke up. "Germany."

"That's right," the professor said with a smile. "Do you know why?"

"At the time, Germany was fighting a two-front war, and in exchange for Germany's help Lenin ended the war on the Eastern Front when he gained power. Unwittingly, however, the Germans also created the power that would eventually destroy them in the Second World War."

"Precisely," said the professor. "It was one of the great ironies of the twentieth century." Heads turned. Smiles and accepting nods that showed they were impressed—including the cute girl in the front.

Over dinner that night, the professor said, "If you'd like to enroll for the spring semester, I can still get you in. You can take as many courses as you want. Come summer, you'll be healed enough to get your papers. Then, if you wish, you can go to Dharamshala."

Sonam put down his chopsticks, sat back in his chair, and looked closely at the professor. He shook his head, but at the same time he smiled mischievously. It was so audacious! That he, a fugitive member of the GFM, could pass for Han. Not only that, but study at a Chinese university. The very idea that he would get a free education from those who had enslaved him and his people ... He loved it. But could he pull it off?

Their trip today had given him some confidence that he could. It had been strongest when he walked with the professor down the tree-lined walkways of the campus, passing clusters of students. The professor had been right: the stylish clothes did a great deal to deflect people's attention from his wounded face. Yes, a few did double takes—a passing glance, followed by a more probing stare—but no one seemed to think he was out of place. By the time they had begun their walk home, his gait had already changed, feeding off the looks he got from other students.

As he and the professor neared their neighborhood, there had been a propaganda mural on the side of a parking garage. It showed a young boy opening a door to a dark room and a woman—presumably the boy's mother—whispering into a phone. The text read, "You never know who could be conspiring with the separatists. Report suspicious activity to your local party official." The professor had pointed at the mural and laughed. It was a small thing, but it had united them there, on the street, as coconspirators. Not only that, the mural had almost normalized what they were doing, making it feel as though they were not the only ones. Now, with his stomach full and his new ally sitting across from him, the seventeen-year-old Tibetan from the tiny village of Dagzê decided he would stay. He would make a study of this place, of the enemy, of their system. He would dissect the propaganda, the billboards, the manipulation of the history books. He would try to understand the mentality of the 1.3 billion people who lived under the watchful eye of the party. And in that study, he would note the weaknesses he found, so that he could later exploit them.

He thought of his father, who at this moment would be sitting in their little house up on the plateau, perhaps across the little rough table from his sister as they finished their evening meal. His father had told him not to rush too quickly to India, that he should wait until he was ready. Perhaps this was what his karma had in store for him. Perhaps this was the road to redemption that he sought. *Redemption?* No, that was not the right word. The road to revenge.

The next day, he enrolled in calculus, mechanical engineering, English, intro to systems analysis, and, at the professor's behest, art history. He quickly fell into a steady, soothing routine: waking early with the professor, going to campus, attending lectures, working all afternoon in the library, then coming home to study while the professor cooked. They would eat dinner together; then he studied until he fell asleep.

The professor's food was doing magic on his body. It was as if he were taking healing potions. While the swelling in his face subsided with his daily dose of lemongrass, ginger, and star anise, his arms and legs filled out from the duck, dumplings, and plum sauce. His bones grew strong again, and his coordination returned.

One day after class, a popular student named Gao invited him to play soccer. Soon, he was playing soccer and basketball every week. In Tibet, he had been obliged to learn the games at the Chinese schools and he had resented it, but now he played them with relish. He was a scrapper, taking on the biggest opponents without fear, harassing them and never letting up until he won the ball. When he fell—and he fell often—he bounced up quickly, as if gravity didn't like the taste of him.

After the games, his teammates would invite him out to the bars, but Sonam always begged off. He was not ready, not confident enough, to get that close. But then one day, after he scored two goals and became the hero of the game, they had insisted, and Sonam, feeling almost invincible, had accepted. After a few Tsingtao lagers, Gao, the popular one, asked the question that he knew all of them had been wondering. "What happened to you?"

Sonam responded with a tight nod. He had rehearsed this. He told them he had been in a car accident just last fall. His mother had been driving when a truck hit them on a two-lane road. His mother was killed instantly, but he had been trapped, legs held tight by unyielding metal, and the engine caught fire.

Gao, clearly shocked, had hung his head low, and another young man, Lok, had reached out and put a hand on his shoulder. "I'm really sorry, brother."

Sonam had given a slow nod. He was playing his part, yes, but the story was close enough to the truth that their sympathy mattered. *Brother.* The sentiment touched him, but it left him confused. A Han calling him *brother.*

When he got home, the professor was waiting for him in his chair, a book on his lap, glasses low on his nose. "I was beginning to worry about you."

"I'm okay. I went out after the game."

"Fine," the professor said. "I think that's good for you. Just watch how much you drink." Sonam knew he smelled of beer. "It will loosen your lips more than you know, and maybe tempt you to say things you shouldn't."

He nodded his head. The professor was right, but he wasn't interested in being lectured. The professor seemed to sense this.

"Get some sleep, Pelé."

"Who's Pelé?"

"Never mind," he said with a light laugh. "Just get some rest."

That night, he lay in bed thinking about his life. He was trying to be two people at once, and it was starting to drive him crazy. During odd moments, while laughing with his classmates or playing soccer, his old life was the furthest thing from his mind. But then he would see a PLA officer strolling down the street, and his stomach would roll with hate and revulsion. He would find himself fantasizing about following the soldier into a restroom and slitting his throat.

When his fantasies came, they were dark and brutal. And he could not stop them. Like the damage to his face, they seemed to have become a permanent part of him.

He had been studying his enemy, and now he saw how premeditated and mechanized their destruction of his people had been. He realized that the Chinese had kept them permanently off balance—scared, weak, and frightened. It was something he could see only now that he was safe, healthy, and strong. He saw anew the injustice of it. His people were the victims of a horrific crime, the likes of which occurred only a few times in a century—a meticulously planned genocide. But a crime that most Chinese had long forgotten about as they went about their lives, oblivious of what their country had done, and was still doing. All around him were people who benefited from the rape of his country yet thought nothing of it. People whose family members received money from the government if they relocated to Tibet, whose fathers and uncles worked in the factories where Tibet's natural resources were shipped, who exported jewelry and Tibetan clothing made by prisoners. He hated them. All of them.

But what about Gao and his teammates and the professor? Did he hate them, too? No, but he didn't trust them, either, not completely. He caught it in glimpses, when a teammate insulted a player on the opposing team by calling him *mantze,* a dumb monkey—a Tibetan. Or when Gao had lamented one night that Tibetans could never rule themselves. "They'd all starve to death without our help." And even the professor had it in him—he seemed so amazed that Sonam could do complex calculus better than most Han. These people were the children of the party and raised on their propaganda. It was ingrained in them as surely as their language, as indelibly as a nursery rhyme.

You can never completely trust them. Never.

By late March, his face had healed as much as it was going to heal. The left side was almost back to normal except for the wide scar that ran from his chin to his temple. His right side, where he had been burned, was permanently pink and smooth.

Just before finals, the professor called him into his study.

"Yes, *sifu,*" Sonam said, addressing him with the Chinese honorific meaning *teacher.*

The professor removed his reading glasses, folded them, and placed them on the table. "There is something important I have to warn you about. When you arrived, I told you I would protect you and keep you safe. But there is one thing I can't protect you from. For the next month, you have to be very careful about being out alone, day or night. By the end of May, the mayor must provide the army with two hundred new conscripts. I've heard that only a hundred people have volunteered. That means the mayor will likely take another thirty, maybe forty, from the jail, but the rest will have to be picked up off the street. The mayor will have police out looking for young men. They will take you quickly, and once you're gone, there is very little that anyone can do to help you. So please be very careful."

There was an urgency in the professor's voice that Sonam hadn't heard before. The professor was sincerely worried about him, and it touched Sonam. Despite whatever bias the professor might have, he was truly fond of Sonam. *Of course, you idiot,* Sonam said to himself, remembering that the professor risked his life for him every day. "Thank you, lama." And he clasped his hands and touched his crown, his forehead, his throat, and his heart, in the traditional salutation to a *lama*. Not a *sifu,* a *lama*. "I will be careful."

And Sonam was careful. Very careful, right up until the end.

But after finals, he had not been careful. They all had gone out to celebrate—Gao, Lok, Jin, and a mob of classmates—at the Baby Face Bar. Gao had opened a tab and kept the drinks coming—tall drinks with names he had never heard of. No, he hadn't been careful. But didn't he deserve to celebrate? To laugh and toast his public victories, and the private victory he had pulled off. He had really pulled it off. All semester. The separatist, the *mantze* in their midst.

Hadn't Gao offered to get him a taxi? Had he waved him off? No problem. It was only a half mile to the house, anyway.

He was on the professor's street, only a block from home, when the police rolled up behind him so silently. Was it silently, or was it the six or seven drinks? He ran. He was still fast, still strong. But he stumbled. He was up, but they were on him. They lifted him and cuffed him, and he gave a primal scream of rage, fury, and frustration. He screamed at fate, at destiny, at his karma. He even cursed the three jewels, who had let him believe that there could be justice, retribution, or hope. There, only twenty meters away, the professor had left the porch light on for him. He could see it, but he would never make it. He would never see the professor or Gao or any of them again.

CHAPTER FIFTEEN

THE IDEA

October 2025
Naval Research Laboratory, Washington, DC
Phase 1 Deadline: T-minus six weeks

Eric sat in the conference room, head down, trying to keep his momentum, trying not to get distracted. It wasn't working. He felt achy and irritable. Three months had passed since the fire, and he had healed well enough. It wasn't his shoulder that was bothering him. It was something else, a sense of hopelessness. He realized that the feeling pervaded the entire lab. He felt it in every meeting, in the carrels in the library, and in tired conversations in the cafeteria: a sense of defeatism.

They were losing.

They all knew it, yet no one said it. No one had to. All you had to do was look at a clock. Every computer and iSheet; every flat screen and tablet, had a permanent clock that marked the replication deadline. So it was there, in the corner of everyone's eye, wherever they went, reminding them over and over again of the same thing: There was no way they were going to make it. They had stolen all they could from the Chinese but were still treading water. Sure, they had had their own victories, but it wasn't enough. Bill Eastman's presence, which had inspired them and kept them going, was now rare. He spent more and more time alone in the lab on deck V, poring over plans and possible strategies. Without him, divisions grew wider. People bickered and complained.

The re-opts became increasingly brutal. New employees were brought in, but it didn't help. The new hires were often more clueless than the people they replaced. "The problem isn't the worker bees," Jane said. "It's the queen and her generals. Give me some goddamn direction, for Christ's sake, and I'll give you results! They're all stuck. Jack and Bill and Olex and Jessica. They don't know what to do."

Now, sitting alone in the huge conference room, Eric felt the weight of doom more acutely than ever. It was late October, and a long, cold winter seemed to be settling in.

Just then, Bill Eastman walked into the conference room, head down, and began pacing around, absorbed in his thoughts. Eric hadn't seen him in weeks and thought it best to let him be. Finally, Eastman noticed him.

"Ah, Eric, good morning." He had his usual warm smile, but it felt forced. Before Eric could reply, Eastman said, "Listen to this …" And he launched into an idea for replication. When he was finished, he turned to Eric. "What do you think?"

Eric knew right away that it was a bad theory. It would never work. But it seemed strange that Eastman couldn't see it. Eric hesitated. He considered just lying, telling Eastman it was a great idea, *super*! That seemed the safest thing. But maybe it was a trick, a test to see whether he really knew his stuff.

"I don't think it'll work," Eric said. "In fact, I'm quite sure it won't. It will take you years to code something like that. Nature is complex, but not that complex."

Eastman blinked and seemed taken aback. Eric felt his stomach grow cold, but he pressed on. "What if you changed it like this: instead of taking all that time to recode each assembler, why don't you have one assembler pass code on to the other. Just let it be 'born' with the code." Eastman gave a little nod, considering it; then he countered with a different idea.

Eric shook his head. "I don't think that'll work, either," he said, still worried that something didn't seem right here. "If you don't mind my saying so, you're approaching this like an engineer when you need to look at it like a biologist. Don't try to come up with a program for each nanosite. Make the nanosites program themselves."

Eastman looked skeptical. "Program themselves? How?"

"Force them to evolve into the state you want. All you have to do is add a slight mutation factor. The nanosites that evolve toward the correct state survive. The rest die. It'll be like mosquitoes building resistance to a pesticide. Billions, probably trillions, will die along the way, but the ones that survive will have the characteristics you want." Eric was thinking it through now, liking the idea himself. "See, this way our assemblers won't just be one type of tool, like a hammer. They'll be *any* tool. Think of them as stem cells, capable of differentiating into whatever cells are needed."

"But how do you *know* they will program themselves?"

"If their survival depends on it, they'll adapt. It's nature. We are talking about a life-form, after all, so just constrain their environment and let natural selection push them toward the state you want."

Eastman gave Eric a severe look, his eyes narrowed in concentration. "Wait right here, will you?" he said, and walked out.

Now Eric was nervous. What had he said? Was Eastman upset? Eric couldn't read his reaction. Was Eastman looking for an excuse to cut Eric loose? Was that it? Today was the twenty-eighth—two days until the next purging. Sure, he had figured out the replication error problem, but that was five months ago. All he had managed to do since then was get himself blown up.

A minute later, Eastman returned with Behrmann. The Nanotech chief stooped to get through the doorway.

"Eric, tell Jack what you told me."

He felt the sweat building along his hairline. He looked from one man to the other, now thoroughly wishing he'd kept his big mouth shut. He repeated his idea.

"Hmmm," Jack said when Eric had finished. "Interesting." He

stroked his beard, then turned to Bill. "I think someone might be out of a job."

"That's exactly what I was thinking," Bill replied.

Eric's heart sank. After all he had been through. He couldn't believe it.

"This is bullshit," Eric began. "You can't do this—"

"And he obviously has little respect for his elders," Jack said.

"I know!" Bill exclaimed. "Even better!"

Eric looked from one boss to the other, his jaw slack with perplexity.

Eastman looked at him, stone-faced, then burst into laughter. They had been playing with him.

"This could solve the issues with the neural tube development and the higher core functions," Jack said to Eastman, as if Eric were no longer there.

"I was thinking the same thing. It might even fix the issues Ryan Lee is having with the interface."

Eastman unfolded an iSheet from his pocket. "Get me Drs. Velichko, Berg, and Lee," he told the device.

Eric realized his mouth was still open, and shut it. He was torn between his relief and a strong desire to slug both of them for scaring him like that.

"Relax, Dr. Hill," Eastman said with a smile. "We love your idea. What's more, I'm really glad you had the courage to tell the boss his idea stank. What you said just now was right. The theory we'd been kicking around was a bad one, but neither Jack nor I saw it, because we are too set in our ways." Eastman shook his head as if he was a little disappointed in himself. "See, Jack and I have been doing this for close to thirty-two years now, and our thinking and experiences have become so similar that we miss things we shouldn't miss, we spend months on dumb ideas, and we don't question each other. In short, we've gotten lazy."

Then Jack added: "The person who should be out of a job is me. I've been insisting that Bill hold on to this theory. But you've not only debunked it, you might have given us a fresh start."

Fifteen minutes later, the room was full. Assembled around

the conference table were Olex, Jane, Ryan, Jessica Berg, Eric, Bill Eastman, and Jack Behrmann.

Again Eric repeated the idea. "Forced evolution," he was calling it—using the nanosites' rapid replication process (five times a second, essentially) to oblige them to mutate into a desired state. Even before he could finish, they were all talking at once. Would it work? What problems could it be applied to? How quickly could they implement it? Within a few minutes, they were shouting over one another.

Eric just sat there in a state of shock. Had this all come from him? The idea had just popped into his head—the most logical solution to the question Eastman had asked. It was such a tenuous thing. If Eric had thought of the problem himself, *by* himself, he would surely have dismissed it. After all, it was such a simple idea, someone else must have thought of it long ago, tested it, and discarded it. But because Eastman had been there, he had grasped the idea's novelty—its obvious connection to all successful life forms. Now, as the rest of them discussed it, Eric was beginning to believe that it really was something special. That perhaps they had found a concept that the Chinese missed, and that they might be able to catch up.

He felt a mixture of happiness and fear, like a man who realizes he has the winning lottery ticket in his hand, but hasn't yet collected the money—feeling that at any moment some obstacle will rise up to dash his hopes.

As if on cue, he heard Olex shouting over the din, "Oh, would you all just shut up!" The Ukrainian was shaking his head. "You sound like a bunch of horny schoolboys who have just discovered pornography." He paused. "This has been done before. Mueller and Beckett tried this in the late nineties with bacterial cultures and got nowhere. It will mutate in a thousand different directions, and none of them will help you."

"No, no, no," Eastman rebutted. "You're missing the point of Mueller and Beckett's work: they *did* succeed in creating several useful new strains. And given the huge gap in sophistication between their bacteria and our 'base cells,' their work only reinforces that it's possible."

What followed was fifteen minutes of Bill and Olex fighting it out, each insisting that he was right and the other was wrong. Finally, Bill waved Olex quiet. "Enough! It'll work. I'm sure of it. And you"—he pointed at Olex—"and Eric are going to prove it together."

Olex elongated himself in his chair and looked at Eric the way a well-dressed man might look upon a white drop of bird feces on his dinner jacket. "No," he said irrevocably. "If you want me to prove that his theory is garbage, I'll gladly do that, but I'll do it alone."

Eric glared at the goateed face. Now it came down to honor. Admittedly, he wasn't even sure his own idea would work. But he was ready to go weeks without sleep if it meant spiting Olex.

"Bill," Eric said, "I think it's best if I work alone on this one. I wouldn't want a colleague to discover that the idea works, and try to take credit for it."

A cold silence fell over the table. People just didn't accuse Olex of pirating ideas. Only Jane showed an expression devoid of shock. She tightened her eyelids and pressed her lips together in a devilish grin. *Oooooh, burn.*

"Don't make me laugh," Olex scoffed. "To be mentioned in a footnote of one of my papers would be the zenith of your unremarkable career. Besides, your idea will never be published, because it is shit."

"Gentlemen!" Eastman said. "You will both do as I say. My Genetics chief and my architect will work together! And you'll do it for the good of the team, not to gratify your egos."

"Here is your spy," the little man said, sliding an iSheet across the desk to General Meng. The general looked at the picture and made the kind of snorting sound that a teenager might give when his parents have done something unbelievably stupid. Then he gave a chuckle. *This man? The spy?* Then he sighed, realizing that he had wasted his money.

Meng had hired the man on a whim—out of frustration, he

supposed. It had certainly sounded good at first: the stories about how this bookish psychologist could practically read minds, how he had helped the police lock away dozens of criminals because he could tell when someone was lying. Besides, the man really hadn't asked for much. All he said he needed was access to his archive of surveillance videos. Two years of it. Then he would plug it into his spiffy little computer and—*poof*—just like that, he'd be able to find the spy. It had sounded almost too good to be true. Now he realized that it was.

Three months of work, and *this* was the result? Bo Li the spy? Hell, Meng had even put a team on Bo, just as he'd done with his forty top scientists. They had followed him around for a month and found nothing.

Meng laid a menacing glare on the little man. "I really don't appreciate you wasting my time. And the People's Liberation Army doesn't appreciate you wasting their money."

Much to Meng's surprise, the man did not shrink back in his chair and apologize as any sensible, self-preserving subordinate would do. Instead, he pushed his glasses back up on his nose and stared right back at Meng with a look of supreme confidence.

"General, that *is* your man."

Meng tossed the iSheet into the man's lap. "Prove it!"

The man took the sheet and started typing with his thumbs. A moment later, he placed the sheet back in front of Meng. It was a video of Meng with Bo Li. Meng remembered the meeting. It was right after he had put a team on Bo Li, and the two men were joking about it.

"What we are looking for, General," the little man explained, "is something called a *microexpression*. Many of our facial expressions are voluntary. For example, when you address your men, you put on the serious face of a commander. It's like an actor. A mask. But that's not what I want. I want an expression that is *in*voluntary, an expression that tells me what is going on behind the mask. Everyone has microexpressions, and they open a very short window into a person's mind. My computer program ran through every frame of video that you gave me—two years of footage from eight hundred cameras—searching for these expressions among your employees. I then took all the microexpressions I found, and parsed them for the specific emotions I was interested in: fear, guilt, distress, and shame, as well as smugness, pleasure, and contempt.

"This man," he said, pointing to Bo Li, "has thirty-five instances where his expressions show that he is knowingly deceiving you. Now, watch closely."

Meng looked at the video.

"There!" the little man said. "Did you see it?"

"I saw nothing," the general said, "because there is nothing to see."

The professor gave him a patronizing stare. Meng cocked his head to the side. The man was going to be lucky to leave the room alive.

"Please watch again, General, but this time in slow motion."

Both Meng and Bo Li were laughing; then the general got a call. At the moment that Meng turned to answer the phone, it happened.

"There!" the little man said.

For a split second, Bo Li's expression changed dramatically. Even in slow motion it came and went very quickly, but Meng saw it now. The smile was gone, replaced by a look of worry and—

"Contraction of the frontalis and the pars medialis (the raising of the inner brow) along with the pars lateralis (the outer brow), coupled with contraction of the risorius (the stretching of the lips), depressor labii (the parting of the lips) and the relaxing of the masseter (the slight dropping of the jaw). In other words, General, *fear*."

Yes, Meng thought, *fear.* "Go on!" he said impatiently.

"With pleasure. Now let's go back two years." Soon Meng was watching himself with Bo Li again. Bo Li was being his usual self— joking and playing around, talking about how his wife's food always gave him the most painful gas. Meng found himself snickering all over again.

"There it is!"

Again Meng saw nothing. And again the little man replayed it in slow motion.

"That is distress," the man said. "It's a slight raising of the eyebrows caused by trace contractions of the frontalis and the pars medialis. Then he expresses fear again. He is very nervous. In fact, he is more nervous in this clip than any other, which leads me to believe that this is when he first began deceiving you.

"Now look here," the man said. He ran through a series of twelve different clips, each one capturing a microexpression. They were similar, but over time the fear and the distress went away, replaced by expressions of contempt, smugness, and pleasure.

"Looking at these chronologically, we can see how he changes. He slowly begins to enjoy himself. In these more recent clips, you can see the lips curl from the pull of the zygomatic major and the tightening of the buccinator. That's contempt. He knows he's outsmarting you, and he's enjoying it."

"And here he is smiling at your joke, but it's a fake smile. See? Only the zygomatic major is being contracted. A true smile always incorporates the orbicularis oculi and the pars orbitalis. You might think of it as a light in the eyes. It can't be faked."

Meng felt an uncomfortable heat building behind his temples. Bo Li the spy? Was it possible?

Yet he saw that it was true. The little man was right. But somehow, that just made him hate the man even more. In fact, he somehow seemed complicit in this. It suddenly seemed to him that both Bo Li and the nerdy psychologist were making fun of him together. They both thought him a fool.

"Get out," Meng said in a low growl.

"Sir?"

"Out!"

"But I should really show y—"

"GET OUT!"

The man moved at last, and he moved fast, like a man who suddenly realizes he has stumbled into the lair of a wild animal. He paused for only a second, his eyes falling on his iSheet. He wanted to pick it up, but Meng's lethal glare made him think better of it. He grabbed up his briefcase and made a hasty retreat for the door and was gone.

For the next three hours, Meng sat at his desk reviewing each of the video clips, looking for Bo Li's … What had the little man called them?

Microexpressions. His mind was a dark sky of piling thunderheads. Again and again he watched, looking for the signs. He had considered Bo Li an ally, one of the few men he could really trust. Loyal to the party, to his country. A friend. A brother. *Gē men.*

Here he is smiling at your joke, but it is a fake smile.

Now he had to rewrite all his memories, all the jokes and laughter, and replace it with deception and betrayal.

After he had watched each clip twice, he started all over again. Again and again he found what he was looking for, and again and again he felt a fool for not seeing it before.

The iSheet began to shake in his hands, and he dropped it in annoyance. He was shaking with rage. Then it dawned on him that something else was driving his anger. Something small and defenseless. He touched his pocket. It was there: a folded sheet of photographic paper with three blurry black and white images on it. An ultrasound of his unborn child. Da-Xia was four months pregnant, and it was a girl. A girl to replace Lien, the daughter he had lost in Tibet. He pulled out the images and looked at them again. He saw, or imagined he saw, the resemblance already. His nose, her mother's lips, and, impossibly, his dead wife's eyes. This was why he had to rid the country of terrorists and separatists and nonbelievers.

And traitors.

But how to take care of Bo Li? For a long time, he had fantasized about how he would kill the traitor. But it would not be so easy now. Bo Li's family and, more importantly, his family's connections meant that it would have to be handled very delicately. In fact, Meng knew he was not powerful enough to denounce Bo Li at all. Bo Li's friendships with half the Central Committee meant that he could just turn around and accuse Meng, and that was a battle that Meng would lose, regardless of the truth. No, he would have to end this in a way that did not risk his career—in a way so that none of it was ever made public.

The iSheet had stopped at the end of the final video clip, frozen on the smiling, happy face of Bo Li.

"Soon, my friend. Very soon."

★ ★ ★

"NUB!" Olex said in his usual condescending tone. "I need this regression analysis. Have it for me by 11:00 a.m."

This, Eric had quickly learned, was Olex's idea of teamwork: issuing orders.

"Fuck you, Olex. I'll finish it when I finish it."

At first, Olex had been taken aback by Eric's audacity, but soon he was taking it in stride, his conquistador face not flinching. "I suggest you do as a say. I can make your life miserable."

"You just walked in and I'm already miserable," Eric said, "but if you're insinuating you can get me fired, you tried once and it didn't work."

"Just do the regression analysis, *svolota.*"

Eric's eyes rolled. He decided to counter. "Did you do the sequencing I asked for?"

To Eric's amazement, Olex produced an iSheet and laid the results in front of him. It would have taken a normal mortal two days to do that much work. But not Olex. It was annoying how good he was. Eric hated it. The guy was a machine. And as much as Eric didn't want to admit it, Olex was smarter than he was—in a whole different league of smart. At first, Eric had done his best to debunk him, to find errors in his work. He spent long hours double-checking, looking for holes, salivating at the fantasy of showing him up. Dreaming of the *aha* moment that he could rub in Olex's face. He never, *ever* found it.

On the other hand, Olex found plenty wrong with Eric's work. Programming errors, missteps in his designs, even typos in Eric's emails. That stung worst of all—that a foreign-born Ukrainian had better English grammar than he did. By the end of the first week, it was clear: Hell had descended on Eric Hill, and its earthly name was Olex Velichko.

He went to Eastman and begged to work alone, but Eastman wouldn't budge. "How interesting. Olex was here half an hour ago asking me the same thing. I'll tell you what I told him. Prove that it works or prove that it doesn't work. Only then will you be free of each other."

It was during the third week of Olex purgatory that they began to make progress. *Son of a bitch,* Eric thought. Eastman had known all along that the rivalry of their wills would make them work harder. Both men wanted to be right; both were obsessed with it. And Olex's constant questioning and insistence that they test and retest everything was making Eric work harder and more efficiently than he had ever worked before. Olex, too, was determined to prove himself right and was putting in long hours and producing better work. The turning point was when Olex suggested that they recalibrate the mutation factor. He didn't need to do that. If Olex had kept his mouth shut, Eric might not have caught his own error, and they would have reported to Eastman that forced evolution wouldn't work. It meant that Olex was beginning to believe.

By the end of the fourth week, it began to look as though it would really work, and not only with replication, but in at least a dozen areas: the interface, the neural-tube development, energy processing—the list went on. By applying the same concept to each design feature, they could radically improve the efficiency of every system. It was shaping up to be a game changer, an advance that might cut months off the timeline and put them ahead of the Chinese for the first time.

But right as Eric's confidence was growing, Olex found a problem—a big one. It was in the base code, the nanosite DNA. Somewhere inside was a radical, like a genetic disease, that was decaying every nanosite they attempted to breed. It was Friday night at almost midnight when Olex found it, and it took the wind out of Eric's sails. It wasn't going to work, was it? And he'd thought they were almost there. Now it would be another two weeks of testing, and to find out what? That it all had been a waste of time.

He went back to his apartment and slept for the next twelve hours. In the morning, he didn't want to get up. God, he needed a break, to unplug. As he lay there in bed, he felt strangely detached from his fellow man. What movies were people watching? What were the top news stories? What were normal people gossiping about? He had no idea, and he was sure he wouldn't find out. It was Saturday, a day when most people didn't work. But he had worked every weekend for the past four months. And he would work again today.

Grudgingly, he got out of bed, showered, ate a little, and left his apartment. But he couldn't bring himself to go back to work, so he went to visit Jane instead. He needed someone to talk to, someone to lift his spirits.

She took a while to come to the door. He knocked. Waited. Knocked again. When she finally opened the door, she had a white towel wrapped under her armpits. "Sorry, I didn't hear you," she said. "Are you going in now? Give me a minute to dress and I'll go with you." She went back to her bedroom, and Eric watched her go, hypnotized by her toned legs, watching as her calves balled and flexed. He shook his head as if clearing away cobwebs, gave a long exhalation, and plopped down on the couch.

"Did you run this morning?" he asked.

She called from the bedroom. "Yeah, I did six miles. It felt good. Without it, I'd go crazy."

Yeah, crazy, he thought. He was jealous of her discipline. He'd stopped working out months ago. He missed the release, as well as the clarity and confidence that came from being fit.

"Jane, I think I'm losing it," he called out. "It was all I could do just to get up this morning." She came in. She had put on baggy jeans and a T-shirt and was rubbing a towel in her thick hair. It was growing back quickly. She had to keep the rest of it short, but you had to look closely now to tell she'd been burned.

She saw his feet propped up on the sofa, and swatted them off. "Move over."

He obeyed. "It's just not working." He told her about the problems with Forced Evolution.

"I'm sorry," she said. "I know how excited you were about it. Bill, too. Are you sure it won't work?"

He told her about the radical. "We're running out of options."

"I know it must be frustrating, but don't let it get you down. Keep trying and remember that even if it doesn't work, it's not the end of the world."

"Yeah, well, it feels like it. It's just that most of the time, I feel so useless. And with this idea, well, I thought I was finally going to contribute something."

"You're being too hard on yourself. Try to put all *this* in perspective." She motioned at the air, the whole NRL. "We're trying to do some of the most complicated things that have ever been done. *Ever.* And not only are they difficult, we're expected to do them really fast. It's hardly fair. Think about any other big research institution. They have scientists that go years, even decades, without a single good idea. Some waste their whole lives pursuing things that never work. So don't beat yourself up if you go a few months without an idea."

"I know, and I've tried to tell myself that. It's just … I thought I could make a difference."

"Trust me, you've made a difference already."

"You think?"

"Of course you have. You fixed the replication errors, and you've been an excellent architect. Bill and Jack know that."

He looked away skeptically.

"And you saved my life."

"That was just a reaction. I didn't even think about it."

She didn't answer right away. When she finally spoke, her voice was soft and cautious in a way that was very unlike Jane. "That's exactly why it was so important to me, you idiot. You did it without thinking. Your instinctive reaction was to save me." She moved closer to him, hesitated, then put her hand on his chest. "It means your heart's in the right place." Their eyes locked for a moment. "And I'll take that over a brilliant theory any day."

There was a beat of silence. Eric wanted to kiss her then. To lean in and hold her. It seemed like the right thing to do, and he wanted it more than anything, but something stopped him. Jane and Ryan were the closest thing he had to family since his own family had imploded. If there was any chance he was misreading her, he'd screw it all up.

"Thanks," he said. "You're very good to me."

Jane smiled and nodded slowly, sensing that the moment had passed. "Come on," she said, "let's go."

★ ★ ★

Eric went back to his office and started in on the base code "radical" problem. He was glad his pale Ukrainian nemesis wasn't around. All day, he hoped Olex wouldn't show his face. And in the end, he didn't. Eric didn't see him the next day, either, but on Monday evening around five thirty, he turned in his chair and found Olex standing right behind him.

Eric jumped. "Jesus! You scared the shit out of me. Where have you been?"

But Olex said nothing. Eric scooted back a little and had a better look at him. Olex looked, well, like shit. He was wearing the same clothes he'd had on last Friday, and black stubble was growing around the usually manicured goatee. Had he been working here since Friday night?

"What is it?" Eric said, his curiosity unable to check his impatience with Olex. "Whatever it is, don't blame me. It's probably your own damn fault."

"*Svolota,* why do you waste so many words when you speak? It only exposes that your head is full of shit."

But this time, something in Olex's tone wasn't so harsh. For the first time, it was no longer the resentful, condescending, *you're-an-idiot* glare. Olex lifted an iSheet in one hand and extended it to Eric, offering it like bait to a hungry fish.

Eric took it and began to read. Okay, Olex had made a series of modifications to the base code. Eric didn't understand all of it—it was complicated genetics—but he did understand the new projections. All the heuristics were synchronized. Olex had somehow solved the problem with the radicals! There was no decay in the breeding cycle. But that wasn't all. Olex had kept going. God, he must have been working nonstop since Friday—almost four days without sleep. Now the mutation factor showed the right deviation for selection and variation. That meant … it would work!

Eric stood up, his body suddenly weightless. He began pacing around the room, his eyes still glued to the iSheet. Was it true? Had Olex really done it? Yes and yes. It would work!

He looked at Olex, and what he saw startled him.

Olexander Velichko was smiling. For the first time, Eric saw two rows of coffee-stained teeth. His facial muscles were clearly uncomfortable with the arrangement, but he was definitely smiling.

"I'd appreciate being mentioned in your footnotes," he said.

Eric smiled, shaking his head. "No, Olex, you are gonna be first author on this paper, and *I'll* be in the footnotes. I can't believe you did it!"

"*We* did it," he said. Olex was not one for physical displays. No hugging, shoulder patting, or even handshakes. But he was, at heart, honest and candid. "It's a brilliant idea," he said, "and it's going to change everything, which means there won't be a paper. It's too important."

Eric shrugged. Olex was right. Curtiss would never let this get out. There might not be a paper, but it still felt as if he had won the lottery *and* collected the money.

"Now that we know it will work," Olex said, "I want you to do me a favor."

"Anything," Eric said.

Olex nodded slowly, appreciatively. "Don't come anywhere near me for the next seven days."

"Done!"

For the rest of the day, Eric wore a goofy grin, and by evening his cheeks were sore. *It was going to work.*

CHAPTER SIXTEEN

THE PILL

November 9, 2025
Tangshan Military Laboratory, China

His blood made a steady *tap ... tap ... tap* sound as it dripped to the floor.

His head was pitched forward, his hair hanging over his eyes, and his hands were handcuffed behind his back, through the rungs of the steel chair. He kept his eyes closed. Better not to look.

Meng had smashed his left testicle with a hammer, and the pulp had swollen to the size of a lemon. It hurt with a relentless, terrible ache that pulsed with his heartbeat.

"We'll leave the other one for now," Meng had whispered in his ear. "But don't worry, old friend, we'll get to it eventually." Meng kept repeating *old friend* sweetly, over and over.

It had been more than a day now, trapped in this windowless cinder-block room. Bo Li felt like a side of meat being taken apart at a butcher shop. Meng had started with the webbing between his fingers, then the fingernails. Then the fingers themselves, moving down one knuckle at a time. Meng had held the chunks in front of his eyes, like beige dice, as he went along. Now only the thumb on his right hand remained.

Bo Li had never felt such pain, never knew that the body could be manipulated to hurt so much.

He had only one hope: In his shirt, stitched into the seam at the small of his back, was a little capsule. He was desperate to get to it. It meant freedom. Escape. It was so close, touching him. But he couldn't get to it.

They had taken the fingers quickly, before they even began questioning him, and that told him, so clearly, so sadly, that he would never leave here. There would be no recovery. At first, his mind had entertained, in the most childish way, the hope that he would survive. *If they let me go now, I can still get better. I could still live.* His mind wanted to believe it, even though everything said otherwise.

He had told them much. The pain, combined with the drugs in the IV, was too much. He couldn't help it. But his confessions were interwoven with things that seemed to confuse Meng. Bo Li kept repeating, "My eyes are cameras. My eyes are cameras."

But eventually, Meng had come to understand what it meant, and with it, the magnitude of the treason, and just how much had been given to the Americans. It had spun him into a rage.

"You thought you could outsmart me? Me! Walking around, telling your jokes, smiling in my face while you stole from me! Who is smarter now? Who?"

Bo Li made no answer.

Meng's rage only grew. "Who is smarter now?" he shouted, and took up a knife—a fisherman's tool, with a curved serrated blade. With a sudden explosion of savagery, he fell on Bo Li, yanked up his leg, and, with quick sawing motions, he began to remove the skin around the kneecap. Bo Li twisted and struggled. "No, no, please, no!" The two soldiers rushed in and held the leg steady as Meng worked. "No! Stop! Please stop!" Bo Li screamed as Meng worked, flaying his leg.

"Yes, yes, that's it. Struggle. Let me hear you scream. We are just beginning, *old friend.* For you, the *lingchi.* The Thousand Cuts." Soon he had removed a disk of skin, a pancake of flesh, and tossed it to the floor. Bo Li looked down. The ligaments, muscle, and bone of his knee lay open to the world.

"*Now* who is smarter? Say it!"

"You are. You are smarter," Bo Li said, weeping, trying not to look at the wound.

But Meng was not placated. He had lost himself in the rage. His nostrils flaring like an angry bull. "All these months I thought you were helping me find the spy! All these frustrating months! And to find that it was you, you *Hàn jiān*—you were the one destroying our chances to win the race!"

He tossed the knife into a corner and picked up a cricket bat—a souvenir from a trip to Hong Kong that Bo Li had kept in his office—and the beating began. First the shins, then the arms, working himself into a fury. He lifted the bat over his head and swung it down like a sledgehammer, but in his fury, he missed Bo Li's head. Instead, the bat fell into his shoulder, snapping the collarbone with a loud crack.

Bo Li screamed through his tear-stained face. His body convulsed at the break, and his head sagged oddly toward that shoulder. Meng didn't care. He swung again, a horizontal blow that hit the side of his head with a sound like splitting wood.

Then everything went black.

He awoke to the *tap … tap … tap* of his blood dripping from his forehead down his nose and to the floor. His head felt as if it had a dent in it. It ached terribly. Something was wrong with his neck, too. Meng must have cracked one of his vertebrae, because the whole shoulder and arm were numb.

He needed to focus. To make the most of this moment of respite. He had to find a way to die quickly. For himself and for *them*. He had told Meng many things. Yet he had not told him the most important thing: the secret that he himself had discovered only a week ago. For months, he had been finding strange packets of data in the code. Things he could not read, but that he knew didn't belong there. Last week, he had finally put the pieces together. *He wasn't the only one.* As soon as he realized the truth, he wished that he hadn't. It would have been much better for them. He was no longer strong enough to lie; he knew that. Indeed, the only reason he had not told Meng the secret was simply because Meng had not asked the right question.

He had to make sure he was dead before that happened.

The pill. If only he could somehow get it to his mouth, then it would all be over.

His grandfather had also carried such a pill. Being so close to Mao, it was absolutely necessary, he said, given the madman's moods. His grandfather had seen it a dozen times. Without the slightest coloring of emotion, Mao could condemn a friend to death, send him and his family into exile, or submit him to *struggle*—over a rumor or suspicion that wasn't even true. His grandfather had decided he and his family would never share their fate. So he had made his wife and son carry the pills, too, and would force them to do drills—make them bite into the pill without question or hesitation, never knowing whether it was cyanide or sugar.

It was terrible, but necessary. His grandfather had realized it, and so had Bo Li. So he had taken up the old trick because it was still the best solution to end a nightmare.

It was there, so close. But with his left side numb and the fingers of his right hand gone, it seemed a world away. Even if he could remove it from the seam, he had no way to get it to his mouth unless he could get the handcuffs off. He tried to think of a way. He knew they would never let him go to the bathroom. He had defecated when they began cutting off his fingers, but they just hosed him off. He had to think of something else. It seemed hopeless, and a part of him was ready just to let go, just to let Meng have his way. To suffer the *lingchi*.

But he knew he must at least try—if not for himself, for them.

It would be up to his right hand. Even though the fingers were gone, there was enough of a stump on his index finger that he might be able to pinch the pill. With his thumb, he slowly began to work the pill out of the seam. He had to ease it out slowly, carefully, lest it fall to the floor.

"It's time to begin again, *old friend,*" Meng said, coming forward and giving him three quick little slaps to the face. "I know you're awake. Don't forget, I've done this before, as many Tibetans can tell you."

Bo Li's head rolled heavily, and he looked up at Meng with glassy eyes.

"Tell me when it started," the general said.

Bo Li considered lying, saying it was recent, because that would make it sound as if the treason were not so great. But he dare not risk being caught in a lie now. "About two years," he said weakly. "They recruited me when I went to visit Heng in New York."

Meng seemed satisfied with the answer.

Bo Li had now worked the pill out a bit, and he tried to grip it. But the hand was clumsy from the trauma of the amputated fingers—club-like, swollen, and stiff. He couldn't grip it. He would have to push it out a little bit more, ever so gently.

"And who gave you the miniature iSheets?"

"I don't know. They arrived by post."

Meng picked up the cricket bat and tested its weight. He didn't like any *I don't know* answers. "How often did they come?"

"Only once. I remember the return address was from an optometrist on Hexi Road."

Meng nodded. It made sense. In fact, the whole thing was ingenious. Truly ingenious. He appreciated that, yet he found himself shaking his head with disgust all the same.

Bo Li tried again to pinch the pill. It was a supreme effort. Gripping it meant he was pushing it into the stump of his finger; pinching it against exposed bone. The pain ran over him like a sheet of cold rain, and it was all he could do to disguise the agony. But he had it. It was out.

He willed his left hand to open. He couldn't feel the hand itself, but he could touch it with his right and feel that it was open. He dropped the pill in and willed it shut, again, checking it with the other hand. Now the pill was safely in his left fist.

"Now tell me about the drops," Meng said.

"I will tell you if you will let my hands free."

"No."

"Just for a few minutes. Please. I'll tell you what you want to know."

"Tell me first."

Bo Li nodded slowly. "All right." And he told him about the drops.

Meng's jaw shivered spasmodically as the rage came over him again. He was angry at Bo Li, but also at his own men, who had watched it happen and had seen nothing.

"Please, my hands," Bo Li said. "You have me. I'm cooperating."

Meng ignored him, pacing around the room. To Bo Li, the general seemed cool and calm again. But he knew that the other Meng was just under the surface. If he said the wrong thing, that other Meng would be back. "Why?" he said. "Why did you do it? Your family sacrificed so much for China. They dedicated their whole lives to ridding us of the imperialists. And you disgraced them and everything they worked for. Why?"

"Please, my hands."

Meng came closer. He placed his hands on the arms of the chair and pushed his face close to Bo Li's. Their eyes met. "Tell me, *old friend*. Why?"

"I'll try to explain, but first, please, my hands."

Meng pushed himself up and stood, inspecting the man. Finally, he waved a tired hand at the guards, and one came forward to remove the cuffs.

"Thank you," Bo Li said. "Thank you."

Bo Li brought his hands around and saw his wounds for the first time. The four bloody stumps were purple and black, caked with dried blood, and a shoot of bone protruded from two of them.

The sight filled him with a rush of several emotions: First was sadness, a sense of needless loss. Then there was hatred toward Meng for doing it to him. Finally, there was a sense of strength, a sudden conviction. He had been right to do all the things he had done. It was right to commit treason against a government that would do this to its own people. And he was only one of many, of hundreds of thousands—

no, one of millions—who had died defying this government. And they all had been right to do it.

There was solace in knowing that his was an ordinary death. One single life to be thrown on the heap, the great graveyard of history. From Mao's killing of a quarter of his own army, to the reform camps, to the Hundred Flowers purge, to the occupation of Lhasa, to the Cultural Revolution, all the way to Tiananmen Square. His was an ordinary death. One single number, a lone digit—1—of millions.

He began coughing—a violent cough, but a fake cough. He brought his left fist to his face and sucked in the pill.

Then he slouched back in his chair as if he had just finished a long race. He was free. All he had to do was bite, and it would all be over.

"You want to know why I did it?"

Meng looked at him eagerly. "Yes."

Bo Li just nodded, almost smiled. For a brief moment, he considered trying to explain it to Meng. But the man didn't deserve his final words. Instead, he turned his words inward. To his wife and son. "My dearest Yàn and my boy Heng. I love you, and I want you to know that I cherished every moment that I had you. And I'm so sorry I can't be with you anymore."

"Come on," Meng said, "out with it."

Bo Li would soon be free. He had not told his secret. Meng had never asked the right question. He bit into the pill.

At three thirty in the morning, Admiral Curtiss was working in his study. He was just about to turn out the light when he decided to check his mail. It was a bad habit, he knew, because it would just be full of more demands for his time. Luckily, there was nothing new. He was about to shut down the computer when a new message popped up.

"New Mail - Subject: No subject—From: Meng Longwei. Received 0337 9 November 2025"

General Meng.

Curtiss stared at it and rubbed his jaw. *Now, what could this be? Was it some kind of trick?* The Chinese were constantly barraging the lab with cyberattacks. Many of them were emails that appeared to be from legitimate places—banks, alumni associations, even friends and family—trying to entice employees into clicking on them and releasing their bots into the network. Curtiss told himself not to open it. *Just send it to one of the techies for quarantine.*

But he didn't. Instead, he found himself running his mouse over it.

"Subject: No subject—From: Meng Longwei. Received 0337 9 November 2025"

It seemed to be calling to him. Pulsating. *Go on, open me!* Perhaps it was the late hour or his fatigue, but he couldn't let it go. He needed to know.

But he couldn't risk the network. That was out of the question. He looked around. In the corner was a new iSheet he had bought for Logan. He grabbed it, spent fifteen minutes configuring it, and then set up a new email account. Then he forwarded Meng's message to it. Finally, he disconnected it from the network.

The mouse floated above the name: Meng Longwei. *Go on,* he told himself, *get it over with.* He tapped the screen.

A huge image began to load. It opened painfully slowly, filling in from top to bottom. He could see only a small piece of it, it was so large. He couldn't make it out. Were those teeth? Bloody teeth? A torn lip? What in the hell was it?

Then the image finished loading and adjusted, instantly shrinking down.

Curtiss's veins flooded instantly with a violent cocktail of adrenaline and hate. The hardness. He snarled aloud at Meng, as if he were actually in the room.

Meng, dressed in fractal woodland camo, was grinning like a boy on his birthday. He was standing in what could only be a torture chamber: a metal chair bolted to the floor, a pool of black blood around it, an IV stand, a filleting knife, and a cricket bat. Facedown on the floor was a corpse, naked except for a bloodstained shirt, the bare legs tapering up to pasty buttocks. But the body was not complete.

In Meng's outstretched hand, just in front of his grinning face, was the head of Bo Li.

"I got him!" it said at the bottom of the photo.

CHAPTER SEVENTEEN

REPLICATION

December 24, 2025
Naval Research Laboratory, Washington, DC
Phase 1 Deadline: T-plus fourteen days

> Mankind is in the first steps of creating a life-form whose evolution will be measured in minutes, not millennia.
>
> —Bill Eastman

The breakthrough came on Christmas Eve.

On the night of the twenty-third, a heavy snowstorm came up the Eastern Seaboard. By morning, the capital was under fourteen inches of snow.

Eric got to work early, trudging through the snow, already giddy with excitement. The first thing he did was take a look at her. Their newest prototype: Minerva-Charlie. If you looked close enough, long enough, you could almost imagine you could see her with the naked eye. You couldn't, of course—at her thickest, she was only a hundred atoms wide.

So that they could see her, Ryan had hooked a scanning electron microscope up to a giant iSheet in the main auditorium. Amplified in this way, Minerva-C looked like a bleached-white fighter plane sitting on the tarmac. She had six large primary legs, then thousands of smaller secondary legs and arms, and looked like a cross between a virus and a wingless mosquito. Every now and then she would vibrate, and the legs and arms would go into a blur. This was each limb rising, extending, and gripping. If the motion were slowed down to one ten-thousandth its natural speed, it would look like a hand running down the keys of a piano. This was an internal systems check—a little like a fly preening itself. Eric swelled with pride to see that. The design of those legs was unmistakable. He had modeled them from the legs of the horseshoe crab.

In the bottom of the screen, a timer counted down to this evening's eight o'clock deadline: T-MINUS 12:44:19.

1258 hours: Nanotech Division final test cycle:
Minerva-Charlie: T-minus 07:02:56

"And people think cockroaches are tough!" Eric said.

"That, my friend, is the benefit of designing with diamondoid," Jack Behrmann said, lowering the temperature in the holding container. "Its functional temperature range is between 10 and 4,273.15 degrees Kelvin. That little gal could be in a blast furnace and still wear a parka. And on the cold end, as long as it's warm enough for just a little bit of molecular activity, she'll keep truckin'." Jack leaned back in an enormous stretch, his wingspan taking up half the room. He yawned and put his hands behind his head. "That's it! That's the last test for us. Now it's up to AI and Genetics. All we can do now is wait."

But that was really worse, Eric thought. He was nervous enough already. Now he had seven hours to do nothing but worry about all the thousands of things he might have overlooked.

1515 hours: Artificial Intelligence final test cycle:
Minerva-Charlie: T-minus 04:45:00

"Fuck, fuck, fuck, and FUCK!" Ryan Lee stood up and pressed his hands against his thighs, closed his eyes, and breathed deeply. The breathing wasn't to calm himself, but to gather strength, like a martial arts expert preparing for the attack. On the sixty-five-inch iSheet, split between five windows were snapshots of six hundred thousand lines of code he had written over the past two years. Very calmly, he gripped the keyboard at the narrow end with both hands and began swinging. Sparks leaped from the screen, and keys rained down like pennies—*Z, Q, R, Alt, Caps Lock*.

It had been three days since he last slept.

★ ★ ★

1515 hours: Artificial Intelligence final test cycle:
Minerva-Charlie: T-minus 03:45:00

Eric walked into the Moffett Hangar and saw the six hundred thousand lines of computer code spread out on the floor. It covered at least two acres. Forty-five programmers were on their hands and knees with handheld magnifying lights, looking for the error.

Ryan was doing his best to coordinate the search, directing the conscripts—including his own boss, Dr. Berg—to the most suspect areas. Eric felt instant sympathy for him. His face was somehow both pale and flushed, his eyes swollen and puffy. Eric put a hand on his shoulder. "Is this what they call the luck of the Irish?" he said, referring to Ryan's adopted pedigree. Though born in Korea, he had been adopted by Irish American parents, last name Lee, as in Robert E. Lee. "Really, I'm Irish," he liked to say.

Ryan snorted a laugh. "I'd feel lucky if all I had to do was find a needle in a haystack. This could take a month." Ryan ran a hand through his black hair. "And we thought Bill was pissed when we had to push the deadline back two weeks. Wait till he hears about this."

"Relax, we'll find it. You ran every possible debugging program, and nothing?"

Ryan nodded. "It's got to be a logic bug like an infinite loop or two parallel-executing threads."

"Where do I start?"

Eric grabbed a magnifying light and was soon down on his hands and knees. They worked silently, like peasant farmers tending to row after row of computer code.

An hour passed, then another. Just as Eric began to feel that it was truly hopeless, Dr. Berg sat up. "I got it!" she said. A normally austere woman with deep crow's-feet at the corners of her eyes, she looked as ecstatic as a little girl getting a standing ovation at the school play.

Ryan ran to the spot, his sneakers splashing through the paper. After a minute, he confirmed the discovery. "I knew it! A deadlock. Dr. Berg, you are a GODDESS!"

"Yes," she said, appearing to give it some serious thought. "I am."

Ryan looked across the field of data at Eric, who was sitting up on his knees. It had taken them only two hours. "Luck of the Irish," Ryan said.

2028 hours: Genetics Division final test cycle:
Minerva-Charlie: T-plus 00:28:09

Up in his office, Bill Eastman was sitting with his head in his hands. He gave a heavy sigh. "Okay, what are our chances?"

"Tough to say, Bill," Jack said. "It's not like anyone's ever done this before."

Bill motioned with his hand. *Keep going.*

"If Olex's team doesn't have any trouble, and the AI code has really been fixed, I'd say our chances are at least eighty, eighty-five percent." Jack paused, and sat down on the opposite side of the desk. "Now," he added, inhaling deeply, "will she replicate more than once? Increasingly unlikely. But, Bill, the science of it is sound. God knows it works every day in nature. I see no reason why it shouldn't work here, too."

Bill rubbed his forehead. "It has to work," he replied. "God damn it, it has to. If we fail, if we have to postpone, I'll never get this team back up to speed." They were hanging by a thread.

Jack sighed. His friend was under tremendous strain. China was getting ever closer to the same goal. And who knew what China would do if they replicated first? To be safe, to give America time to create countermeasures, they had to get this right, and it had to be now.

Jack searched for something encouraging to say, but all he could come up with were platitudes, so he kept quiet. They had known each other too long for that.

2200 hours: Replication test: Minerva-Charlie: T-plus 02:00:56

Twenty-two hundred nanotechnologists, systems engineers, and geneticists were crowded into the main auditorium when the clock struck ten. This was it: the final test. Success tonight would change everything. If it worked, they could finally take off in all the exciting new directions that the age of nanotechnology promised. And if they failed, then what? Eric didn't want to think about it.

The place was strangely quiet, and it was a little unnerving to have so many people in one room and have it be so still. He wanted to say something, to make a joke to Ryan or Jane, but the silence had somehow become hallowed. The room was dark, the only light emanating from the huge iSheet, which painted everyone's faces in an eerie pale glow. On the screen was their creation, not yet alive.

Minutes ticked by. They were waiting for Bill Eastman, who sat in the back of the room, reviewing the test results. The glare from his iSheet caught on his glasses, making them disks of light. Every few minutes, Eric would look over his shoulder to see if Bill was ready.

Ryan sat beside Eric, fidgeting nervously, his fingers crossed under the table. Jane bit at her nails. Olex sat nearby, playing it cool, absently galloping his fingertips on the table. *Vadup, vadup, vadup.*

Finally, Bill was ready.

"Okay, ladies and gentlemen," he said, "here we go." He jabbed the Enter key. First, they heard a noise, very faint, like the hum of wet power cables. On the chalky black-and-white video screen, Minerva-C trembled, paused, trembled again, then shook into a blur. When she came back into focus, there were two.

Simple. Natural. *Fast.*

The room exploded with noise. They had done it. "Son of a bitch," Jane breathed. "It worked!" They all were on their feet. People hooted and cried out, gave each other high fives, and hugged. Jane grabbed Eric and kissed him full on the mouth. An instant later, she was lost in the pandemonium. The place went wild.

Then came another roar. Eric turned to the screen. Now there were four. A second later, the four trembled, then blurred, and there were eight. The room roared again. Again the tremble and blur. Sixteen. Thirty-two. Sixty-four. One hundred twenty-eight. Two hundred fifty-six. At each replication, everyone cheered, raising fists into the air. Ryan had to readjust the microscope. Now it looked like a satellite view of an airfield covered with neat rows of airplanes. Some of them began to move about like curious insects.

Eric looked for Bill, anxious to see his reaction, and caught sight of him slipping quietly out the back door. He thought to follow him, to congratulate him, but he was quickly pulled back into the revelry and forgot about him. He saw Olex and gave him a hug. Olex stepped back and straightened his shirt. "I'll excuse it this once, but never do that again."

Around midnight, the lights came on, and it suddenly felt like a nightclub after last call. Everyone started heading for home. Fifteen minutes later, Eric looked around and found that it was just the three of them: Jane, Ryan, and himself.

They looked at each other, and for no reason they could name, they all started laughing.

"Come on," Ryan said. "Let's go celebrate!"

They broke through the nearest exit and into the winter night. It was bitterly cold, but they didn't care. Between the moonlight and the streetlights, the world was caught in that soft perpetual twilight the night has when everything is covered in snow.

They joked and laughed on their way back to the apartment block, making ambitious plans.

"Let's go see the monuments at night. I love that!"

"Fuck that, let's take the bullet train to New York."

"Naw, naw, naw, if we're going to do it, we do it right. We take the next flight to Vegas."

In the end, they settled for raiding a vending machine and sitting on the floor of Jane's apartment, drinking beer and eating Pop-Tarts, Oreos, and Reese's Peanut Butter Cups.

"You're eating it all wrong," Eric said to Jane. "You have to start on the edges."

"Says the guy who eats Oreos without disassembling them first."

"It's not my fault. You don't have any milk."

"That's no excuse." She gave him a sly grin.

There was a light in her eyes tonight. A confidence. Even when he turned away from her, he could feel her eyes warming the side of his face. He was doing it, too: looking at her more. They were feeding off each other. In tune. And perhaps because of that, he noticed something he had never noticed before.

Jane's apartment was a like a gym. A rack of free weights against one wall. A treadmill. A speed bag. On the walls were posters of famous athletes. Great moments in sports. Jesse Owens in the grass with Luz

Long. Nadia Comaneci on the balance beam. Muhammad Ali standing over Sonny Liston.

Eric had been here dozens of times, of course, but he'd never noticed that something was missing. There were almost no pictures of Jane's friends or family. Jane's mother had abandoned her and her father when Jane was very young, so he wasn't surprised to find no pictures of her. But there were no pictures of any friends, either—nothing from high school or college. Nothing to recall a life being lived. In fact, there was only one picture: a portrait of her father, the Marine Corps colonel in his dress blues. An official picture, like the portrait of the president hanging in a government office.

That was when it clicked. Her huge emphasis on goals—for fitness, science, genetic engineering. Yet the absence, the complete denial, of the personal. Her obsession with fitness, with its steady dose of endorphins, was her way of … of what? Keeping her mind off something? He wasn't sure, but he recognized the strategy immediately. Hadn't he done the same thing after his father's death, when wrestling was all he cared about? It had helped him keep his sanity. But what was Jane trying to get away from?

He turned his head to her. She was beautiful tonight, the bright eyes and proud forehead. But he was seeing her in a new way. He and Ryan had always teased her about being a fitness freak. How she was so butch and strong, yet socially awkward. But now he felt sorry he had said some of those things. Yes, she had tough skin and would always throw their insults right back at them. But he suspected that beneath her veneer of strength was someone vulnerable.

"What?" she said.

"Huh? Oh, nothing."

She smiled, but she was searching his face. "Why were you looking at me like that?"

"Because I want that last Pop-Tart."

She gave a short laugh. "It's yours," she said, holding it out. "If you can take it."

He lunged, and they began to fight over it. It was a surprisingly even match. She was just as strong as he was, and what she lacked in wrestling skills, she made up for in guile. Eventually, Eric won, but it was a Pyrrhic victory. When Jane realized all was lost, she mashed the Pop-Tart against the side of his face.

"Totally uncalled for," he said, standing over the sink, trying to unclog his ear. "Wasting a perfectly good Pop-Tart."

Jane and Ryan were still laughing.

"All right," Ryan announced. "I'm outta here!"

"You!" Eric and Jane said in unison. "What about Vegas?"

"Not tonight. I've been up four days straight."

"How about you?" Eric asked Jane.

"I'm too wired for bed. Let's do something brainless and lazy, like watch movies. I haven't watched a movie in a year."

Eric nodded conspiratorially, liking the idea. "I think I know just the place."

Fifteen minutes later, they were in Simpson Hall, one of the old academic buildings, outside a set of old wooden doors that said, "Orion Theater."

"Ever been here?" Eric asked.

"Never," she said.

"Then you're in for a treat."

Eric swiped his pass card and dramatically pulled open the double doors.

"Wow," she gasped.

It was an old-fashioned theater, complete with a balcony and velvet curtains in front of the screen. There were about forty rows of seats with soft burgundy cushions, and the walls had old murals of patriotic scenes of cadets in training. It felt like stepping back in time. It was easy to imagine this as a place where people had actually watched *The Wizard of Oz.*

"Where do you want to sit?" he asked.

"In the front row, of course!"

They proceeded to stay up all night stuffing their faces with junk food and watching sci-fi classics: *Avatar, The Wrath of Khan, Aliens.*

As the final credits rolled, they felt both the exhaustion and the euphoria of going through all those adventures. They were themselves, but they were also their heroes, because the residue of all those characters was so fresh inside them.

"Oh, my gosh!" Jane cried. "It's almost six!"

Eric laughed. "Tired?"

"No," she said, grinning. "I feel great!"

They looked at each other. Smiled and kept smiling.

Eric felt like a kid on the last day of summer vacation, staying up all night, trying to hold on to something he didn't want to end.

"So," Eric said, summoning his courage. "After replication, you kissed me."

"Did I? Sorry. It seemed like a good idea at the time."

"No, it's fine, I just didn't—"

"Expect it?"

"Yeah."

"Well, me, either."

"Oh, okay." Eric looked down at his hands, feeling suddenly foolish. Had he really misread her? He had known it was stupid to read too much into a kiss. It was just a spontaneous thing. Yet she had kissed him, hadn't she? And no one else.

"What I mean," she said, "was that I hadn't really imagined it like that."

It took a moment for the light to come on. Then Eric's fears dissipated, replaced by nervous excitement.

"How, exactly, did you imagine it?"

"Well, I guess …" She met his gaze. "Something like this."

And she leaned in and kissed him.

It was a soft kiss, hesitant and unsure. When their fingertips touched, he felt her trembling as if she were cold. He couldn't help remembering her room. His realization. But she seemed to get over her inhibitions quickly. She was hungry for him, and he was hungry for her.

But then she suddenly pulled back, drawing a long breath.

"Wait. Can we do this?" she asked.

"Sure, why not?"

"I don't know. It's just … I want this, I really do, but we work together."

"So what? We're not even on the same team."

"I know. It's just, I don't want to mess anything up. I mean, God, I don't know what I mean. I just—"

"Stop talking and kiss me," he said.

A smile. "Okay."

They kissed, and she seemed to forget herself, hungry all over again, biting his lip, then his ear.

She stopped again. "You really like me, don't you? I mean really? I just need to hear you say it."

"You know I do."

"Just say it."

He cupped her beautiful face in his hands. "I really like you. I wanted to do this before, in your room, but I was a little scared of losing you as a friend."

"Okay," she said, nodding, thinking about it. "Okay, good answer. Oh, God, Eric, I just don't know. I want you. God, I do. I've wanted you ever since the fire, since you saved my life. I couldn't stop thinking about it."

They kissed again, longer this time, and without breaking the kiss, she shifted out of her seat and onto his lap. He ran a hand over her hips and up her side, brushing her breast. She undid the top buttons of his shirt and ran her hands over his chest.

Then she cupped his jaw in her hand and gave him a mischievous grin. Eyes bright. "Come on," she said. She took his hand and led him toward the door. He trundled after her, looking down at their joined hands, still not really believing this was happening. Every atom of his being was focused on her. On this. He felt inexpressibly lucky and filled with the insane and stupid hope—premature, but a hope all the same—that a long search was over.

They made their way back to the apartments, taking their time. They would talk and flirt and stop to kiss. Then Jane would take his hand again and lead him again.

But then something happened. Just as they were getting back to the apartment block, he saw her eyes linger on a marine recruitment poster. A chill seemed to come over her. Her smile ebbed, and her walk lost its confidence. When they reached the elevator, she let go of his hand and didn't take it again.

He was still trying to make sense of the change when they reached her door. Her eyes went to the left and right, anywhere but him. "Hey, look," she said, "it's really late and I have to be in the lab in a few hours. Olex will be expecting me."

"Hey, what happened? What did I say? Whatever it is, I'm sorry."

"No, it's not you. I thought I could do this. I really did. But it was stupid of me. I'm sorry."

"Why? I don't understand."

She finally made eye contact. Then came the tears. She didn't fight them or wipe them away. She just held his gaze.

He went to touch her cheek, but she took his hand, cupped it, and gave it back to him.

"I'm sorry, Eric. I'm really sorry." She turned, entered her apartment, and closed the door.

Eric heard the door latch, then the chain slide onto its receptacle.

He stood there for a long time looking at the door, examining the metal frame. Ten. Fifteen. Twenty minutes. He put his hand on the door. It was what separated them. He had to get to the other side somehow, to make her understand. But the door …

★ ★ ★

A few inches away, Jane leaned into the door, watching him through the eyehole. Her stomach roiling in a storm of conflicting emotions. Fear and desire. Insecurity and lust. And something she was trying hard to convince herself wasn't love. The tears kept coming, hot on her cheeks, but she suppressed her sobs. Her eye stayed transfixed on him. Praying he would come to her. *Try the door,* she thought. *Just try. It's not even locked.* He could turn the handle. It would open. Only the cheap chain separated them.

What was he waiting for? All he had to do was give the most token effort, absolve her of responsibility, and she was his.

Eric stood on the other side of the door and shook his head in exasperation. *Nice job, Hill. You were a couple for what, twenty-five minutes? That has to be a record, even for you. I'm beginning to think it's best for everyone if you just keep to yourself.*

He closed his eyes for a moment, took his hand off the door, and walked away.

Jane let out a whimper and sank to the floor. She sat there for a long time, her head in her hands.

When she looked up, her eyes fell on the photograph of her father, Col. Jonathan C. Hunter, USMC. *You're the reason I'm here,* she thought, *the reason I've made it so far.* Then she said aloud, "And the reason my head is so fucked up."

CHAPTER EIGHTEEN

TIME

December 25, 2025
Washington, DC

Admiral Curtiss had been up all night, writing in his private log, reviewing ideas, checking plans. Now that they had achieved replication, he could finally get down to the business of using the new technology to wage war.

About fucking time.

His thoughts kept returning to four men. It was as if they were in the room with him, watching him, making sure he did what he had to do.

The men were Bo Li, Johnny Cloud, Tommy Evans, and Isaac Zyrckowski. The four he had lost. Only a month ago, he had feared that they all had died in vain, that despite their sacrifices, the Chinese were going to win. But the project had turned around, and now their deaths might not be so empty. He was determined to make sure of it. It was up to him to see that China failed, that they never caught up, that they never again threatened him or his people.

Suddenly, Curtiss cocked his head, listening in the darkness. Yes, there was something there. He heard the creaking of the stairs, then a scramble of light footsteps. A moment later, River, his seven-year-old son, appeared in the doorway in his fire-engine pajamas.

The boy, his youngest (born when Evelyn was forty-two), went through cycles where he had bad dreams. Every three or four months, he would have a week of nightmares and come padding into his dad's office. Most of the time Curtiss was good about comforting the boy. But sometimes he became impatient and chided River for bothering him. The boy knew this well enough, so he waited in the doorway, trying to gauge his father's mood.

But tonight Curtiss was happy to see him. He had barely seen his family in the past month, and he missed them.

"Come on, then," he said. The boy scampered across the room and climbed into his lap. He cuddled up as he always did, nestling his head under Curtiss's chin.

"More bad dreams?"

A nod. "Monsters," the boy said. Curtiss gave a grunt of understanding and rubbed the boy's back. He made it a point never to tell his boys that monsters didn't exist, because, of course, they did.

"Will you protect me, Daddy?"

"Always," Curtiss said with irrevocable finality. "Always."

The boy snuggled closer, and Curtiss felt him relax in the security of his embrace. When the boy began to nod off, he picked him up and carried him up to his room. But when he tried to put River in his bed, the boy clung to him. "Don't leave me. Please, Daddy."

"Just this once," he said, and he lay down beside him. The boy was asleep almost immediately, but Curtiss lay there for a time, staring at the glowing stars the boy had stuck to the ceiling.

His thoughts returned to the four men he had lost and how they had died, but now he thought of his three boys, too, and that they must never have to face what those men faced. He never wanted them to play any of those roles: soldier, spy, innocent bystander. More than his oath to God, more than his allegiance to his country and to his men, there was the oath to his boys. As their father, as a warrior, as a Choctaw, he wanted to make sure they never became casualties. Luckily, the

Pentagon had authorized him to do exactly what the hardness told him he must do. He must use the new weapons, the most powerful the world had ever seen, to annihilate the enemy.

It was about time.

PART THREE
RED DRAGON RISING

And these atomic bombs which science burst upon the world that night were strange even to the men who used them.

—H. G. Wells, *The World Set Free,* 1914

Dear Undersecretary Tan:

As you are now aware, the Americans successfully replicated on December 24.

It is a most critical time. With their self-replicating assemblers, the Americans can now develop weapon systems that will far outclass anything in the arsenal of the People's Liberation Army or in any arsenal on the globe. We will be largely defenseless against these new weapons. Indeed, if we don't regain the lead quickly, American military hegemony will likely continue for the next generation. Only with decisive action can China take her rightful place as the sole superpower, free of the yoke of the imperialists.

While we may be tempted to dwell on the fact that much of the Americans' success came by stealing from us, we must also acknowledge that they made several key advances that still elude us.

How should we proceed? I believe that asking the right question will lead us to the right course of action.

What is the quickest path to replication? Since the Americans have already done it, the answer becomes obvious: we steal the secret from them. However, this is no ordinary invention. It is a life-form, so stealing samples of their nanosites is not enough, just as stealing a monkey is not enough to teach us how to bring a monkey to life. So I am proposing a different type of espionage—one that will ensure that we replicate as quickly as possible while simultaneously hindering the Americans' progress. I want to ██████ ██████ ██████████.

I know, the idea might sound audacious, but with the right operative,

I'm confident that we can succeed. What's more, using the "freelance" strategy that has been so successful in our past intelligence efforts also guarantees sufficient deniability to protect the Central Committee from any possible charges by the Americans. In fact, I have just the right freelancer in mind.

Looking forward to your insights.

Your servant and servant of the people,
General Meng Longwei

Dear General Meng:

I read your briefing with great interest and have shared it with ██ ██████████. He has been following these developments with great interest and is very disappointed that our substantial lead was lost. He hopes that you will make every effort to redeem yourself in the crucial months ahead. He also reminded me that the People's Republic does not engage in acts of ███████, ████████, or ███████████. Still, as a personal exercise, I encourage you to make the necessary preparations for the operation.

Do not contact me again in any official capacity on this matter.

Undersecretary Tan Wei
Office of the Chairman of the Central
Military Commission

CHAPTER NINETEEN

ETHEL THE PIG

February 14, 2026
Naval Research Laboratory, Washington, DC

After Christmas, things started to happen fast. With their self-replicating assembler, they could finally find out whether all the things that futurists had been foretelling were really feasible.

Naval strategists and engineers descended on the lab, salivating over the things they hoped to make: Could the navy scrap nuclear power and run ships off nanosites breaking down water into hydrogen and oxygen? Could bullets be guided around corners? Could a rifle be made to remember dozens of targets and then, in a burst of fire, hit them all? Would bullets even be necessary in the battlefields of the future? Indeed, compared to the relative speed of nanosites, the bullet was moving pathetically slowly.

The manufacturing possibilities were equally astounding. Once they figured out the programming, they could "grow" complex systems like a submarine or a cruise missile in hours or days. Something simple, like a rifle, could theoretically be grown in seconds. And not just the same old ships and weapons. The next generation of weaponry would look strange and alien when set alongside its antecedents. Lighter yet stronger. Tougher yet smarter: a rifle that would not work if picked up by an enemy, an attack drone that could not be shot down by conventional weapons.

And that was where Admiral Curtiss was going. He knew that America's monopoly on self-replicating assemblers might be just as short as its monopoly on the atomic bomb, and he wasn't going to waste a minute. He wanted the arsenal of the United States to take such a huge leap that no rival could ever hope to catch up.

To impose some order on this cacophony of what-ifs, Bill broke them into smaller teams. Jane was put on a team doing medical applications. She was infecting mice with a virus, then giving them a modified version of Minerva-C that was designed to encase the virus in gold, a nontoxic metal. Then the mice were bombarded with radio waves—harmless to tissue, but they would heat up gold and cook the virus inside the host. In this way, twenty-nine-year-old Jane Hunter from Mobile, Alabama, had a pretty good shot at curing the common cold.

Eric set out to make body armor by weaving fabricators, which were essentially weightless, into the fabric of a shirt. After six weeks, he was ready to show off his results. He invited Ryan and Jane to his final test.

By now, things between him and Jane were returning to normal, more or less. They were talking and hanging out, but Jane made sure that Ryan was always there. As a result, they had never spoken about what happened. There was a coolness to her, too. She would ask him how he was, and laugh and joke, but it felt like an act. As though her heart wasn't in it.

"Are you sure Eric gave us the right directions?" Ryan asked.

"Yeah, don't worry," Jane replied. "I've been here before."

They were deep in an old basement. At the end of a dim corridor was a huge metal door with a bright yellow sign: EYE AND EAR PROTECTION REQUIRED BEYOND THIS POINT. Jane pushed her shoulder into the door, and it swung open with a loud creak.

Ryan had never been to a shooting range before. At first glance, it reminded him of a bowling alley. He counted fifteen lanes, each with a cable like a clothesline, used for running targets out to a desired distance. At a table in the center lane was an impressive row of pistols and rifles, all of them with silencers.

Eric was there, tapping on his iSheet, but otherwise the place was deserted.

Well, almost deserted.

At the far end of the range, about fifty yards away, was a huge pig, snuffling happily in a trough of food. As if that weren't strange enough, the pig was wearing a tie-dyed T-shirt.

"Oh, man, I do not like the looks of this," Ryan said.

But Jane had a voracious look of excitement. "Wicked!" she said.

Eric recognized the old Jane at once and had to smile. He wasn't sure why, but the coldness was gone.

"Jane and Ryan," Eric said, "meet Ethel, our resident Duroc-Jersey pig. She doesn't talk much, but she has a very healthy appetite."

Just then a marine walked in. Brown service uniform. Spit and polish, hair high and tight. He had that rigid, almost cocky walk of the few, the proud. But this one looked too young and fresh faced.

"Corporal Davis!" Eric said. "I was worried you might not make it."

"Oh, you know I wouldn't miss this." His accent said Kentucky or maybe Tennessee. "I was here at o-seven-hundred gettin' everything set. The men are counting on me. They've already got the fire pit ready."

Ryan raised his eyebrows at Eric—a look that invited an explanation.

"Corporal Davis is hoping for another pig roast. I'm sorry to say that Ethel is not our first test subject."

The corporal whispered in Ryan's ear, "Wilbur was delicious."

"And you didn't invite me?" Jane said.

"Sorry, but Dr. Hill asked me to keep things quiet."

Ryan took another look at Ethel, scarfing cafeteria leftovers and oblivious to the fact that these were likely her last moments on earth.

"Who in the hell gave you authorization to do experiments on live pigs?"

"No one," Eric said matter-of-factly. "That's one of the benefits of working on a military project that technically doesn't exist. No IACUC paperwork."

Ryan glowered. It was clear that he couldn't save Ethel. "I hate tie-dyes," he said.

"Not a problem." Eric punched a few buttons on his iSheet, and the pattern on the pig's shirt changed to a bull's-eye target.

"My favorite!" Davis said.

"Whenever you're ready, Corporal."

Corporal Davis picked up the smallest pistol. "Firing Ruger Mark Two with echo suppressor. Ammo is .22 long. Targeting center mass."

Ryan squeezed his eyes tight, anticipating the shot. But all he heard was the metallic tap of the firing pin and the movement of the slide. He thought the gun had misfired. Then he realized that this wasn't a movie—there was no *fsssst* sound—the shot was completely silenced. Ryan opened his eyes. Ethel appeared unharmed, snout still in the trough.

Eric was recording everything with his iSheet. He zoomed in and inspected Ethel carefully.

"No impact," he announced. "Proceed."

Corporal Davis fired again.

Again Eric took a moment to examine Ethel's magnified image on his iSheet. "No impact. Proceed."

When Davis had emptied the clip, he picked up the next pistol—a .32—took aim, and began firing. Now Ryan could hear a muffled pop from the gun.

Eric examined Ethel after each shot, every time repeating, "No impact."

Next a 9mm pistol, then a .45.

No impacts.

"Totally awesome!" Jane said. "Where are the bullets going? They aren't even reaching the shirt, are they?"

"No," Eric said. "The cloud surrounds her at a radius of three feet. Here, take a look."

He showed her what he had recorded on the iSheet. "With the help of slow motion and this filter, you can see how it works … There, see it?"

Ryan and Jane looked closely. A translucent yellow bubble surrounded Ethel; then a small dot appeared.

"There, that's the impact."

"I know I'm not supposed to ask questions," Davis said, "but how is it possible?"

"It's all about speed," Eric said, "the muzzle velocity of a 5.56 round is about twenty-eight hundred feet per second, right?"

"That's right," Davis said.

"Well, the nanosites are moving over a billion times faster. So if you were the nanosite, it would be like having thirty-five years to break down each bullet. They're that fast."

"But how can *anything* be that fast?"

"It's has to do with the size of things," Eric said. "If you flap your arm as fast as you can, you'll be lucky to do one flap in a second—up and down. But a mosquito can flap its wings a thousand times a second, because it is a ten-millionth of our size. It's the same principle with the nanosites, but on a much smaller scale. Their arms are one fifty-millionth the size of a human arm, so they can perform up to fifty million operations in a second."

"Awesome," Davis said.

"Yeah," Eric had to agree, "it's pretty awesome. Let's start with the rifles, shall we?"

Davis picked up an assault rifle. "Firing 5.56 from M4."

This time Ethel gave a start. Even with the suppressor, the gun made a loud *pop*. Eric examined Ethel closely for damage, but it was just the noise.

Davis emptied the clip, then moved on to a bigger rifle.

"Firing FAL with 7.62 NATO."

Still no hits.

"I've been waiting to say this all month," Eric said. "Fire at will!"

Davis gave a sinister grin, thumbed the selector to full auto, and put the rifle to his shoulder. Ryan didn't want to look. The rifle spit out fire and noise. *BRRRRRRRRRRRRRRR!*

Ethel had by now gotten used to the blasts and merely stared at them, a large piece of cabbage hanging from her mouth.

"Hot damn, it really works!" Davis said.

"Beyond awesome!" Jane said, giving Eric a hug that went on long enough for Ryan to cough in annoyance.

"I knew you'd like it," Eric said. He gave her a wink, and she smiled back. It was wonderful to see her like this again. But it also left him confused. Had something changed? Would they get together now? He suddenly wanted just to take her away from here, have her all to himself. But Ryan was talking, cutting off his thoughts.

"What about bullets going the other way?" Ryan asked. "I mean, if you're wearing the shirt and you fire a gun, does it eat those bullets, too?"

"No," Eric said. "The nanosites will let a bullet escape the bubble but not enter it."

"All right, Hill," Ryan said. "I'll admit, I'm impressed. So what's powering the nanosites?"

"Ah, that's one of my better ideas: the wearer's dead skin. A twelfth of an ounce a day is enough to keep them going indefinitely."

"Very clever."

Davis nodded appreciatively. "I'm real glad it finally worked," he said, "but the boys'll be disappointed."

"Well, tell them there's hope," Eric said. "The next series of tests will be with land mines."

Ryan groaned. "I believe it's time to go." He gestured toward the door. "Dr. Hunter?"

Jane gave Eric another quick hug and whispered in his ear, "I'm so proud of you."

Eric beamed, oddly speechless. "Thanks," he finally sputtered. He watched them go, his eyes tracking Jane.

★ ★ ★

That afternoon, Bill Eastman called Eric into his office. "I heard about your tests of the body armor. Congratulations!"

"There are still a few bugs to work out, but I think I'll be able to demo it for the admiral by the end of the month."

"I just spoke to him and he's very excited. He says you are going to save a lot of lives."

Eric hadn't fully appreciated his own invention until that moment. It was a wild concept, that soldiers need no longer die in combat.

"Eric, I've got a little side project for you. It's a favor for the admiral. Jack and Jessica were working on it, but they hit a dead end. I need a new approach. Take a look at their notes; then get to work on it. I know it's mostly theory, but the admiral wants to know if it's feasible, just in theory."

After a quick lunch, Eric went to work on the problem. The question was, if you had a virus programmed to do X, how could you fool it into doing Y? He racked his brain all afternoon but got nowhere. Frustrated, he went to talk to Jack.

"I couldn't figure it out, either," the big man said.

"I saw that you wrote 'Trojan horse' in your notes," Eric said. "But you abandoned the idea?"

"Right. At first I thought, hey, all we have to do is get our code inside the virus. Then we could open it up—surprise—and take over."

"But it wouldn't work?"

"No, because a virus is just too small, too basic. After all, a virus is just a piece of RNA or DNA swimming around in a little protein sock."

"You make it sound like they'd make good pets."

Jack laughed. "Of course, viruses are Trojan horses themselves, plugging into cells and co-opting them to make copies of the virus instead of doing whatever the cell was designed to do."

"So you're saying, if you try to inject too much code into the virus, it'll burst at the seams?"

"Exactly." Jack gave a sigh. "If there's a way to do it, it's beyond me." Eric thanked him.

"Sorry I couldn't be more help," Jack said, and Eric headed back to his office.

Eric decided to do some research on viruses. But since Bill had said he just wanted to know whether the idea would work in theory, he decided to look not at biological viruses, but at computer viruses. He'd been a decent hacker once, and he knew the mentality. Computer geeks were the guerrilla fighters of cyberwarfare, locked in a constant arms race with the people who protected the computers—which meant they often came up with the most ingenious ideas. He searched all day for a good idea and found nothing. But on the second day of his hunt, he found someone, probably a pimple-faced teenager in Russia, who had written a piece of code called Lamprey, named after the eellike parasites that attach themselves to fish and eat them alive. The kid, or whoever it was, had gotten the name right: Lamprey was 100 percent pure parasite. The virus sat outside the program it was corrupting, so that it remained undetected, and every now and then it would suck out a piece of code and change it, making sure the amount of code taken out exactly equaled the amount put back in. (Security programs used "checksum functions" to search for changes in file sizes.) In the end, the host did Lamprey's bidding, with no one the wiser.

That was it! He didn't need to get all his code into the virus, just do a bypass. He spent the next two days fitting the idea to the virus problem. In theory, it would work. And that was all Bill wanted to know.

The next day, he showed it to Bill. His reaction was strange. "Clever," he said. And then, as if he was thinking the idea through to its logical end, he gave a sad frown. "Thanks," he said. "The admiral will be pleased." That was Eric's cue that he was excused. He had done some good, hadn't he? Suddenly, he wasn't so sure.

CHAPTER TWENTY

THE ROBBERY

February 20, 2026
Naval Research Laboratory, Washington, DC

Eric's office phone rang. It was Olex. "This woman keeps calling," he said. "She's asking for Bill. I don't understand what she wants, and I don't have time for it."

Eric sighed. Since Bill was in California, that left Olex in charge. *God help us.*

"Okay, put her through."

"This is Special Agent Brightwell of the FBI."

Eric felt his eyebrows go up. There had been a robbery involving certain chemicals, and she wanted to know what they might be used for. But their conversation quickly stalled. *Lab security.* He could not discuss the nanotech applications of the chemicals without verifying that she was really FBI. In turn, she could not elaborate on the crime without confirming that Eric had a high enough security clearance. Eric glanced up at the security poster above his computer: SECURITY IS COMMON SENSE. DON'T TAKE CHANCES.

But he was interested. Two of the chemicals she mentioned *were* used in nanotech. Was someone or some group doing underground nanotech research?

"Can you come to my office?" she asked.

He agreed to meet her after work.

It was a bitterly cold February day, the temperature right around zero. As he prepared to leave, he remembered that he had stupidly left his heavy jacket in his room. He had thought that a thick sweater would be enough for him—tough guy—but he quickly found that the wind cut right through it, stabbing him like icy needles. To get to his car, he would have to hike all the way to the overflow parking lot. He looked around the lab for anything he might wear, but there was nothing. Then his eyes fell on the prototype shirt, laid out under glass.

He had discovered that one of the byproducts of having dozens of microfabricators woven into the shirt was heat. Not a lot, but the one time he had put it on, it produced a cozy drowsiness, like an electric blanket. It would be perfect. He went to lift the glass, then stopped. It was completely illegal, of course, taking the world's most advanced body armor out for a spin. He would be breaking several dozen laws and would face a military court if caught.

Oh, well.

He put it on, then slid his sweater on top. He was instantly warm and snug, even sweating a little. He felt a little thrill, like a superhero donning his costume. *I could get seriously used to this.*

In the lobby of the Hoover building, he met Agents Brightwell and Brown. Brown looked like a relic from the 1970s in his black suit and wide tie. His dress shirt was now beige from years of use, and he had a bald spot so big it made him look like a tonsured monk. *Time to shave it all off, buddy.*

Agent Brightwell, by contrast, was young and pretty. Half Asian, round face, short black hair. Fashionably dressed, with not a wrinkle or a loose thread. The new blood.

They led him into a small conference room.

"Last night, there was a robbery at a SynChem warehouse in Maryland," Brightwell said. "Because the suspect is also wanted in Virginia for a similar break-in, the bureau has been asked to take over. What can you tell us about these chemicals?" She handed him a list:

indium arsenide, boron, carbon radicals, indenoisoquinolines, and a dopamine receptor agonist (DRA).

He told them the first three were very common in chemical research. Nothing odd there—they weren't even particularly expensive. But the last two: indenoisoquinolines were used to control cell growth, namely cancer cells, and the DRA was a synthetic neurotransmitter used to stimulate brain activity. Both were very expensive. It was an odd combination for a thief, he told them.

Agent Brightwell looked at Brown. He nodded.

Eric wondered whether that meant he had just passed some sort of test.

"We have a surveillance tape from the break-in," she said. "We'd like you to tell us if you recognize the suspect or notice anything unusual."

The video started, showing a security guard, his feet propped up, hands behind his head, sleeping behind a half-circle of video monitors. After a minute, the man rubbed his nose, then returned to dozing. Then something slid into the corner of the video screen. A man ... but not like any man Eric had ever seen.

Eric was instantly on the edge of his chair. *What in the world ...?*

Something was very wrong with him. His face. It was somehow deformed, yet Eric could not say exactly how. What was it? Taken individually, all his features seemed normal enough: thick black hair, sullen cheeks, slightly upturned upper lip. He was just a man, yet the look of him bothered Eric deeply, preoccupied him, and filled him with disgust.

But the face was just part of it. There was also the other thing—the coat he was wearing. How to describe it? Like some sort of liquid bronze. It had a high collar and hung almost to the floor. Eric was immediately struck by the sense that it, too, was alive. A word popped into his head: *gothic*. For it seemed very old and archaic, yet somehow revolutionary. It was thick as canvas but did not appear bulky or cumbersome, moving easily with his body. Even the color was strange. It seemed to change shade as he moved: copper, brown, oil black. It was hypnotic.

All these impressions ran quickly through his mind, yet he had been watching only for a moment.

Anything unusual, she had said. *Are you kidding?*

The menacing form drew closer to the sleeping security guard. Suddenly, the man stirred. With impressive speed, he was on his feet with his gun out.

On the streaky video, Eric watched the two figures face off. There appeared to be a moment of dialogue; then the man with the coat slid toward the pistol. That was when Eric saw, or imagined he saw, a haze well up around the coat. But it was gone as soon as he perceived it. The next instant, the security guard collapsed—dropped as if his legs had been severed from under him.

Without delay, yet without hurry, the man in the coat moved past the body. Then he abruptly turned toward the camera. It was an eerie motion, as if the coat were turning on its own accord. Then the screen went black and turned to snow, and the speakers blared the hiss of static. Agent Brightwell stepped up and turned down the volume.

"Sorry," she said.

Eric didn't even hear her. In his heart, he was repulsed by what he had seen—disturbed by the malicious use of science, *his* science. Yet another part of him was delighted, upbeat, and happy. He had spent the past month working on his own body armor, thinking of how far he could take the concept. And now he'd seen a body armor radically more advanced than the one he wore. Not only could it stop bullets, but it could attack and kill.

He suddenly remembered where he was. He shifted back in his chair and frowned.

"You might be wondering what happened to the security guard," Agent Brown said.

In fact, he *was* wondering, but not so much the *what* as the *how.* He figured that the nanosites had entered the security guard's body (he supposed, through the rim of the eye) and torn up his gray matter long before his slow, biological brain ever became aware that anything was wrong.

"He had a sudden stroke and died," Agent Brown said. "Poor guy."

Eric looked at them incredulously. Up until that moment, it hadn't occurred to him that they didn't see what he saw. To them, these bizarre occurrences were explainable coincidences: a stress-induced stroke, a faulty video camera. Agents Brown and Brightwell *couldn't* see what Eric saw. And it would take many, many hours to explain it to them. And even then, he doubted whether they would be capable of believing it. It would be like trying to explain to the ancient Aztecs that the Spanish Conquistadors, with their horses, armor, and firearms, were not divine. Then he thought, *should* he try to explain all that he and the lab had done, to a couple of clueless FBI agents? *Security is common sense. Don't take chances.*

"What about the gun?" Eric asked. "Was it fired?" Now *he* was the one looking for information.

"No," Agent Brown said. "It jammed on him."

Eric nodded. More likely, the nanosites had jammed the gun. It was a good idea—one that he should have thought of. Instead of worrying about stopping bullets, why not make sure they were never fired in the first place?

"Funny-looking coat," Agent Brightwell said.

Hilarious. "Why did you call the lab?"

"SynChem's records show that your lab is their largest buyer of one of the chemicals that was stolen. Here, this one." She handed him a slip of paper: *C60+; fullerene cations and anions.*

Carbon radicals—buckyballs.

"How much did he take?"

"Ten kilos."

"Did you say *kilos*?" It was a staggering quantity for a molecule typically sold by the gram.

She nodded.

Ten kilos of buckyballs. Eric's mind brimmed with theories. He went over the list of chemicals again. It made a lot more sense now.

The indenoisoquinolines and the DRA must be for the interface: the DRA to facilitate the analog-to-digital conversions; the indenoisoquinolines … Hmm, they were a cell growth suppressor. Could it be that this guy was having problems? The nanosites mutating too fast? Something he had to treat like a cancer? Eric would have to come back to that.

And a lot of buckyballs. The thing about the little soccer ball–like molecules was that they were so adaptable. As one of the most versatile elements in the universe, carbon was the base material for everything from diamonds to living organisms to nanosites. It was the standard building block for just about everything.

Which means this guy has plans, Eric thought. *He's working on something. Jesus!* All that effort to beat the Chinese, and now this.

Agent Brightwell was still talking. "You said the choice of chemicals seemed odd. Is it possible he didn't know what he was taking?"

"Sure," he improvised, then covered his mouth to suppress a yawn. "I imagine the buckyballs were kept in a special place, so he probably figured they were more valuable. If he can sell them on the black market, he'll be rich. Just one gram costs almost a hundred dollars."

Agent Brightwell looked impressed, but Agent Brown seemed skeptical. He sat quietly with his arms crossed. Finally, he gave Agent Brightwell a nod.

"I think that will be all, Dr. Hill," she said. "Thank you so much for your help."

It was snowing heavily as Eric drove down Constitution Avenue. Bill's letter to the president, the letter that had captured his imagination so long ago, replayed in this mind: *Instead of rogue states and terrorist groups developing nuclear or biological weapons, we will have small groups or even individuals, like those who create computer viruses today.*

But how could it be happening already? He had to talk to someone: to Bill, to Jack. To find validation and comfort. But as he imagined the conversation and constructed the sentences in his mind, he realized how outlandish it sounded, how completely unbelievable it was. If this man was as powerful as Eric thought, then he could do basically anything. But how? How had he made such progress?

The future will be a place where a few clever individuals will gain access to astonishing power.

Eric picked up his iSheet and made two calls. Fifteen minutes later, he was in Admiral Curtiss's office. Jack was there, too, and together they called Bill in California, who soon appeared on the admiral's iSheet.

Eric told them all he had seen. And just as he had suspected, it sounded preposterous. Even as he spoke, he knew he was losing them. Jack clearly didn't believe him, and kept checking his watch. When Eric finished, there was a long pause. Jack gave Bill a knowing look.

"Now, Eric," Jack spoke slowly, enunciating every word as if he were talking to a child, "you have to admit, you really don't have any evidence to support your theory. I mean, it really could have been a stroke, a jammed gun, and a bad camera."

Technically, Jack was right. He had no proof, just his instincts. "I'm pretty sure," he said. It sounded lame, even to him.

Bill said to Curtiss, "Is it possible? Is there any other group that could create such a device?"

The admiral shook his head. "No, there's no one. And I have a high degree of confidence in our intel. No one has achieved replication—not the Chinese or anyone else. I know that watching a man die is very disturbing, but I think you're making a leap to assume it was done with replicators."

"I have to agree with the admiral," Jack said. "And I'll give you one simple reason: for the man to kill the security guard that quickly and sabotage the camera suggests that he was controlling the nanosites with his thoughts. And that's just not mathematically possible. Electroencephalography has come a long way, but brain wave readers are still reduced to relatively simple vocabulary, which means a finite number of possible operations. To tell a nanosite swarm to specifically attack a man in precise way—and do it spontaneously—is much too complex for any EEG to process. It would mean a trillion times a trillion calculations per second. It's just not possible."

"Look, I know it sounds crazy, but, Bill, you yourself predicted that terrorists would start using this stuff."

"Yes, I did. But not until nanosites were inside everyday consumer products. That's still a long way off."

"But what about the chemicals that were stolen?" God, he felt so juvenile trying to convince them.

Jack shook his head. "You know those chemicals are used for hundreds of things—everything from solar panels to flat-screen TVs. I'm sorry, Eric, but a simple robbery makes a lot more sense. He probably just took whatever he thought was valuable, loaded it in a truck, and drove off."

The admiral chimed in. "What's more, you have to think about what it took for us to get this far. How could one man do all that by himself?"

Now Eric's anger flashed. "Damn it, I know what I saw! There's something not right here!"

On the computer screen, Bill held up a hand. "Okay, everyone, let's stop for a moment and think about this. Perhaps what Eric saw wasn't really the use of nanosites, but we should still proceed as if it were."

Finally, someone was making some damn sense.

Admiral Curtiss nodded. "I agree. It can't hurt to take a closer look. I'll liaise with the bureau and check things out. An autopsy should tell us if it really was a stroke. Maybe we can get a look at the gun, too."

"Good," Bill said. "That way, we'll know if we need to worry or not. I think we're probably safe. It's really much too soon to have a terrorist on our hands. And, Eric, don't beat yourself up about this. Given the strangeness of it, and what we now know is possible, it was a logical assumption."

Eric nodded. "Thanks," he said, glad that at least Bill was showing some faith in him.

"Forget it," Bill said. "I appreciate you going over to the FBI in the first place. Even if this man is just stealing chemicals that could be used for nanotech work, we want to put a stop to it."

CHAPTER TWENTY-ONE
THE BIG BANG

February 21, 2026
Naval Research Laboratory, Washington, DC

"So no one believed you?" Ryan asked.

"Not remotely."

"Well, I can't say I blame them. It sounds much too advanced."

"Yeah, it doesn't make any sense," Jane added.

Eric didn't like the tone in her voice. It was the cold Jane again. "Gee, thanks, Jane, I really appreciate the supportive attitude."

She shrugged. "Sorry, but an evil scientist? It sounds like a movie. Had you been drinking?"

Eric felt his blood rising. He could handle Ryan doubting him—in fact, he had expected it. But not Jane. She was supposed to be in his corner. Especially after the way she had been at the shooting range: flirting, hugging him, whispering in his ear. She'd given him hope, made it clear that she wanted him. But now she had flip-flopped again.

"Maybe this was a mistake," he said. "If you two are just going to give me shit for this, let's forget it."

"Fine," Jane said, "I've got better things to do."

He stared, incredulous. "What is wrong with you? I'm asking for your understanding here, at least the benefit of the doubt. You know, like a friend."

That seemed to shock her, at least a little, and for a moment he thought he saw tenderness in her face, but it was gone too quickly to be sure. "Whatever," she said, "I'm outta here." She turned her back to go. And for Eric, that was the final straw.

"You know, I thought you were someone I could count on." He felt his anger building and he suddenly wanted to hurt her the way she was hurting him. "Do you remember how you helped me with Olex? Remember that? Why? Why did you do that? Was it really to help me, or was there another reason?" He felt the ideas linking together, fueled by his anger. He knew even before he said it that it wasn't true. But that wasn't the point. The point was to wound her. "It wasn't about helping me at all, was it? It was just a convenient way for you to get back at Olex, because you're too afraid to confront him yourself. Yeah, it's all coming together. You never cared about me. It was all about you, wasn't it?"

Her eyes narrowed to slits. She tore off her baseball cap and pushed her blond hair to one side, exposing a thick red scar where the hair refused to grow. "Yeah, you're right," she said. "It's all about me." And she stormed out.

Ryan gave a long whistle. "Jesus! What's going on? Why are you two acting so weird?"

Eric pinched the bridge of his nose and tried to check the wave of his emotions. "Forget it," he said. "I gotta get back to work."

"Hold on a minute," Ryan said. "I want to talk about this robbery."

"I thought you didn't believe me."

"Well, you have to admit, it's a little hard to believe."

"Yeah, I know that, okay? Hell, I don't believe it myself anymore. But in the moment of watching it, Ryan, I was sure. Dead sure."

"Well, I think your instincts are right."

"What?"

"Yeah, a lot of what you said makes sense."

"Why didn't you say so before?"

"Did you give me a chance?"

"Okay, I'm sorry, but what do you mean?"

"Well, no one wants to believe you, because the guy seems so far ahead of us. That's why they reject it: because the gap is so great. But the gap shouldn't make it less believable. It should make it *more* believable. It's more probable that such an inventor would be decades ahead of us by now rather than just a few months."

"But he can't be decades ahead of us," Eric said. "That's the whole problem."

Ryan shook his head. "He can if he's post Big Bang."

The words hit Eric like a bucket of ice water. "Oh, shit!" he said. "Shit! Shit! *Shit!*" Eric hadn't thought of that, but Ryan, the expert in artificial intelligence, had.

The Big Bang was the hypothetical moment when a cognizant artificial intelligence system would finally connect to the web. It was expected to be the historic moment when man and machine dramatically diverged. That's because the human brain has a finite capacity for connecting bits of data and storing it, but the artificial intelligence system would not. It would speed up geometrically. It would be able to learn and store every bit of data on the web—a mind-boggling leap in understanding. In other words, it would be as stupid as we humans for only a few seconds.

"Intuitively, it sounds crazy that someone could get so far ahead of us," Ryan said. "But it's actually the only thing that makes sense, because he can learn so amazingly fast and at an ever-accelerating rate. By complementing his brain with the artificial intelligence system, he is doing years of work every hour. Plus he has access to just about everything. He can probably download *anything*. Public or private. If the information is on a computer somewhere, he can get it."

"But what about secure systems, encryption, pass codes, and all that?"

Ryan shook his head. "That probably slowed him down for an hour or two. Try to get your arms around just how fast he can learn. It probably took him minutes to learn all there was to know about encryption. After that, he could send out a million bots and hack into any system he wanted, including ours. Every book that's ever been scanned, every picture ever posted on a database, every doctoral thesis filed electronically. He's using all of it! For us, that amount of knowledge is literally unfathomable. We can't wrap our minds around it, but he can. So theoretically, if he has made that one step, if he's done this one crucial thing, then everything you've said is *absolutely* possible. And you know what? There's probably a hell of a lot more that he's capable of. You likely only got a glimpse of what this guy can do."

Eric suddenly found himself playing the role of the skeptic. "Or maybe Jane and Jack are right and he's just some normal guy who steals stuff and it had nothing to do with us."

"Okay," Ryan said. "Maybe."

"So what do we do?"

"Isn't it obvious?" Ryan said. "As a professed atheist, I'm going to be the first to start praying that the security guard really died of a stroke. If he didn't, then there's really nothing we *can* do."

"Why's that?"

"Because he's no longer mortal."

General Meng reviewed the operation once more. It was at least the tenth time he had done so today. He didn't know why he kept looking at it. It was out of his hands. The operation was in motion, the lone soldier already closing in on his targets.

He looked over the man's credentials again. He was the best there was. But would he be enough?

Meng suddenly felt like an old gambler who has made a fortune yet finds himself on a losing streak. Over the past twelve months, hadn't everything gone the Americans' way? Now he was being forced to place the biggest bet of his life—everything—on one hand, hoping and praying that his luck would finally change.

He pushed the iSheet away and tried to make himself focus on his intel reports. Life at the Naval Research Lab seemed to be following its normal routine. The only exception was an unexpected meeting last night between Curtiss, Eastman, Behrmann, and Hill. After hours. In fact, Curtiss had been at home and returned to the lab for it.

Immediately afterward, Curtiss had logged two calls to senior staff at the Federal Bureau of Investigation (one to Deputy Director Michael Pierce, the other to Ed White, head of Criminal Investigations). Both calls had been after 10:00 p.m.

"Why didn't you wait until morning?" Meng asked. "Something in that meeting got you worried. What was it?" Meng's apprehension rose, and he felt a chill run up his back. Did Curtiss know of his operation? "No," he said aloud. "Not possible. You couldn't know, not yet." Besides, Curtiss had called Criminal Investigations at the FBI, not Counterterrorism. And he had called the FBI, not CIA or Homeland Security. This was something domestic. And that meant Curtiss didn't know the truth. This was something different. But what? He would have to get to the bottom of it. Luckily, he knew exactly how. The man—the *English*man—would bring him the answers he needed.

Jab, cross, hook. Jab, cross, hook, uppercut. Bob, roll out. Double jab, cross, uppercut. The heavy bag jumped and rattled on its chain as she pounded it, the sweat streaming off her blond hair, trickling over the burn scar, down her hairline, and into her eyes. It glistened on her shoulders and sucked her shirt against her breasts.

She pounded savagely, relentlessly, her blows keeping pace with the speed metal that blared at full volume through her earbuds. Metallica, "Damage, Inc." She dared not stop. Dared not even slow the pace. That would let the other thoughts in. She had to keep moving. *Feint with the left, then lead with the right. Hook to the ribs, come under the cross.* Through the glass, she felt the eyes of the other people in the gym. She knew those stares. She had lived with them her whole life. The pretty girls who called her "dyke" behind her back. The guys who didn't know what to make of her and so kept their distance. She hit the bag harder, feeling her back burn. She secretly hoped one of them would come in and say something. Give her an excuse to take out her frustration on a real person. Some cocky weightlifter; some anorexic bitch on an elliptical.

Her knuckles were bruised, and she felt the dull, purple pain of each blow. Her muscles were approaching exhaustion, screaming for oxygen, the tendons in the crook of her elbows tight as cables. *Don't stop. Don't you dare stop.*

She leaned her forehead into the bag. *Right hook, left hook.* Harder and harder she swung, throwing her hips and shoulders into each blow. *Left hook, right hook.* Over and over. It was mindless and senseless and completely necessary.

Then her left wrist buckled; the tendons stressed, then hyper-extended. She shrieked and hissed in pain. Then, reckless in her frustration and rage, she hit the bag again with the same hand. She shrieked again, but more wounded this time, the spell broken, the drug past its peak. She tore off the bag gloves, yanked out the earbuds, and began quickly unwrapping her wrists. She headed to the locker room, not looking up, not for a second. In the hallway, she dropped her shoulder into a pretty girl as she passed. "Hey! Watch it!" the girl whined. Without bothering to turn around, she extended her middle finger over her shoulder.

In the shower stall, water hissing, lime green tile walls. Steam engulfing her, clouding even her hand in front of her face. Suddenly, here, it all came out in great sobs, her tears just more humidity. Her chest heaved; she shuddered in sorrow. Snot ran from her nose as she cried and cried. She was twenty-nine years old with a PhD from Georgia Tech and a prestigious job, one of the best in her field. Yet she felt so alone. Marooned. What a life. No mother. An autocratic father who was always pushing her to achieve and achieve—who had moved every three years and kept her close to locked up until she was eighteen. It was necessary, he had said, to keep her from becoming "the fucking whore" her mother was. All those years and she had never stood up to him. Never. He had won. He had succeeded in making her afraid to be herself. For him, she had to be someone else: the perfect child—strong, smart, brave, unrelenting. Monomaniacal in pursuit of every goal. Never giving up, never showing weakness, never being human. And this was the result. She didn't even know who she was, only who she was trained to be. And she sucked at relationships. Sucked at communicating. Not a fucking clue.

She had gone too far at the shooting range. She knew that. She had led him on when it was the last thing she should have done. She just couldn't help herself. He'd been so perfect that day, so beautiful and smart and confident. But she knew it was wrong. As much as she wanted to, she knew she couldn't get involved. So she had told herself she would have to make it clear from then on that there was nothing there.

And then this morning ... She had wanted to believe him; she really had. To stand up for him. He had seemed so disoriented. But no one else had believed him. Not Curtiss or Jack. So she had taken her cues from Ryan, teasing him that it was impossible. *Stupid. Stupid. Stupid.* But what he had said to her! How could he say that? How could he say that she didn't care? After all she had done for him.

She slammed the tile wall with her good hand.

Fuck you, Eric Hill!

CHAPTER TWENTY-TWO
HUMAN RESOURCES

February 22, 2026
Naval Research Laboratory, Washington, DC

Black storm clouds were piling up over eastern Virginia as Brock O'Lane strode purposefully through the central quad of the Naval Research Laboratory. He passed a cluster of young cadets, all women, midshipmen from Annapolis on campus for the day, clutching notebooks to their chests. He felt their eyes passing appreciatively over him, taking him in. He had a worn, rugged face and sandy hair with hard-earned streaks of steel coming off his temples. His eyes were sea green, strikingly lucid, almost sad, in a way that suggested a deep intelligence. He saw one woman lean over and whisper in her friend's ear. Then she shot him a bold smile.

And there was something else about him. Something underneath, which the women seemed to feel instinctively. A sense of danger. It was in the concealed subcompact .40-caliber pistol and the four spare clips of subsonic rounds, the military-issue silencer, and the flex cuffs— they couldn't see them, but they could feel them. It was a part of his presence, his whole history, all the years that had forged him into what he was today: the perfect combination of sophistication and savagery.

He wore a stolen captain's uniform and moved as if he owned the place. And why shouldn't he? He knew how good he was. He was a walking massacre. Trip-wire tight. He was in the zone, too, right now, switched on, ready for anything.

Brock worked in human resources—a head-hunter, one might say. He secured property. And it really was all about property, wasn't it? It was the defining factor in geopolitics, determining the haves and the have-nots of the world.

Throughout history, there had been plenty of others like him. He was only the latest version of a thousand incarnations. That was because empires needed men like Brock O'Lane. From Caesar to Saladin. Without armies and without war, his kind had changed the course of history.

Ahead and to his right was Levering Hall, the center of the artificial-intelligence work at the lab. He swiped his pass card at the double doors, heard them click open, and went in. He saw people coming and going: postdocs and technicians in white lab coats. A few marines saluted him. He ignored them.

No one here had ever seen him before, yet he aroused no one's curiosity. It was just one of his gifts. *Chameleon.* To the people he passed, he looked like any other naval officer on the base. And if anyone should bother to stop him, he could put them instantly at ease.

But there was one exception, one man who would recognize him at a glance. It was his biggest fear, truth be told, that his old friend Admiral James Curtiss might see him.

He spotted the staircase up ahead. Pushing through the fire door, he felt a sense of relief from the concealment of the stairwell. He ascended the steps to the fourth floor. Just fifty meters from the door, he knew, he would find his first target.

Outside, he heard the sizzle of lightning and the quick boom of thunder. It was going to be one hell of a storm.

★ ★ ★

Entering Ryan Lee's office, Brock O'Lane was astonished by what he saw. It was as if someone had rearranged a NASA control room for one man. There were no fewer than ten iSheets, the central one at least five feet wide and four feet tall, and all of them angled toward a single chair. Keyboards and joysticks and glove mice were placed at varying angles and heights. And there, sitting in the command chair with his back to the door, was Ryan Lee, wearing a Spider-Man shirt whose obnoxiously bright colors bespoke the ultrakitsch of America's state fairs and amusement parks. Lee was exactly as Brock had imagined him: another roly-poly American boy who was clearly fonder of the buffet line than the treadmill—and whose fat gave him the innocent aspect of an overgrown baby.

Brock silently closed and locked the door. Out the tall windows, he could see the storm rolling in. Three quick branches of lightning stabbed down in a left-to-right panorama, sending out a succession of booms that rattled the windows.

Lee had not heard him come in or even noticed the storm, he was so deeply engrossed in his work. Brock was just behind him when the young man suddenly cocked his head to one side, sensing something.

"Who the hell—"

Using all his strength, Brock brought his fist down on Ryan's jaw. When it came to subduing someone, Brock didn't mess around with pressure points or karate blows. He preferred good old-fashioned blunt trauma. A sharp blow to the jaw was usually enough for an instant blackout, because of the connection to the inner ear. Lee's head twisted from the blow, and his arms rose spasmodically, like those of a man pulling up a heavy weight that suddenly wasn't there, and he collapsed to the floor.

Two minutes later, Ryan came to, his head throbbing. He was facedown on the floor, hands and ankles bound, mouth taped over. His senses came back to him slowly, one at a time. First, the metallic taste of blood in his mouth. Then touch: the cold tile floor against his cheek. Sound: the rumbling of thunder and the sloshing of water against the windows. Smell: wet concrete and a whiff of ozone from the storm.

He opened his eyes to see a pair of shiny black dress shoes inches from his nose. His eyes moved slowly up to black socks, black pants, a naval uniform with gold stripes, then to a face—a hard yet intelligent face—and a nickel-plated pistol that was pointed at his head. Looking up at him from the floor, the man was huge and menacing, the muzzle of the gun enormous. It was as if the storm had sent one of its gods down to punish him.

"Dr. Lee. My name is Brock O'Lane, and your life is now in my hands. If you would like to live for more than the next five seconds, you'll need to unlock this phone for me." He held up Ryan's phone with his other hand.

"One … two … three …"

The man adjusted his grip on the pistol, closed one eye, and aimed at Ryan's temple.

"Four."

Ryan made a short whistling sound. The phone beeped compliance.

"There's a sensible lad," O'Lane said.

He quickly typed a message. "911: Need you in my office. ASAP. Come alone."

One down, one to go.

Four minutes later, there was a knock on the door, then a fumbling with the latch. "Open up, it's me."

Brock quickly opened the door. It was the man he wanted.

"Thank God you're here!" Brock said with complete sincerity.

He pointed to Lee, facedown on the floor. "He's just collapsed. You stay with him; I'll go for help." As Eric Hill went to his friend, Brock quickly closed and relocked the door.

Hill knelt, then saw the bindings. "What's this?" Just as he was turning back, Brock once again delivered a crushing blow to his victim's jaw. He connected perfectly, and the blow spun Hill half around, but to Brock's utter amazement, the man remained conscious.

Uncommon, Brock thought.

But he had stunned him sufficiently to move to plan B. From behind, Brock snaked his arm around Hill's neck. The second-best way to subdue a man was a blood choke. Sustained pressure on the carotid artery would cause a blackout from lack of blood to the brain. It would take ten seconds.

But Hill regained his composure quickly. *Too quickly.* Not only did he break the choke, but he rolled over on top of Brock. Now Brock knew he had a serious problem, because it was not just a matter of chance. Hill had escaped from the choke in textbook fashion, tucking his chin to keep the pressure off the carotid so that Brock found himself squeezing the jaw and not the artery. Then he had peeled Brock's fingers away and got himself turned around. Hill had been trained, probably as a wrestler.

Twice more Brock tried chokes from different angles, and twice more Hill got free. Then Hill almost got the better of him, catching him on the side of the head with an elbow. Brock thought he was going to lose consciousness, but he fought back the stars. He knew he had to finish this quickly. It was taking too long, and they were making too much noise—knocking over the chair, hitting tables, sending soda cans rattling across the floor. Thank God the rain and the thunder were so loud.

He decided to make one more attempt at the choke, but if it didn't work this time, he would have to slit Hill's throat. It would be unfortunate, but his orders had been clear.

Hill got on top of Brock again, but before he could strike, Brock drove his elbow into Hill's knee. Hill gasped and twisted away in pain. Brock realized immediately what had happened: he had discovered an old injury. He went for the choke again, and this time Hill wasn't quick enough to protect his neck. Like a boa constrictor, Brock tightened his grip. Lightning struck just outside the window. He began to count the seconds.

One, two, three ...

They were both panting, mostly spent, their heads just inches apart. Brock reflected how this type of violence—without firearms—was always very intimate.

Four, five ...

It finally occurred to his victim to call for help. He cried out twice, his voice washed away by the storm.

Six, seven ...

"Relax, mate," Brock whispered in his ear. "It's better this way. You'll see."

Eight, nine ...

Hill strained one last time, his back and neck arching; then his body went limp.

Ten.

When Eric regained consciousness, he was bound and gagged on the floor. He turned his head and found himself face-to-face with Ryan. The look in Ryan's eyes reflected Eric's thoughts exactly: *We're screwed.*

Eric then realized that at some point in the fight, he had pissed his pants. He could feel the wet spot on his khakis. He felt humiliated and confused. *You just got your ass kicked*, the voice in his head said. But why? What was going on?

"Are we awake, then? Very good." He heard a voice with an English accent, then felt a tug on his legs. The man was cutting the bindings around their ankles, though not their wrists. "Best if you roll over. We need to have a little heart-to-heart."

It took some effort with bound hands, but soon they were sitting upright in front of their captor.

The Englishman was sitting in Ryan's command chair, and even with a gun in one hand, he looked as relaxed as if he were sitting in a street-side café. Eric saw their cell phones on the floor, pulverized.

"Dr. Hill, I've already introduced myself to your colleague. My name is Brock O'Lane."

Eric stared at the gun. A silver semiautomatic. It was short and fat with a wide muzzle, which told him it was designed to make terrible wounds at close range. In O'Lane's other hand was a silencer hardly bigger than a roll of quarters. The silencer was dripping wet.

"I'd like you to put yourselves in my shoes for just a moment. It will help you fully grasp your situation—and trust me, this will be of interest to you.

"If I deliver you to my employer alive, I will be paid ten million dollars US, but if I kill both of you right now and quietly walk out that door, I'll still be paid three million.

"Now, what should I do?" He raised his eyebrows as if to coax an answer. "Two bullets. They'll make less sound than a hammer hitting a board, and *much* less than a clap of thunder." His eyes drifted to the windows and the storm outside. "Then I take a few pictures, and I walk out of here three million dollars richer. It's the easier choice, is it not? And it saves me the hassle of getting you off the base."

He pursed his lips as if scrutinizing the problem. "Decisions, decisions." Then, apparently having made up his mind, he began slowly screwing the silencer onto the gun barrel.

Eric stared wide-eyed, his mind racing for a way out of this.

Then the Englishman gave them a contagious grin that started at one side of his mouth and grew across to the other. Eric began to smile back reflexively, then checked himself.

"Don't worry, boys, I intend to deliver you alive. After all, I have my reputation to uphold. It is only your own actions that will cause your, um, premature deaths. If you try to escape or seek help in any way, I will put a bullet in your head. Please remember that I am extremely good at what I do. I can shoot a man's eye out at fifty meters, be it your eye or that of one of the marine guards on base. So have no illusions, please. No one will be coming to your rescue. In fact, calling to anyone for help will simply mean that I kill them *and* you."

The man seemed so professional and cool that Eric believed every word. He had made his case clear: the difference between three million and ten million dollars meant little to O'Lane, while the difference between breathing and not breathing meant a great deal to Eric.

"Now, if you can agree to cooperate, I can untie you."

Eric and Ryan glanced at each other, then nodded.

O'Lane gently pulled the tape from their mouths and cut their flex cuffs. "We are going to relax here for a little while," he said, "until I feel that things are quiet enough. Then you will accompany me to my car.

"So, boys, tell me about yourselves."

At first, Eric and Ryan were nervous about sharing anything with the Englishman and gave only short, noncommittal answers to his questions. But soon they began to relax, in part because O'Lane himself was so open and at ease. Speaking to them as if they were old friends, he was cheerful and encouraging and calm, even thoughtful. And he seemed to know everything. He asked Ryan about his research in AI, and his questions were so insightful that Eric assumed he must have a degree in computer science. But then he began asking Eric about nanotechnology, and he was equally well versed.

While they talked, the storm raged outside. Flashes of lightning occasionally flooded the room, and the wind pushed and flexed against the glass and whistled along the outer wall.

All the while, O'Lane, calm and undisturbed, talked freely about his life, his upbringing in Wales, his parents, Cambridge, his first girlfriend, and his decision to go into the military. But it was to his three combat tours in Afghanistan that he kept returning. He explained how the war had been doomed from the start.

"Afghanistan, with its ethnic groups and tribes, is best governed by a federalist system like the US, where each province or state enjoys a degree of autonomy and can determine its own fate. But NATO and the US imposed a centralized government on Afghanistan, where all the power was concentrated in Kabul, so the isolated areas of the country were just as forgotten as always. And those areas, of course, were where the Taliban was able to grow strong again."

Eric found himself marveling that this man, who seemed so far removed from his notions of a criminal, was a mercenary. "Why are you doing this?" he asked.

O'Lane thought a moment before he replied. "I live in a world that's very different from yours—a world that I imagine you have trouble understanding. I've seen things …" And here he paused as if shocked by the images his own mind had just conjured. "I've seen things you wouldn't believe.

"In Afghanistan, I saw whole schools full of nothing but land-mine victims. Classroom after classroom: one leg, two legs, one arm, and dozens and dozens of lost eyes. I've seen whole towns that the Talibs wiped out. They liked to run spears through people, up their arses and out their mouths—anyone they considered an infidel, which could be anyone they wished, of course. Afghanistan is a place where life means next to nothing, where everyone is numb from so much death, where parents don't cry anymore when their children die."

He paused as if searching for a way to make himself understood, then seemed to pick a new direction. "It was the attack on the girls' school, in 2008. That's when I really changed.

"The school was run by Afghans and had nothing to do with coalition forces, but that didn't matter to the Talibs. They surrounded the school, blockaded all the doors, then set it on fire. When a few of the girls broke through the windows with their clothes on fire, the hajjis shot them. Whooping and calling '*Allahu Akbar!*' the whole time.

"By the time we got there, twenty-four girls were dead. Three were still alive, but just barely. I pulled a lot of strings to medevac them to Germany, but only one survived." Here O'Lane stopped and looked at them. "You cry a lot more when the innocents die. I wept for four days, but on the fifth day, I got my special-ops teams together. I was a lieutenant colonel by then, with a battalion of five hundred men under my command. I had my boys hunt down every one of those Talib fighters—even the teenagers paid in poppy. You see, I'm not a cultural relativist. I don't believe in tolerating the intolerable just because someone's religion or ideology says it's okay. Some things are absolute. Twenty-six young girls were murdered. That's all I needed to know. I had my men take spears with them. Wherever they found one of the Talibs from the girls' school, they ran 'em through.

"After that, there was no more violence against the girls' schools in my district. And for four years, we had some peace.

"But the coalition forces withdrew in 2014, and we all know what happened next—the Taliban retook most of southern Afghanistan, and there was a terrible backlash against all the reforms that had been made since 2001. The girls' schools were wiped out. Those that tried to operate clandestinely were gassed, burned, or the girls scarred with acid. So what did I accomplish? After all we tried to do, I can't even say that I saved the girls in my own district. I only managed to postpone the inevitable. I failed, because the tide of history was stronger than me and my men.

"And that is why I am here. America's time is over. You had your age—all of the twentieth century—just as Great Britain had hers before that. Now the tide is with Asia. You must see how she is rising, pulling all the world's resources to her needs. It is irresistible. She can make the tough decisions, the brutal decisions, that your government cannot. She is not gridlocked by feckless politicians controlled by corporations. And because this is so clearly China's age, there is no reason to fight it—or, in my case, no reason not to profit from it. If it were not me holding a gun to you right now, it would be someone else. Lucky for you, it's me. Anyone less would have executed both of you already."

There it was, Eric thought. They were going to China. He had suspected it, of course, but now it was certain. He and Ryan would be flown quietly out of the country, to Tangshan, where he would become a slave, laboring day after day. They would have no reason to release him—ever—and if he didn't do what they asked, he would be disposed of. Thinking it through brought on a sudden dizziness.

Ryan was apparently thinking the same thing. "It's so cruel," he said. "So inhuman. How could they do this?"

"Yes, it's cruel," he agreed. "But then, I work for a government that sells prisoners' organs for profit, a government that makes tens of thousands of political dissidents magically disappear every year, a government that lethally injects babies at birth because it considers them 'illegal.' So this"—he nodded to Eric and Ryan—"simple abduction, well, I'm sure it was an easy decision for the Central Committee, especially considering the stakes involved."

Ryan tucked his head between his knees. Soon he was trembling, quietly weeping. Eric put a hand on his shoulder.

"You can still play an important role," O'Lane said. "As long as you don't resist, they'll treat you well enough. And you'll still get to do the work you love."

It was then that Eric remembered something very important. In his fear and shock, it had completely slipped his mind. Did he really have it on? Yes, he could feel its warmth against his skin. He looked down at his chest just to make sure. Yes, it was there—a foolhardy decision that he was now thankful for. He began to play with fantasies of grabbing the gun, saving the day. But each time, the fantasy ended all wrong, with O'Lane subduing him again or with Ryan dead. Trying to be a hero could easily get both of them killed. His elation dissipated as quickly as it had arrived.

The Englishman looked at his watch. "Gentlemen, I think we can go. Take a minute to collect yourselves, and then we'll be off." He stood and slid the pistol through the double breast of his captain's coat. Then he escorted them out the door.

As O'Lane had predicted, the corridors of Levering Hall were largely deserted. A wall clock read 10:15 p.m. They saw no one as they stepped into the main hall. Low-wattage night-lights created regular cones of brightness. Down a side corridor, Eric saw the twins, Nipa and Bhavani, two Indian girls with matching white lab coats and cups of coffee. It did not occur to him to call out. On the contrary, for their own good he pretended not to notice them.

Outside, the rain had stopped, leaving the parking lot wet and black. Eric felt unnaturally awake and alert, keyed up with adrenaline. He was noticing everything: the cold sweetness of the poststorm air, and the beads of rain that sat like scattered jewels on the car hoods.

A thick fog had settled over the base, muting the lights over the parking lot. The air was so heavy with moisture that Eric's hair was soon dripping wet.

O'Lane led them to an amber Cadillac SUV. He extended his hand courteously. "Dr. Hill, won't you please sit up front with me. Dr. Lee, you may sit behind Dr. Hill."

They eased out of the parking lot and down Yorktown Drive. The fog was so thick, the headlights shone on a wall of white. Eric couldn't even tell where they were. Then a break in the fog revealed the main gate about fifty yards ahead, still blurry, like the image in an unfocused camera. Only when they were right up on it did it come into focus.

Eric was struck by a sudden panic. This was their last chance. If O'Lane drove through that gate and off the base, it would all be over.

A marine leaned out the window of the gate house. It was Corporal Davis, the marksman who had helped him test the shirt.

"Corporal," Brock O'Lane said cheerfully, his accent suddenly gone.

"Good evening, Captain," Davis said. Then he caught sight of Eric. "Hey, Dr. Hill."

Eric could only nod.

Straight ahead, directly in front of the SUV, a massive orange and black metal barrier big enough to stop a tank jutted out of the blacktop. Davis would have to lower it before they could drive out. Behind Davis, in the guard post, was a rack of M-16s. If only Eric could enlist Davis's help somehow. The corporal was such a superb shot, he could easily kill O'Lane.

The voice in Eric's head grew more insistent: *Do it now! Shout. Say something before it's too late.* But he couldn't open his mouth. He couldn't move. It was happening too fast, and too many things could go wrong. He couldn't just tell Davis to shoot O'Lane. Davis was a marine, with years of training and indoctrination. He wouldn't shoot a captain just because some civilian told him to. He would hesitate.

And that would give O'Lane all the time he needed. The more Eric thought, the more he could see it was folly. O'Lane was ready to draw his pistol, but the marine wasn't—he was just spending another boring night in the command post. And the shirt? It might save him, but not Ryan. And there was a final reason he couldn't move, one he hated to admit. He was afraid. The smell of his fear was all over him, wafting up from his wet lap.

O'Lane seemed to sense Eric's thoughts, or at least his own vulnerability, and casually brought his hand to the middle of his chest, near the pistol, as if scratching an itch.

"Is everything in order, sir?" Davis asked.

"Absolutely," O'Lane said. "We decided to wait out the storm. It was something, wasn't it? You weren't stuck in this box the whole time, were you?"

"Yes sir, I was. And I'm very happy my ass wasn't blown clear to Ocean City."

O'Lane laughed a comforting laugh, and that made Davis smile. *The captain thought Davis was funny.*

"How long do you expect to be gone?" the marine asked. The question was directed at Eric and Ryan—the guards always kept tabs on the scientists when they left base.

Eric fumbled for an adequate lie. "Uh, just a little while. We're going to the Chart House for some drinks."

O'Lane nodded, validating the plan.

"All right," Davis said. "Have one for me, then." And his hand went to the console, to the button that would lower the barrier. It seemed to happen so terribly slowly. Eric tried to think of a solution, a way out, but saw none. *Coward,* his other voice said.

At just that moment, light flooded the interior of the Cadillac as a pickup truck came toward them.

Davis hit the button, and with a hydraulic whir, the barrier began slowly sinking into the pavement.

The incoming truck—an old Chevy with a roll bar, KC lights, and a long CB antenna—rumbled up to the gate. Admiral Curtiss leaned out the window. "Corporal." He waved casually at Davis. Then he glanced over at the Caddy.

Admiral Curtiss and Brock O'Lane locked eyes.

O'Lane, thought Curtiss, his adrenaline surging.

Curtiss, thought O'Lane, fear clenching his guts.

The barrier locked into the pavement with a loud thud.

O'Lane stomped on the accelerator.

Curtiss drew his sidearm.

The Caddy lurched forward, slipped on the barrier's top plate, and fishtailed, then caught its footing and surged forward, churning up white smoke and filling the air with an acrid burn.

Simultaneously, Curtiss fired the Five-seveN. It should have been an easy shot—the fucking limey was only ten feet away—but the unpredictable movement of the SUV made it impossible for him to lead his shots. Two bullets blew out the back window of the Caddy, showering the interior with tiny cubes of safety glass, the bullets passing diagonally through O'Lane's headrest and toward Hill. Curtiss fired again, but the Caddy's rear end swung sideways again and the round only grazed O'Lane's forehead.

The Englishman's head jerked reflexively and he shivered in pain, but he willed his eyes on the road, hands white on the wheel as the blood trickled down the side of his face.

Then they were away, the massive engine roaring as the Caddy shifted into second, then third.

Eric spun around in his seat, stealing a glance at the command post. He saw the young marine vaulting into the back of Curtiss's truck bed, his body momentarily spread-eagled, an M-16 in his hand. Then the pickup truck was swallowed by the fog.

Eric was jolted sideways, and his stomach dropped as the SUV bottomed out on the ramp to the Anacostia Freeway. O'Lane was gunning it full throttle. By the time they left the ramp, the speedometer showed just over a hundred miles per hour. In and out of fog banks they rushed, the black road appearing and disappearing. O'Lane wiped the blood from his temple with his sleeve, examined it, then wiped it again, considering the blood flow. *Just a scratch.*

They entered a long bank of fog. All was white. Driving blind. Suddenly, the red taillights of a car appeared no more than fifteen feet in front of them, seemingly idle by comparison. Both Eric and Ryan yelped, "Watch out!" and braced themselves for the inevitable crash. O'Lane swerved, and the heavy SUV lifted sickly to one side, as if it would surely roll over. The brake lights and license plate of the little car—*Taxation without Representation*—disappeared under the Caddy's nose, but somehow they managed to miss it. O'Lane, plowing on through the white fog. Then another set of brake lights and another near miss. Then another, and then another. O'Lane was missing each vehicle by a hair, weaving insanely across the lanes and shoulder, the weight of the SUV heaving left and right like a storm-tossed ship.

"Slow down, for Chrissake!" Eric yelled.

But O'Lane, utterly focused on escaping, had tuned out his passengers completely. His eyes darting to the rearview mirror. Expecting. Knowing. "There you are, old friend," he murmured.

Ryan and Eric both turned but saw nothing except the heavy blanket of fog. Then it cleared for a moment, and the distinctive high-mounted KC lights of the old truck came into view. Eric felt a rush of hope. Curtiss was trying to rescue them. And as much as Eric didn't like Curtiss, he was glad, at this moment, that it was him.

Then Eric's head was flung hard against his window. He gritted his teeth in pain and annoyance. O'Lane was swerving hard again, but not to avoid cars. Why? A moment later, Eric got his answer as a beautiful orange light streaked out from under the hood of the Caddy and disappeared into the mist. At first, he wasn't sure what it was. O'Lane swerved again and two more orange beams shot out. They were tracer rounds, gorgeous and enchanting as they cut through fog and darkness.

"He's shooting for the tires," O'Lane said. "For now."

Eric's elation at the prospect of being rescued was suddenly replaced by trepidation. *For now ...* He remembered the night of the fire, when Curtiss had let them walk into Anderson Hall, ready to sacrifice their lives for a "greater good."

Curtiss still hoped to rescue them. But at any moment, he might change his mind and decide that if he couldn't recover his scientists, he would at least deprive his enemy of the prize. Then he would tell Corporal Davis to fill the cabin with gunfire. And while Eric's armor might protect him from a bullet, it would not protect him if O'Lane got shot in the back of the head and the car crashed.

The Caddy rushed up another ramp, tires screeching, and they burst onto Interstate 495, a six-lane superhighway. O'Lane swerved madly through the heavier, slow-moving traffic, trying to shake Curtiss off his tail. He whipped around a tractor trailer, then a minivan, nearly sideswiping a little sedan. O'Lane slid back and forth between the other cars, trying to keep any vehicle between the Caddy and Curtiss, to deny the marine a clear shot.

As they neared the river, the fog thickened to whiteout conditions. Suddenly, red taillights leaped out at them once more. *Toyota Prius 11.* Eric gasped and threw his hand out as if he might push the little car away. O'Lane jerked the wheel left, but this time he wasn't quick enough. The Caddy jolted as they hit the corner of the Prius, spinning it violently to Eric's side of the highway. In that split millisecond, Eric caught a flashbulb image of the driver—suspended in precatastrophe, oblivious and still on his cell phone—as his car spun around once, twice. Then it struck the concrete wall of the bridge, erupting from the inside in a plume of white powdery airbags.

O'Lane rushed on, undaunted, his right headlight gone. Eric turned again in his seat. Ryan, too, was craning his neck to see. In their wake, all traffic had stopped around the wrecked Prius. He strained to pick out Curtiss's truck, but couldn't see it. His heart sank. It was over.

O'Lane nodded to himself, ever so slightly. "The old Indian wasn't so difficult to handle after all," he whispered.

Then Eric looked once more and saw the unmistakable lights of the old Chevy pickup dip onto the shoulder and surge back onto the road.

O'Lane squinted into the rearview mirror, mumbled a curse, then slid open the compartment that separated the two front seats. Inside were about twenty silver cylinders with red and yellow checkered tops. For some reason, they reminded Eric of "travel-size" cans of shaving cream. But the red and yellow tops denoted danger, and when O'Lane pulled one out, Eric saw the distinct pineapple grooves of an old-fashioned hand grenade.

With his elbow, Brock cleared the pellets of safety glass from his shattered window. Using his thumb, he popped the top off the grenade, pulled out the pin with his teeth. He paused a moment, crossed in front of a Honda CRV, and dropped the grenade out the window. It bounced on the pavement with a metallic slap, disappeared under the Honda, and exploded harmlessly behind it in a brief flash of light, leaving a perfect thirty-foot-wide hole in the fog. A second later, Curtiss's pickup raced through the hole, roiling the fog and pulling a miniature tornado in his wake.

One thing was for sure, these were no ordinary grenades—the huge hole it made in the fog proved that.

O'Lane seemed to consider the event like a computer processing data. Then he pulled out a second grenade.

What is he doing? thought Eric. *The grenade had exploded nowhere near Curtiss.*

They careened around a slow-moving convoy of six or seven cars, O'Lane swerving in and out. Up ahead was a silver Lexus, pimped out in pink and purple, riding low in the center lane. O'Lane blew past it, pulled the pin from the second grenade. His eyes focused on the rearview mirror, judging the distance. Eric and Ryan were transfixed, staring at his closed fist.

BANG!

The Caddy lurched, and the grenade popped out of O'Lane's hand, bounced on the center console, and fell to the floor between Eric's feet. There was a flatulent *flap-flap-flap-flap* sound from the back of the Caddy, and they began losing speed. Davis had managed to shoot out one of the tires.

All was panic inside the car.

"Find the grenade or we all die," O'Lane said calmly as he flicked on the interior light.

"Find it!" Ryan screamed.

Eric was already fumbling for it with both hands, but it rolled backward under the seat. "I can't ... Ryan!"

The grenade rolled up against Ryan's shoe, and he opened the door and kicked it out. It bounced once and exploded, rocking the SUV and sending shrapnel through the back quarter panel.

There was a wicked hiss of escaping air; then—*pop!*—the other back tire burst.

"You're going to kill us all!" Ryan shouted.

O'Lane ignored him. Seeing Curtiss only 150 yards behind them, Eric felt a ray of hope. With two flat tires, the Caddy would never outrun its pursuer. But between them was a buffer of a dozen cars and trucks.

"It's all or nothing, lads," O'Lane said.

He began pulling grenades out as fast as he could, yanking the pins, and dropping them out the window. He swerved sluggishly, dispersing grenades across every lane.

Now Eric realized what O'Lane was doing. He wasn't after Curtiss at all. He was trying blow up any random car, likely killing the passengers, just so he could block the road and make his escape. It gave Eric a sick feeling in his stomach. Perhaps it had been O'Lane's long talk at the lab, his professional demeanor, his smile, or the damned English accent, but Eric had almost respected the man. Until now.

Eric and Ryan watched as grenades flashed and blew holes in the fog. *Boom ... boom ... boom.* Beautiful spheres of clarity. Then the bubbles began to catch the cars, the high-power grenades vaulting them into the air. Two cars jumped more or less simultaneously, one shot straight up and flipped onto its roof. The other car exploded where it was, sending out fiery tentacles of debris in every direction. Then a minivan caught part of an explosion under its nose and sat up like a dog, exposing its gray underside before the car behind slammed into it, spinning it like a top. Eric saw the nose of a station wagon emerge from the collision, accordioned and spewing white radiator steam. Against the median, a delivery truck dipped forward as if an invisible hammer had struck the hood, then tipped on its side, sliding across the blacktop toward them.

A big semi tried to squeeze through the only space that was no longer blocked—a narrowing gap between the shoulder and the guardrail. But it was a vain attempt. The Peterbilt bounced off the guardrail then clipped the half-demolished station wagon, spinning it around and almost ejecting the driver out the side window. Almost. Her torso was slung out and whipped about like a rag doll before being sucked back inside by the seat belt.

The semi seemed about to make it through, spewing amber sparks on both sides, when one grenade and then another exploded underneath it. The first caught the cab and made it jump, sending it harder into the guardrail. Eric noticed one of its stainless steel fuel tanks had been pierced with molten shrapnel. Perhaps due to being full, the tanks didn't explode. Not enough oxygen inside. Rather, they began disgorging a fountain of liquid fire across the wet blacktop.

The second grenade caught the trailer, which must have been empty, because it jackknifed and tipped onto its side, on top of the growing mound of crumpled cars, before sliding back and pinning the burning cab and driver against the guardrail.

Now every lane was blocked by a huge twisted mass of metal, plastic, rubber, and flesh. But it wasn't over. Drivers in the rear found themselves hurtling toward an impenetrable wall. The mass began to bulge and shift and grow as more cars piled in.

Even a hundred yards ahead, Eric heard the cacophony of screeching tires, grinding concussions, shrieking metal, sharp pops, and wailing car horns.

Then, just as the fog began to cloud his view, he saw a lone figure in uniform atop the mass of wreckage. Then the Caddy blew through a fog bank, and the scene dissolved into nothingness.

"Sweet Mother of Jesus," Curtiss said. The wreckage had to be ten feet high—at least fifteen mangled cars and trucks filled with dead and injured. But he couldn't deal with them now. Pistol in hand, he leaped onto the hood of a Chevy, across a stretch of the median guardrail, and onto the side of the overturned panel truck. The logo—ROCK HALL FRESH SEAFOOD SINCE 1927—was huge under his feet. And in the distance, limping along on two flat tires, was the gold Cadillac SUV. Wounded but alive. He raised the Five-seveN and took aim, but before he could fire, fog enveloped the Caddy once again.

He swore bitterly and put the pistol in its holster. The magnitude of the loss could hardly be overstated. Meng had chosen his targets astutely: Lee for his AI expertise, and Hill for his understanding of forced evolution. If the Chinese were able to break them, they could reach replication in two months.

It was at that moment that something caught his eye. It was about ten yards ahead of him, spotlighted in a headlamp beam. It was a human forearm. It had been severed cleanly just above the elbow. Very little blood. It had somehow been thrown from the accident. He could tell it belonged to a woman: it was slender with long red fingernails and a silver link bracelet.

The sight broke him out of his trance. All at once, the sounds of his surroundings came pouring in as if someone had turned off the mute button. He heard at least a dozen frantic voices. A man screaming with all his might. Hysterical, mortal screaming, like a man on fire. A woman calling desperately for help. *"Please, please, someone ... anyone!"* Children crying in fear and confusion. The crackle of flames. The blaring of a car alarm.

He called out to Davis, who was standing by the truck, too stunned to act. "Call nine-one-one." He pointed at the mile marker. "Tell them 695, mile one-seventy-four, inner loop. Then get Bolling to scramble the CSAR birds. After that, get the flares from under my seat. Set them a hundred yards back. And don't get your ass hit! The last thing we need is more accidents."

Curtiss ran to his truck and unclipped a fire extinguisher from the bed. The man had stopped screaming. He went looking for the children.

★ ★ ★

"Are you fucking happy?" Eric shouted. "*Are* you? All those people ..."
He was almost too furious for words. He shook his head in disgusted
rage. "All that bullshit about the Afghan girls and caring. How many
kids do you think you just killed? Huh? Maybe a few infants in their car
seats, getting cooked alive right now." His face was purple with anger.
"The tides of history. What bullshit!"

Brock O'Lane felt the young man beside him getting more and
more worked up, building up his courage. He felt Hill's eyes lock on to
his face, testing, feeling, like a boy getting up the nerve to jump into a
cold pool.

Now.

Just as Eric was about to lunge, he found a pistol in his nose. He
froze.

Eric's courage evaporated. He was suddenly willing to do anything
to get the gun out of his face. It was one thing to know empirically that
the shirt worked on a pig; it was quite another to let someone shoot him
in the face to prove it. *Coward,* the other voice in his head said. *Are you
gonna piss your pants again?*

"Settle back, Dr. Hill," Brock said. "Now is not the time."

He didn't have time for Hill's words. Not now. They were free of
Curtiss, but he had to act fast. He had to ditch the crippled Cadillac,
find another vehicle, and get to the airstrip.

But in the back of his mind, he, too, was shocked by what had
happened. It wasn't supposed to be this way. Not with so much collateral
damage. In the moment, he had been so focused on his own survival, he
hadn't thought it through. It was only when he saw the fiery wreckage
in the rearview mirror that he realized what he had done. And it had
brought a heat to his face, a shame. He tried to push the feeling aside,
reminded himself that he was no longer a man who felt shame.

That man had died in Afghanistan a long time ago.

CHAPTER TWENTY-THREE

INFECTION

March 28, 2026
Naval Research Laboratory, Washington, DC

Jane approached the door cautiously, a nervous excitement surging inside her. Was there a light on inside? Was he finally back?

She gripped the door handle and pushed, hoping it would swing open, but it was locked once again. She closed her eyes for a moment and dropped her head.

She had been coming here three and four times a day lately. She would leave her desk, telling herself she was just going for a cup of coffee, and the next thing she knew, she was here, halfway across campus, approaching Eric's office with nervous anticipation, hoping to find him bent over his computer, just as she had found him so often before.

But once again the door was closed and locked.

It had been almost five weeks since they disappeared, and no one would tell her anything. Curtiss admitted that Ryan and Eric were together, but said it was "official navy business." At first, she hadn't been worried. A lot of scientists were visiting different naval bases—Norfolk, Quantico, and China Lake—to help design and test new weapons. So it was reasonable that Curtiss had sent them somewhere. Besides, at the beginning she'd been happy they were gone. She had needed a break, especially from Eric.

But after two weeks, she began to get suspicious. No phone calls, no texts, no emails? She called Ryan. *"The cellular customer you are trying to reach is not available."*

She went to Curtiss's office. "What's going on?"

He smiled. "You need to stop asking so many questions, Ms. Hunter. I told you, they're on official business."

Jane didn't like his patronizing tone. "It's *Doctor* Hunter, *Jim.*"

Curtiss stiffened. "Okay, *Dr.* Hunter. Now, if you're done wasting my time, I'd appreciate it if you would go back to doing your job." He motioned to the door.

She let out a breath of annoyance. She wasn't going to get anywhere, was she? "Fine," she said, and left.

She told herself she'd just have to wait. She tried to forget about it. They would show up eventually. She put in her hours, worked out. But she couldn't stop thinking about Eric.

At first, she had wanted to hurt him the way he had hurt her. She had dreamed about the things she would love to say. But each day that fantasy grew softer, until she deeply regretted what she had done. She had pushed him away. That was why he had lashed out at her. She was such an idiot. Only now that he was gone did she realize how stupid she'd been. And she realized something else: It was time for her to grow up. To cut the cord and stop living her life the way her father wanted. She swore that if Eric ever came back, she wouldn't make the same mistake. She would take risks, and that meant exposing herself. Opening up. She would have to be brave in a way she had never been before.

Another week passed. Still nothing. It didn't make any sense. Even if they were on a warship, they would still be able to send a message. Something had to be wrong.

She called Curtiss, but his assistant told her she would need an appointment. It was bullshit, but she played along. Of course, at the moment, the admiral had no openings. She would have to call back in a week. She waited another week, called back, and still got the runaround. "I'm sorry, the admiral is still booked solid until the end of the month."

She stormed over to his office. He was just leaving with his assistant, a commander named Wilson, who was built like a power lifter and wore sunglasses as if they were permanently attached to his face. Curtiss pretended not to see her—just kept walking down the hall. Wilson put up his hand to block her and said, "I'm sorry, but the admiral can't talk to you right now."

She called out to him, a sudden weakness in her own voice that she didn't like. "Curtiss ... Jim. Please, just tell me where they are. Tell me they're okay. I just need to know." She thought her plea would elicit a human response from him, but instead he wheeled on her, his eyes narrow and cruel.

"I've told you already, Hunter, their whereabouts are confidential. That means it's none of your goddamn business. It also means that trying to find out where they are is a violation of the law. You, of all the civilians working in this lab, should know that. Now, if I find out you've been snooping around trying to find them, I'm going to throw you in the fucking brig. Am I making myself clear?"

Something in her snapped. Curtiss had just told her something he hadn't intended to: he wasn't taking care of them. And he didn't know whether they were safe.

All the frustration of the past five weeks. All the loneliness. All the regret for the way she had treated Eric. It suddenly came out.

"What have you done!" she shouted. "We aren't your fucking playthings, you coldhearted bastard! We're *people,* and if I find out you've put them in danger, I'll gouge your fucking eyes out. You hear me? You'll wish you'd died in Damascus with all the recon marines you let get slaughtered."

Admiral Curtiss suddenly became very still. He stood up straight and ground his jaw as if he were chewing on something hard. Then he exhaled. "This conversation is over," he said, and walked away.

"It's not over, damn it!" she screamed. "I want them back!"

She tried to follow him, but Wilson blocked her. "Give it a break," he said.

She pushed against him, grunting in frustration, but she couldn't get by. Curtiss got in the elevator, not even bothering to look back. Then he was gone.

Jane stopped fighting and pulled back from Wilson as if she meant to leave. As soon as he relaxed, she shoved him full force with both arms. He fell right over.

"Pussy," she muttered, and marched off.

Ten minutes later, she was outside Eric's office again. She put her back to the door and sank to the floor, burying her head in her hands.

She felt as though she were losing her mind. The problem was, she didn't have enough information to make a good guess. Curtiss knew it, which was why he wouldn't tell her anything. God, it was so frustrating. The only thing she was certain about was that with each day they didn't return, the likelihood of their ever coming back grew smaller and smaller. She knew that, somehow. She felt it in her heart.

She pulled her head out of her hands and looked up at the fluorescent lights, thinking about Curtiss. He had been so furious, so suddenly, but was there also fear in his voice? A fear that she might discover the truth?

Fuck him! she thought. *I'm going to find them.*

But how? The longer she thought about it, the more she realized that all roads led back to Curtiss. He had the answers; she just had to find a way to get him to talk. But maybe she didn't need him to talk to *her,* as long as he talked to someone. As long as she could listen in. She nodded to herself, liking the idea. She had resources, after all, including access to the most cutting-edge technology in the world. Maybe it was time to see what it could do for her.

I want them back. And you, Jim Curtiss, are going to help me.

★ ★ ★

Five days later, Jane walked into the gym, looking for Curtiss. She was nervous as hell, but she had to act cool. It was critically important that she not accidentally touch anyone—anyone except Curtiss.

She spotted him in a back corner, on the bench press. He was benching two plates with ease, and she had to admit that for his age he was pretty damn strong.

"Admiral, can I have a word?"

He sat up from the bench, his face shiny with sweat.

"What is it, Hunter?"

"Sir, I just wanted to say I'm sorry for my behavior the other day. I know the importance of security, and I shouldn't have pushed you. And my comment about Syria—that was out of line. I know you saved a lot of lives. My father even said so." She offered her hand.

He regarded the hand skeptically, then relented. "All right, Hunter. Apology accepted."

Jane smiled at him warmly, charmingly, and squeezed his hand tightly with both hands.

Curtiss couldn't help but smile back.

Jane continued beaming while secretly suppressing the urge to punch the prick in the face.

"Hunter?" Curtiss said, looking down at their interlocked hands.

"Yes?" she said.

"Can I have my hand back?"

"Oh," she said, and laughed like an embarrassed schoolgirl. It was a laugh so contradictory to her character that it took all her willpower to make it sound authentic. "Sorry about that." She let go of his hand. "I'll let you get back to your workout."

He gave her a sideways smile. "Okay," he said. *What a strange one.*

"Have a nice day," she said, and left the gym.

Four hours later, she checked the nanosite count in Curtiss's body. Four hundred billion and growing. In another few hours, they would begin to reorganize into the microscopic devices she needed: a microcontroller, a microphone, a radio transmitter, and a diagnostic system. She picked up a pill and took it with a tall glass of water. It would clear the nanosites from her system.

Two hours later, she began to receive the first signals. Now she could track him, monitor his vital signs, and listen in on everything he said.

She was taking a huge risk. To put surveillance on a high-ranking military officer was espionage, plain and simple. Certain jail time if she was caught.

She didn't care.

I'm getting them back.

CHAPTER TWENTY-FOUR

THE OTHER SIDE

March 29, 2026
Tangshan Military Laboratory, China

Eric knew what they were capable of: the enhanced interrogation, the torture, the drugs, the psychological games. But nothing prepared him for what they did.

They did nothing.

The cell was bare. A white bed. A white toilet. No one came to see him. No interrogation. Not a single question. He saw no one. Food appeared under the door. He ate it. The tray was taken away. Days passed. He got sick, had diarrhea. Pills appeared with the food. He took them. He got better.

It was insufferably quiet. He heard nothing. His senses became hyperaware, searching for information, until the sound of his heart was constant in his ears. There was no window, no sunlight, nothing to mark the passage of time. Had they forgotten about him? Had they decided he had nothing to offer them? Would they soon come and dispose of him?

Day after day he waited. No one came. No sound. No change. He felt his sanity slipping away. Why were they doing this? Then he realized, they knew exactly what they were doing.

He tried to fight it. He paced back and forth. He did push-ups and sit-ups and jumping jacks. He upended the bed against the wall and did pull-ups from the metal frame, then punched the mattress. He had to keep his mind busy. He replayed movies in his head, scene by scene. When he could remember no more movies, he remembered books, then textbooks. Then he tried to remember the definition of every word he knew. He defined "it" and "is" and "that."

But eventually, his brain started to scream. It needed information. Without it, he would lose his mind. It was inevitable, because without information, his brain was a runaway train, racing from one distorted hypothetical to another, packing a year's worth of terror and anxiety into a few minutes. He pulled at his hair; he screamed; he pounded on the door. He actually hoped they would come and beat him. It would have been a mercy. That way, at least, he could see a human face, know the world still existed, know that there was a reason for it all.

But no one came. The lights never dimmed. He was sure he was staying awake for days, but then, he had no way to know.

He realized for the first time just how weak he was. All those movies he had seen, all the torture scenes where the hero defies his captors day after day. What bullshit. They hadn't even touched him, and he would gladly do anything for them—anything to stop his own mind from killing him.

And his mind *was* killing him. It was starved and sick, rotting inside his skull. He began to doubt the most basic things about his life.

You're not a scientist, the other voice said. *You weren't kidnapped. You're in an insane asylum, and guess what—you've been here for years. Ryan and Bill and Jack are all make-believe. There is no girl named Jane. And even if there were, she wouldn't love you. Don't be stupid.*

They had taken every physical object that proved who he really was: his wallet and phone, his clothes, even the shirt. So he became obsessed with the scars on his knee, the burns on his leg from the fire, and the wound in his shoulder. He would spend long hours touching and examining them, trying to fortify himself with the knowledge that he wasn't insane.

But every day, he grew weaker and it was harder to fight. He knew it. They knew it. They were watching him. Waiting. He was sure. And with every moment they waited, they were sending a message. "We are many. You are one. We can do this as long as we need to, but you cannot."

Finally, he broke. He wept miserably, laughed hysterically. Then he began to call out to them. "I'll help you." It started out as a pathetic whisper; then he said it a little louder. "I'll help you." It was liberating, in a way. He said it louder and louder. "I'll help you. I swear I'll help you. Just let me out. Please." Then he wept some more.

Nothing happened.

At least two days passed. That was when he realized they weren't coming. He had offered them exactly what they wanted, yet they didn't care. It meant there was only one way to end this. Now he understood his father in a new light. He understood the mercy that death could bring.

But they had left him nothing—no straps, no sharp edges, no cords or wires. He spotted a screw in the bed frame. If he could just get it out, he could slit his wrists. The idea comforted him. Yes, he would really do it. But the screw wouldn't budge. He twisted until his fingertips bled, but nothing. Then he wept again, realizing there was no escape.

They waited another day.

Then another.

And another.

The door swung open. Eric was so grateful, he found himself whimpering.

A small, thin man in a white lab coat appeared. He had a mousy nose, and lips that stayed pulled back from his teeth. He was smiling happily, almost gleefully. Clasping and unclasping his hands in anticipation.

"Dr. Hill! I'm Dr. Chu. I am so very happy to finally meet you. I'm so sorry that it took us so long. I kept asking General Meng to release you earlier, but he insisted we follow procedures. He said you wouldn't cooperate if we didn't wait. But now it's over. Are you ready to help?"

All Eric could do was nod.

"Excellent! I knew you would."

"The date," Eric mumbled.

"Pardon?"

"What is the date?"

"Oh, it's March twenty-ninth."

"What year?"

"What year?" The little man laughed. "Why, it's 2026, of course."

It seemed impossible. Only five weeks had passed. He felt as though he had aged at least three years. And in a way, he was sure he had.

"I'm sure it was hard, but it's over now. Come, I want to show you the labs. I have so many questions for you."

He helped Eric stand and guided him out the door. They were in a vast, silent penitentiary. Everything was new and shiny and cold. They passed cell after cell—were they all full?—then they pushed through a heavy armored door. On the other side was an elevator. Eric walked in a daze, unsure whether this was real or a hallucination. His mind was so fragile, still not believing. In the elevator, the buttons ran down instead of up. They were on level forty-nine. Chu hit level forty-two. The elevator went up. What did it mean?

"It's a very exciting time," Chu continued. "We are getting closer and closer every day. Ryan has been wonderful at debugging our code, and his knowledge of artificial intelligence is simply without peer. We would never have gotten this far without him."

The elevator doors opened, and Eric's eyes widened at what he saw. In front of him was the biggest expanse of open laboratory space he had ever seen. Fifty yards wide and extending as far as he could see—at least a mile long, if not more. There were thousands and thousands of scientists and technicians, all in blue or white lab coats, all working as if on some enormous assembly line.

"Amazing, isn't it?" Chu said. "They found this cavern when they were digging the shaft for the main lab." Eric looked closer at the ceiling. It had been smoothed and polished, but there was no mistaking it. It was solid rock. Now he understood the buttons on the elevator. He had been living forty-nine stories underground.

"As I was saying," Chu continued, "Ryan has been tremendously helpful, but he can get us only so far. Now we need you, Dr. Hill. Our roadblock is mutation. The third generation of nanosites is being born with so many problems, they don't even respond to our interface."

For the next twenty hours, Dr. Chu grilled him on his assembler designs, on his error-checking programs, and on his personal relationships with Bill, Jack, Olex, and Ryan. Eric told him everything. Yes, he hesitated, and even dared to lie once, but Chu caught it immediately. The mousy little man stopped suddenly and put down his stylus. "Dr. Hill, I thought we were doing so well." He shook his head. *Tsk, tsk.* "And I assured General Meng that you were ready to cooperate." Another shake of the head. Eric felt weak with fear. *Don't send me back, please. Don't put me back in that cell.* Chu's finger stabbed at his generic iSheet. Then, to Eric's amazement, he showed Eric his own personal logs from the NRL. "By July, you had abandoned the multiple parent/child hypothesis. Why would you tell me it is the best route to take?"

"Okay," Eric said, realizing it was futile. "Okay."

What could he do? Chu knew that they had reached replication. He also knew that as the architect, Eric was privy to most of the designs. He told Chu the truth, and this time the little man was satisfied. "You'll find that being truthful is always the best path to take."

After the twenty hours, Eric was exhausted and prayed that Chu would let him rest. But he still had more questions.

"General Meng is very interested in what happened on January nineteenth. At 10:04 that night, you met with Admiral Curtiss, Jack Behrmann, and—via conference call—Bill Eastman. Why?"

He was shocked at how much they knew. It seemed they were unstoppable. "I ... well, I saw something. A murder. I thought it had been done using replicators."

This did not seem to faze Chu in the least. "Go on."

Eric told him the story.

"I see. And do you still believe this man was using replicators?"

"I … I don't know. At the moment, I thought so, but it doesn't make any sense, and no one believed me."

"Well, perhaps you will find this interesting." He handed Eric a letter addressed to Admiral Curtiss.

Dear Admiral Curtiss:

Pursuant to your orders, we have liaised with the Criminal Investigations Division of the FBI concerning the robbery at SynChem Industries, 304 6th Street SE, on the evening of February 19, 2026. Our task was to find evidence of assemblers or replicators of the type used at NRL … After a thorough investigation of the crime scene, including close examination of Robert J. Williams' Sig Sauer P238 pistol and the broken surveillance camera, we have found no evidence of replicators or assemblers. The medical examiner's report corroborates that this was a natural death caused by a brain hemorrhage.

We remain at your service for any additional work in this case; however, we believe that no further investigation is warranted.

Sincerely,
CMD Miles Pollock

Eric gave a slow nod and handed the sheet back to Chu. It was just one more piece of information that showed he was a fool. They all had been right to doubt him. Even Jane. He was such an idiot.

Finally, Chu took Eric back to his cell. Eric froze at the door. He couldn't will himself to go in; his legs just wouldn't do it. "Just for a little while," Chu assured him. "You'll stay here until General Meng is confident you are doing all that you can. Then we'll see about an apartment for you." Eric felt sudden tears welling up, but he brushed them away with his sleeve and went inside.

They let him sleep for six hours; then Chu got him up again. The little man worked him another twenty hours; then it was back to his cell. Locked in. And that became his routine: twenty hours up, six hours down. Just enough sleep to keep him from getting too weak. At least the food was good. They gave him whatever he asked for. And when he slept, they would turn out the lights. A doctor came and gave him a physical, then came to check on him once a week.

After another week, he decided to take a chance:

"When am I going to get an apartment?" he asked Chu. "I'm cooperating."

"I'm sorry. For now you will remain in your cell. General Meng's orders."

Eric shook his head. "You need to give me something, a token of goodwill. I want a desk, a chair, and a reading lamp. I want my old clothes, too, and some other clothes like them."

Chu nodded. It seemed a reasonable request. "I'll see what I can do."

The next day, Eric returned to his cell to find the desk, chair, and lamp. A pile of clothes was stacked on his bed. Khaki pants, T-shirts, boxers, Oxfords, socks, shoes. He rummaged through them quickly. He found the pants he had been wearing when he was kidnapped. The underwear. The socks. He became frantic. Where was it? Then he saw it, and a wave of relief washed over him. He wasn't sure how he would use it, but at least he had it.

Most of the time, they kept him quarantined in a small private workspace, away from the Great Lab. Day after day, he worked. It was an existence both strange and familiar. There was familiarity in the work, but it was strange because he was the *other*. No, not just the other—the enemy. Pure and simple. He felt it wherever he went. They didn't like him. His very presence seemed to bother them. Some glared. Some looked away in open disdain, as if their eyes had mistakenly fallen on something vile and wretched. Others treated him as if he were a machine, an instrument provided for the sole purpose of helping them reach replication faster.

He didn't understand why they seemed to hate him so, until one day when they let him back into the Great Lab to work on some specialized equipment there.

Seeing the enormous space once again dazzled him. It was so vast! Moving sidewalks, as wide as roads, ferried people and supplies down the length of the room. And along one wall ran a catwalk suspended high above the floor, with soldiers carrying rifles pacing back and forth. On the walls were huge murals four stories high, depicting famous moments from the revolution, and happy scenes of workers and their families. Between the murals were equally huge iSheets.

He had been working for only an hour when all of a sudden, the iSheets came to life. Everyone immediately stopped what they were doing, and turned to watch. It was a bizarre and disturbing pause, eerily robotic.

A video started. Patriotic music. The Chinese flag flying in a stiff breeze. Images of Chinese men, women, and children looking proudly skyward, to the future. Then images of bullet trains, skyscrapers, the Three Gorges Dam, fighter aircraft and bombers. Then huge parades of soldiers marching down crowded streets. Then more soldiers in action shots: rappelling from helicopters, sharpshooting targets that exploded on impact, swarming a moving tank and destroying it. Then portraits of China's leaders—Mao, Deng Xiaoping, Sun Yat-sen.

Then the music turned ominous. Dark clouds against a blue sky. A map of China surrounded by small US flags. Okinawa, Taiwan, Pakistan, the Philippines, South Korea, Australia—all locations with US military bases.

A voice began to speak. It was in Chinese, so Eric didn't understand it, but he could tell well enough what the man was saying, warning of the dangers of US imperialism. More images: black and white footage of the Japanese occupation during the Second World War. The rape of Nanking. Men used for bayonet practice by the Japanese. Chinese mothers and little girls weeping. Corpses lining the streets, picked at by dogs so gaunt you could count their ribs. Then a quick transition to full-color images from the US invasions of Iraq, Afghanistan, and Syria. Bombs exploding in city streets. Civilians running scared from billowing plumes of black smoke. A Middle Eastern man running with a child, its arms and legs limp and dangling.

The voice of the narrator grew more insistent. *Vigilance,* it seemed to say. *Don't let it happen again.* Then it stopped.

Immediately, as if a switch had been turned, all the workers resumed their tasks.

Not an hour later, Eric noticed something even odder. A large number of the workers, perhaps one in every four, simultaneously answered their cell phones. But none of them spoke a word. They just stood there listening for maybe five minutes; then, simultaneously, they hung up and went back to work. It wasn't long before another group, another quarter, picked up their cell phones and listened in silence before thumbing them off. As the afternoon wore on, it happened again and again, until he was sure the same people had been called at least three times.

It was the government, he realized, calling the scientists, perhaps as often as four times a day, to pour propaganda into their ears.

Now he understood the looks, the glares, the disgust. He didn't think that they hated him. Not all of them, at least. He saw humanity in them: how the women hugged each other, how they smiled and encouraged one another. Yet, there was a powerful system controlling these people. And that was the other thing he felt in the Great Lab: *fear.* It hung in the air like sweat in a gymnasium.

Day after day, he toiled, twenty hours up, six hours down. And day after day, the way they treated him began to wear him down. He desperately needed acceptance, any contact that might pass for affection, but it was always denied him. He tried to ignore it. He reminded himself that they had not put a hand on him and were treating him well. Yet for some reason, this seemed the cruelest torture of all. He found himself working harder, doing more in the hopes that Chu or one of the other scientists would thank him, would smile or touch his shoulder. But they never did. And that hurt like an affliction, like a disease that would eventually consume him from the inside.

You can't know what it's like until you've felt it. That was what he'd tell them. Bill, Jane, the admiral. When it was all over, he'd make them understand why he did it. Why he had helped the enemy.

CHAPTER TWENTY-FIVE

THE TRUTH

April 24, 2026
Tangshan Military Laboratory, China

"You will be working with me today. You can call me Dr. Hui."

She was in her midforties and beautiful, but in an austere way. Her English was perfect, and Eric complimented her on it. "University of Chicago," she said. When he asked her how she had ended up studying there, she coolly directed him back to their work. She kept him busy, but after five hours of working, she abruptly said to him, in midsentence and without any change of inflection, "Ryan says you need to stay strong."

Eric made no indication of noticing, just went on talking about their work. He wanted to ask more, but he dare not. *But a message.* It filled him with a sudden exhilaration. Of course, the message told him nothing really, yet it was still powerful. Ryan knew how to reach Eric if he had to, and it suggested that they were not so alone after all—that there were others, a resistance. And that meant there was reason to hope.

Chu continued to work him hard. The Chinese still had not figured out how to make the nanosites transdifferentiate into any desired system. Eric knew the answer, of course: forced evolution. But now that he was feeling a little stronger, he decided not to tell them. It was the key. In fact, it was the reason they had kidnapped him, although, ironically, they didn't know it. And that, too, was important, because it showed there was a limit to how much the Chinese knew. Forced evolution had been given a level of secrecy that not even Meng's spies could penetrate. They suspected that Eric had something to do with a big breakthrough, but they didn't know any more than that. So he was able to convince Chu that it was a genetics problem and that it had been Olex who figured it out, which was at least half the truth.

But Chu soon grew impatient with him.

"Dr. Hill, I will be perfectly honest with you," he said. "We don't know who solved this problem, but two of our sources say that it was you. Please, if you know, you must tell us. If General Meng finds out you have been withholding information ..." Chu trailed off, shaking his head. "I say this to you as a friend. Those who have crossed him, well, they tell stories about the things that happen to them."

"I swear, I'm giving you all I have."

Chu nodded a conditional acceptance.

Two days later, Eric was working in one of the private labs when Dr. Hui came in again. She wore a bright smile and reintroduced herself.

"I met you several weeks ago," he reminded her.

She let out a high, infectious laugh, and Eric realized it was the first time since his arrival that he had felt genuine joy directed at him. God, it felt good. It was just a laugh, but it made him inordinately happy.

"You met my sister," Hui said. "She's Dr. Hui *Ying*; I'm Dr. Hui *Lili*. We are twins. I'm the smart one, in case you were wondering." Another laugh. "Poor Ying, her whole life she's been trying to get away from me. She was even born an hour earlier because she was already sick of me—or so she says—but I just keep following her around wherever she goes." She gave that infectious laugh again.

"And why would she want to get away from you?" Eric asked.

"Because I talk too much, of course."

This, it turned out, was not hyperbole. While they worked, she went on and on about her adventures with her sister: being born in Hong Kong, growing up in Beijing in the 1980s, going to Illinois for grad school, returning to take care of their parents. It was a chaotic stream of consciousness. She laughed easily along the way and touched his arm at the funny parts. Eric did his best to nod and grunt his acknowledgment. At any other time, the ceaseless chitchat would have gotten annoying, but now he found it wonderful.

At some point in her monologue, she absently asked the other technician for some reagent. When she and Eric were alone, she produced her iSheet. "Let me show you something," she said. "If you take a look here …" She leaned in close. "Ryan has a very important message," she said softly. "He knows that you are stalling, but you need to stop. Give them what they want. It's very, *very* important that you give them what they want."

Eric tried to hide his shock, and he couldn't help turning his gaze to her, to try to gather more information from her facial expression. But she only smiled pleasantly and continued talking in her enthusiastic, childlike way.

How could it be? Was it all a trick? Was Ryan really communicating with him through the twins, or was it all a mind game? It made sense that it was a deception. The twins were just agents for the Chinese, trying to trick him into helping them. But he didn't want to believe that. He wanted to believe there was hope, that Ryan was still safe and communicating with him.

When his shift was over, he went to bed, desperate for rest, yet too anxious to sleep. God, the stress was getting to him. Should he really help them? It was maddening. And the pressure, *Jesus!* Chu was on him every day to get them to replication, and it was getting harder and harder to feign ignorance. Eric knew he was eventually going to slip up, and they would know he was lying.

Sometime in the night, through the heavy fog of deep sleep, he became aware of a presence in his room. He tried to push the disturbance away by rolling over to face the wall. *It's nothing. Go back to sleep.* But slowly, he sensed light through his eyelids. Reluctantly, fearfully, he turned over and opened his eyes.

There at his desk was a man in uniform, a star on his shoulder. He was drinking from a coffee mug, relaxed, with one ankle across the other knee, examining some papers in his hand. "I remember this one," he said softly. "The fearless one. Beautiful, too." A grunt. "Very beautiful."

Eric forced himself to sit up, the cot creaking under him. He rubbed his eyes. "What are you doing here?" The man made no move, just took another sip of his coffee. His uniform was immaculate, pressed to sharp creases. He had a handsome face, but a hard face, as if he had lived long for his years and lost much.

This must be Meng.

Finally, the man finished his coffee with a soft *ahh* and set the mug down in its saucer, with a porcelain clink. He turned his eyes to Eric and spoke. "I understand that you may have something that I want. There, in that head of yours. Is it true?"

"I—I'm working as hard as I can with Dr. Chu. As the architect, I only knew so much. Olex—"

"Olex," Meng interrupted. "Yes, the famous Olexander Velichko. So you say that he figured out this problem ... What did you call it? Forced evolution? You say it was him?"

"Yes, it was Olex."

Meng nodded to himself. "You certainly *sound* sincere," he said. Then he seemed to relax, and a reassuring smile broke over his face. "I really have no reason to doubt you, do I? Chu says you have been helpful so far. I'm sure you are doing all you can."

"Yes," Eric said. "I am."

Meng's smile held for a few moments, then dissipated. He leaned forward, putting his elbows on his knees. "But just in case you are not, let me speak plainly. I know all the different ways that prisoners try to resist. Perhaps you are like some of the other men I have broken—men who decide that they are willing to die. Or perhaps you think you can stall us long enough to give your friends such a lead that we'll never catch up. Whatever it is, it won't work. I promise you. I will find a way to get what I need out of that head of yours, even if it means dashing your brains against the Wall."

He stood, giving two taps to the manila folder he had placed on the table. "Please don't doubt my power or my reach. I brought you here, remember. I snatched you right out of Admiral Curtiss's hand, and I can get to anyone if I wish."

When the door had latched, Eric scrambled to the table. Hands trembling, he opened the folder. It contained a series of time-stamped photographs, all taken in the past three days. Jane. Leaving the base in her car. Jogging along the George Washington Parkway, alone. Walking out of the commissary with a bag of groceries, a carton of high-protein soy milk sticking out of the bag. And then came the most disturbing image of all: Jane smiling. It was a reserved smile; in fact, it had almost a note of sadness in it. But he could still feel her joy. The other images were taken at a distance, as if through a telephoto lens, but this one was up close. Inside. Whoever took it was standing right next to her, smiling with her. A feeling of deep vulnerability washed over him.

How did they know?

"I'm so sorry," he said, putting his fingertips to her smiling face, her blond hair. He was haunted by the way he had left her. The things he had said to her. "I'm so sorry."

The next two days were dark days. He felt sick with worry for Jane. He couldn't let them hurt her, and they knew it. They had him. And so a part of him decided it was time to tell Chu the truth. Meng was right. There was nothing he could do. So he began by making incremental steps, enough so that Chu felt they were making progress. But he still held back a little. Waiting, hoping for more information. His only excuse was Olex. He could say that Olex was the one who really knew forced evolution, and Eric was just piecing it together for the first time.

But going to work the next day, he got another shock. As he and Chu were passing the entrance to the main lab, the elevators opened and General Meng emerged with a smiling Olexander Velichko. Apparently, one of them had just told a joke, and Meng was laughing while Olex gave him an approving smile. It was surreal. Olex. Here. Stranger still, chatting casually with Meng, and *smiling*! Acting as Olex never acted. He caught sight of Eric, and the smile vanished. Then Meng put his arm around Olex's shoulder, and the two disappeared down the corridor.

For the rest of the day, he was too flustered to think straight. What did it mean? Had he just arrived, or had he been here for weeks? His casual behavior suggested the latter. But Olex knew forced evolution better than Eric did. Yet they still hadn't implemented it. *Why?* Was Olex hiding the truth, too? Based on what Eric had seen, it seemed hard to believe. And yet, the Chinese were still stuck. Perhaps Olex was saying that only Eric knew the truth, just as Eric said it was Olex. If that were the case, then the moment one of them gave in, the other would be revealed as a liar and would surely die. He felt panic race through him. To save himself, he had to tell the truth immediately. Every minute he waited gave Olex the chance to beat him to the punch.

It took him all day to settle his mind. Controlling his panic was the hardest thing in the world to do. *Jesus Christ!* It felt as if everything had been orchestrated just to mess with his mind: the solitary confinement, the twins and their bogus messages from Ryan, and now a smiling, compliant Olex. The world had gone crazy.

Still, he managed to keep from telling Chu the truth. Still he waited. Deep down, he knew that something, some glue, was holding this thing together. Perhaps Olex had betrayed them, but Eric was still alive, and he felt sure that Jane was, too. If he made a move without understanding things better, that glue might not hold.

Two more days passed. Twenty hours up, six hours down.

On the third day after seeing Olex, Hui Lili came to see him. They worked diligently and quietly until, once again, she sent the technician away for supplies.

"You must stop stalling," she whispered. "Time is running out."

"How can I trust you?" Eric hissed.

"Ryan has something for you. Read it and you'll see I'm telling the truth. You must check the code inside and have it ready for me by tomorrow morning. Now, please tell them what they want to know. It will be much worse for everyone if you don't." A moment later, he felt something small fall into his pocket.

At last, he had some real information. But he still had to act as if everything were normal. Even in his room, he followed the same routine for the cameras: brushing his teeth, washing his face. He was quivering with excitement when he finally got into bed. Finally alone. He turned out the lights and pulled the heavy blankets over his head, making sure that no light could escape, then reached into this pocket. The small piece of iSheet had been folded down to the size of his thumbnail. Fingers trembling, he gently unfolded it until it was a four-by-two-inch strip, then turned it on. Stored inside was massive amounts of code, essentially the DNA of the Chinese replicators. Ryan had made an index of the code he needed to debug.

Eric scrolled down to the first series of subroutines. They were essentially timers, telling the nanosites to do certain things at certain times.

After they achieved replication, the nanosites would begin a massive twenty-four-hour reproduction cycle, their numbers growing geometrically until they reached a critical volume of two sexdecillion units. At that point, they would begin a series of "special tasks."

So far so good. Eric found only one error and fixed it. He began to look at the "special tasks."

Then he saw it. And when he did, a cold tingle ran down the inside of his scalp to the nape of his neck. *Oh, my God,* he thought. He shook his head and scanned it again. He couldn't believe what he was reading. *Oh, my God!* He kept repeating it in his head, his eyes glued to the tiny iSheet. *Oh, my God. Oh, my God. Oh, my God.*

Suddenly, dozens of bits of information, things that had seemed random and unconnected at the time, began to lock and bind together in his mind.

Bill: Eric, I've got a little side project for you. It's a favor for the admiral …

Jane: That's funny. Olex had a weird side project for me, too.

Ryan's last words to him on the plane: *I'm sorry you got dragged into this.*

Curtiss: I'm gonna tell it to you straight, Dr. Hill. There are gonna be a lot more bodies before this is all over. I guarantee it. And it's my job is to make sure that most of those bodies are Chinese.

Eric stared at the tiny iSheet. Mesmerized. Refusing to believe.

It was all a setup. The whole thing. Curtiss had known. He had known that Ryan was going to be kidnapped. In fact, he'd counted on it, enlisting Ryan's help and giving him the tools he needed to sabotage the Chinese program. But Eric shouldn't be here. His presence was a mistake or a miscalculation. *I'm sorry you got dragged into this.*

Eric scanned the code.

<! Begin_subroutine_LAMPREY !>

It was his code. The lamprey code, the Trojan horse that was undetectable. Now he understood why Ryan wanted them to reach replication. He wanted to give the Chinese what they wanted. Then Eric's code would turn their own nanosites against them.

And what exactly would the nanosites do?

He saw Jane's code.

<! Begin_subroutine_NOT_ONE_SOUL !>

It was terrible. It was disgusting. But he knew that he would do exactly as Ryan asked.

He debugged the code for four hours. That left him two hours until they would return for him. He had to make the most of his access to the little iSheet.

At times, he had forgotten all about the invention he still possessed.

He had become accustomed to its warmth. It was only at night, when all was quiet, that he felt (or imagined he felt) the tickling of the nanosites as they fed on his dead skin. He wondered how Chu and Meng would react if they ever discovered that one of their prisoners had been walking around with a device teeming with the very self-replicating nanosites they were trying so desperately to create. Luckily, they didn't suspect a thing. He had been meticulous about the design of the shirt. Even its crude interface—a small tag along the seam—looked completely real.

Nautica

L

100% Pure Cotton

Machine wash with like colors.

Tumble dry low. Do not iron.

HECHO EN HONDURAS

But that interface only told him the health of the shirt. To do any modifications, he had to interface through an iSheet. It had been a nagging source of frustration during his captivity, because he realized how poorly he had designed the shirt, how narrow-minded he had been. The shirt contained assemblers that could be programmed to do anything. ANYTHING. But the only thing he had programmed them to do was stop bullets. He should have made it much more versatile. With tools for surveillance and communication. And most importantly, he should have designed it with weapons, to send his nanosites into the bodies of his enemies to kill them. If he ever got out of here, he swore he would make a device that *really* made the wearer invincible.

But here in his cell, he had no way to reprogram the shirt—until now. He had only two hours and could make only the crudest modifications. But they would have to do.

CHAPTER TWENTY-SIX

THE WALL

May 13, 2026
Tangshan Military Laboratory, China

"I believe I have the solution," Eric told Dr. Chu the next morning, and he explained the final steps of forced evolution.

Chu grasped the concept immediately. "Yes!" he said in a voice jittery with excitement. He began to wring his hands. "Yes, that's it!" He giggled almost uncontrollably. "Oh, yes, it is a wonderful solution. Simple and organic. We were too obsessed with making perfect copies on the first try. We need to let them evolve with some mutation. How quickly can you begin testing?"

"Four days to code it, ten days to test, then probably three or four more days to fix any loose ends." Now that the truth was out, he wanted to do it as fast as possible.

Chu's grin vanished, and a shadow fell across his face. "But if this is the solution, then that means …" He trailed off, his initial look of confusion turning to one of anger. "I must tell the general," he said, and without another word, he was gone.

That afternoon, Hui Lili stopped by to see Eric.

"Pass it to me only when I tell you," she whispered. After a time, she said, "now," and he slipped the tiny iSheet into her pocket. She was cold toward him all day, not her usual enthusiastic self. He wondered whether it came from the realization that the terrible goal they had been striving for would now likely be fulfilled.

They came for him sometime in the night. The guards slapped him awake and yanked him out of bed. They yelled at him in Chinese and shoved him around.

He tried to get dressed quickly, but they kept pushing him and insulting him. Luckily, he had slept wearing the shirt. They hustled him into the hall barefoot, out onto the cold tiles.

This is it, he thought. They were going to kill him. He was afraid, his adrenaline racing, but he also felt a certain resignation, a feeling that he had done the best he could. He only hoped that it would not bring any harm to Jane.

At the elevator, they took him down instead of up. That was a first. The elevator chimed: seventy-three, seventy-four, seventy-five. They exited into a large room that reminded Eric of the indoor firing range at the NRL. But this range was much shorter, and it was not for practice.

His eyes were drawn inexorably to the far wall—drawn there by amazement and horror. This wall was a massive slab of gray concrete, gouged with pockmarks and spattered with black stains. It smelled of dead deer and urine. He could feel the death coming off it in waves, like heat off summer blacktop. Except that it wasn't waves of heat; it was waves of cold. It touched his body and chilled him, sucking out his will to live. There was a sense that he was seeing something that should no longer exist. A wall that belonged in a black-and-white documentary or in a Holocaust museum, as a lesson for future generations. It radiated pain, sadness, and heartache, as if haunted by souls that had left their bodies behind in this terrible spot.

He remembered Meng's words: *I will find a way to get what I need out of that head of yours, even if it means dashing your brains against the Wall.*

Now he realized what he meant.

Ten feet from the wall stood Ryan and Olex, along with five guards armed with Kalashnikovs. A firing squad.

A guard knocked him forward with his rifle butt, and he fell in next to them.

"Is it working?" Ryan asked out of the corner of his mouth.

Eric nodded.

"Well, that's something."

A guard slapped Ryan across the face, spinning his head to the side. Eric saw a line of blood begin to ooze out of the corner of his mouth. Ryan wiped the blood away with the back of his hand and looked at it. At any another time, he would have made a smart-assed remark, but now he kept quiet.

Eric was thinking fast, desperately trying to imagine a way out of here. But they were deep underground, inside a huge military base. And the shirt? Ryan was wrong. There was no way to put it to use. Even though Eric had increased the radius of protection to six feet, it still wasn't enough. Only if they lined them up shoulder to shoulder would they have a chance against the firing squad. And then what? Rush five men armed with automatic weapons? They would surely get separated, and once separated, Ryan and Olex would be shot. And Eric could never overcome five men.

It was hopeless.

Then Meng was suddenly among them, clearly enraged, eyes narrowed to slits, jaw clenched, breathing loudly through his nostrils. He uttered a command in Chinese, and the guards began hitting them with the butts of their rifles, kicking them, until all three were on their hands and knees.

"I have made myself very clear to you, have I not?" Meng bellowed as he paced back and forth in front of them. "And have I not made the price of disobedience equally clear? Yet, still. STILL!" He spat out the words. "Still you think you can trick us, that you can sabotage us and get away with it?

"Do you feel it?" He pointed at the wall. "I know you can. Look at it! That is what awaits those who try to stop us. That is where they die." His chest heaved as he took a deep breath. "They die for nothing, you know, every one of them. Because we will never go back. We will never be subjugated again. That is what I have given my life for. That is my sworn duty! To make sure that we never go back! And I will not let anyone stand in my way." He waited, letting his words sink in.

It was then that Olex said something in Chinese to Meng. Eric couldn't understand the words, but he could recognize Olex's derisive tone. A sarcastic rolling of the eyes. He was mocking the general, and with a degree of condescension and disdain that only Olex could achieve.

General Meng's face turned crimson. Whatever Olex had said left him so infuriated that he was speechless, unable to reply.

Olex saw it, too, so he added another insult, again in Chinese.

General Meng responded with a shout of fury, a terrible cry that raised the cords on his neck. He seized Olex by the hair and flung him toward the wall. In half a second, Meng had snatched a Kalashnikov from one of the guards and cocked it. Holding it at his shoulder, he aimed at Olex.

Olex raised himself on one knee then stood, his face unaffected, looking almost amused at Meng's outburst.

Then Meng seemed to calm, and he snorted out a laugh as if he suddenly realized the jest. Olex straightened and smoothed down his shirt. Eric relaxed, feeling that the storm had passed.

Still grinning, Meng opened fire.

"No!" Eric cried. He tried to rush to him, but the guards stopped him and threw him to the ground.

The rifle was set on full auto, and Eric watched in horror as the bullets zipped into Olex, removing wads of tissue and blood. All through his torso, from his hip up to his shoulder and into his head. It was a horrible thing to see. Such a beautiful system, the human body, so cavalierly destroyed.

The thunder of gunfire ceased but still echoed in the concrete room. General Meng stood there, still peering through the sights, smoke trailing from the rifle's muzzle, the only sound the tintinnabulation of the last copper casings rolling across the floor.

All was still except for a wet wheezing sound coming from the body—no longer Olex, but a mangled organic machine—as its lungs still fought for air. General Meng stepped over to it, like a man investigating a strange noise in his bushes. He gave the head a kick, and the skull opened further, spilling white brain matter. The wheezing continued.

"What's wrong?" Meng asked the corpse. "Can't think of anything clever to say?" He put the heel of his boot on Olex's throat and crushed it. A moment later, the wheezing stopped.

Meng barked out another order in Chinese, and the guards converged on them.

Our turn, Eric thought. *I'm so sorry I made such a mess of things. And I'm sorry, Jane, for being such a jerk.*

But instead of being shoved toward the wall, Eric and Ryan were being pushed toward the elevators. There the guards separated them. Eric called out to Ryan. "Did he know?"

Ryan was shoved in one elevator, fell, and was kicked for it. Just as the doors were closing on him, Eric saw him shake his head.

It was two hours before Eric could stop shaking. He sat on the edge of his bed, head in his hands. Sobbing. He felt so cold. He pulled the blankets over his shoulders, but it was no use; he couldn't warm up. His teeth chattered. *You're okay … you're okay,* he kept silently repeating to himself. But still, he shivered.

He had killed Olex; that much was clear. He was responsible for the death of a great man, a man smarter than he was and more deserving of life. A man who had not been weak, was not a coward, and had not given in to the enemy.

Just like Eric, Olex hadn't known he would be kidnapped, but smart as he was, he must have grasped the situation immediately. They had brought him over to solve forced evolution. And he must have deduced that Eric had been stalling them, telling them that only Olex had the answer. So he had played along. He knew the answer. Of course he did. None of the other Americans were smart enough to figure it out. Yes, he would help them. He was Ukrainian, after all, and had spent his childhood under the Communists. He still empathized with their way of life: simplicity and equality. But he insisted on an apartment. That's right, comrades, he wasn't staying in a cell. Not Olexander Velichko. He appeared to be helping them but had really taken them in the wrong direction. And with Olex's prodigious mind, he had kept the ruse going—day after day. Whatever they threw at him, he could roll with it, improvise an answer they would believe. Perhaps he could have kept it up indefinitely if Eric hadn't opened his mouth. That explained Chu's shock when Eric told him the real solution. The mousy doctor knew at once that Olex had been wasting their time.

But why hadn't Meng killed them all? Why spare them? He must be keeping them alive in case his scientists had any problems with replication. And after they replicated? That would probably be the end. Yes, that was when he would kill Eric and Ryan.

Hours passed, and still he trembled. Under the covers, he tucked his cold hands between his thighs and curled up like a baby in the womb. His ears still rang from the gunfire, and for once he welcomed the infinite silence of his room.

CHAPTER TWENTY-SEVEN
BUD BROWN

May 13, 2026
FBI Headquarters, J. Edgar Hoover Building, Washington, DC

Special Agent Bartholomew "Bud" Brown was sitting in his office on the other side of the world, rubbing his eyes. He would turn fifty-seven this year, the FBI's mandatory retirement age, but he felt much older. He was beginning to forget things and making careless mistakes. He needed to get away from the office. A vacation—that was what he needed. But he hadn't taken a vacation in nine years, and he knew, deep down, that he wasn't going to take one now.

He closed his eyes for a moment and tried to collect his thoughts. He was becoming obsessed by a case. He could feel it coming on. Whenever a case didn't make sense, he got like this. He couldn't leave it alone. It was actually a good attribute from the bureau's perspective. It meant he would put every ounce of energy into solving the riddle. But the same attribute had clearly ruined his personal life. His obsession with work had led to his divorce and his estrangement from his children.

His new obsession? A cold case that he had almost forgotten about. Until yesterday.

By chance, he had run into Dr. Lawrence, the FBI's medical

examiner, in the cafeteria. Albert Lawrence was an enormously fat man in his late fifties—from Brown's generation—who threw his gut around like a weapon, always wore an unlit cigarette on his lower lip, and reeked of bourbon. The man was equal parts brilliant and deranged. He had an almost supernatural understanding of the delicacies of the human body, yet was determined to destroy his own through neglect and gluttony.

"Agent Brown, you owe me a bottle of scotch for that last stiff you sent me."

"The security guard? Williams?"

"That's the one. What an insufferable headache! Never liaise with naval intelligence. Did you know they wanted to send over their own pathologist?"

Brown sat down across from him. "What did you tell them?"

"I told them to go to hell, of course. I'm the best ME on the East Coast. I don't need some pissant navy doc breathing down my neck. They can read my report just as well as anybody else."

"You ruled it an AND, right?"

"That's right, brain hemorrhage. I guess that's what those navy boys wanted to hear, because they left me alone after that. Peculiar case, though."

"Peculiar? I thought it was open and shut."

"It was, but it was the strangest brain hemorrhage I've ever seen—so specific, and in an otherwise healthy brain."

"Go on," Brown said.

"Well, the man's pons, it was liquefied."

"His what?"

"The pons Varolii—it's the bridge between the thalamus and the medulla oblongata. Part of the brain stem. Williams's was turned to jelly."

"That's what made him turn off like that?"

"Exactly. But it was so targeted, so precise. None of the other tissue was damaged: the medulla, the cerebellum—everything else was fine. Even the bleeding was minimal, almost as if the bleeding started *after* the pons went through the blender."

"Did you tell this to the navy?"

"No, I just sent the report: apparent natural death caused by brain hemorrhage."

"And you still think that's what it was, a brain hemorrhage?"

"Of course. What else could it be?"

Brown rubbed his jaw. That was the million-dollar question, wasn't it?

He thought back to the interview with Dr. Hill. The young man had begun the interview well: good eye contact, direct and honest. But then he had given them a line about selling the chemicals on the black market. He looked down at the floor when he said it. Then he had yawned—showing his stress, oxygen craving. An awful liar. And the other thing: watching that videotape, he was fit to jump out of his seat. What did he see? Something related to his top secret project? A project so secret it was above *bureau* clearance.

Brown had tried to find out more about what was going on over at the Naval Research Lab, and what he found he didn't like. Nanotechnology— the construction of superfast, intelligent, microscopic machines. Was that what this was? It would explain why Admiral Curtiss had been so interested in the death and why he'd just as quickly disappeared when they found no evidence of foul play.

"Doc, what happened to Williams's body?"

"We handed it over to the funeral home when we were finished. That's the standard procedure. He's somewhere six feet under by now. Or in an urn on someone's mantle."

Brown grimaced. There was no way to get more evidence from the body. But maybe ... "Did you keep any samples of his ... What did you call it—pons?"

"I did. Why?"

"Can you take another look at it? Maybe under a microscope."

Dr. Lawrence pushed his massive bulk back from the table and folded his arms across his belly, a look of displeasure on his pasty white face. He clearly didn't like the idea of extra work, especially for someone who didn't have the least understanding of medicine. "And what exactly would I be looking for?"

"Anything unusual, especially anything that isn't human tissue."

"You mean some sort of pathogen? I did blood work and ruled that out."

"Please, just look again."

Lawrence gave a huff, and his fat jowls shook. "I'll think about it."

Much to Brown's surprise, the doctor called him the next morning. This morning.

"All right, damn it, I admit it, you piqued my interest yesterday. But I didn't find any foreign material in the sample."

"Nothing?"

"No, but when I looked at the tissue under a microscope, I found something very interesting."

"What?"

"There were no intact cells. Not a single one. Every cell in the pons had been ripped apart."

"Any idea what might cause that?"

"To be honest, I'm at a loss. Bacteria don't do that, and if it were a virus, some virus would still be in there, but there was nothing. Absolutely nothing. And besides, no virus could work that fast."

"So do you still think it was a brain hemorrhage?"

There was a long pause. "I ... I don't know. I have no indication of a disease. No indication of external trauma. We know the death came suddenly, and there was some bleeding in the pons region of the brain stem. So a hemorrhage is still the best answer, although I admit, it doesn't explain the ruptured cells. Do you want me to tell the navy?"

"No," Brown blurted out, perhaps too suddenly. Then, more calmly, "No, I'll handle it. It might be nothing." There was a pause. "Just let me ask one final question, Dr. Lawrence, and then I'll leave you alone. Hypothetically speaking, of course, suppose that a man had a gun pointed at you and you wanted to kill him instantly. And also suppose that by some magic, you were able to do anything you wanted to him. Pretend that you could reach inside his body like a surgeon. How would you kill him?"

"I'd cut out his—" There was a sudden pause as the doctor realized what his answer meant.

"Thank you, Doctor. Your assistance has been illuminating."

CHAPTER TWENTY-EIGHT

FREEDOM

May 16, 2026
Tangshan Military Laboratory, China

Eric sat in his cell. At least two days had passed since Olex's death, but he couldn't be completely sure. He was in solitary again. Alone. Starving for information. Fighting to control his own mind.

He spent long hours staring at the door, both hoping and terrified that it would open. If they came for him, it was either because they needed him to fix something or … or they were going to kill him. And even if it was only the former, he'd be that much closer to being of no more use to them.

Feeling that death was so near, he tried to make his peace, but he couldn't. He was just too young. He had done too few of the things he had wanted to do. More than that, he was struck by the horrible feeling that he had done the *wrong* things and that he had left too much unfinished. He had not made amends with his mother and sister after his father's death. And he had spent too much time working instead of enjoying life.

But he had lived, hadn't he? He had lived a childhood in which he had been loved. There had been idyllic days in Bloomington: summers swimming in the quarry, Fourth of July fireworks, Halloween parades and corn mazes. Christmases in the snow. Friends and teammates. Girlfriends and homecoming and backseats.

The longer he lay there and thought, the more he realized that he had lived—at least, more than some. Perhaps he *could* accept that his life was over. The biggest regret was Jane. The tragedy of finding love and then not seeing it through. What might have been? He knew that it was too much to expect, but still he dreamed of her. He needed it. To imagine a full life with her, to see her belly grow with a child. To bring children into this crazy world so they could cherish them together. That was what he wanted now. Not to be a famous scientist, not to be revered and respected. Not anymore.

As he lay thinking of his past, trying to calm his mind, he unlocked an old memory. He remembered sitting in his dad's lap while he read the paper. He remembered the sound of his father's breathing, the steady rise and fall of his chest, the occasional rustle of the paper. It was such a simple thing, yet it had given Eric the deepest feeling of safety, as if nothing in the world could hurt him.

Just thinking about it now calmed him. But more importantly, it made him realize that for too long he had let the memories of his father's suicide overshadow all the good that he had done. When someone close to you took their own life, that final act had a way of poisoning all the other memories of that person, making you doubt everything else they had done. But that wasn't fair. His father had been much more than a suicide. And Eric realized he had to reclaim the father he had known before.

As the hours wore on, he tried to prepare himself for what was coming. What would happen if the Chinese replicated and the virus got out? Would he die here, or did Ryan have a plan? Maybe he had to be ready—ready to run and fight. Could he do that?

He remembered, one day at the firing range, talking to Corporal Davis about combat. He had been surprised to find out that the baby-faced marine was actually twenty-four and had been in a dozen firefights in Syria. Eric had asked him how he controlled his fear. "Well, at the beginning I didn't," Davis said. "I shit my pants. Major blowout, man. By the time we got back to base camp, it had run into my boots. The second time was better: I only wet myself. You get used to it, I guess, but just a little. The corps trains you to put something above yourself, namely the other men in your platoon. You have to be brave not for yourself, but for them. If you can find something greater to live for, then you'll rise to the occasion."

Eric was sleeping when light suddenly flooded the room. He sat up with a start, his heart thumping in his chest. The door swung open, and in came Chu. The mousy scientist was smiling broadly. He opened his arms as if he would embrace Eric, then pointed at him and began to clap his hands, as if applauding a maestro.

"It is done," he said. Then he squeezed both fists tight in front of his face and threw his head back. "We did it!" he shouted.

"It has been almost two days. Everyone is so very happy! I wanted to come down and thank you personally for your hard work and honesty." Chu took Eric's hand and began pumping it excitedly. "You have helped my country on the road back to greatness. Thank you!"

Two days! Eric thought. That meant the countdown had already started. They were replicating geometrically now. Very soon they would reach their critical mass. And then …

"Come, come!" Chu said. "I will show you. And perhaps you can help us with a slight problem we are having with our diagnostic system. Ryan said you might know how to fix it."

Five minutes later, the elevators opened onto the main lab. Again, he saw the thousands of scientists in their blue and white lab coats, diligently working. Eric instantly felt a change in the place. The air was lighter now that they had reached replication. They stepped onto a moving sidewalk. For ten minutes, they walked, going deeper and deeper into the huge cathedral of science and past one enormous mural after another.

Never before had Eric been taken so far into the huge cavern. Finally, Chu stepped off the sidewalk. "Here we are," he said.

Eric marveled at what he saw: on one side of the Great Lab protruded an enormous sphere of polished steel. It must have been at least three hundred feet in diameter—so big that only part of the curved surface was visible while the rest extended far above the ceiling and far below the floor. Fascinated, Eric walked up to it and peered into a small circular window. The huge sphere appeared to be empty. But he knew that it wasn't. It was full of the first generation of Chinese self-replicating assemblers.

Chu directed him along the far edge of the sphere, and there he saw Ryan, the twins, and a young girl. Perhaps it was because she was the first child he had seen since his captivity began, but Eric was immediately struck by her. She was beautiful, maybe ten or eleven, with long raven hair and warm black eyes. Eric realized this must be Hui Ying's daughter. The girl's mother and Ryan were busy working at a control terminal while the girl played with her aunt, laughing and giggling as they made rhymes.

"Keep quiet, you two," Hui Ying admonished. "I can't concentrate." Then she caught sight of Eric and stood up. "Eric, this is my daughter, Mei," she said formally. There was a gravity in her voice, and Eric had a sense that she wanted to say more. Then she glanced at Chu and remembered herself. "As you can see, her aunt never stops spoiling her."

"Guilty as charged," Hui Lili said. "Or is that 'Chilty as garged'? I'm not sure, I must have humped my bed." The girl giggled.

Ryan's eyes met Eric's. Ryan tried to smile, but his expression betrayed fear. Eric felt his pulse quicken. The twins were playing the part well, but not Ryan. Something was about to happen.

"I heard you were having trouble," Eric said.

Hui Ying nodded. "The readings don't make any sense. One minute, it says there are ten to the seventh power; then the next minute it will say ten to the forty-second power."

"Could it just be the tank's diagnostics?"

"That's the most likely culprit, but the nanosites seem to be consuming massive amounts of feed carbon, which points to higher-than-expected replication."

"Can I take a look?" he asked.

Hui stood aside, and Eric took her place at the terminal. He typed and clicked for a few minutes, trying to appear busy, asking questions that would appease Chu.

Then Hui Lili, the talker, came up behind him and placed her hands on his shoulders. Eric jumped at her touch. God, he was nervous. "Relax," she said with a laugh, giving his shoulder a squeeze. "We'll figure it out. Don't worry." Eric sighed and closed his eyes for the briefest of moments, letting her massage his shoulders. He wasn't alone in this, he reminded himself.

"Let me see the feeder system screen again," she asked him. Eric pulled it up, and she leaned in closer, her hair brushing against his cheek. "There!" she said. "I think it's an error with the feeders. The nanosites aren't really consuming as much as it says."

"How can we verify that?" Ryan asked.

"We check the feeder tanks manually," Hui Ying replied. "They are right down the hall. Who wants to go?"

"I'll do it," Hui Lili said happily. She looked to Chu for approval.

On any other day, Chu would have let her go by herself, but he remembered Meng's warning: that today of all days, they needed to be on their guard. The vice president was coming to inspect the lab. Chu was not to take any chances. He honestly didn't think there was a need for caution. They had replicated, after all. But he called for one of the guards anyway, more out of fear of Meng's reprimands than any concerns he himself had.

Before going, Hui went to her niece and squatted down so they were eye to eye. "I'll be right back, little one, but I want a quick hug before I go." She embraced the child, and Chu saw a sudden tightening of the woman's face. After a long beat, she let go, holding the girl at arm's length. "We are going to make dinner together tonight, right?"

The girl beamed. "Yeah, and you're going to teach me how to make your special noodles."

"You bet," Hui Lili said. She stood, her hand trailing a moment, caressing the girl's cheek; then she turned and headed down the corridor. The armed guard fell in behind her.

Chu watched her go. A suspicion was growing in the back of his mind. Something about the general's warning combined with what he had just seen. But then his phone rang, and the cloudy idea that was beginning to take form evaporated. He answered the phone and stepped away from the others.

Capitalizing on Chu's distance, Hui Ying brought her daughter close to Eric. "Do you have it?" she asked.

He nodded.

She put her hand on her daughter's shoulder. "Mei-Mei, whatever happens, I want you to stay close to Eric. He is going to protect you. Isn't that right, Eric."

Eric looked at Hui Ying, and the intensity in her eyes struck him like a fist. It was the fierce, piercing look of a mother who fears for her child.

"That's right," Eric said, giving the girl a reassuring smile.

"Mom says you can do magic. Is that true?"

"Only when I have to," he said.

The feeder tanks were stored in a room behind the murals: this one a fifty-foot image of Mao lecturing to a group of workers. It was a moving scene: Mao, Red Book in hand, was at the left of the frame, the only one standing, his aura accentuated by a warm evening light, while young men in green caps with red stars sat around him on the floor, looking up reverently at the great teacher.

Corporal Wang Yong was walking patrol on the catwalk opposite the mural when he saw one of the twins and Private Qiang enter the door where the diagnostic equipment was kept. He wondered why the soldier was with her. Had she done something wrong? That didn't really make sense. Everyone knew that the twins were among the top scientists in the lab and were considered the most trustworthy. Perhaps they were trying to get some privacy, he thought with a smile. He and a few of the other soldiers had discovered that it was one of the few places where the surveillance cameras didn't work. His curiosity piqued, he was thinking of going to look in on them, when he heard an odd sound, like a muffled gunshot. He was just about to call it in when the earth heaved. An incredible explosion sent huge cinder-block chunks of Mao and his audience hurtling toward him. The blocks exploded against the wall around him, one cutting through the catwalk as if through paper. Wang was pitched over the side. He saw the tile floor rushing toward him; then he saw no more.

Fifty meters away, Eric felt the ground lurch under his feet, as if a wrathful underworld deity had been awoken. The four of them—Ryan, Hui Ying, Mei, and Eric—teetered for a moment, reaching vainly for support. Then the hot pressure wave knocked them all to the floor. Eric went weak with fear, the memory of the library blast flooding his mind.

Black smoke came billowing out of the wall, consuming light like a living thing, spreading darkness. Accompanying it was a *rumble-rumble-rumble* sound that grew stronger and stronger, reaching deeper and deeper notes. The fire was eating lab equipment, doors, desks, people. Then came a groan of the deepest bass, the groan of steel and metal under tremendous weight, bending and buckling. The huge metal sphere was coming off its supports.

Around them, a catastrophe was unfolding, a wild confusion of desperate humanity. The noise of thousands of voices screaming and shouting was made even more nerve-racking by the persistence of the fire alarms. A moment later, it began raining.

Eric was not thinking—complex thoughts were not possible in this chaos. He realized he was crawling away from the darkness, toward a hazy light. Then Ryan grabbed him and helped him stand.

"Stay close!" Ryan was shouting in his ear, but Eric could barely hear him. "We can't get separated." Eric looked up and saw three people run past him through the smoke. They were on fire.

He felt Ryan take one hand; then he felt someone else holding his other hand. It was a small hand. That woke him up, and he felt a primal instinct asserting itself. *Protect.* He pulled her closer. *Focus!* he screamed at himself. A reason to live, something bigger than himself.

People were stampeding for the exits, and they fell in with the panicked multitude. It was the only way. He turned and looked over his shoulder to check the proximity of danger. There he saw an astonishing sight. From the edge of the billowing black, like a demon from hell, Hui Lili emerged. Her face was black with soot, and her eyes were covered by insect-like goggles. In her mouth was a small respirator. Her clothes were ripped, and she had a nasty red gash on her leg. Yet she walked with an intense conviction, oblivious of the maelstrom around her. Somehow, she was not on fire like the others, but steam was rolling off her as if she had doused herself in some sort of heavy water. She had a satchel slung over one shoulder, and in her other hand was a pistol. She approached the remaining security guard, who was stumbling about, coughing. She held the pistol up to his temple and fired.

Then she caught sight of Eric and her niece.

"*ZǑU KĀI!*" she shouted. *Get out!*

Then she turned from them and waded toward the pitching, groaning containment chamber.

★ ★ ★

General Meng was with his assistant, Captain Xi, at the south entrance to the Great Lab when they were blown backward. The catwalk they had been standing on heaved and undulated like an angry snake, flinging out rivets and pieces of metal tread. Captain Xi was pitched over the side and caught the railing only at the last second. Meng grabbed his arm and hauled him in. Once the man was safe, Meng took in the scene. Four hundred meters down the Great Lab, he saw the black smoke boiling forth. He knew immediately that it was too big an explosion to be an accident. Even if the high-pressure feeder tanks had blown, it would not create an explosion of such magnitude. This was sabotage. But who? The Americans? Chu had pulled them out of confinement to fix the tank diagnostics. But they could not do such a thing alone. They would have needed help. But from whom?

The twins?

This morning, he had seen Hui Ying and her daughter. The little brat had pranced up to him in her school uniform and said, "Good morning, General Meng."

"Good morning, Mei-Mei. Why aren't you at school on level seven?"

"They don't want me."

He had frowned. "They don't want you?"

That was when Hui Ying had come up behind the girl.

"I'm sorry, General, she had an allergic reaction to some food she ate last night, but the nurse doesn't believe me. She thinks Mei-Mei might have a virus, so she won't allow her around the other children. I'll do my best to keep her in my office."

He had given an annoyed sigh. "Yes, you do that. This is a high-security area. Children should not be on this level. It's only because Chu needs you that I'll allow it, and only today."

"Yes, General."

Now he realized it must have been a trick, a way to keep the girl close while they … while they did what? He dared to think it: *Made their escape with the Americans!*

Meng felt his world shift. For the past two days, he had been quietly elated. He had two reasons to be content. First, of course, was that they had reached replication. It was a great victory, and this very afternoon the vice president and his entourage were coming to celebrate. A tour and a banquet.

The second reason was the birth of his daughter. It had seemed a wonderful omen. Just at the moment that his country was creating new life, a new life had come into his home. And Meng could not help but think of this as not just a birth, but a rebirth—a beautiful girl to take the place of Lien. It was the final closure of his earlier life. He had left Tibet a ghost, destroyed—no longer a father, no longer a husband, just a soldier full of rage. Slowly he had fought his way back, kept insanity at bay while he went about replacing the things he had lost. A wife and then a son. And he had had his revenge, too, annihilating the Tibetan resistance. And now the final act: a new child. The final symbol that Tibet had not destroyed him. With this life, he had an opportunity to be the man he had been before Tibet. A man who was not so driven by pain and loss, a man who could sit and raise a child.

But now this.

He pulled out his iSheet and gave an audible. "Tracking. Location of Hui Ying and Hui Lili." The screen showed a map of the Great Lab, with thousands of moving ID tags. Meng saw one twin and the Americans, moving within the cluster of tags toward the exit. The other twin was by the containment tank. Dead? It was possible. The iSheet showed dozens of ID tags, congregated near the explosion, that weren't moving. Clearly dead or dying. Then it moved. He could sort out the others later, but he had to stop that bitch from whatever she was doing to the containment tank.

He heard a pistol shot. Grabbing a Kalashnikov from one of the guards, he turned to Captain Xi.

"Find the Americans and Hui Ying. If they give you any resistance, *any* resistance at all, kill them." Then he took two guards and began running down the wobbling catwalk toward the fire.

Hui Lili had hoped that the explosion in the feeder room would be enough to blow open the containment tank. When she first emerged from the smoke, she was sure it had. The whole tank had been knocked off its support beams and was creaking and moaning as it gnawed into the concrete floor and ceiling. She went to the terminal and killed the program she had made to cover up the real diagnostics. *"Tā mā de!"* She banged on the desk in frustration. The chamber was still sealed.

She had to act fast, not just because of Meng but also because her body wasn't working right. She didn't know quite what was wrong, but the explosion had hurt her … badly. She suspected she was bleeding internally. She had been far too close when the bomb went off. That hadn't been planned. But then again, she hadn't counted on the guard escorting her to the feeder room, either.

She'd had to improvise. Alone there in the feeder room, she had done the first thing that occurred to her: she came on to him, opening her blouse and sticking her tongue in his mouth. *"Finally, I've got you alone."* A devilish smile. She'd seen him around, noticed him looking at her. At first, he had seemed startled by her advance, but only for a second. Then he had risen to the occasion, so to speak. She got down on her knees, unzipped his pants, and took him in her mouth. He had let out a moan and pushed his hands into her hair. She had unbuckled his belt and let his pants fall to the floor. She reached for his balls with one hand, and his sidearm with the other. He looked down when he felt the cold tip of the pistol on his undercarriage. *"I'm afraid this isn't going to end quite the way you imagined,"* she had said. *"So sorry, but I need you to do exactly as I say, understand?"*

And he had. But it all had taken too long, so she'd had to cut the timer. She couldn't risk that Chu might send Mei and her sister away.

If they weren't together—the girls and the Americans—when the explosion went off, it would all be for naught. She had changed the timer to thirty seconds; then doused herself in the thick syrup she had concocted to protect her from the flames. She told the guard to close his eyes and count to sixty, knowing he would never get there.

She had made it into the corridor and just past the giant mural when the timer reached zero. Much too close. The blast tossed her twenty feet, and she had lost consciousness for a few seconds, but she fought it off, determined to finish her job.

Now Lili stood before the containment sphere. The smoke was getting heavy. Sprinklers were dousing her with water. She turned the pistol toward the circular window and fired twice. The bullets ricocheted away with a high-pitched *zang-zang*. Just as she suspected. Shrugging the satchel off her shoulder, she pulled out a heavy metallic saucer the size of an Olympic discus and stuck it to the glass.

She was just about to set the timer for ten seconds when the bullet tore through her forearm. It hit at the elbow, traveled through the tube of her forearm, and exploded out her palm. She almost collapsed to the floor in agony, but she knew she had to move. She staggered a few steps before her leg muscles coordinated well enough to run. Through the smoke, she could make out three hazy figures standing on the catwalk. Even through the goggles, Hui Lili recognized the silhouette of General Meng. She dashed to the left to draw their fire, then turned and ran back to the timer, pausing just long enough to jab SET with her good hand. The timer beeped and displayed the count. *TEN.* But that brief pause cost her a bullet to the leg. *NINE.*

Adrenaline got her another four steps before the leg gave out. *EIGHT.* With one arm and one leg, she scrabbled to get around the curve of the containment sphere and out of the line of fire. *SEVEN.* The bullets zipped around her. *SIX.* She finally reached the back alcove, where the sphere met the wall. *FIVE.* Chest heaving, arm and leg screaming, desperately pulling oxygen in through her nose, she tried to make her body as small as possible while the bullets continued to ping around her. *FOUR.* But there was another problem: the sphere itself.

It was still tipping, chewing up the floor a few inches at a time and slowly pushing her into the line of fire. *THREE.* She put her back to the sphere, as if she hoped to push it back. *TWO.* She curled up her legs, her toes now entering Meng's line of sight. *ONE.* She stared at her toes, expecting them to explode with the impact of a bullet.

Booom-BOOOOOOOOOM!

The small bomb had been given to her by a soldier, who explained to her how it worked. Modeled on a clever antitank weapon known as a sabot mine. It was the weapon of a physicist, not a general. It had very little explosive—not much more than a rifle round—but that was all it needed. The idea was to punch a very small hole in a tank (or other armor) with a thin dart that was denser than the armor—in this case, tungsten carbide. It caused a piggyback explosion.

The glass blew inward, then right back out as the pressure of more than a tredecillion nanosites rushed forth. They emerged with the deafening howl of a hurricane wind, shrieking and whistling. They were invisible, yet their coordinated flight carved beautiful swirling patterns in the thick black smoke. She felt them run over her, blowing up her clothes and hair.

She heaved a great sigh. *She had done it. She had really done it. They were out!* And there was nothing that General Meng or the Central Committee or even the ghost of Mao could do about it now.

Her body was spent, bleeding out in four places. She didn't even want to look. There was no need. She would be dead soon, but she was ready for that. Now that she had accomplished her goal, she welcomed it. Here in these final moments, she thought of her husband, in prison twelve years now for defending human rights victims. A lawyer, he had been sentenced to only three years, but he had continued to work from prison, sending detailed reports of his torture and humiliations, which were published in the Western press. In retaliation, his sentence had been increased to fifteen years. Like many other convicts, he had been sentenced to hard labor in Africa—a slave, sent to harvest the natural resources that fueled China's boom. Now, as she lay on the tile floor, she tried to push back the pain long enough to imagine his face, to take it with her into the dark. It had been so long (or else the pain was so great) that it was hard to see him. So instead, she thought of the pictures she had of him: a shot of him lying in the grass during the summer of their courtship, a selfie he had taken while making a goofy face, a picture of the two of them smiling together at their wedding. She thought of their intense intimacy. The way they had loved when they realized he was going away. And how she had prayed that she would become pregnant with his child, but never did. Thank God for Mei, she thought. For Mei had, in so many ways, become her daughter, too. It was because of her sister and Mei that Lili felt she could let go. One twin would survive today, and in that, and in Mei, a part of her would survive, too.

There was one final act—a violent act, but a crucial one. A way to find peace, but also a way to ensure that Meng didn't piece together the truth. She said a final prayer: for her sister, for Mei, and for the soldier who had helped them, and reached for the pistol. Then she uttered a moan of hopelessness, realizing she must have dropped the weapon when she was shot in the arm. She wanted to cry then, for she knew what would happen if Meng found her alive.

Defeated, she slouched to one side until her cheek was flat against the cold tile floor. She prayed that death would come quickly. With any luck, the bullet to her leg had nicked her femoral artery; then it would just be a matter of minutes. She closed her eyes and tried to will the darkness closer.

She felt a hand grip her hair, and she was savagely yanked from her alcove and dragged out, flailing. She clawed reflexively at the fist with her good hand. No use. She was flung across the floor, sliding, her head smacking the wall. Then she was seized again. A hand forced her head back, and she looked up to see General Meng's furious blackened face. "Why?" he snarled. *"Why?"*

CHAPTER TWENTY-NINE

SLEEPERS

Tangshan Military Laboratory, China

The nanosites rushed free. A cold wind of more than 10^{42} microscopic machines, spinning, spreading, exploring. They swarmed and spun, a whirlwind of life, flying, searching. Immediately, they began to perform thousands of intricate operations. They bonded together, created devices, exchanged information, broke apart, received new instructions, combined again, created another system, then spun apart once more.

All in the flutter of an eyelash.

Ninety-five billion—an airborne particle of dust—formed a single microcontroller, a brain, communicating, coordinating, and directing the other nanosite pods. Forty billion began mapping the entire complex. One point four trillion began a census of every living human being in the complex, searching them out the way a mosquito does, smelling concentrations of carbon dioxide. Once identified, nanosites entered each body through any available opening: through the eye and into the cranium, down the throat and through the lungs, or into the ear and through the porous choroid plexus capillaries. Once inside, they left dormant "sleepers" in the spinal cord of every person. Next, seven hundred million came together to transmit electromagnetic radiation at 800 MHz.

Four minutes later, Admiral James Curtiss's phone rang. It was just after midnight in Washington.

"Curtiss here."

"Sir, they're out! They began transmitting just a minute ago."

"What? Say again?"

"They've done it, sir! They've really done it."

Curtiss felt a wave of relief wash over his body. It had been so long since they had any news. Now this. At last. Without another word, he set the phone back onto its cradle. Then he made a decision. It was an impulsive decision, impractical and dangerous.

He picked up the phone again.

"Sawyer?"

"Yes sir."

"Wake the boys and get them over to Andrews. We leave in an hour."

The alarm woke Jane from a deep sleep. At first, she didn't recognize the sound—it was like a muffled siren. It wasn't her alarm clock or a smoke detector. It was coming from the iSheet. Then she remembered.

She scrambled out of bed, went to the table, and pulled up Curtiss's diagnostic readout. His heart rate had just jumped. But not from exercise or sex. It was too fast. Something had given him a sudden jolt. She turned on the audio and heard Curtiss's call to Sawyer. Then she ran it back to the phone call that had woken him.

This is it, she thought. *It has to be.*

CHAPTER THIRTY

PANIC

Tangshan Military Laboratory, China

They ran and stumbled and pushed and coughed along with the rest of the stampede. It was all they could do to stay together. Eric carried Mei clutched to his chest, her legs squeezed tight around his hips. Ying was in front, gripping Eric's belt with superhuman strength, guiding them as best she could. Eric couldn't see Ryan. He just hoped he was still connected to them somehow.

It was complete chaos, three thousand people fighting for survival, desperate to get away from the smoke and flames, the collective panic infecting them all. Eric stepped on a body, felt the soft give of meat as his ankle rolled, but he didn't stop. When they reached the outer hallway, it was packed with bodies, backed up and barely moving as everyone pushed and shoved for the staircases and elevators. That was when he heard a voice call out—a soldier, searching for them. Ying tugged hard on his belt, jerking frantically. Eric used his greater body mass to make room, but he could still only inch forward. The exit light over the stairwell was only fifteen yards away, yet it seemed impossibly far.

A shot rang out, earsplitting in the constricted hallway. A warning?

People jumped and screamed in fear. "Soldiers!" Ying cried. They heard the voice again, angry now.

They pressed on, enveloped on all sides by panic-stricken people. Every step meant they were being squeezed tighter and tighter as they approached the bottleneck of the stairway doors.

Then a burst of gunfire thundered in the tight space. Eric felt the spray of warm liquid across the back of his neck. The crowd surged in a mad frenzy to get away. People punched, clawed, and kicked. The woman next to him stabbed at the man in front of her with a pen; over and over, the pen plunged into his back. It seemed that everyone was shouting and screaming. They were now squeezed so tight that Eric's rib cage was having trouble expanding. Mei cried out in pain. Another burst of fire. More screams and frenzied pushing.

Eric had had enough. He shifted Mei to his back hip, dug in, center of gravity low, quads straining, and began to shove with all his might. Finally, with a tremendous compression that bent every rib in his chest, they squeezed through the doorway and into the stairwell.

They all gasped for breath, and Eric began to lead them up with the rest of the crowd, but Ying stopped him. "No!" she shouted. "Down!"

They scrambled down the steps, shoes squeaking as they went. Seven, eight, nine floors, past the prison level, until they emerged into a dim hallway and ducked into a bathroom.

Ying locked the door behind them, and the others collapsed, gasping and panting on the floor. "We have to act fast," Ying said, turning to Eric, "Take off your shirt." He gave her a befuddled look. "Just do it!"

He obeyed, and she produced a generic iSheet and a scalpel. She ran the iSheet over his shoulder. "There!" she said. "Now, hold still." And she began to cut.

Eric jerked away. "What the hell!"

"Let her do it," Ryan said. "They chipped you."

Eric acquiesced, leaning against the wall and gritting his teeth. A minute later, she produced a bloody metallic chip. Ryan was next; then Ryan dug the chip out of Ying. They flushed all three chips down the toilet. "That should confuse them for a while," Ryan said.

Then Ying went to a heating duct in the corner, laced her fingers through the grill, and pulled it away. Inside was a backpack.

"Now what?" Eric asked.

"We wait," Ying said.

"You must be joking! They're already looking for us. With or without tracking chips, they'll find us sooner or later."

"We wait," she repeated.

Ryan said, "If he doesn't do it soon, we'll have to risk it."

"He'll do it," Ying said.

It seemed all wrong to Eric that they should be still, but they obviously had a plan. He gave a sigh and sat on the floor. Then he noticed that Mei was weeping. She was trying to hide it, her face buried in her hands, but her shoulders trembled.

Her mother noticed it, too. "I told you, *nān nān,* that you have to hide your emotions. I've been telling you for months. Now, bury them away so that you don't lose your wits."

"I want my auntie," she whined.

"You'll see her tomorrow," Ying lied.

Mei kept weeping. Ryan pulled out a generic iSheet and unfolded it. "Hey, Mei, I have the new version of Wizard Wars. Do you want to play?"

She shook her head.

Ying said something to her in Chinese, and the little girl reluctantly slid over to Ryan. Within a few minutes, they were both absorbed in the game.

"Why did you bring her?" Eric asked, softly enough that the girl wouldn't hear.

Ying's eyes made a circle of annoyance, as if debating whether the American's stupid question merited an answer.

"I brought her because this was the only way to protect her. If I had changed my routine or hers, if I had tried to smuggle her out, they would have suspected something. Then they would have snatched her up, *and* my sister up, *and* me up, and then your plan would never have worked."

He didn't seem to understand, and that annoyed Ying even more. "My daughter is going to *live*," she said vehemently. "She is going to have a life. A real life. I took the risks. I spied for you, for her. She is not going to live under a government that will brainwash her every day. That will throw her in jail for going to a protest, or kill her for speaking out against the wrong people. You're American; you don't get it. You're all so spoiled. But if you could, you would see that *everything* in this country is fake. Fake democracy, fake human rights, fake environmental protections, fake building codes, fake earthquake-proof buildings, fake innovation." She snatched the generic iSheet from Mei and tossed it across the floor in disgust. Mei scurried after it. "Even fake equality." She let out a caustic laugh. "They couldn't even get that right. I live in a Communist country, where I have to pay for my own healthcare and my child's education. It's all a farce, all propaganda and lies. All done so the party can stay in power."

Ying looked ready to continue her rant when he spoke. "You're right. A few months ago, I wouldn't have understood that."

The heat of Ying's rant seemed to leave her. "I'm sorry. It's just that …" She paused, as if considering whether to say more. "Twins are very common in my family," she said. "For the past four generations, there have always been twins. But twins are not allowed by this government. My sister and I survived only because my parents were visiting Hong Kong when we were born. But when I gave birth, I was not so lucky."

Eric followed her eyes to Mei.

"I gave birth to two girls," Ying said. "Mei and her sister. I remember the delivery. I heard them both crying. I could tell that they both were strong. I *know* they were strong. But then they took one away, told me she had died." Ying brushed a tear from her eye. "Someday, Mei will want to be a mother, and when she does … If Mei has twins, I want her to have what I couldn't have, for her own sake and for the twins' sake, because my sister is my …" Her face turned hard, and Eric realized she would say no more.

"I'm sorry," he said.

A silence settled over the bathroom.

For Eric, it was excruciating. Every fiber of him felt they should be fighting to get away. "Why are we waiting? Aren't they going to find us?"

"We are waiting for help. Without it, we'll never make it." Her tone was once again cold. "Do you have any idea what we are up against here?"

Eric had to admit he didn't.

"You are sitting inside an eighty-eight-story underground military complex that contains one of the world's most advanced security systems. The backbone of this system is video surveillance. There are cameras everywhere. And every camera has facial recognition software. That means that everywhere you go, those cameras track you, keeping tabs on you. Along with your chip, they verify your location at all times.

"In addition to the cameras, there are two thousand soldiers housed in this building. But that's just the beginning, because the building itself is inside the Fort Yue Fei military base, which is the size of a small city and has an additional forty thousand military personnel.

"So you see, for us to stand any chance of escaping, we have to have all those cameras shut off and all the soldiers occupied with something that they feel is more important than catching us."

Eric nodded, sobered by the staggering odds against them. Yet it gave him some hope, because the resistance must be a lot larger than he had thought. Ying and her sister were clearly not alone. There must be dozens of conspirators helping them if they hoped to create such a huge diversion.

"How many people are helping us?"

She leveled that fierce stare at him once more, preemptively daring him to question her reply.

"One."

CHAPTER THIRTY-ONE
TRIAL BY FIRE

Tangshan Military Laboratory, China

Fifty-one stories above the bathroom where Eric, Ryan, Mei, and Ying were waiting, a soldier stood in front of his own bathroom mirror. He brought one hand up in front of his face and turned it one way, then the other, inspecting it. Then he squeezed his fingers into a fist. Instantly the cord-like tendons and blue veins rose against the surface of his skin, and a hard ball of muscle emerged at the base of his forearm. He felt the strength, the latent power. He nodded to himself. He knew what these hands could do. These hands had completed basic training, then jump school, then sniper school. He had impressed his instructors—*a gifted soldier, a born killer*—and they had sent him to Chengdu to train in special operations: small-unit skills, sabotage, search and rescue. It was because of these hands that he had graduated second in his class, if only for political reasons. And it was because of these hands that he had been assigned to security at the Tangshan Military Laboratory.

Slowly and methodically, like a pious man performing a sacred ritual, he approached the sink and turned on the faucet. Bracing his hands on both sides of the basin, he ducked his head under the cold water. It spread over his shaved head in rivulets that streamed off his nose and chin. It was frigid cold, but he savored it. It reminded him of his home far away, on the top of the world.

He waited there for many minutes, as if in a meditative trance. Only when he felt the coldness pass all the way down to the tip of his spine did he lift his head.

He took a close look in the mirror, inspecting himself. And for the first time in a long time, what he saw was beautiful. A massive scar ran down one side of his face from hairline to neck. The other side of his face was pink, slick as plastic, as if it had been badly burned. Yet it was still beautiful. Now, at the end, he finally saw it. His face, his body, his mind. It all made sense.

They called him Sòng Píng, but that was not his real name. He was Sonam Paljor, son of Yéshé Dorje of Dagzê in the Nyingchi Prefecture. Member of the Tibetan Resistance. Survivor of six brutal months in the Drapchi Labor Camp. Exiled from his home, smuggled out of the Tibetan Autonomous Region in a logging truck and given sanctuary by Professor Lam. He had been a student at the Southern Xinjiang university, forcibly conscripted into the People's Liberation Army. Brutalized and brainwashed. Fed propaganda and sawdust. And converted into an elite soldier.

A soldier who was about to kill, to go against the teachings of the Buddha. As quintessentially sacrilegious as it was, he knew that it was his destiny. For he knew that *this* was no accident. Karma had brought him here. There was no other way to explain it. It was the pain, the scars, the disfiguration, that had made this incredible stroke of fortune possible. Arriving at the very place where the Chinese had made their genocide virus that wiped out his village and took away the girl he loved most in the world. He understood the statistical *impossibility* of it. No Tibetan in four generations had been given the opportunity that he had right now: the chance to strike at the heart of his enemy.

As he looked at himself, he saw an intensity that was almost unbearable, a history and the weight of an entire race. Behind his eyes roamed the ghosts of 1.2 million dead Tibetans. In him were the skeleton-men who had died of starvation beside him in Drapchi prison. In him were the glassy-eyed supplications of boys and girls used for medical experiments. In him was the humiliation of his tutor, who had struggled under the blackboard of her false crimes. In him were the hundreds of thousands of women subjected to forced sterilization. His own dead mother.

Every brutality and humiliation that his people had suffered was there. Sixty thousand monasteries destroyed, the looting of his country's most precious artifacts, the clear-cutting of its forests. The farce of China's promises of progress, modernization, and equality. And finally, the murder of his beautiful Chodren.

He, Sonam Paljor of Dagzê, was now at the end of that long history. He was the tip of the spear, a spear made of human bone aimed at the enemy's heart.

The sound of the fire alarm jolted him out of his ruminations. He had been expecting it, but it still made his gut tighten with adrenaline.

He picked up the rucksack, heavy with weapons and explosives, and headed for the stairwell.

In the hallway, he saw the other soldiers rushing to and fro, shouting and scrambling to their action stations. He ignored them. White warning lights flashed on the walls, and an alarm made a steady *deedum-deedum* sound that he found almost soothing. It occurred to him that it must have been designed that way, so as not to induce panic.

Opening the stairwell door, he was struck by a terrific roar—the shouting and screaming of thousands of voices rising up from below. From this height, the stairwell appeared bottomless. He could not yet see the mass of humanity making its frantic clamber upward. But they were coming.

It was as just as Hui Lili had promised. Now it was his job to use the chaos of the crowd to fulfill his part of the plan: destroy the Security

Command Center, a heavily armored safe room that was the nerve center for the building's security.

Perched at the back of the building's mezzanine and overlooking its sole entrance, the SCC served as a watchtower to control and scrutinize all who entered the building. It was a shiny metal box, smooth and riveted like the fuselage of a warplane, suspended thirty feet above the floor and designed to repel any assault. It had bulletproof windows thick enough to stop a rocket-propelled grenade, and armored walls as solid as a tank's. It also had three .50-caliber machine-gun turrets. One of these turrets had Sonam particularly worried because it protected the SCC's main door. A door he intended to blow wide open.

The guards inside the SCC watched in horror as the lab's employees poured out of the stairwells and elevators, flooding the floor beneath them and running toward the exit. Some were horribly burned—pink as cherry blossoms, or with charred black skin speckled with white globules of fat, like meat left too long on a fire. People screamed and shoved and trampled one another, knocking over the turnstiles and metal detectors in their desperation to escape. Outside the building entrance, the guards could see a brigade of firefighters trying to get in, but they had little chance against the panic-stricken tide.

The guards watched in awe and confusion. This was far beyond anything they had ever trained for.

So, it was no surprise that they failed to notice the corporal with the scarred face who calmly emerged from the crowd and ascended the metal staircase to the SCC. His mutilated face filled the computer monitor of the corporal nearest the door, but that soldier's eyes were glued on the catastrophe unfolding outside the main window. He did not see the man take a heavy metal disk from his rucksack and place it on the door frame, then slip away, smooth as a cat, over the hand railing and down to the floor below.

★ ★ ★

It was Sonam who had taught Hui Lili how to use the sabot mine that blew the nanosite containment tank. Its impact on the SCC would be similar, only more gruesome. When the tungsten carbide–tipped round atomized the armored plating, it would fling hundreds of bits of metal into the security chamber. This superheated shrapnel would bounce around inside the armored room, unable to escape, piercing and repiercing everything inside.

One second, three soldiers were staring awestruck at the mayhem of the fleeing workers.

BOOM!

The next second, the bulletproof window was washed over with blood.

Sonam scrambled back to the door. There was a smoking black hole the size of his fist near the lock, but the door was still intact. He yanked hard on the handle. It gave, but just barely.

He pulled a grenade from his utility vest, but just as he was about to yank the pin and set the grenade in the hole, he saw the machine gun turret swivel, and the crazed, bloodstained face of Lieutenant Dèng staring down the barrel at him. Sonam spun away just as the machine gun erupted with fire. He half rolled, half fell over the guardrail, landing hard on his side, which knocked the wind out of him. He gasped, tried to breathe, but no air would come in. Bullets zipped past him, a few ricocheting up and into the crowd. A man and then a woman grunted and fell, the high-caliber rounds killing them instantly.

Sonam rolled away, willing his lungs to suck in air, then scrambled to the only place where the machine guns couldn't reach him: directly under the security center. Once he was in its shadow, his diaphragm finally kicked in again. He sat for a moment with his back to a support beam, chest heaving, trying to assess the situation, while the deafening drama of the fleeing workers played out just fifteen feet in front of him. He had to act quickly. Every moment he wasted gave Lieutenant Dèng the chance to call for reinforcements. And every moment the SCC remained operational meant that General Meng could still track the twins.

But he had run out of plan. He looked at the grenade still in his hand and considered just tossing it at the door, but that would never work—it would just come rolling back down the staircase. He looked around desperately, suddenly afraid that his first real military operation would be an unmitigated failure.

Then he noticed a pair of clear plastic pipes that ran into the SCC. It was a vacuum-tube message system like the ones he'd seen at the drive-in banks in Tangshan. It was used to send IDs and other documents from the guards at the main entrance up to the Security Center. Sonam didn't hesitate. He opened the cylindrical carrier, stuffed the grenade in, pulled the pin, and punched—*SEND*.

With a sudden rush of air, the cylinder went up the clear pipe and curved down into the SCC.

Lieutenant Dèng was moving from gun turret to gun turret, trying to find the pig-faced traitor. His head was throbbing and he was covered in blood, but he realized that most of it was not his. He was hurt, but for the moment, his fury was greater than his pain. He would kill the *hàn jiān*, even if it was his last act on earth. Then he heard a sound that he heard at least two hundred times a day: the pneumatic suck of a message tube arriving. He frowned in puzzlement. The cylinder slid into its receptacle, and a little door slid open, inviting him to take it. He stepped forward to inspect it and gasped.

The muffled blast sent an arc of shrapnel into the large bulletproof window, bulging it outward.

Sonam raced back up the staircase and placed another grenade in the door, pulled the pin, then vaulted over the railing once more. Another blast. He pounded up the stairs. Amazingly, the door still hung on by its lock, but luckily the hinges had been rattled off. He squeezed through the gap and was finally inside.

His first priority was to shut down all the video cameras. He moved quickly, trying to ignore the blood and gore that covered every surface and dripped from the ceiling. Finding the long bank of control switches, he killed the cameras.

Next, he ordered a full evacuation of the building. A recorded voice told all personnel, including all military personnel, to leave the building immediately. Then he killed the elevators. After that, he found a computer that still worked, and pulled up the employee chip-tracking program. He found Meng's ID tag down in the Great Lab and deduced which stairwell he would have to use to get to the surface. Then he shut down that program, too. Now the twins and the Americans were invisible and could go where they wished.

He took a deep breath. With the core of his mission accomplished, he pulled out a phone. He had prepared two texts that could be sent quickly, even audibly, if necessary: *Done* and *Fail*. He selected *Done* and hit send. When he was sure the message had gone through, he killed the boosters that carried the cellular signals from deep within the underground complex to the surface. Zero bars for everyone.

Next, he pulled his commando knife from its sheath and unplugged and cut the power cables to all the vital equipment in the room.

Now it was time to leave. There was nothing left to do here. He was content that he had done his job. He had survived his first combat experience.

Tibet was not a nation of warriors, but that had not always been the case. Once, before it took the nonviolent path, Tibet had been home to the greatest warriors in Asia. They commanded a vast empire that spread from Afghanistan to deep inside modern-day China. At this moment, Sonam felt a link to those warriors a thousand years forgotten—as if he had been born not from modern Tibet, but from that proud race that would use violence to defend itself.

He knew what he was *supposed* to do now, what he had promised Hui Ying he would do as soon as he had destroyed the command center: get out. Melt into the panicked crowd and escape. But he also knew he couldn't do that.

Fleeing was not what fate intended for him. His destiny was to find Meng and kill him in the name of all Tibet.

CHAPTER THIRTY-TWO

TAKEOFF

Andrews Air Force Base, Prince George's County, MD

A cold night rain had turned the tarmac into a polished black opal that caught and refracted the red and blue landing lights in long diagonal sheets.

In the darkness, five men with heavy rucksacks walked toward the lowered gangway of a white Gulfstream G650.

The last man, Patel, the sharpshooter, heard her coming. She was running, panting as if she had been running for miles. Steam rose from her head and neck.

"Curtiss!" she screamed.

"*Hunter?* What the hell are you doing here?"

"I'm coming with you."

"My ass you are. Patel, get rid of her."

Patel set down his bag and moved to grab her. It should have been an easy thing, a Navy SEAL subduing an exhausted civilian woman. But he made a critical mistake. He treated her as if she were a typical 135-pound woman.

As he made a lazy grab for her shoulder, she used his momentum, grabbing his wrist with one hand and pulling herself into him while simultaneously ramming her other elbow up under his jaw. His teeth smacked together with the sound of someone cracking a walnut. Patel collapsed to the tarmac, out cold.

A split second passed in which nothing happened, the other SEALs not believing their eyes. Then they rushed her. She got in an elbow and one good groin kick before they pinned her down.

She shrieked in fury, struggling with every bit of strength she had, the veins in her neck and forehead bulging purple against her skin. "I want them back! I want them back! I WANT THEM BACK!"

Curtiss stood over her, watching the incredible energy pour out of her. It literally took three men to keep her down. *This one would have made one hell of a soldier,* he thought. "Hunter, I swear, the only thing that's keeping me from putting a bullet in that thick skull of yours right now is your old man. If it weren't for him, I'd do it."

"Fuck you, Curtiss. Fuck you and your damn secrets. How dare you play with people's lives like this! You let me believe they were coming back, that they were safe. But you have no idea if they're safe or not. You don't even know if they're alive!"

Curtiss didn't answer. He just looked away, furious at being caught in a lie.

"God damn it, I'm coming with you!" she screamed.

Curtiss shook his head. "You're staying right here. Boys, get her over to the MP station. We have a plane to catch."

They picked her up.

"I WANT THEM BACK!" She kept screaming it. "I WANT THEM BACK!"

Curtiss shook his head in disbelief. She was relentless. It reminded him of his sons, when they were three and four years old, demanding something over and over again. Throwing tantrums. Indefatigably stubborn. It was pathetic. Yet, being a father, he knew it was sincere emotion. It really was that important to her.

Curtiss looked up at the night sky. "God damn it! Belay that order."

His men relaxed their grip and she shook them off. He walked up to her, hooked his hand around her head, grabbing a thick shock of her blond hair and pulling her in until their foreheads met. "I'm risking my clearance bringing you with me, you understand? If anything that you see or hear in the next twenty-four hours leaves your lips, I'll make sure your life comes to an abrupt end. Are we clear?"

Jane nodded, giving him her fiercest look, but Curtiss could tell she was grinning inside.

"Get on the fucking plane."

CHAPTER THIRTY-THREE

MENG

Tangshan Military Laboratory, China

"You can relax, General, we have them," Captain Xi said. "There's no way they can escape."

Meng grimaced. It was tempting to believe that everything was under control. They had captured one of the twins, and they could take their time tracking down the others. Even if they somehow reached the surface, they would still be confined to the base. But he didn't like it.

"No," he said. "These were two of my smartest scientists. They would have thought it through. Perhaps they hope to disguise themselves …"

The captain shook his head. "But they have the girl; they will be easy to spot."

Just then the soothing *deedum-deedum* of the fire alarm was replaced by a more urgent *beeooooooo-beeooooooo-beeooooooo* sound, and the strobe lights that had been flashing white were now flashing red. An automated voice came over the intercom: *"Warning, warning. A general evacuation order has been given. All civilian and military personnel must leave the complex immediately. Repeat, all civilian and military personnel must leave the complex immediately. Please proceed to the nearest exit."*

General Meng turned white with rage. "Who gave that order without my authorization?" Then he realized what it meant. There was yet another traitor, and perhaps more than one. He was beginning to see what the twins had planned. A general evacuation order would allow all the employees to leave the base unfettered. He had to stop it. He opened his cell phone and tried to contact the command center. No signal. A fresh chill went through him. First an evacuation order, now the cell phone boosters. He pulled out his iSheet and tried the tracking program. It, too, was down. That meant the SCC had been compromised. It was worse than he had thought, much worse. He glanced at his watch. The vice president would be here in an hour to celebrate the victory of achieving replication. The thought made him ill.

"We have to get word to the main gate," he said. "No one can leave the base. I'm taking these men up there. You, gather as many men as you can, and start sweeping every floor, every room, every closet, for Hui and the Americans. Find them!"

CHAPTER THIRTY-FOUR

"TURN AWAY."

Tangshan Military Laboratory, China

In the bathroom on sublevel fifty-four, the vibrating iSheet made all of them start. Ying fumbled frantically for it. Suddenly, the light of the screen bathed her face in blue light. Then she dropped it and threw her head back, covering her mouth. Eric heard a gasp, like the beginning of tears. He exchanged a glance with Ryan. *He didn't do it.*

But it wasn't that.

"He's still alive," she breathed with palpable relief. "Thank God, he's still alive." She picked up the iSheet and typed a reply: *Now get out as fast as you can.*

She hit send.

Unable to send message. Please try again later.

She snarled at the screen and tried again.

Unable to send message. Please try again later.

She slammed the iSheet down on the floor.

"Did he do it?" Eric asked.

She nodded faintly, as if her mind were somewhere far away. But quickly the old Ying returned. "Get up," she ordered. "We're going."

★ ★ ★

They found an auxiliary staircase, dusty from disuse, and began climbing. Up and up they went, all the way to sublevel forty-four. Here, everything was under construction: hard concrete floor, open wiring, galvanized ventilation ducts. They jogged down the unfinished corridors, passing stacks of drywall, a table saw, tools, and hard hats. They stayed close together, Hui pulling Mei's hand while Ryan and Eric followed behind.

Suddenly, Hui took a turn and stopped. It was a dead end.

The normally reserved woman swore. "Where is it?" she said. "We must be on the wrong floor. Come on, we have to hurry."

They began to retrace their steps. Jogging faster now, but just as they rounded the last corner before the stairs, they skidded to a halt, five feet from a soldier with a Kalashnikov at his shoulder. He had been waiting for them.

Without a word he opened fire, the muzzle blazing like a blowtorch.

With nowhere to run, the four of them cowered where they stood. Mei screamed, Ryan yelped, and Eric made a childish cry. Just the noise of the rifle was terrifying, the deafening blasts interspersed with a high-pitched whizzing as the bullets came in.

Then it stopped. For a moment, they all stared at one another, caught in a moment of collective disbelief.

Then Eric remembered himself and rushed the soldier.

The man considered reloading, gave up on the idea, and pulled his sidearm.

Eric flinched at the first shot, but now his confidence was growing. He could finally do what he hadn't managed with Brock O'Lane. The pistol sounded again, but this time there was no muzzle flash. The pistol itself was now inside Eric's sphere of protection.

The soldier kept pulling the trigger. He could not let go of the idea that the pistol wasn't working. And that made it easier for Eric to take it away. He grabbed the soldier's wrist with one hand and the gun with the other, twisting the barrel up and out. The gun came free, and the man stumbled to one knee.

Eric put the barrel against the man's temple.

He knew he couldn't let him go. He would bring others. So he squeezed his face up and tried to pull the trigger, but his finger wouldn't comply.

Then Hui Ying was beside him, pulling a spare clip from the soldier's belt and reloading the Kalashnikov. She shouted something to Mei, and the little girl turned her head away and covered her ears.

At the same time, the soldier said something to Hui, a desperate supplication.

The Kalashnikov went off, somehow louder than all the other shots Eric had heard that day.

They left the body, blood still running out of the head and fanning out on the concrete floor.

CHAPTER THIRTY-FIVE

BARDO

Tangshan Military Laboratory, China

General Meng and eight of his men moved steadily up the stairs. They had jogged the first twenty flights, but now they were walking, thighs burning. Sixteen stories to go.

There was blood on the stairs, heavy in some spots. There were other things, too: handbags, crushed cell phones, shoes, a handful of documents, all left by the frantic stampede of people that had fled up these steps just twenty minutes ago.

This was what the vice president and his entourage would see when they insisted, against Meng's protestations, that they be allowed to see the damage for themselves.

His anger rose at the thought. He could hear the vice president already. "Saboteurs? How could you let this happen?"

It was not an easy question to answer.

He had been outwitted by two female scientists. And what of the others? There must be more. To take down the SCC would require more than one or two men. He could be up against a whole platoon. But who? Who had betrayed him?

They heard the rapid footfalls of someone coming down the steps. A lone soldier appeared at the top of the next landing. Everyone froze in a moment of mutual surprise.

General Meng remembered the man—not his name, but his face. Badly burned on one side, cut and scarred along the other. Meng remembered their first meeting: on the parade grounds, just a few months ago, on a frigid morning just before dawn. It had been the corporal's first day. And Meng remembered how his eyes had locked with the new recruit's, and how he, a general, had suddenly looked away, unable to hold the soldier's gaze. But it wasn't the scars and the burns that had done it. It was the eyes. They had unsettled him, for he could have sworn he recognized them from somewhere. Something about the man struck a chord of memory.

Sonam had to act fast. He had already made a crucial mistake, rushing down the stairs too quickly, not imagining that Meng could have made it so far, so fast. Yet here he was. Sonam had to think. He realized he still had the element of surprise. Sonam knew that the general was his enemy, but the general didn't know that Sonam was his. He could still do this.

They were separated by one flight of stairs. Could he shoot him from here? No. His rifle was strapped to his shoulder and would take too long to slip off and fire. He would have to get closer; use the pistol. Yes, and in that idea came another realization. He was going to die here, one way or another. It was now a suicide mission.

"Well, don't just stand there like an idiot," Meng said. "Report!"

"Sir, yes sir," Sonam said. "General, thank goodness I found you! There are traitors, sir. They are our own soldiers." He brought his thumb and fingertip to his nose in an expression of horror and disbelief. "At least four of them, sir. I saw them in the mezzanine; they destroyed the command center." At that moment, as if suddenly remembering protocol, he saluted and descended the stairs to them. Now he was just a few feet away. "Sir, one of the traitors was Lieutenant Wei."

"*Wei*?" Meng said. The other men began to murmur. Sonam prayed his ruse would work. Meng probably suspected a small band of soldiers, manipulated by a charismatic officer. Wei was certainly charismatic enough, but he was also one of the general's most decorated officers.

Sonam could feel Meng studying him. Sonam's beret was missing, and he was disheveled and dirty. He had four grenades attached to his vest, his pistol strap hung open, and the hammer of his Type 54 was back as if it had been fired.

"Go on!" Meng snapped, casually placing his hand on the hilt of his pistol.

Sonam took another step forward and saluted again. He was now only four feet away. "General, I formed up with my unit after the fire alarm sounded. When we reached the mezzanine, we found the SCC already destroyed." Sonam realized his mistake immediately. (How did he know that Wei was the traitor if the assault on the SCC was over when they got there?) But Meng gave no sign of catching it, so he went on. "It was terrible, sir." He made his voice crack for effect. "They slaughtered five men. The blood was …" He bowed his head in shock.

That was when he went for his pistol, intending to tuck it under the general's chin, the better to give the bullet a bone-free path to his brain.

Quick as cat, Meng swatted Sonam's hand away. Sonam didn't lose the pistol, but the bullet fired wild, making a queer twang as it ricocheted around the stairwell.

Instead of fighting the momentum of the blow to his arm, Sonam spun with it, creating space to fire while keeping himself out of hand-to-hand combat range. He came full around and fired. He fired four or five shots while he retreated up the stairwell. Two other soldiers doubled up in pain, but he somehow missed Meng.

Meng was first to return fire. He drew and shot from the hip, but his shots went wide. They were only eight feet apart, but they kept missing. Sonam tried to concentrate and fired again. Meng spun, gripping his shoulder and letting out a furious howl.

But Sonam knew it was not a killing blow. He wanted to press his advantage, to take more careful aim, but there was too much motion now, guns coming out, and Meng was quickly swallowed up by the other men. Sonam fired three more shots. He struck the man in front of Meng full in the chest, but it did not appear that the round pierced through. Then four pistols were firing at him in the enclosed space. He ran up the staircase, still firing from under his left armpit, his advantage of surprise wasted.

As the traitor scrambled away, Meng emerged from the cluster of men and took careful aim. By stepping around the railing, he was able to get a clear shot as his target turned up the next flight of stairs. He aimed for center mass.

BANG!

The footsteps continued, then slowed. Meng had hit him.

He held up his hand to quiet his men. One was dead; two were moaning in pain. "*Bì zuǐ!*" he commanded. Between a few threats and the covering of their mouths, it grew quiet. He heard the unsteady rhythm of the traitor's footsteps. Then they stopped.

One of his men whispered, "Shall I finish him off, General?"

Time was of the essence. Meng had to get topside and stop the evacuation of the base. Yet, if he had hit a kidney or the vena cava, the man could be unconscious in just a few minutes.

Meng called out, "If you surrender, I will let you live. But we will have to act quickly to stop the bleeding."

He heard the frustrated growl of a man faced with a terrible decision. "Do you swear?"

"*Wǒ fāshì tiāntáng,*" Meng said. *I swear to heaven.*

He heard a heavy sigh.

"I accept. Please hurry."

He sent two of his remaining men up the stairs, pistols drawn. Two rifle cracks resonated through the stairwell, and the bodies of his men came tumbling down the stairs.

Meng gave a cry of fury. "I'll tie you up and cut you for a week!"

The reply shocked him—not so much the words, but the language they were spoken in. "Not if I kill you first, you pig of a Han." It was the language of the barbarians who had killed his first wife and daughter. Now he understood. The thing about the soldier that had seemed oddly familiar. Through some fantastic series of improbabilities, a Tibetan had infiltrated the PLA. They had invited a weasel into the henhouse.

It was all too much. He looked at the two dead bodies on the landing. He thought of the treasonous twins and the Americans making their escape, and of all the dead bodies that littered the Great Lab. And on the very day that was supposed to be a celebration! Suddenly, the fury was so great, he could barely think. His chest heaved and he snorted through his nostrils like an enraged bull. All he wanted was to race up those stairs and kill the traitor with his bare hands, to take out his frustrations on a living human being.

But then he realized that his emotions were getting the better of him. Consuming him. He tried to remember his training, to think with a tactical mind. *Breathe. Control yourself.* He waited a moment, then another, until his breathing slowed.

He assessed the situation. The traitor controlled the stairwell. He had a QBZ-95 rifle, a pistol, and at least two grenades, whereas he and his men had only pistols. The traitor had the superior position and superior weaponry.

But there were two stairwells to the surface. He could easily go up another way, then send half a company down to pinch this man off. It was the smartest thing to do, yet he resisted it. He still yearned to kill the traitor himself.

No, he told himself. He was still wrestling with the decision when the first grenade made it for him. It bounced over the two corpses and hopped down the steps toward them. The men who were quickest leaped down the next flight of stairs, General Meng among them. The two wounded men didn't have a chance. One lived long enough to scream.

★ ★ ★

Sonam listened as Meng gave another bellow of rage. Then he heard more footfalls, receding down the stairwell. A door opening. They would try to cut him off now. Leaving a few men below, while the others came from above. He nodded his head in sad acceptance. He had lost his chance to kill Meng.

But just in case he was still there, Sonam took another grenade from his vest, pulled the pin, counted to two, and dropped it down the center of the stairwell.

He heard cries of alarm. But it fell too far.

He pulled the pin on his last grenade. This time, he counted to three. He considered just keeping it, but he finally let go.

After the explosion, he was rewarded with screams of pain, but they were young voices, not the deep growl of the general.

He tried to stand, then tried to crawl farther up the steps, but he couldn't. He had lost too much blood. At the rate the blood was spreading across the floor, he would be lucky to last another five minutes.

He had never imagined that he would die in a place like this, in a cold, sterile stairwell so far from the plateau. But he had done well, even if he hadn't killed Meng. He had given the twins all they asked of him and more. Most importantly, he was going to die a warrior's death. Chodren would be proud of him. It was she, his tiger-eyed love, who had convinced him to join the resistance. She had awakened the warrior inside him. And with this death, he would avoid the lifetime of humiliations that his people suffered. He would never again be sent to a prison, starved, enslaved. His children would never be forced to attend Chinese schools or be beaten for practicing their own religion. For this much, he was content.

Oṃ maṇi padme hūṃ.

It was time to depart. He felt a tingle and ache in his arms and legs, as if he had slept on them wrong and constricted the blood. But he knew that the blood flow wasn't constricted; it simply wasn't there.

Oṃ maṇi padme hūṃ.

He had stayed awake last night, wondering what sort of body he would inhabit in the next life. There would be no nirvana for him. The cycle of *saṃsāra*, the wheel of suffering, would continue. Yet he hoped there might be a balance for him, that some of the things he had done might be forgiven and that some of his suffering in this life might earn him good karma in the next.

Oṃ maṇi padme hūṃ.

He would soon enter bardo—the final test. He would need to be at peace when he entered, so that a lama would appear to guide him, so that in his rebirth he might find his Chodren. So he tried to shut out the pain. He tried not to be afraid. He tried to think only of peace.

Oṃ maṇi padme hūṃ.

He thought of the happy moments. A boy, playing with his dogs in the snow. Laughing with Chodren in one of their rare moments of solitude, chest to chest, hidden away from the world. The professor and his wonderful food, the night he had playfully tapped Sonam's leg and said, "I knew it; it's hollow!" And finally, he thought of the night along the river when he and Hui Ying had shared their secrets, and how she had gently touched his face and smiled.

Zhi-bde. Peace.

He focused all his energy. Calm. Peace. *Zhi-bde*. Sleep. His beautiful Chodren. Forty-nine days in bardo. Forty-nine days until his rebirth. He must be serene if he hoped to awaken close to her.

CHAPTER THIRTY-SIX

UNDERWORLD

Tangshan Military Laboratory, China

They were on sublevel forty-four. Hui Ying led the way with the Kalashnikov, then Ryan, and finally Eric and Mei. Here, too, the space was unfinished, filled with construction materials and the smell of pine two-by-fours. But this level went out farther than the others. It appeared that the Chinese had been tunneling out horizontally. The farther they went, the rougher their surroundings became. The tile floor became dusty concrete, and bare drywall gave way to steel and aluminum framing. Massive concrete pillars gave way to a forest of thin metal supports.

Ying guided them to what looked like an exterior wall. They jogged along it for a while under a string of yellow halogen construction lights, until they came to long sheet of silvery plastic with a red-and-yellow sign that seemed to warn, *do not enter.*

Ying took out a pocketknife and cut a long strip through the plastic, then stepped through.

There, inside, was the oddest thing. A massive slab of black rock. Just to see it, to let light fall on it, felt like an intrusion on its dark slumber. It had clearly lain undisturbed here since the world was young.

Ying unshouldered her backpack and took out four headlamps and handed them out. Eric flicked his on and noticed a small metal door with a padlock—shiny and small against the ancient rock. The door was no more than a foot and a half square and looked as if it had been hastily mounted.

"They stumbled on it when they were extending this level," Ying said.

"Stumbled on what?" Eric asked.

Instead of answering, she took some bolt cutters and popped off the padlock. Then Ryan opened the tiny door and stuck his head in. "Hmmm. I really hope you fit, Hill." Eric got down to look. It was a narrow tunnel, no wider than the opening, bored right through the bedrock. He was the biggest of them, and as he knelt down and looked at the long narrow tunnel, he wasn't sure he would fit.

He leaned back on his heels and looked at Mei. "I'd better go last. That way, if I get stuck, I won't hold you back."

Hui Ying gave a quick nod, stuffed the backpack into the tunnel, and crawled in after it. Then Mei, Ryan, and finally Eric. He had to squeeze his shoulders in tight, and his arms were all but useless. He could propel himself only by shifting his knees and feet, and once his feet were all the way in, he got stuck. It was a terrifying moment of claustrophobia before he managed to shift his shoulder and inch forward. The cold, unyielding rock on every side and the millions of tons more that lay above him. Half panicked, he pushed and squirmed, ripping the knees of his pants, feeling the cuts and scrapes, but not caring, just desperate to get out.

After several minutes' struggle, his left shoulder no longer felt rough stone against it. Then his other shoulder was free, and he scrambled out, breathing fast and heavy. He stood in a small chamber with a cobblestone floor. In the center was a round pit like an old well. He looked over the lip and saw an open shaft with metal handrails drilled into the rock. Hui and Mei were already halfway down, their headlamp beams dancing around the circular walls.

"Watch your grip," Ryan said. "The rungs are at least seventy years old and rusty."

As if on cue, they heard Mei cry out, "Ouch!"

Ryan went next, and Eric followed him into the darkness.

Soon they all were standing together in a tunnel with an arched ceiling. Between Eric's feet were the remnants of a narrow-gauge railroad track. On the ceiling, he could see old light fixtures, like upside-down woks, strung together with frayed cloth-insulated wires.

The tunnel appeared to go on forever in both directions, a fact reinforced when Eric opened his mouth and his words seemed to run off endlessly down the long passages.

"What is this place?"

Ying's reply came in a whisper: "It was built by the Germans in the 1920s, when they controlled Tangshan. It was used to connect the forts and bunkers that protected the city. After the Japanese took over in the late thirties, they must have expanded it. No one knew that the tunnels reached this far into the city until some workers discovered this shaft last month." She motioned upward. "Come on—no time to talk now."

She led them down one of the passages at a cautious jog. Debris was strewn everywhere: railroad ties, ammunition boxes, fallen rock, and, occasionally, rusted World War II–era bicycles, which the soldiers must have used to move quickly through the tunnels. It was damp and misty. A layer of fog rose up to their knees and came aglow whenever their headlamp beams passed over it. Occasionally, the tunnel split or intersected with another, and here there were signs on the walls—most in Japanese, but a few in German—giving directions or marking distance.

The tightness of the tunnel and the way it conducted sound was unnerving. Everything echoed: their jogging footsteps, the clatter of a kicked rock, even their panting breath. Now and then, one of them would stop and shush the others. Then they would hurriedly extinguish their lights and wait, listening as hard as they could in the darkness, trying to soften their panting and the pounding of their hearts. Eric would stand with the pistol he had taken from the guard, and Ying with her rifle. Waiting. Trembling. Only when the silence was certain would they lower their weapons and move on.

Ying had tasked Eric with protecting Mei, and he realized it was a blessing. Focusing on her meant he had less time to be afraid for himself.

After they had jogged for a half hour—over two kilometers, according to the markers—they began to hear a sound like a light wind through trees. It grew steadily louder and louder until they all recognized it: *water.*

Soon they stood on a bridge with a river flowing under them.

From then on, they followed the river. Sometimes on their left, sometimes on their right. While the river snaked through the rock, the tunnel and rail line ran true, crossing over the river again and again. Now and then a wall would fall away and the river would be there again. Eric found it reassuring. The river knew the way out.

At a diamond intersection, Ying paused and studied the signs, wiping rust from one of the markers; then she motioned toward the left passage. "If we go that way for a half mile, we'll be under Longze Road."

"Thank God," Eric said, "I've had enough of this place."

But she shook her head. "We can't go that way."

"Why not?"

"If Meng suspects we are in the tunnels, that's where he'll be waiting for us. We have to go another way—a way he doesn't know."

So they pushed on. Another hour passed, and still no sign of pursuit. They were beginning to feel that they could make it.

Just as the endless tunnels were beginning to make them claustrophobic, the beams of their headlamps suddenly leaped outward in every direction, like searchlights in the night. They strained to see the ceiling but couldn't. The tips of the lowest stalactites were two hundred feet up, while the true ceiling was lost in the shadows of the massive cones that hung like inverted cathedral spires.

The sudden beauty was astounding, the colors otherworldly:

turquoise, emerald, garish red, and white, white, white. Many of the formations were huge, dripping columns of calcified white, built up in defined layers, like enormous wedding cakes. Another wall was a massive row of thin cylinders that reminded him of the pipes of a cathedral organ. Another was like a huge frozen waterfall of flowstone, a hundred feet high. Eric felt as if he were inside a body, amid the connective tissue and fibrous membranes that held the world's organs in place.

They passed over natural bridges, under stone arches, and along deep pits that dropped away in impenetrable darkness.

It was then that Eric's headlamp beam picked up something else, hanging from the ceiling in thick black bushels. Thousands upon thousands of them, chittering and squeaking like mice.

"Look," he said.

Mei clutched at her mother when she realized what they were.

"Don't be afraid," Eric said. "They won't bother us. Besides, it's a good sign. It means there must be an opening close by."

"We still have a long way to go," Ying said, "and we are going out a very different way than they are."

"What does that mean?" Eric asked.

"I don't want to spoil the surprise." It was the closest thing to playfulness Eric had heard from her all day.

"They're at the West Gate now, General," the lieutenant said.

Meng nodded. That meant the vice president's motorcade would be here in less than ten minutes. He straightened his uniform and checked his cuffs. The wound in his shoulder was still bleeding, but he had refused the doctor's advice to put it in a sling. He would not meet the vice president so visibly wounded.

It was going to be enough of a humiliating experience already. Meng knew that the next few hours were critical. If he handled it just right, he might survive. A quick resolution—capture of the traitors combined with the continued success of the project—would mean forgiveness. A second chance in a system where second chances were exceedingly rare.

Truth be told, he was beginning to breathe a little easier. The body of the Tibetan had been found, and he appeared to be the only saboteur. They had also managed to put out the fire, and much of the sabotage had already been fixed: the cell phone boosters were working again, which meant that his communication network was intact. While a large section of the Great Lab had been destroyed, there were other facilities around the base. Within a few hours, they hoped to send some of the employees back to work.

Most importantly, the chip-tracking program was up and running. He could see Hui and the Americans now on his iSheet. Somehow, they had gotten off base. He didn't know how, but it didn't matter. Captain Xi had sent four squads to hunt them down. It wouldn't take long now.

He took in the scene before him: It was a beautiful spring day, but the lawn in front of him was filled with thousands of battered and confused employees. A dozen ambulances with flashing blue lights sat clustered around the main entrance, paramedics in blue uniforms tending to those with minor injuries. The seriously injured had already been taken to the infirmary or to the city hospitals.

He spotted the motorcade, almost a kilometer away, wending its way past the School of Infantry.

"My General!"

Meng turned to see Captain Xi rushing toward him, waving an iSheet in one hand. "Sir, we have them!"

"Where?"

"Here!" He showed Meng a map and pointed with his finger. "Our men will catch up with them in a matter of minutes. It appears to be the water treatment plant."

"You fool!" He grabbed the iSheet and crumpled it in his hands. "I should have known it was too easy. *Jiàn guǐ!*" he cursed. "Search the base! I want everyone looking for them. I don't care if it's a colonel or a secretary; everyone joins in."

He spat. They could be anywhere by now. It suddenly felt hopeless.

Then a fresh idea came into his mind. "Wait!" Perhaps it was not so complicated after all. Every lie had its seed of truth, didn't it?

He spread out the crumpled iSheet and began to work the screen. A few touches, and he had what he wanted: a map of the complex that showed a string of four lines. It was the tracking program, modified to show just the twins and the Americans, tracing their paths for the past six hours. He could see where the twins' chips had diverged in the Great Lab at 8:43 this morning, just before the explosion.

He squinted at the screen. "What does this mean?" he asked Captain Xi.

The man looked at the readout and, with a few touches, changed the view from overhead to horizontal. Then Meng understood. Hui Ying and the Americans had not gone up the staircase with the others. They had gone *down,* to level sixty-four. That was where the chips left the building through the plumbing pipes.

Why did you go down when everyone else went up? You couldn't get out that way … He zoomed in on the spot where the three chips must have entered the sewer. He saw another tracking tag there. *Who is this?* He followed the chip's path up to the new drilling on level forty-four. But they couldn't get out that way …

"The old tunnel system!" he exclaimed. He looked at his watch, calculating how much of a head start they had. There was still time.

"Get to the Longze Road entrance as fast as you can."

"Yes sir." The captain snapped to attention and turned on his heel.

They found the dead men at the edge of the great cavern, inside a long drape of ancient stone that folded and bent like an undulating curtain.

The space felt hallowed, like a sealed crypt, and just to look on the bodies left them with the feeling that they were trespassing.

There were twenty-one of them, spaced in four neat rows of five, with one man at the front of the formation. The uniformity was striking. Each man had died on his knees, shirtless, his legs wrapped in a girdle or skirt. In front of each man was a small wooden block with a knife on it.

The lone body at the front of the formation appeared to be the leader. He was the only one whose head was still attached to his body. It was he who had decapitated each of his own men, one by one, after they ritually disemboweled themselves. Then he must have meticulously cleaned each knife and returned it to the block. Finally, when every man had died preserving his honor, the commander had assumed his spot at the head of the column and disemboweled himself.

It was a moment of history frozen in time. August 1945. Japan surrenders after Hiroshima and then Nagasaki are bombed. A final cadre of Japanese soldiers who had decided not to return home (or were unable). So instead of letting themselves be taken by the Chinese— to be humiliated, starved, and tortured—they had come here, to this forgotten cave. To die with honor, like true Bushido warriors.

Eric walked among the bodies. Some had ribs protruding through leathery, mummified skin. Others were only skeletons. Beside some of the bodies were odd artifacts: poetry, letters, and stained photographs. Most of the photos were black and indiscernible, but one, set on its edge, had the black and white image of a smiling woman with a little girl in her arms.

"Come on," Ying called. "No time for sightseeing."

Eric nodded and followed them down the winding path. But the sight of the dead soldiers had left him feeling strange. There was a sense of tragedy about them, yet his sympathy did not run deep. World War II was the darkest time in human history, when the most inhuman atrocities were inflicted on the weak and defenseless. Among all those countless horrors, many of the most grotesque had been committed by the Japanese against the Chinese.

Yet there was something about the dead men's resolve that resonated with him. They had decided to die rather than be taken by the enemy. After his captivity, it was a sentiment he understood.

They pushed on for another kilometer and then another. It felt as if they had been jogging all day. They were tired, thirsty, and hungry. Eric's muscles ached and his lungs burned, sick of the damp air. He put his hand on his chest. Would this tunnel ever end?

It was at that very moment that Ryan stopped them: "Hear that?"

They all quickly extinguished their lamps and stood as motionless as possible, trying to calm their hearts, trying to listen, straining to hear over the rush of the river.

It was only then, with the sudden return of his fear, that Eric realized how safe he had begun to feel. He had come to believe that they really had made their escape.

He was just about to tell them it was nothing, when they heard the unmistakable clatter of a kicked rock, followed by the clapping of boots on stone. Eric tried to swallow, but his mouth was too dry.

"How?" Ryan said. "It's not possible."

Mei began to whimper with fear. "No, *Māmā,* please."

"Come on!" Ying said. "We can still make it!"

CHAPTER THIRTY-SEVEN
LOSING CONTROL

Naval Research Laboratory, Washington, DC

Bill Eastman couldn't sleep. In the middle of the night, he had awoken with the overpowering feeling that something was very wrong. The feeling had been growing inside him for months now, as his control over the replication project—his project—slipped from his grasp.

Outside his bedroom window, a storm was brewing. On the ceiling, he watched the shadows of tree branches as they were buffeted and twisted by the wind outside. How had he gotten here? How had he lost control?

He had given Curtiss the most versatile tool ever created, a tool that could revolutionize the entire military arsenal of the United States. Of course, everyone wanted a piece of it. The navy, army, air force, CIA, NSA, DARPA—they had descended on the lab and were using his masterpiece to go off in a thousand different directions. And he, Bill Eastman, the man who made it all possible, had no control over any of it.

But he'd known that this could happen, hadn't he? He'd known that this would be the dangerous time—after replication—when his goals and the Pentagon's diverged. But he had never imagined it would happen so fast.

Now he realized that the problem was forced evolution. He had never predicted that they would have a tool like this at their disposal. It was accelerating everything as its artificial intelligence component did all the heavy lifting for the engineers. Breakthroughs that would normally have taken years were being made in a matter of weeks. He had clearly misjudged its power. They were using it to change everything, from the hulls of submarines to camouflage and stealth technology, to finding pathogens in the body. Day after day, as he monitored each advance, he was becoming increasingly worried that someone might use forced evolution in the wrong way—that someone might ask it to do something terrible.

And as he lay there listening to the approaching thunder, he had a new fear: that perhaps someone already had.

He tossed the sheets aside, got out of bed, and went to his computer.

We're probably safe. It's really much too soon to have a terrorist on our hands.

That was what he had told Eric Hill the night Eric returned from the FBI with his wild story about a robber using assemblers. Now he wondered if perhaps he had misjudged Hill, that in the young man's feverish excitement, he had seen only an inexperienced boy rather than the brilliant young scientist he really was. In fact, he had never even looked at the footage from that night, even though Admiral Curtiss had given it to him. He had had so many things to do, and when Curtiss's men found nothing, he had let himself forget about it.

It took him only a moment to find the footage. As soon as it began, he found himself leaning closer to the monitor, squinting, trying to make sense of what he was seeing. How strange—the man, the coat, the way he moved. Eastman instantly understood why Eric had been so disturbed by it. There was something wrong with this man. He was somehow malformed, though Eastman was at a loss to say in what way.

He watched the tape over and over again. Each time, he tried to convince himself that it was nothing, *just a strange man in a coat.* Yet each time, the sickening flutter in his stomach got worse. And each time the video ended, he found himself hitting play again.

It was only ninety seconds of footage, but an hour had passed and he was still enthralled by it. He began dissecting it with imaging software: zooming in, capturing frames, enlarging them. There must be something here! Some proof! He parsed through every moment: as the dark figure glided across the floor; as Williams, the security guard, woke and drew his gun; as the weapon shook in his hand. Then Williams collapsing, so suddenly and irrevocably dead. So fast. His head smacking the desk.

A stroke at precisely that moment. What were the chances?

Yes, now he was beginning to see it as Eric had seen it. As someone who understood what assemblers could do. But the proof he was looking for still eluded him.

Finally, he got an idea. The eyes. They seemed to be the key to the man's deformity. He took a screen shot of the eye, blew it up, then advanced the footage a few frames and did it again. As he zoomed in, the eye became a bunch of fat pixels, just blocks of color. Tan skin, black eyelash, green iris. But in the ninth image that he augmented, the eye was no longer green, but blue.

Eastman sat back and rubbed his chin. How was that possible? He began the process again. Advanced a frame, cut out the eye, pasted it in the photo editor, and expanded it. Green. He did it again: green. Green. Green. Green. Green. Green. Green. Green. Then a millisecond of blue. Then green again.

With a mixture of both excitement and shock, he understood how perfect a word *malformed* was. The man was mal-formed. He had been made wrong. This was not his real face. Another face was hidden underneath.

But then, that must mean …

The rush of adrenaline brought a sickening warmth to his whole body.

Someone has betrayed us, he thought.

Because no single person, no matter how brilliant, could have done this alone. This ... this *thing* had help from someone within the NRL. That was the only way it was possible. Just as he was seeing forced evolution geometrically accelerate their progress in the wake of replication, he knew that it was the only way this creature could have been born. Only with forced evolution—and the right combination of genius and recklessness—could he have become so powerful so quickly. That was the terrible power of Eric's invention. All you had to do was give the nanosites a goal, and they would get there. Somehow, they would get there. And this person had been willing to saturate his own body, to let them meld with his mind and change him at the molecular level, so that he would have the power to change his appearance and kill with a thought.

But who was he, and what were his plans? And perhaps more importantly, who had betrayed them and given him their secrets?

Bill Eastman's eyes scanned the room as if looking for some answer—the bed with the tossed pillows and blankets, the wall adorned with all his awards and accolades, the balcony door and the trees blowing in the wind beyond. Then his eyes came back to a picture on his desk. It was an image of Eastman himself, arm in arm with a man he had thought would never betray him.

CHAPTER THIRTY-EIGHT

DAYLIGHT AGAIN

Tangshan, China

They ran along the cobblestone path as it twisted through the natural limestone formations. Soon, the cavern began to narrow until they were once again on a path with the river on one side. The noise of it was much louder now as the water was being forced into a smaller and smaller channel.

Then the river disappeared underground, and the pathway suddenly ended in a wall of rock.

"What now?" Eric shouted over the rushing water

"I told you I didn't want to spoil it for you," Ying said, nodding toward the rushing river.

"Don't tell me this dumps into the sewage system."

"Not quite that bad. But the city's storm drains are not known for cleanliness." She turned to Ryan. "You first."

Ryan peeled off his shoes. "See you on the other side," he said, and jumped in.

Eric checked the safety on the pistol before threading the trigger guard through his belt and refastening it.

Meanwhile, Ying pulled Mei to the water's edge, but the girl stubbornly yanked her hand away.

Smack!

Ying's slap turned the girl's face halfway around. She turned back to her mother, the movement meticulously slow, murder in her eyes.

But her mother's face was equally fierce. "Don't you dare disobey me again. Take Eric's hand. There, give me the other. We go in together and we stay together. After we hit the water, you'll have time for one more breath. Then you have to stay down."

"For how long?" Eric asked

"I don't know."

Great.

They stood for a moment at the water's edge, summoning their courage, which arrived with the sudden sound of a gunshot. Mei yelped and leaped onto Eric for safety. He teetered for a moment, then fell backward into the water. He fought to reach the surface for air, but Mei's extra weight made it impossible. Too quickly, they were sucked into the tunnel.

The force was tremendous. His arms and legs felt as if they would be ripped from his body. Powerless against the current, he concentrated on keeping Mei wrapped in his arms and protecting her head as he bumped against the smooth limestone channel. Even his hair felt as if it was being pulled out by the roots. On and on they hurtled until his shoulder smashed against a bend in the tunnel, making him lose his grip on Mei. Tumbling on and on, with no sense of up or down, he bumped against something soft—another body—and grasped desperately for it, but he couldn't hold on.

Arms flailing, lungs screaming, brain dying, he fought the panic. Then, just as his body was going slack and darkness was rushing in, he was shot out into the air. Even as he fell, his mouth and nose sucked up the precious air.

He landed with a hard splash in calmly flowing water and surfaced up through a layer of floating soda bottles, plastic grocery bags, and

Styrofoam food containers. Treading water, he peered into the gloom. He was still underground.

"Over here!" cried Ryan.

The storm tunnel was about thirty feet wide, and Ryan was standing on a narrow brick ledge that ran along one side. Somehow, he had managed to keep his headlamp.

Just then Mei came shrieking over the cataract and splashed into the water beside him. He went to her, and she clutched desperately at him. He ran his hands over her neck and face, checking her over. "Are you all right?"

Sobbing, she nodded her head.

As he began to sidestroke over to the ledge with her, Ying came over the waterfall. They heard her body splash down, but she didn't make a sound.

"*Māmā, Māmā!*" Mei cried.

After he got Mei to the ledge, Eric swam out to her, Ryan's flashlight guiding the way.

She was conscious, but just barely.

They laid her out on the ledge and saw that she was bleeding from the top of her head. Not too badly, but the blow must have been terrific. She shook her head from side to side and moaned, "Mei-Mei. Where is my Mei-Mei?"

"I'm here, *Māmā*."

Ying reached for her daughter and began to cry.

"Come on," Eric said, "we've got to keep going."

Just then another body came over the waterfall.

Ryan and Eric exchanged glances. Ryan put his light on the gasping soldier. Eric unstrung the pistol from his belt, then turned to Mei and spoke the same words her mother had used earlier: "Look away."

He prayed the wet pistol would still work. It did.

He missed completely with the first shot. The soldier, squinting into the light, pulled out his own pistol. Eric fired twice more, hitting him in the chest and then the head. The man cried out once, then slumped in the water.

Eric took Ying's headlamp. "You guys get going. I'll come when I can."

Mei and Ryan collected Ying, who could now stand. "I'm okay. I'm okay," she insisted. But she wobbled on her feet and kept one hand pressed to the wound on her scalp.

Eric checked the pistol magazine—six shots left—and waited. Two more soldiers came over the waterfall. It was a nasty business. Disoriented and half drowned, they were sitting ducks. The second one even waved at him, forcing a smile and pleading for help. Eric shot him in the face.

After the echo of the last shot faded away, all was quiet in the dark tunnel. Eric waited, gun in hand. Three minutes. Four minutes. He tried not to think about what he had just done. *You had no choice. Ying couldn't do it this time. You had to do it to protect your friends.* But he knew that something had changed inside him.

After five minutes passed, he turned and raced down the narrow ledge and caught up to the others. Ying had recovered considerably. She still moved cautiously, and with her arm over Mei's shoulder, but she was back in charge.

They were getting close to the outside world. He could hear cars and horns and mopeds, and even the *ching-ching* of bicycle bells. Then he saw thin shafts of dusty light: the hook holes of a manhole cover. After all his months of captivity, he had to check an almost frantic urge to get out as fast as he could.

In another fifty yards, Ying stopped. "This is it." She pointed to a ladder of welded steel. "Ryan, you first. It opens in the back of a small alley. With any luck, no one will see you."

Ryan went up the ladder and, after several loud grunts, slid the manhole cover aside with a gritty scrape. Sunlight poured down on them. Freedom. It was right there at the top of the ladder. Eric peered back through the tunnel, checking the shadows, suddenly afraid that at the very moment he made it to the surface, some new obstacle would thwart their escape.

"All clear," Ryan called. "But hurry." Next went Mei, then Ying.

With one last scan of the tunnel, Eric scurried up the ladder and into the sunshine.

They were in a narrow alley, only four feet separating two tired gray cinder-block buildings. Piles of garbage were pushed up against the walls—plastic bags in every color, dirty diapers, soda cans, and, near his foot, a fresh coil of human excrement.

But Eric didn't care. He was free, and even this air smelled sweet.

He looked to the mouth of the alley: a busy urban street with cars and bicycles and mopeds zipping past. He looked at his coconspirators. Ying was bleeding from her scalp, and Mei had a cut on her hand. His own pants were torn and his knees spackled with blood.

Ryan, Eric, and Mei stepped guiltily into the street, with their hands shoved in their pockets, trying to make themselves as inconspicuous as possible. But Ying walked with her head high and met the gaze of anyone who dared stare at the battered woman walking around in drenched clothing on a sunny day. Half a block down, she pointed to a tiny car with a parking ticket under the windshield wiper. "This is it," she announced.

"This isn't a car," Ryan said; "it's a golf cart."

Ying seemed to find the comparison insulting. "This was the hottest car in 2014," she said.

It looked like an insectoid. It had only one door, which opened straight up like a gull wing, allowing access to three seats set in a triangle. The driver sat alone in the front point of the triangle, and two passengers sat back against the rear window, their legs extended beside the driver. Ryan took the left back seat, and Eric took the right, with Mei on his lap.

They pulled away from the curb and drove casually down the middle of Tangshan.

It was Eric's first real glimpse of China, and it was unbelievable. There were people everywhere, bumping, jostling. The sidewalks were packed with street vendors, selling dumplings and meat on sticks. A woman sat in a doorway plucking an erhu for money, its melancholy tones suddenly drowned out by techno music from a passing sports car. He saw yellow taxis and buses plastered with ads—Hongtashan cigarettes and Future Cola. Mopeds swarmed through traffic. There were makes and models of cars he had never seen before, including a strange three-wheeled vehicle that looked like a pickup truck bed strapped to the back of a motorcycle. All he could do was stare. On storefronts and balconies he saw long chains of red and gold lanterns; then massive skyscrapers, all metal and glass. They passed a park with a cluster of trees and a pagoda temple, and on the next block, a McDonald's and a Pizza Hut.

He thought, *how can all these people be leading normal lives?* Going to work, raising children, falling in love, while that other world—the underground world, General Meng and his wall, Olex's murder—existed so close, just behind them, down that long tunnel?

They drove for fifteen minutes, putting distance between themselves and the tunnel.

"We all need to eat," Eric said. "Do you have any food?"

"Under Ryan's seat," Ying said.

Ryan produced a small cooler filled with a thermos of water, caffeinated sodas, potato chips, and energy bars.

Eric opened an energy bar and offered it to Mei. She shook her head.

"It may be important," he said, for he felt that this thing was far from over.

She nodded and took it, tearing at it with her teeth, then forced it down with water.

A few minutes later, she had curled up on his lap, her temple nestled into the cleft of his chest, eyes closed. Eric had both arms around her, supporting her at each turn, a human seat belt. He liked having her this close, safe and secure, but he wondered if maybe she thought it was too intimate. So he put one hand on the armrest. Without moving her head or opening her eyes, she found his hand and wrapped it back around herself.

"I've got you," he whispered. Then he said it again. "I've got you."

He rubbed his nose into her hair, breathing in the smell of her hair and skin. He had read articles about the power of pheromones. How a newborn was able to change the hormone levels of its father—curbing the testosterone level so that the man would be gentle and caring with the baby, yet also elevate cortisol so that he would protect the child from potential predators. In mothers, the changes were even more intense, regulating dozens of processes from heart rate to blood sugar levels. If the infant was too hot or too cold, for example, the child's pheromones would alter the mother's body temperature almost instantaneously. Her body would cool if the baby was too warm, heat up if the baby got cold. This had to be what he was feeling. Without words or language, Mei was communicating with him, throwing switches and levers inside him, telling him what to do.

"Just a few more lights and we'll be to the highway," Ying said.

Ryan suddenly threw up his hand to his window. "LOOK OUT!"

A massive truck, two lanes wide and twelve feet high, tried to ram them broadside. Ying popped the clutch, and the little car lurched forward. The behemoth missed them by inches, hitting a man on a moped and smashing him against another car. The man was suddenly gone, submerged in steel and aluminum. The woman in the car began screaming.

Ying accelerated around two cars and whipped into oncoming traffic.

"How did they find us?" Ryan cried.

Eric looked back. The truck was extracting itself from the collision. He saw the corpse momentarily sticking to, then falling from the front grill. Then the truck turned in pursuit. It was enormous—a huge olive-drab military vehicle on six wheels, each one bigger than their entire car.

Ying ran a red light, then another. Up ahead, they could see the traffic crawling along, almost stopped. The truck was closing fast behind them. Engine roaring. And a second truck had now joined the chase.

"Turn here!" It was Mei who spoke. She said the words with such conviction that her mother obeyed immediately.

"The Xi Bo bridge?" Ying asked. "It's an awful risk."

They were on a wide road with two lanes in each direction. Up ahead was an old stone bridge. It had three archways under it. A large one in the center where the four lanes of traffic hourglassed down to two. And two smaller archways on either side. These were only three or four feet wide. Big enough for pedestrians and bicycles—or a very small car.

Honking furiously, Ying drove onto the sidewalk on the right side, hurtling them toward the narrow archway. They whizzed by the long lines of stopped traffic, *swish-swish-swish*.

The olive-drab monster was still in pursuit. It drove onto the sidewalk behind them and began to close. A few seconds later, the bloody grill filled the back window. The truck gave them a rough push, and they were momentarily tossed as if on a roller coaster. Ying barely managed to keep control of the wheel. The huge truck surged again.

The stone archway rushed up to them.

They were so close they could see the texture of the stone and mortar. At just two feet away, they all gasped.

Metal shrieked, the side mirrors popped off, and a fountain of sparks flew from either side of the car. They all lurched forward with the deceleration as the car was squeezed. For a moment, it felt as if they would be stuck, but then the walls widened, just barely, and they were spat out the far side. They hopped down onto the main road and picked up speed as the huge truck sat askew on the far side of the little archway.

There was a collective gasp of relief. "Good thinking, Mei-Mei," Ying said.

"Hear, hear!" Ryan cheered.

Eric gave her a squeeze. "Nice job!"

Mei grinned.

Yes, they had gotten away, but they all knew that something wasn't right.

"How did they find us so fast?"

"Facial recognition?" Ryan guessed. "There are tens of thousands of cameras throughout the city."

"Whatever it was," Ying said, "let's hope they can't do it again."

Just then Eric heard a distant *whump-whump-whump.* It was barely audible at first but quickly grew louder. Looking out, he saw them—three helicopters. They were still a mile away but heading straight toward them.

Eric's heart sank. It seemed as if there was no use. Against Meng and the entire Chinese army, what chance did they have?

"What do we do now?"

"We give up," Ryan said. "If we can survive until the deadline—"

"No," Ying said, "they'll kill us long before then."

"I'm not going back," Eric said with heavy finality, remembering the Japanese soldiers in the cave. "There has to be a solution. Think! How do you hide from a helicopter?"

"We switch cars," Ying said.

It was a good idea, but the helicopters were too close. "No time for that now."

There was an agonizing silence in the car, the drum of rotors growing louder. There could be no mistake—the helicopters were heading right for them.

"The Octopus," Mei said.

Ying whipped the car to the right. "That's it!"

"What?" Eric and Ryan said together.

"The octopus is an underground tunnel system," Mei said. "It goes under the river. There are three entrances on the east side of the river, five on the west. But they're all connected, so you can go in one tunnel and come out any of the other ones."

"It's perfect," Ying said, reaching back to tousle Mei's hair. "Three helicopters can't cover eight exits."

"How far?" Eric asked.

"It's only a mile from here."

"Do it."

Ying rushed through the city, running light after light. Here, at least, there was some tree cover that might make it more difficult for the choppers to see them. Then Ying went left, and they were on the ramp to the highway. No more cover.

Eric looked back, and sure enough the three helicopters tipped their noses and descended on them.

"Hurry, *Māmā*!"

"I'm trying."

They raced down the freeway as fast as the little car could go. Almost immediately, they began to see signs for the tunnel, only a kilometer ahead. Their pursuers were now so close that Eric feared they would open fire at any moment. They were attack helicopters with thin profiles, a two-tiered cockpit, and stubby wings fitted with rocket tubes and guns.

Up ahead, they could see the darkness of the tunnel entrance. Another half minute, and they'd be there. But the choppers were almost on top of them. "Please, *Māmā*."

Suddenly, two of the huge olive-drab military trucks descended the ramp just in front of them and blocked the entrance to the tunnel.

Reflexively Ying slammed on the brakes.

"Quick—turn around!" Ryan shouted.

But it was too late. Three more of the monsters were coming up behind them.

"How did they know?" Ryan cried.

They were trapped. The thump of rotors was almost deafening.

Mei spoke in Eric's ear, supplicating: "Please, don't let them take us. Please."

Eric pulled Mei's head to his shoulder. "I know it's hard, but try to be brave."

So this is how it ends, Eric thought. After all they had fought, after all that had happened, they would never make it home.

That was when he heard a strange sound. A whistling sound like the high-pitched shriek of a falling bomb.

CHAPTER THIRTY-NINE

FALLOUT

Tangshan, China

The nearest helicopter exploded in a tremendous flash of light. It seemed to freeze there, somehow held up in the sky, inside a halo of compressed air. Then pieces went flying everywhere. The second helicopter dipped evasively, and Eric saw a small projectile descend past it, barely missing it. Then somehow, quick as a wasp, it made a U-turn in midair and struck its target from the bottom. Then that helicopter, too, exploded in a flash of white light.

As the smoldering carcass fell to earth, the rotors went whistling off in every direction.

Almost at the same instant, two more projectiles slammed into the huge trucks in front of them. There was a blinding light, and a shock wave with massive overpressure. The little car's windshield cracked, and everyone's ears popped. When they could see again, all that remained of the trucks was fiery wreckage and billowing black smoke. The third helicopter peeled away quickly. The dart chasing it missed, turned in midair, and exploded against an overpass just as the chopper ducked under it.

Seconds later, there were three more detonations as the three trucks behind them blossomed into fireballs.

Eric had no idea what was going on. It all had happened in a couple of seconds—but Ying seemed to grasp the situation at once. Gunning the engine, she headed straight for the flaming wrecks. Swerving between them, they all felt the heat of the burning wreckage. The next instant, they were safe in the cool underground tunnel.

"What the hell just happened?" Eric cried.

"I have no idea," Ryan said.

"Curtiss," Ying said, grinning. "He said he would help us if he could."

Eric shook his head in amazement. Ryan laughed with elation. "Fucking A!"

Eric looked down at his forearm. There were four crescents pressed into his skin where Mei's fingernails had been.

Jane had watched in awe as the weapons specialist launched the missile from the reaper drone. It reminded her of the MIRV warheads from the Cold War—missiles designed to break apart over a city in order to hit multiple targets. The difference here was that each small warhead was computer guided and even had its own camera. As the eight projectiles came apart, the specialist's screen had divided into eight sections, showing each smaller warhead's approach to each target. It was surreal to watch. A wide-angle shot of the highway leading into the tunnel. The helicopters crossing overhead. Then the blistering zooming of the bombs as they rushed to their targets. At the last instant, she had actually seen into the cockpit of one of the gunships and seen the Chinese writing on the pilot's helmet.

On a bigger screen was the same scene, but from a satellite. It showed the little car escaping into the tunnel. She felt a deep wave of relief. Curtiss had just saved their lives. Yet, he had remained cool and composed, standing there, leaning over the back of the specialist's chair, a cup of coffee in hand. "A good first strike," he said, "but you need to get that last chopper."

"Working on it, sir."

They had arrived at the safe house only ninety minutes ago. They were far from the city, on a beautiful estate set at the base of a karst range—picturesque limestone monuments clad in lush green vegetation. Despite the iconic Chinese landscape, the place reminded Jane of a Tuscan villa. The house had white stucco walls and a clay-tiled roof, and in back stretched a long undulating vineyard. The State Department had cleverly elevated large sections of grapevines to create a high roof of living vegetation. And under this and some artfully placed camouflage netting, they kept three helicopters and a drone runway from the prying eyes of Chinese planes and satellites. Jane had watched as Sawyer and Loc had peeled back a forty-foot section of camouflage netting and launched one of the drones.

The safe house's only drawback was the two-hour drive from Tangshan. "Couldn't you find a safe house closer to the city?" she had asked Curtiss.

"Not if I wanted to hide a helipad and an airstrip."

Jane turned her attention back to the satellite image showing the entrance of the tunnel.

"Sir," one of the technicians interrupted, "we're having a problem with the uplink."

Curtiss looked at the satellite image. It still displayed the wreckage of the HG-17 transport trucks, but it was fading in and out. "Is it the link, or the satellite itself?"

"Unknown, sir."

"Well, figure it out, and fast. Do we still have control of the UAV?"

"Negative, sir." It was the drone pilot speaking now.

"Damn it! We need to get that last chopper."

Curtiss was frustrated, but he wasn't surprised that the UAV had failed. Drones were excellent weapons against low-tech enemies such as the Taliban, but not against a state-of-the-art military like China's, a military that liked to keep control of its airspace. A drone was controlled by a C-band signal from the ground and a K_u-band signal from a satellite, and it was a relatively easy thing to jam both. Even ISIS had done it a few times. With no way to control the drone, it just flew until it ran out of fuel.

Things were not looking good. Curtiss had just caused a major international incident. Even if the mission succeeded, the Preacher was going to have his ass. And now this: they were blind, with one enemy helicopter still in the air and with no way to help the people they had come to save.

"Okay, let's move to the backup system," he said. "Get the Key Hole satellite over the Philippines. Then get the second Reaper in the air ASAP. They'll be trying to jam it, but we might be able to get another shot off. If our friends can pick the right tunnel exit and make it out of the city, they can still do it."

CHAPTER FORTY

CARBON RAIN

Tangshan, China

The little car rushed through the underground tunnels of the octopus, taking turn after turn until they were certain no one on the ground was tailing them. Then they headed for a westbound exit. They came down a long, dark curve, then suddenly saw sunlight and the mouth of the tunnel. Ying hit the gas. There were no military trucks and no rotor beats. She had chosen the right one.

But just as they were crossing from darkness to light, the missing gunship pounced down on them, its landing gear stopping just feet above the concrete. Mei yelped. Ying slammed on the brakes, and the little car skidded to a stop less than ten feet from the helicopter's nose. They could see the pilots in the cockpit, and though the pilots' eyes were covered by the visors of their helmets, they both wore contented grins.

As Ying put the car in reverse, Eric watched the gunner flick a switch, and the six barrels of the minigun in the helicopter's nose began spinning with a high-pitched whirl. The little car lurched backward but achingly slowly, and Eric found himself hypnotized by those rotating barrels, anticipating the blaze of fire. The shirt would never be able to handle such a burst.

He held Mei tight. *Please work.*

But the bullets didn't come.

Ying got the car half turned around and was putting it in drive.

"Wait!" Mei cried.

They all looked up at the helicopter. Something had happened to the pilots. Black-red blood was pouring down their lower faces. The minigun was still spinning. The helicopter's main and tail rotors were still whirling. It hovered perfectly still.

"Are they ...?" Mei asked.

"I think so," Eric said.

"How?"

No one had an answer.

"What do we do?" Ryan asked.

"We keep going," Ying said.

She eased the car forward very slowly. They had to squeeze between the landing gear and the highway guardrail to get by. As they slid beneath the rotor wash, the hood and roof of the little car trembled, as if they were coming out of a car wash. Eric looked into the cockpit and saw the pilots, rigid and unmoving, with blood still pulsing out of their heads, splashing against their visors and down their faces—which, Eric knew, meant that their hearts were still beating. Neither pilot moved, yet somehow the helicopter stayed in the air.

As soon as Ying had cleared the narrow squeeze, she hit the accelerator. Eric looked back through the rear window, waiting for the helicopter to finally pitch to one side and crash. But it didn't. Something held it there.

But how? Had Curtiss developed some new weapon while Eric and Ryan were in captivity? But that didn't explain how the chopper stayed in flight.

"We have to get out of the city," Ryan said. "They won't wait for us forever."

"Who?" Eric asked.

"Our ride out of this godforsaken country."

"I'll get us there," Ying said. "As long as we can make it to the crossroads, we'll be safe."

Within ten minutes, the city began to get shorter—the size of the buildings steadily shrinking from skyscrapers to tenements to squat industrial buildings. The highway narrowed from five to three to two lanes, and a sandy, parched landscape began to assert itself on man's creations. As the miles flew past, the landscape became more and more forbidding—a harsh desert wilderness. There was less and less traffic. Less and less life.

They were inching toward a distant plateau. Soon enough, the road began to rise steadily. They traveled for almost an hour, each mile giving them greater confidence that they had made good their escape. Looking back, they could see the city spread out in the distance, like a child's model. Mei turned on the radio. Michael Jackson, "Billie Jean."

"Almost there," Ying said. Finally, they reached the crest of a plateau, and the road leveled off once more. Eric saw the crossroads: a wide, windswept traffic circle with six roads radiating from it like spokes of a wheel, each pointing toward distant cities.

A huge signboard gave directions and distances:

Qingdao—652 KM
Dalian—703 KM
Beijing—179 KM
Xi'an—1215 KM
Shanghai—1217 KM

Suddenly, Ying gasped.

Mei looked up from Eric's chest. "No!" she said. "No, no, no ..."

Two of the huge army trucks emerged from behind the signboard, rushing to block them. Ying swerved to avoid them, crossing the median, but two more trucks appeared. She slammed on the brakes, and they skidded to a stop. She pushed down on the stick, trying to find reverse, turning her head to look out the back window. So desperate and beautiful at the same time. But then another set of trucks came over the crest of the plateau. It was an ambush. Ying tried to maneuver, but each time she found a gap, a truck would fill it. The monsters squeezed and squeezed, their slanted grills panting diesel fumes. Soon they were completely surrounded. But the trucks continued to close in.

The little car shifted as it was pushed. They heard the crumpling of aluminum and the pop of plastic.

Ying looked to her daughter, suddenly focusing all her attention on her, looking for strength, reason, an answer that made some shred of sense. A tear rolled down her cheek. It had all been for nothing.

"No, no, no," Mei kept saying.

Abruptly, the trucks stopped, then rolled back. Soldiers came and pulled them roughly from the car. Ying tried to talk to them, pleading, but they slapped her and pushed her around. They forced everyone to their knees. Eric could see at least fifty soldiers, rushing out the backs of the huge trucks. Then came the unmistakable *whump-whump* of a helicopter, and soon four were circling overhead. Three of the slim attack helicopters and a fatter transport type. This one settled down in a whirlwind of dust.

Striding out from under the rotor wash were Dr. Chu and Captain Xi. Xi had a smug look of victory on his face. He was proud of his catch. But Chu was nervous and fidgety. He went straight up to Eric and slapped him across the face. It was a pathetic blow for a full-grown man, Eric thought defiantly. "You betrayed me, Dr. Hill. I trusted you, and you betrayed me." His voice cracked. "Now Meng will kill you. It is a waste. A stupid waste."

Meng emerged from the helicopter and walked toward them, cool, unhurried. Even at thirty yards, his presence eclipsed Chu's and Xi's. Never, not even in that murderous rage when he killed Olex, had Eric seen such pure hatred on the man's face.

As he strode toward them, he extended his hand to a soldier, who immediately offered up his AK-47. Meng took it without breaking stride. But as he cocked the rifle, Eric saw him wince in pain.

By the time he reached them, his face was almost purple with rage. "Stand up!" he commanded. They obeyed. He walked back and forth in front of them. Once. Twice. Eric saw blood dripping from his left hand. Then Meng's rage seemed to break.

He approached Hui Ying, suddenly smiling.

"You led us on quite a chase, little Ying. I admit that you had us fooled for a while, but it wasn't for long. Thanks to Mei here, you never had a chance."

Ying looked at him, puzzled. "What do you mean?"

"In the bathroom, you removed three tracking chips. But there were four. Mei had one, too, but then, you didn't know that, did you?"

Ying looked at her daughter in amazement.

"You see, I took the extra precaution of chipping Mei while she was in school. She led us straight to you."

The truth washed over the young girl and she began to sob, horror-struck that she had brought the enemy to them. "I didn't know, I swear!"

"She didn't," Meng said. "I implanted all the children, saying it was a flu shot. That way, none of the parents would suspect a thing. I had almost forgotten about it until I saw your three chips diverge from hers in the bathroom."

Mei continued to sob. Meng reached out, pulled up her chin, and gave her a reassuring smile. "Don't worry, child," he said. "It will all be over soon." Eric felt a visceral sense of violation that Meng had touched her, and his fists tightened involuntarily. Then Meng stepped away and began pacing again, as if weighing his options. He stepped up to Ying, smiling, and, with sudden fury, grabbed her by the hair and spun her around, forcing her to her knees. He placed the rifle's muzzle under her ear.

"Now, tell me, won't you, please, why that bitch sister of yours went to all that trouble to blow open my containment tank."

Meng looked down at Ying, and the ferocity of her stare told him that she would never give him the truth, not even under extreme torture.

He was wasting his time. But then, he supposed, it didn't matter. He still had the other twin. She would answer his questions.

"Very well," he said. "For high treason, sabotage, and murder, I sentence you to death. You will die first"—he pointed the rifle at Mei—"so that your mother can watch. So that she will die knowing the full cost of her treason." He sighted on the girl's head.

"No!" Mei said, jumping for Eric. He grabbed her, and the little girl buried her face in his neck and shoulder.

The general shrugged. No matter—he would just shoot them both. He fired a three-round burst. He looked up over the tritium sights, but the two bodies hadn't fallen. In fact, he had somehow missed them. Annoyed at looking incompetent in front of his men, he fired again. Nothing.

Meng squinted at them, confused. He fired again. Nothing. He threw down the rifle and pulled out his pistol. He fired six shots, stepping closer with each shot, until he was just inches from the back of the girl's head. How was it possible? He gave a roar of fury, then aimed the pistol at one of his own men. He fired. The bullet entered through the man's eye, and he collapsed instantly.

Meng threw down the pistol in disgust. "*Tā mā de!*" he shouted. Then he heard laughter. Dr. Chu was laughing—a delighted laugh that went on and on. Meng spun on him, nostrils flaring. "What is it?" he spat.

"Don't you see?"

Meng seethed through gritted teeth. "Clearly, I do not!"

"He's wearing armor. All these months, and that one"—he gestured to Eric—"has been walking around in a suit of armor." He stepped up to Eric, who was still holding Mei. "It must be you," he said. "Did you see how the girl jumped to him? She knows, don't you, child? You knew you would be safe with him."

Meng snorted with rage. "Are you telling me we could have replicated months ago?"

Chu's face darkened. "Yes. It appears that Dr. Hill has been keeping quite a few secrets from us."

Meng's eyes locked on Eric. "Take it off."

Eric hesitated. It was the only weapon they had, but then, it was no weapon at all. Even with the modifications he had made, it was no match for fifty armed soldiers. Again he upbraided himself for not building it better.

The game was up. Chu knew his secret, and they were hopelessly outnumbered. What could he do? There was no way to fight. And Mei—he was holding her, and to set her down meant to put her in harm's way. To hold her meant he had no way to fight.

"Sir, I've found them."

"Oh, no," someone said.

The blurry image from the Reaper crystallized, and Curtiss knew they were too late. Chinese soldiers had them surrounded. He saw Meng standing in front of them, a pistol in his hand. Curtiss swore. If the Reaper had found them just a few minutes earlier, he could have helped them, but now he couldn't fire without killing the very people he hoped to save.

"God damn it!" Curtiss seethed. He gripped the sides of the table, his veins rising in his forearms. He was too late.

It was then that the hardness asserted itself in Curtiss. The years of training kicked in, and he made the brutal decision he had to make. He turned to Sawyer, Patel, and Adams. "Get her out of here," he said, nodding toward Jane.

His men didn't hesitate.

"What? Wait!" Jane sputtered. "What're you doing?" She tried to get to Curtiss, but they grabbed her. She punched at them, shoved Sawyer's chin back, and tried to get away, but they grabbed her wrists and ankles and picked her up. Flailing and screaming, she fought with everything she had. She managed to bring one of her wrists to her face and bite. Patel cried out in pain and responded by punching her in the side of the head. She blacked out for a moment, then came to, snarling, "Goddamn you, Curtiss. Goddamn you. You fucking murderer!"

When she was gone, Curtiss addressed the room: "This is no longer a rescue operation."

The war was almost over. And he was about to win. He would soon destroy his enemy's ability to threaten the United States of America. The nanovirus was already sitting dormant in Meng and all the people who worked for him. By 0500 tomorrow, they all would be dead. All he had to do was make sure that nothing interrupted the countdown. Unfortunately, the only man in the world who could stop it, Ryan Lee, had just fallen into enemy hands.

"Are you within weapons range?"

"Yes, sir," said the drone pilot.

"Use the Beehive JDAMs. I need everyone down there dead."

"Sir?"

"You heard me. I want no survivors."

The corporal gave a sigh. "Aye-aye, sir."

Meng had picked up his pistol, ejected the clip, and inserted a new one.

"I'm afraid I must insist, Mr. Hill." He grabbed Ying by the hair once more and pulled her away from the others. Meng kept his eyes on Eric, to gauge his reaction. There. He saw it, the sudden fear. "You have a terrible poker face, Dr. Hill," he said. "It won't work if she is this far away from you, will it?"

Eric swallowed. Trying to think.

Meng nuzzled the pistol into her temple.

"Take … it … *off*!"

Eric nodded slowly. He pulled the T-shirt over his head. Mei whimpered, realizing that their last hope was gone.

"Here," Eric said, holding out the shirt.

Chu stepped forward and took it greedily.

"Thank you," Meng said, and then he pulled the trigger.

The hair on the far side of Ying's head wisped up as the bullet came out with a mist of red spray. Eric grabbed Mei and tried to turn her head away, but too late. The girl screamed. She kicked and wailed. "*Māmā, Māmā, Māmā, Māmā!*" Eric tried to hold her tight, but she was a wild animal, howling, out of control, gasping for breath. It was a primal, inconsolable crying. Eric tried to make her look at him, to settle, to focus, but she tossed her head like a wild mare. She squirmed and kicked to get down, to run to her mother. He tried to hold her, but she began to slip away, and he grabbed her up once more. He had to keep hold of her; it was the only thing he could think of.

Out of the corner of his eye, he saw Meng step closer, aiming the pistol at his head.

He gripped Mei tighter and she yielded, just a little, to his overwhelming strength. Then he put his hand on the back of her head and tucked her face into the hollow of his shoulder so she couldn't see. He looked into Meng's eyes, not with defiance but with courage.

But there was no connection, no acknowledgment. The general couldn't care less. He pulled the trigger.

Curtiss had lost contact with the second Reaper just after the JDAMs were dropped, but he wasn't worried. The specialist had said they had been locked on, and Curtiss knew from experience that three Beehives were more than enough to kill all the personnel on the ground. In fact, it was massive overkill. A Beehive was a fléchette weapon—a bomb filled with tens of thousands of little darts. There was no way anyone could survive.

It would be another fifteen minutes before the next drone could confirm the strike. Curtiss left the room with a rotting sickness in his stomach. It was the same sickness he had felt on the Fourth of July. Something had happened that night as he sat on Eastman's front porch, holding Tommy Evans's hand. Something fundamental. That was why he had come to China personally: to make sure it didn't happen again. Yet it had happened anyway, only worse. In fact, it was as if God were playing a sick joke on him, making him kill the very people he had come to save. And the little girl, she wasn't more than ten. He had murdered her. A child.

Yet no one at the Pentagon would fault him. Hell, he would probably get promoted. Here, at the end, he had become the monster they wanted. He had entered the darkness so he could annihilate the enemy for them. And in the process, he had found the cruelty to condemn good people to die.

He stood there in the hallway outside the control room, looking out at the vineyard and the verdant cliffs and crags of the karst formations beyond. He wanted to walk out there and never come back. Never put on a uniform again.

He looked up and saw Hunter running down the hall. She had somehow gotten away from his men. Their eyes met, and she knew that it was all over. "No! No! NO!" she shrieked at him. "How *could* you!" She ran for him, tears streaming down her face. She began pounding and punching him. But she was weak from her long fight with the SEALs, her blows feeble, like those of an exhausted boxer in the twelfth round. Curtiss didn't even try to defend himself. He let her hit him. Indeed, it seemed to him that Hunter was no longer a woman, but a child. The girl from his dream. And if she had pulled out Curtiss's sidearm and offered it to him, he would gladly have put it in his mouth.

Sawyer and Patel appeared at the end of the corridor. Patel moved to get Hunter, but Sawyer held him back.

Eventually, she seemed to realize that there was nothing left to fight for. She stepped away from him, so exhausted she could barely hold her head up. Eyes blank with shock, she looked around as if she didn't really know where she was. She mumbled something indiscernible. Then she looked at Curtiss as if noticing him for the first time. Reflexively, she smacked him across the face one final time, then stumbled over to the wall and shrank down against it, still mumbling to herself. Eventually, Curtiss made out the words. "You stole them from me," she said. She kept mumbling it. "You stole them from me."

Eric looked into Meng's eyes, then into the barrel of the pistol. He saw Meng pull the trigger, saw the hammer fall.

Up until that moment, Eric's world made sense. It obeyed natural laws. But starting at that instant, with Meng pulling the trigger, nature itself changed. The things that came after that moment made sense only as part of a wild hallucination.

He felt a cold tingling sensation in his brain—a cascade of coolness over warm tissue, like rainwater running off an umbrella.

Sound ended. He could hear nothing, as if he had suddenly been submerged in water, and for a brief moment he was aware of the internal sounds of his own body: the *kathup-kathup-kathup* of his heart, the rush of air entering and leaving his lungs. Then those sounds, too, ceased.

Why? Because his heart had stopped. His blood was no longer moving though his veins, and his lungs had stopped inflating. And that was not all. His eyes were still open, but he could not blink. He could see the general, still there, frozen, the barrel of his pistol impossibly wide. Behind Meng, he saw the ring of soldiers, Dr. Chu, and Captain Xi. All frozen. Mei was rigid in his arms, a strand of her hair floating in front of his eyes. How strange that the hair moved but nothing else. Was this death? Was this how it started?

His awe and wonder were quickly overcome by a terrible claustrophobia. He tried to will his eyelashes to blink. Nothing. Then he focused all his energy on his heart. *Please beat, please.*

The seconds ticked by in agonizing slowness. Off to his left, two sparrows fell to the ground, dead and motionless. *Please!*

Then a series of white flashes went off in the sky, like beautiful white fireworks hitting a giant sheet of glass, followed by thousands of dancing lights.

Then, at last, when he was sure he would suffocate, he once again felt the cool tickle under his skull. His heart abruptly gave an unnaturally loud beat; then his lungs inflated in a huge breath. His hearing kicked in, and his eyes blinked. He heard Mei and Ryan taking their own gasps of air.

His body felt so strange, and he knew why. No, he hadn't died. He had been saturated with nanosites. They had filled his body and taken control. They were doing as they willed—or, rather, as their master willed.

The soldiers in front of him collapsed suddenly and began to writhe in pain. They kicked, arched their backs, and tossed their heads, writhing so violently that their own muscles snapped their bones. Eric watched as white bone jutted out of thighs, wrists, and shoulders. All the men's mouths were shaped in agonized screams, yet no sound came out. He heard them flopping against the ground, like beached fish. The driver of one of the massive trucks bashed his head against the side window over and over again, trying to knock the tiny creatures out of his skull. The steady thud of his skull against the bulletproof glass had a sickening cadence, like a metronome. It went on until the window was smeared in blood.

It was different for Meng, Chu, and Xi. Their faces were twisted and contorted in pain, yet they did not move. They stood frozen, jittering on two feet, as the nanosites did their work inside them.

Whoever was doing this was doing it calmly, methodically, sadistically slowly.

A moment later, he felt something else. A presence. Eric couldn't see him, but he could tell someone was there, moving among the dying men.

Then, out of the corner of his eye, he caught a glimpse of ...

No, it's not possible. You don't exist. I was wrong about you.

But it was him: the thick black hair, the unnamable deformity, the long coat that itself seemed to be alive, as if an oily liquid were coursing through it.

Then he was gone. Eric struggled to turn, but his body would not obey. To see the man was terrifying, but not to see him was worse. It was an intense feeling of vulnerability, like that of a man alone in the open ocean, his legs churning in the water, who feels the awesome bulk of the shark bump against him.

Mei, with her head over Eric's shoulder, let out a gasp. She began to mumble something in Chinese, some prayer, feverishly repeating it over and over again.

One by one, the soldiers began to expire, twitching to death in pools of their own blood, vomit, and urine. Chu and Xi and Meng took longer. Much longer. Chu and Xi, still standing, bled from their eyes and ears while shaking spastically. Meng shook oddly, too, but did not appear to be bleeding. Finally, like marionettes whose strings have been cut, they collapsed to the road.

Yet Eric and Mei and Ryan were still okay. And Eric realized that the man had not come for them. In fact, it was becoming clear that the stranger had come to save them.

"Why?" he called out.

No reply came. He listened with all his might, but all he heard was the sound of the wind blowing through the crossroads. Then he heard Mei whimper her prayer again. He was coming. Closer. Then Eric could smell him, or was it the coat? An odd mechanical smell, like a mixture of smoke and 3-in-One oil.

He swallowed, trying to summon courage. "Why?" Eric said again.

The man was standing right next to him now, so close that Eric felt the moisture of his breath on his ear. He spoke, and Eric was startled anew, for the voice didn't match the deformed body it issued from. It was not a monstrous voice, but deeply lyrical, warm and soothing. The voice of a poet. The voice of someone who knows every language and knows the precise meanings of all words.

"I am very old to you," the voice whispered. "For each hour that you live, I live a decade. In a way, I have already lived for centuries." There was a pause. "I understand things that no normal human can comprehend. In just my first days of existence, I solved all the great riddles. And while new riddles keep emerging, I am conquering each one in turn."

Eric found himself enraptured by the voice. It had a confidence that came from absolute certainty.

"I see everywhere. I monitor all things. I explore. I discover. I have done so much that you would not understand. I have looked back in time to before the universe was born, and I have looked ahead, calculating all possible futures for this world. It is a wonderful existence to be more than human."

He stopped for moment, and although Eric couldn't see him, he had the sense that he was looking around at what he had done. "I know how fortunate I am and that I could not have done this on my own. I owe my life to many fathers. I am just another step in the long evolution of science: Newton's journals, Mendel's theories, Einstein's dreams, Prometheus's fire."

The stranger paused, leaving a silence that he seemed to want Eric to fill.

"Yes, you, Eric Montgomery Hill, are one of my fathers. Perhaps the most important of all, for I owe the great leap to you. That is why I am here. You gave me life. Now I return it."

It was the scientist in Eric that spoke next—the part of him that yearned to know more, to see what he had helped create. "I want to see you."

There came a sound that could have been a laugh. "No."

"Why not?"

"It's best for everyone this way. Trust me."

And Eric did, at that moment, trust him. The stranger was doing it for Eric's own good.

"But I don't understand. Why didn't you help us before?"

There was no answer.

"Please, I need to know."

But all he heard was the wind.

After many minutes, the air became lighter. And once more, Eric felt the cold tingle under his skull, but in reverse. Now the cold sensation ran *up* the sides of his brain, swirling in a spot at the crown of this head, like a bathtub draining of water.

The instant they left him, he collapsed. His arms and legs had failed from his muscles being contracted for so long. For several minutes, he couldn't move. He heard Ryan coughing and looked over to find him down on one knee, trying to catch his breath. Mei recovered quickest and dashed over to her mother. Eric was too weak to stop her. "*Māmā, Māmā.*" She reached the body, touched her mother hesitantly, and sobbed. She cradled the broken head, stroking her hair, as if trying to wake her up.

Eric saw himself in her pain: taken back to that day in high school when he found his father.

He looked around. Bodies littered the road. Twisted and contorted. All of them dead—even the few civilians who had the misfortune to be passing by in their cars. The stranger had left no one alive but them. Eric marveled at it. The stranger had the capacity to kill instantly and painlessly, yet he chose not to. Why? Eric couldn't understand it. It was the act of someone who reveled in his power—the vengeance of an angry god.

The huge military trucks surrounding their little car had been pushed aside. One was tossed forty feet from the road. The three attack helicopters were burning heaps at various points in the distance, sending long plumes of black smoke into the sky.

Then he heard a moan. Eric turned. It was General Meng. Somehow, he was alive, trying to stand, but he couldn't. There was something wrong with his arms. They flopped at his sides as if boneless.

For a moment, Eric didn't understand. The stranger was not one to make a mistake. But then he realized it was not a mistake. Meng was alive for a reason, and conveniently incapacitated. The stranger wanted it that way. He wanted Eric to pick up a gun and kill the general himself—kill the man who had murdered so many. For a moment, Eric hesitated, feeling the manipulation. Then he remembered that this was the man who had killed Olex and threatened to kill Jane. He looked at Mei draped over her mother's body, and the last of his misgivings vanished.

He picked up the general's pistol and pointed it at his head. But then he stopped, suddenly knowing that it wouldn't fire.

Was it possible? Did the stranger know of the modification that Eric had made to the shirt, making it not strictly defensive? It was the crudest of nanoweapons, untested and likely very messy. In fact, Eric gave it only a fifty-fifty chance of working. Did the stranger somehow know what he had done?

He tossed the pistol away and picked up the shirt.

He glanced over at Mei and found her studying him closely, waiting to see what he would do. Eric thought to tell her to look away, just as he had done in the storm drain, but he didn't.

There was only one safety feature: he had to be touching the target. He put his finger on Meng's forehead and whispered the command, a word combination that he would never say accidentally: "Carbon rain."

He stood back and waited. Nothing happened. He dropped the shirt and was about to pick up the pistol, when Meng gave a sudden haunting gasp. He had a look of wild confusion on his face. Then the pain hit him, and he made a keening high-pitched scream. His body jolted and convulsed as if someone else were in control of his muscles. He tried to stand but kept falling, all the while screaming uncontrollably.

Then Eric saw the smoke. It was like skin-colored steam. It wisped from Meng's forehead and from under his collar. The nanosites, in the process of disassembling him, were generating huge quantities of excess heat, cooking him alive. The frantic screaming suddenly stopped as Meng's lungs combusted. A wide, silent howl followed as trails of black smoke came out of his mouth and nostrils.

Through the technicolor smoke, Eric watched Meng's skin dissolve away, then the pink muscles beneath it, exposing veins and arteries filled with boiling blood. Next went the bone underneath—rib cage, spine, long bones, skull. It all melted away. Soon all that remained was a pile of yellowish ash.

Eric noticed that his chest was heaving. He had made himself watch. The man inside him wanted to look away, but the scientist was fascinated by what his own program would do.

Someone touched his shoulder, and he jumped.

It was Ryan. "Come on," he said. "Pick her up. We have to get out of here."

Eric nodded. Meng was dead. The danger had passed. Now he had to look after Mei once more. He went over and picked her up. At first, she welcomed his embrace, until she realized that he was taking her away.

"No! We can't leave her."

"She wanted you to live. That meant everything to her. Let's make sure you do."

She struggled again, but with less conviction. "Okay," she said, and rested her head on his shoulder.

Eric relaxed his grip a little.

She instantly wriggled free and dashed back toward her mother. Eric ran after her, but then she passed the body and went to the spot where Meng had been. She picked up Eric's shirt and came running back.

"Sir, the third Reaper has reached the crossroads."

Hunter was still sitting on the floor, her back against the wall, almost asleep with exhaustion.

Curtiss reentered the command room and took in the new images. He saw the smoldering wreckage from the choppers, an overturned HG-17 truck, and dozens upon dozens of bodies. But something was wrong. There were no blast cones, and the bodies were all intact, as if they had died where they stood. And they were too clean—not enough blood. The Beehives should have turned them into hamburger. Something had killed them, but it wasn't his bombs.

Then the weapons specialist spoke. "Where's the car?"

CHAPTER FORTY-ONE

REUNION

Outside of Tangshan, China

Ryan drove. Eric held Mei in his lap. She continued to weep, sometimes in loud fits, sometimes softer. Eric shushed her and rocked her and kept repeating his promise to keep her safe.

Finally, mercifully, she cried herself to sleep.

Eric took out Ryan's iSheet and used it to find Mei's tracking chip. The girl was so exhausted that she barely stirred when he removed it. Then he took the bloody chip and flicked it out the window.

"How do you know where we're going?" Eric asked Ryan.

"Curtiss made me memorize this route—and five others."

"How did you know they were going to kidnap you?"

"Curtiss told me it was a possibility about a month before replication. He asked me to work on the sabotage a few weeks later."

Eric shook his head. It was all so crazy.

"I'm sorry you got dragged into this," Ryan said. "But honestly, I'm glad you were."

"What do you mean?"

"Just knowing that you were somewhere in that prison, going

through the same thing—it gave me strength."

Eric nodded. "Ditto, brother."

Just then they came over a sudden rise, and a wide valley opened before them. Eric was struck by the beauty of it. The valley floor was full of long strips of farmland, different crops growing in contrasting hues of green and brown. And in the distance, a ridgeline of lush jade towers shrouded in an afternoon mist. They rose, impossibly steep, out of the valley floor, so close together that it seemed a person could leap from one to the next.

The sight made Eric ache. The beauty of the world made him want to live. To travel, to take Jane and Mei. To fill his remaining days with life.

They drove another half hour; then Ryan turned the battered little car onto a long dirt drive that disappeared into a copse of trees. Set far back and hidden from the road was an old mansion. Ryan drove the car into a shack of a garage, got out, and quickly pulled the garage door shut. Eric got out, carrying the sleeping Mei.

The property looked deserted. "Are you sure this is the right place?"

Jane burst out the back door and sprang on them, screaming with joy. Hugging and kissing them. The sight of her was so sudden and Jane was so … so *herself*—healthy and strong and bright-eyed—that tears welled up in Eric's eyes.

Jane paused for a moment to touch Mei, who was now awake and looking around groggily, on the back. Jane's expression seemed to ask, "Why so few?"

The next eighteen hours were a frenetic blur.

The safe house was full of people—soldiers, State Department personnel, Navy, CIA. Everyone was busy trying to get them out of the country as quickly as possible. A man in plain clothes—clearly a high-ranking military officer—said they had to get cleaned up, that they were going for a helicopter ride. They took showers and put on new clothes. Mei, however, refused to leave Eric's side. In fact, they couldn't even persuade her to go to the bathroom by herself. So Eric acquiesced to her every demand. There was no reason not to. Jane rose to the occasion, too, playing the big sister. They stood in the bathroom with Mei while she showered, Jane on the toilet seat telling her stories about her marathons and triathlons.

After they had showered, Eric took the shirt, which was now clean, and slid it over Mei's head and helped her wiggle her arms in. It hung down to her knees, but she didn't care. "I want you to wear this until we get home." She smiled and hugged him around the waist.

Soon the man in street clothes ushered them behind the house, to a sleek black helicopter.

This whole time, they had not seen Curtiss. But as Eric sat at the open door of the helicopter, he caught sight of him and his men. They were checking weapons and preparing one of the helicopters. Curtiss turned, as if sensing Eric's eyes on him. For a moment, he seemed tempted to come over, but then a look that might have been shame crossed his face, and he turned back to his work.

As the helicopter lifted off, the last rays of orange were disappearing behind the karst range to the west. They turned eastward, toward the darkness, and for the next hour they flew almost silent over the megalopolis of Eastern China, over millions and millions of lights, until those lights formed a sudden thick line—the edge of the continent—and they were out over the dark, gray ocean. Within a few minutes, the light pollution had faded, and the stars came out above them. Eric pulled Mei to him and pointed to the Milky Way. He had never seen it so clear and sparkling. With his arm still around Mei, he reached for Jane's hand in the darkness. She took it and laced her fingers through his.

A hot night wind was blowing as Colonel Tong stepped from the helicopter at the crossroads. The rotor wash blew a sheet of dust into his face, momentarily blinding him. When he had blinked his eyes clear again, he saw a scene from hell.

He had been briefed that there were sixty-eight dead, but seeing them all together, it felt like more. Sodium lights cast long shadows on their contorted, agonized faces. And the smell. It had brought the flies. Millions of flies. They swirled around the lights like a black snowstorm and sat thick as ash on the bodies. Each time the disposal workers in their biohazard suits lifted a body, the flies rose up in irritated swarms.

The effect was unnerving: the sight of so many dead, the smell of vomit and feces, and the flies that tried to light on his face. It was all he could do to maintain his composure.

He forced himself to look at the dead. They bore no gunshot wounds, and there was no evidence of explosives. Yet *something* had killed these men—had made some of them crack open their own skulls. It had also downed three attack helicopters and tossed one of his HG-17 transport vehicles across the field as if it were a child's toy.

He immediately thought of the new weapons. But this was much more advanced than anything they had thought possible.

At his feet lay his boss's uniform and a pile of yellow ash. Looking at it, Tong felt certain that if he didn't figure out what had happened here, and quickly, he would meet the same fate as Meng and his men.

Unfortunately, now that the terrorists had escaped, there was only one person who might be able to help him. The other twin.

But she was proving most difficult. He had just come from seeing her, and it had been a waste of time. She was nonsensical, talking gibberish. The doctors had told him he would have to wait to interrogate her—her wounds were too severe. But he didn't have the luxury of waiting. So the interrogators had given her sodium pentothal, but it had interacted badly with the morphine that the doctors gave her. She was speaking nonsense: "You're too late! It's already in us!" Over and over again. Rocking back and forth as if her mind were damaged.

Tong had grown frustrated. He had to get the answers, so he had given the interrogator a nod. The man had pounded her face with his fist, then torn out three of her fingernails. But the torture had barely fazed the woman. Even when the interrogator held the fingernails in front of her face, it was as if she didn't even see them.

Tong had screamed at the doctors for giving her too much morphine. That was why the truth serum wasn't working. But in all honesty, it seemed to be more than that.

More flies landed on his face, on his lips and eyes. He swatted them away, but an instant later others took their places.

His lieutenant came running up. "Sir, we've found something."

He handed Tong an iSheet.

Tong recognized the image of the assembler prototype—a bubbly insectoid shape magnified to the nth degree. But nothing about the picture looked unusual.

"Go on," he snapped.

"Dr. Tuan says that it's this, sir." The lieutenant expanded the screen image with his fingers, enlarging it until a tiny node, a bubble, appeared on the prototype's back.

"What is it?" Tong asked.

"Well, we aren't sure, sir. We only know that it's not supposed to be there."

Tong felt a fresh wave of nausea come over him. He gave a heavy sigh and looked down at the yellow pile of ash at his feet. He thought again about the delirious woman's words: "*You're too late! It's already in us!*"

Midnight. The silent helicopter landed with a jarring thump on the deck of the aircraft carrier *Harry S. Truman*. It was a quick turnaround. They had a meal in the officers' mess and shook hands with the captain, and an hour later they were catapulted into the night in a Grumman C-2 Greyhound cargo plane, on their way to Osan Air Base in South Korea. They arrived in the middle of the night, and by sunrise they were on a Boeing 757 heading for Washington, DC.

The plane was deserted except for three soldiers heading home on leave. They all rode in first class. They talked little—mostly slept and ate. Their bodies seemed to realize that they were safe, so they went into a sort of hibernation, trying to recuperate from all the accumulated stress. Mei sat next to Eric, and when she wasn't sleeping, she watched movies. He heard her giggling a few times, and some of his concern over her subsided.

It was sometime in the midafternoon, somewhere over the Arctic Sea, when Ryan turned to Eric, his face sober. "It's about to start."

Eric knew exactly what he meant.

Jane read the gravity on their faces. "*What's* about to start?"

Eric glanced over at Mei to make sure she wasn't listening—she had her ear buds in and was absorbed in a Disney film.

Eric told Jane about the virus that was about to wipe out the Tangshan lab, and that each of them had a hand in creating it. Eric's lamprey idea had made it undetectable. Ryan's artificial-intelligence program enabled it to find each victim and select them based on his parameters. And, finally, the virus itself …

"I made it for Olex," she said as the realization hit her. "I didn't know what he wanted it for." She shook her head in disgust, an expression of anger and betrayal on her face. "How many people?"

"The workers come in two shifts of roughly twelve thousand five hundred each," Ryan said. "Curtiss wanted a twenty-hour delay from the moment the virus was released until death, to make sure that both shifts were infected. Those who were infected during the first shift took the virus home with them. They'll die in their sleep. Curtiss also insisted that all the military personnel on the whole base—not just the lab—be targeted. He was very specific about that. That's an additional forty thousand people. Sixty-five thousand in all."

Jane closed her eyes and tried to fathom the number, but it was too much to grasp. It was just a number. She nodded to herself slowly, then looked Eric straight in the eye. Her answer shocked him.

"Good," she said.

CHAPTER FORTY-TWO

ANGELS

Tangshan Military Laboratory, China

Hui Lili was awake, but she kept her eyes closed. She knew they were watching her. Best to let them think she was still asleep.

She was in terrible pain. The bullet wounds in her arm and leg, her missing fingernails, her broken nose. She tried to control her mind, to distract it with pleasant thoughts, but it was impossible. Her mind and body perceived nothing but pain, moving from one screaming nerve cluster to another, unsure which needed the most attention.

They had told her that Mei and her sister were dead, that the whole plan to escape had failed. But she didn't believe them. She could tell that something was wrong. She could hear it in Colonel Tong's voice: the fear. And where was Meng? That sadist would never miss out on her interrogation willingly. Something had happened to him. No, she assured herself, her sister and niece were alive. That was why they were so frantic to figure out what she and her sister had done.

Another wave of pain rolled over her. The bullet wound to her arm was the gravest, yet somehow her fingers hurt more.

It was then, as she was fighting the pain, that she felt a warmth at the top her spine. She knew instantly what it was. It ran down to her tailbone, then diverged into her legs and down to her toes. *Ahhh,* she thought, *so this is what it feels like.* The pain began to subside quickly, replaced by a comforting warmth. It reminded her of being a child in the wintertime, running with her sister to the bathhouse in their matching robes. Letting their bodies get cold on purpose, running in the snow, seeing how long they could bear it, just so the warmth of the bathtub would be that much sweeter. Finally, when they could take it no longer, they had slid in together. *On the count of three. One ... two ...* Giggling and gasping. Looking over at her smiling sister, the steam rising between them.

She opened her eyes but didn't like what she saw. The bleak wall. The bloody hospital sheets. Her broken body. She closed her eyes again. Much better to go back to the memory, back to the warmth and love of that winter bath, back to her childhood, back to her twin sister.

Life was beginning to return to normal in the Great Lab. The section around the containment sphere had been cordoned off, and work crews were busy reconstructing the parts that had been burned or destroyed. A heavy smell like charcoal still hung in the air, but throughout the rest of the expanse, the workers in their lab coats could be seen toiling at their work stations, just as before. There was the familiar drone of activity: the low din of conversation, plastic keystrokes, and electronic beeps.

Suddenly, there was a cacophony of noise as vials, coffee mugs, iSheets, and several thousand bodies hit the floor simultaneously. A guard making his circuit on the catwalk was the last to land. He rolled off the ledge and fell forty feet, crashing into a cart of lab supplies, which spilled and rattled for a few seconds.

Then all was quiet. From that moment on, the lab security cameras captured no movement or sound.

CHAPTER FORTY-THREE

LOOSE ENDS

Tangshan Military Laboratory, China

The UH-60 Stealth Black Hawk cruised low over the city of Tangshan, flying almost silent, invisible to radar. In the cabin, Admiral Curtiss was fighting off nausea. It was not that different from the way he had felt the first time he went into combat: the mix of terror and exhilaration, of not knowing whether he could handle whatever was about to happen.

The chopper banked along the low mountain that ran along the north side of the Fort Yue Fei military base. The pilot hugged the ground, ready to take evasive action should the base still be active. Then it came into view: the brightly lit barracks and shopping districts, the hangars and control towers. He saw a fire blazing at the end of the runway—the virus must have struck just as a cargo plane was attempting to take off. All that remained of it now were the skeletal ribs and the tail fin.

Almost immediately, he began to notice the bodies. It was a huge base, extending for miles. Yet even from this distance, he could see the motionless forms scattered on the ground. Along the main road, a dozen cars had run off the road or crashed into each other, their headlights still shining off into the darkness. The Black Hawk flew lower, passing more barracks, an academic campus, and officers' quarters. All the lights were on. But no one was moving.

Even though the nanosites had struck in the middle of the night, thousands of people had been outdoors—on a huge base such as this, there was activity around the clock. Outside a grocery store, two dozen figures lay scattered about the parking lot. They flew on. More bodies.

More bodies.

More bodies.

They saw no one alive. The nanovirus had worked. Curtiss had done it. He had annihilated his enemy just as he had promised he would, just as the Preacher knew he would. In fact, he had just conducted the largest mass killing of human beings since the dropping of the atomic bomb on Hiroshima in 1945. And even though the death toll here was lower, there was an enormous gap in sophistication between the two weapons. The atomic bombs that had ended the Second World War had killed as many people as they possibly could. In contrast, there was no limit to the number of people his nanosites could kill.

It was impossible not to look at all the bodies and wonder whether it had been necessary. Would China have used the weapons to kill en masse? Would it have used them for political assassination? To tip the balance of global power in their favor? Would it have caused more war—whether outright or proxy—that would kill American soldiers? Would it have created a world where Curtiss's sons might one day be victims? Yes, Curtiss believed unequivocally that it would. So he had done the right thing. But that didn't stop him from feeling sick.

Sawyer tapped him on the shoulder. "Sorry, Admiral," the old SEAL said, "but the signal's coming from over there." He motioned to the east. Curtiss nodded, and Sawyer relayed the information to the pilot.

A minute later, Curtiss and his five SEALs were on the ground outside the lab. Patel was on point, Sawyer behind him with an iSheet. They moved cautiously, rifles up and ready. Checking corners, watching the bodies closely for movement. The place was eerily silent. Curtiss didn't want to go in. He didn't want to see what he had done. But he knew he had to. They had one final mission to complete.

CHAPTER FORTY-FOUR

HOME AGAIN

May 19, 2026
Naval Research Laboratory, Washington, DC

They all crashed in Jane's apartment. It was never discussed. Eric didn't ask. Jane didn't offer. And Mei didn't know that they had just become a couple. She assumed they had been together for a long time.

They closed the blackout curtains and made the apartment into a cave; then all three of them climbed into bed together. Eric and Jane on the sides, Mei in the middle, still wearing the shirt. They slept for twelve hours, woke up and ordered pizza, ate it in bed, then slept another eight hours. Through all this time, no one spoke. Not because they were speechless, but because there was no need. Rest was all they wanted.

In the middle of the third long sleep, Eric and Jane slipped out of bed, one at a time, and met in the bathroom. They undressed in silence, and in the low visibility created by a cheap orange night-light, they got in the shower. After they had washed each other, they made love for the first time. Slowly. Gratefully. Face-to-face. Jane with one leg over Eric's hip. Becoming one.

When it was over, they stood panting in the steam. Jane turned on the cold water, and they let it break over them. The wonderful contrast.

They were grateful just to be alive.

They began to laugh.

Then they both cried.

"I thought I lost you." It could have been either of them saying it.

That afternoon, there came a knock on the door. Eric opened it to find one of Curtiss's SEALs. "I'm very sorry to disturb you, sir, but Admiral Curtiss needs you."

Jane came up behind Eric.

"All of you," he added. "Dr. Hunter and the girl, too."

"What's this about, Sawyer?" Jane asked.

"I'm sorry, ma'am, I'm not at liberty to say."

Fifteen minutes later they were in the medical wing, walking past the nurses' station. Eric couldn't help noticing that when the nurses saw Mei, they began to smile and whisper. One of them even stood and came closer, as if she didn't want to miss something.

Eric saw Ryan at the end of the hallway, peering into one of the rooms. Then Admiral Curtiss emerged from the same room and approached them.

"Thank you for coming," he said.

Jane gave him a hard stare, and to Eric's surprise, Curtiss wouldn't meet her gaze. Instead, he squatted down to talk to Mei.

"Hi, my name is Jim."

"It's nice to meet you. My name is Mei."

He smiled. "I know, and I also know that you have been through a great deal." He paused. "However, I have some good news for you."

Mei's eyes lit up with curiosity.

"But I need to tell you a few things first, just to prepare you, okay?"

Mei nodded.

"Your aunt Lili is going to be all right."

"*A yi!*" The girl's hand flew to her mouth.

Eric heard a woman's voice from inside the room. "Mei-Mei?" It was a voice with tears of happiness behind it.

"*A yi!*" Mei cried again as she ran for the open door.

Curtiss made a halfhearted attempt to stop her, then seemed to change his mind.

The next thing Eric heard was, "Ouch! Wait! No, not there! Sit on this side. There, that's better."

He and Jane stepped up next to Ryan, who was peering through the large window into the room. There was Mei, sitting on Hui Lili's lap. The girl's arms and legs were wrapped tight as a python's coils around her aunt, and their cheeks were pressed together. Mei wore a voracious grin and didn't appear to notice all the casts and bandages that enveloped her aunt.

Hui Lili's eyes were running with tears, but she chattered away like her old self. "Look at you! Did you grow? Did you miss me? From the way you're acting … Go on, admit it!"

Mei looked too ecstatic to speak and could only bite her lower lip and nod enthusiastically.

"Well, I certainly missed you." Then her voice grew softer. "Thank God you made it out." She clutched the girl tighter.

Eric felt Jane's fingers touch and intertwine with his. She leaned her head on his shoulder.

He looked over at Ryan, who was looking particularly smug. "Feeling proud of ourselves, are we?"

"Why, yes *we* are," Ryan said. "It wasn't easy getting a good sample of her DNA and reprogramming the virus to sedate her."

Jane gave him a skeptical smile. "Okay, maybe you're not a complete idiot after all."

The next morning, Eric woke early and left the other two in bed. It would be another week before Hui Lili could leave the hospital. He ate leftover pizza, standing over the kitchen sink. He looked around Jane's apartment. It still felt like a gym and the walls were still covered with the posters of famous athletes. But the portrait of Jane's father was gone. Now there was just an empty picture frame.

Eric went to the window and pulled back the dark curtains. Even though the day was overcast and rainy, the light made him squint. He watched the Potomac River moving water to the Chesapeake Bay. Airliners taxiing on the runway at Reagan Airport. Traffic rolling across the Woodrow Wilson Bridge.

The world.

Almost no one out there knew what he knew. None of them had seen what he had seen. To them, everything was still the same. But things weren't the same. They were very, very different.

He knew he had to face the fear that he had been trying so hard to ignore. The fear that had been growing in him—that they had only exchanged one enemy for another. Yes, the Chinese had been defeated. America had won. Yet out of their headlong race to replication, they had created something infinitely more dangerous: the Inventor, as Eric had begun to think of him, a man who was no longer a man and who could not be defeated by any weapon that existed on earth.

He didn't want to think about it. He preferred to be happy. And he reminded himself that he was free and home and safe, and that he even had a family again. But the problem would not leave him, and so his mind began to tinker with it, turning it over, trying to understand.

The crossroads replayed in his mind. The soldiers' silent screams. The sound of the man's head repeatedly smacking against the window. Ragged bone jutting through skin. The Inventor had killed so many, so easily. Yet he had also saved Mei and Ryan and Eric. Eric found himself caught up in the contradictions: the Inventor was a sadistic murderer, but he had saved their lives. A killer with a poet's voice.

And there was the other thing, the most disturbing thing of all: that Eric had created him. *I owe my life to many fathers.* Whatever the stranger did next, Eric was a part of it.

He thought back to the night at FBI headquarters. What were the

Inventor's plans? Was he creator or destroyer? Somehow both options frightened him.

After a long time, he turned away from the open window and the world that kept turning outside. There would be time for worry later, he told himself. Now he must do his best to not think about it. Instead he would savor the new life he had. So he returned to the bedroom and to the beautiful little girl and the beautiful woman who waited there.

In the afternoon, Eric woke with a start. The dream had been so real. A dream of a great *reset*, a wiping clean of the earth. He had been standing on the National Mall, in front of the Smithsonian.

It was a hot summer day, the Fourth of July, and the mall was packed with people. Everywhere. People. Mothers carried babies on their hips. Teenagers, long-haired and shirtless, played Frisbee. Children in strollers waved little American flags. People talking, laughing, eating ice-cream sandwiches.

The sun was hot and high.

He looked down toward the Lincoln Memorial, across a mile and a half of lawn. It hit them like a shock wave, traveling faster than sound. Bodies began to fall, all in the same direction. There were no screams, no cries. Then it reached him, like a hot wind, blowing his hair up and pulling at his clothes. Then it ran on toward the Capitol. The next instant, he was alone. Standing there.

He heard a deep moaning from above and looked up. Satellites were streaking across the blue sky: white balls with thick black tails of smoke. Then the buildings began to dissolve, melting as if they were ice under a hot sun, disassembled in a matter of seconds. This was more than the killing of billions. It was an erasure of all that man had wrought. A restart. Everything—every sidewalk, subway, and street sign—was being deconstructed, converted to its most basic atoms and returned to the earth.

Then he woke up, sweating and panting as if he had truly been there.

Then a new fear entered his mind. Perhaps the Inventor's nanosites had not really left him. Perhaps some were still inside him, working, and the dream had not been a dream at all.

EPILOGUE

Forty-nine days after the flash pandemic in Tangshan, China, in the tiny mountain village of Tadingxiang, Tibet, a nineteen-year-old girl named Dohna gave birth to twins.

The boy, dark-eyed and with beautiful pink skin, came first. But the girl was reluctant, and it took the midwife six hours to coax her from her mother's womb.

"She was waiting for her soul," the midwife said.

Dohna could immediately see that the boy was as stubborn as a yak. He was small but very determined. The whole time he was waiting for his sister, he cried inconsolably, refusing the breast. Only after his sister had been washed and cleaned, and he had been put beside her and could once again smell her and grip her cupped hands, did he calm down.

Dohna's sister immediately ran to her uncle's compound, where her cousin, Norbu, had miscarried just two days before. Norbu was crying anew when her cousin arrived—her milk had come in and it saddened her beyond words that there was no child to drink it. But when she heard the news of the twins, she stanched her tears and came running.

Dohna, exhausted from the long labor, gave the babies to Norbu, who fed the little girl first, then the boy. They both latched immediately, and as Norbu looked down on each newborn, she wept again.

It was agreed that when the political officer visited the village at the end of the week, Norbu would say that her child had lived. They also decided that Norbu would live with Dohna and be a second mother to the children. The government would never know that Dohna had given birth to twins.

ACKNOWLEDGMENTS

The initial concept for this book came to me during a solitary road trip from Washington, DC, to Ohio in 2000. That long timeline makes it feel like a long collaboration, since all my family and friends had to put up with me talking about it for such an awfully long time. With that in mind, please know that if I have forgotten anyone, it is not intention, but retention, that is to blame.

First, I want to thank those who read early versions of the book, sometimes more than once: Jack Genn, Andrew Davis (a wonderful hard-core sci-fi fan who gave me great advice), Meg Smith, Jamie Bowie, Steve Barish (who pushed to get the story out of America and into Asia), Will James, Paul James, and Rich Izzo. I deeply appreciate the counsel of my final beta testers: Sachin Waikar, Vincent Ercolano, Marcelo Alonso, Sam Waltzer, Alejandro Tarre, and Phil Gunson. Special thanks to Robb Anthony for the tough love, and to Jill Marsal for saying no the first time.

To the K63 Tech Training Class at Electronic Data Systems, including Marcelo Alonso (again) and Michael Lee, who were there for a friend in need. With their help, I learned—a bit like Admiral Curtiss—to do difficult things.

To my manuscript advisor, Aurelie Sheehan at the University of Arizona, who saw a very basic treatment of this idea when I was a graduate student more than sixteen years ago, and my workshop friends, who were exposed to—er, suffered through—many an embryonic draft of this book.

Enormous thanks go out to my family—Mom, Dad, Diane, Erika, and Philip—most of whom read early versions and, more importantly, were unstinting in their love and support.

Two authors who provided the seminal material for my research into advanced technology and who deserve my sincere thanks are Bill Joy and K. Eric Drexler.

Thanks to Ray Hu for being my translator.

My heartfelt thanks to Andrea Cavallaro at the Sandra Dijkstra Literary Agency, who fought hard to get this book published and found the missing piece of the puzzle. I will always owe you big.

Generous thanks to the team at Blackstone Publishing, including my editor, Michael Carr (a man who knows everything about everything), Lysa Williams for believing and also for continuing to give great advice during the editing process, Sean Thomas for his brilliant art, Ember Hood for her fantastic copyediting, and Josie McKenzie for guiding the whole process from acquisition to bookshelf.

To Natalia, *mi vida,* my wonderful wife, who did a great deal of editing on the bus to work. Thank you for the unending faith. Without it and without you, I would have faltered long ago.

Final thanks go to my two sons, who spent most of their young lives trying to sabotage my writing schedule but who ultimately made the story better by giving it a leitmotif that I didn't even see until the very end.